"Clever writing and pacing make this story not only believable but serve to draw the reader in as all the characters are likeable in their way, but all have their flaws, cracks in their characters... One can tell when good writing is unfolding right before their eyes." **STARRED REVIEW**, James Fisher, *The Miramichi Reader*

"This is a beautifully cadenced novel of loneliness and desire. The evocation of the physical world is wonderful, the synthesis of the weather of the heart and the elemental landscape is stunning. Prose of grace and clarity is ballasted with real narrative drive as past ghosts emerge. Powerful, evocative, haunting, *The Thickness of Ice* is an extraordinary novel." Eoin McNamee, Eoin McNamee, Man Booker Prize finalist for *Blue Tango*, screenwriter amd author of 19 novels.

THE THICKNESS OF ICE

THE THICKNESS OF ICE

Gerard Beirne

Baraka
Books

Montréal

ISBN 978-1-77186-339-1 pbk; 978-1-77186-345-2 epub; 978-1-77186-346-9 pdf

Fiction Editor: Blossom Thom
Cover by Maison 1608
Book Design by Folio Infographie
Editing and proofreading: Blossom Thom, Robin Philpot, Anne Marie Marko, Leila Marshy

Legal Deposit, 2nd quarter 2024
Bibliothèque et Archives nationales du Québec
Library and Archives Canada

Published by Baraka Books of Montreal

Printed and bound in Quebec

Trade Distribution & Returns
Canada – UTP Distribution: UTPdistribution.com

United States
Independent Publishers Group: IPGbook.com

We acknowledge the support from the Société de développement des entreprises culturelles (SODEC) and the Government of Quebec tax credit for book publishing administered by SODEC.

Société
de développement
des entreprises
culturelles
Québec

Funded by the Government of Canada
Financé par le gouvernement du Canada | Canada

for John Keeble,
a true teacher

Winters are tense times. The winds gust in continually carrying the fierce chill off the vast solid bay. Beards, moustaches, eyebrows, the hairs in our nostrils are taut with frozen moisture. I am knee deep in snow, the beach hidden as though it did not exist, the ice on Hudson Bay forced upwards at the shore as though the waves had been caught unawares, frozen at the height of their crest. Poised now as if they have made a discovery hitherto unknown.

From out of anywhere, the gauze of blowing snow, a bear could just as easily appear, its great white hulk lumbering into view. The sweep of its huge grasping paw. Death, you see, is everywhere. It is less the mystery than we would assume. I could step forwards, not much more than a short distance, and I might never step back.

Esther, my love, I should turn away from the onslaught of the weather much as I should have turned away from Jack Butan on that peculiar day that has skewered itself into every other day since. If I could undo what I did, I would, but there is no undoing death, I am not a foolish man. I am not a violent man either. Before or after that irreconcilable event, I have never raised a hand to harm anyone. It would have served no purpose for me to admit what I did. It would benefit no one, not the man whose life I so unjustly took, not the people whom the law is written to protect, not least myself. And so I have told no one, and no one knows.

The case, it is said, remains open, but history has already closed it. The many people of this small town have already

1

finished the story. They have no wish for it to be retold, for the end to be rewritten. And yet, it seems, the end is about to be rewritten. Our history is about to be changed. Esther, all I ask of you in your unearthing is that you discover the reason why. Take my hand, and we will walk into this together.

CHAPTER 1

In summer I worked at the terminal in the port emptying Hopper cars of grain. In winter when the bay froze over, and the port shut down, I hibernated, stepping out only to measure ice. Each week, year after year, from freeze-up to break-up, I took my auger, walked out onto the ice and drilled a new hole. I pushed the stainless-steel flights together, attached the adaptor, brace and cutting bit, and slowly bored through the frozen water. My parka, my balaclava, my thick thermal gloves. The snow that fell, the bitterly cold winds with their promise of numbness and frostbite. The crunch and squeak of my boots on the slippery surface. The gaping mouth of snow and ice that stretched as far as I could see. I lowered my gauge within the bore hole, pulled the bridge against the underside of the ice and measured its thickness. Then I returned to the warmth of my truck, disconnected my auger, and filled out my weekly report.

I have measured ice in this way ever since that day it gave way, and my world fell in.

✦

Esther first walked into my sight from behind the veil of her exhaled breath. It was late June 1994. The temperature had dropped below zero the night before. The pale sun had risen before five that morning and had yet to warm the chill from the air. The bleak streets of Churchill were almost empty. I was waiting for the grocery store to open and had taken a stroll along the stony beach. Break-up had come late. The bay was filled with hefty icebergs and expansive fractured sheets of ice. The wind blew in hard, crashing the sheets against one another, groaning and creaking, shattering at their edges, splashing into the frigid water. An Arctic tern flew in low, swooped slowly past and tipped its head towards her.

I turned and witnessed the mist of her breathing, and as her breath disappeared Esther stepped into my view. I would like to say that the sea froze over once more, that the ice sheets reformed and that the winds abated, but the truth is more opaque. Esther stood amongst the dunes oblivious to my presence, and I for my part turned my gaze away soon thereafter. I could say I turned back to her and that she had disappeared in the way of melting ice, but instead I can only tell you that I carried on walking and Esther went her way too.

It was on a whim that I went for breakfast at Gypsy's Café where I saw her again. She was seated at the table next to mine. Her cheeks red from the cold. Her bushy long brown hair tied behind her. Her ordinary face that I would soon discover the beauty in. She caught my glance, and each of us blushed. I nodded an embarrassed greeting. Esther briefly smiled and averted her eyes. And it was, I believe, in that moment of turning away that the first glimpse of her beauty was revealed to me. I, Wade Sinclair, who had squandered beauty so many years previously, who had accepted a lifetime of solitary moments.

Do not ask me why but the next morning I returned. I ate my breakfast and watched for those raw moments of beauty to ripen. There is no explanation for my behaviour. For six-teen years, I had spurned the thought of any woman. I could see no place in my life where a companion could dwell, no place for the intricacy of love, no belief that any other love could, in fact, exist.

She traveled here alone to join one of the many tours to observe the birds. Hudsonian Godwits, Spruce Grouse, Ptarmigan, Boreal Chickadees, Smith's Longspurs, Pacific Loons, Harris Sparrows, and the rare Ross's Gull in their pink breeding plumage. Instead, she found me.

Although I am by nature a quiet man, it is not an intrusion in such a location as this to speak with someone you do not know. Scores of birders pass through each week of the summer, scores of wildflower enthusiasts, whale-watchers later in the season, and of course the multitudes in early winter in search of the great white bear. There is always someone or something arriving and someone or something departing. Humans, bears, birds, flowers, ice, water. But they are always coming and going in groups, and so when I saw Esther seated alone, I greeted her once more. I sat one table away. The café was filling, birders arriving for breakfast before setting out on their day's excursion.

I asked the obvious question which in truth required no answer. "Are you here for the birds?"

"I am," she replied. She told me she had traveled here from Winnipeg. She had lived there all her life but had never been here before, hard as that was to believe.

I disagreed. "I have lived here for most of my adult life, and I have never been to Winnipeg."

"Worlds apart."

Yes, worlds apart. But somehow our worlds came together. We stepped upon each other's unmapped shores. Each morning I arrived for breakfast, and each morning we talked.

Esther told me of her previous day, the birds she had seen, the places where she had seen them. She asked about me, and I told her of my work at the grain terminal when the shipping season was open, when the waterways flowed free. I told her of my home at the rocket range, and she shook her head in disbelief. We spoke of such things, and then after her food was eaten, she would excuse herself. There were schedules to be adhered to, tour bus departures to be present for. I would sit there and watch her leave.

Although she stayed in one of the motels with other members of her tour group, she did not mix with them. She seemed as alone as I was. Was this part of the attraction? Undoubtedly it was. For what do we ask from love if not more of ourselves?

The day before she was to leave, she walked right up to my table and brazenly sat down beside me.

"I am to leave tomorrow." She brushed strands of her hair from her forehead. "I am not sure how to say this," she began, "although I have very much enjoyed the beauty of the tundra, the enchantment of the birds I came to see, I believe I have enjoyed our conversations, brief as they were, even more." A line of moisture glistened above her upper lip.

"Yes," I agreed, "I will miss them when you go. I have not been much in the habit of talking recently. There are many things I ought to have said that I did not."

She smiled. "I am a better listener than talker too. I heard more than you have spoken."

We drank our tea, ate our toasted muffins. "Where do you go today?"

Esther shook her head. "Yesterday we almost caught sight of the Ross's gulls. Our tour guide pointed them out as they flew away disturbed. They were but dots in the sky. The rest of the group is going out for one last look, one last chance to see them up close. I cannot help but wonder if we have not frightened them away, spying on their courtship. I don't want to go back. It is said that here is the only place in North America where they nest which is part of the reason why I came, I suppose, but now I am afraid that my presence will drive them away."

She looked immensely sad. She asked if I would show her instead the grain terminal, the rocket range, things she was incapable of disturbing. We walked down to the port, and I led her around the outside of the closed terminal. I pointed out its features, and I explained their significance, where the railcars were received, where the grain was cleaned and stored, where it was shipped to the vessels. The receiving conveyor, the car haul equipment, the head, garner, scale, and distribution floors. The storage bins, the gallery, the shipping conveyors. We looked out at the ice sheets in the harbour, the chunks of floating bergs. I spoke of icebreakers and shipping lanes, passageways over an open sea. I explained how, like the immense tundra, there were only small parts of the vast oceans we could navigate.

We seek out paths wherever we go, and Esther and I had not left those paths. But now, in her quest for the truth, she has strayed into an unexplored world where there is no guarantee of a safe passage through.

That day, we did not make it to the rocket range as she had initially requested. We walked along the shore, along the sidewalks, the edges of our lives. What we spoke about, I cannot be certain. Our words fluttered between us like birds we were so accustomed to that we barely noticed them. We ate lunch at the cafeteria at the town centre. Esther told me how tired she was of her life. "Sometimes, I feel as if whole years have been wasted." She worked in a stationery supply shop, a photocopy operator. "Who would want to duplicate my life?"

Late afternoon she said she needed to pack, to prepare for the journey back. I walked her to her motel. We said goodbye. She stepped up on her toes and kissed my cheek. We shared blushes, our plumage turned pink.

✦

When the polar bear hunts, it hides the black tip of its nose. It places its paw upon it, camouflaging itself upon the white snow. The seal will not see it. Esther, as you kissed my cheek and bid me goodbye, you hid your nose did you not?

I had no phone, and we had not exchanged addresses, but Esther sent me a letter, general delivery, two months later. She spoke of her affection for Churchill. She recalled the beauty of the tundra, its wildlife. To live among the Ross's gulls would not be an intrusion she deduced, it would be a consequence. She was planning to return. She could even envisage a longer stay. A few weeks later, I replied. You would be welcome back, I assured her, but I warned her of the approaching winter, the harsh climate. Over the ensuing months, we wrote and replied, more and more frequently. The landscape, its ecology, its geology. The weather and the climate. She was fast losing sight of Winnipeg, she said. It was disappearing within a northern blizzard. And then one morning, she wrote, the blizzard cleared. One by one the flakes of snow ceased to fall, the winds died out, and when they did, there you were. Wade Sinclair, I believe I love you.

Shortly thereafter, we were planning her move. Esther uncovered the tip of her nose, but it was too late by then. I love you also, I wrote in reply.

✦

"It is unreasonable I know," Esther had written to me in one of her letters, "to be so fearful of the white bear especially since I have chosen to live among them, but I am. I am frightened to death." Without this fear, I wrote back, you would surely die.

So Esther came in May when the bears had long since departed and before they would gather once again. She came when the temperatures were warming up, when the ice was not gone but was soon to go. She did not want to arrive in a time of false promise, nor did she want to arrive in the dead of winter.

The day she came, the ice was 180 cm thick. I woke that morning at sunrise. From my bed where I lay, I saw small gaps in the cloud cover like tracks of water in melting ice. The strong northern gusts of wind had given way to gentler southern breezes. Esther was making her way to me.

I drove to the station to meet her. She had boarded the train in Winnipeg the night before and headed north. First through the wheat belt, the immense flat fields of swaying yellow stalks. And then through the boreal forest, the endless spruce and pine trees, the occasional glimpses of steely blue water, the low grey mounds of granite shield before arriving in the mining town of Thompson twenty hours later, and from there the slow night crawl to Churchill through the swampy muskeg. Esther dozed and woke to the screeches of metal on metal, raised voices calling through the chilled air. The eerie flash of lights shining in the darkness. Shadows of men clearing snow from the tracks and heating line switches to prevent the train derailing further ahead. Esther peered through the dark window. Flakes of snow drifted against the cold pane. This was why she had taken the journey by train, she said. To see the landscape alter before her eyes, the flat fields of wheat transform into tall boreal forest. To have the day disappear into darkness so that when the light reappeared the tree line would be left behind. The tall vegetation of her life dwarfed, stunted in its growth in a bid for survival.

Esther opened her eyes at dawn, the sky overcast. The sedges, the mosses, the grasses, the heaths draped in snow. The train vibrating on the frozen tracks. A man she was betting her life on awake in his bed looking out at the same cloudy sky. Esther closed her eyes briefly, but when she reopened them the sun was still rising, the tundra still passing.

She said she needed to make the long journey here slowly to give her time to adjust, but what journey should I have been taking to adjust to my new way of life with her? I had made no preparations whatsoever. I was here without Esther, and then I would be here with her. My life was inhabited by one, and then it would be inhabited by two. I was fifty-two years old. Outside lay an abandoned rocket range that had once been the busiest range in the world. Three and a half thousand rockets launched in a forty-year span. An army base that had a population of thousands razed to the ground. I was alone here as much as I was surrounded by people. I missed Esther. I feared her coming.

I turned in to Bird Cove on my way to the station, parked my truck, took out my auger and walked down to the snow-covered beach. Pockets of early meltwater pooled between the rocks. Water dripped from the thick edge of ice ridged at the shore. It was 7:50 a.m. The train was due in forty minutes. The sun brightened the sky through the gaps in the clouds. A sign of better days to come, perhaps. The frozen waters spread into the bay. The wreck of *The Ithaca* was lodged in the ice as though it had only recently been trapped there by the swift winter freeze-up. If Esther were here at this moment in time, I could tell her its story, and she would have no reason to dispute it. Not to know that it floundered here thirty-four years previously, in an 80 mile per hour storm, bound for Rankin Inlet. Not to know that it was here I met Tess and floundered also, caught up in her storms. The cold grip of our handshake that I can feel yet in my palm and fingers.

I walked out on the ice, set up my auger and drilled through the hard shell of winter. From the distant horizon, a storm of snow geese, blowing over the coastal ice ranges to their breeding grounds in the Arctic, their cries like the screech of brakes on metal tracks. It is time to meet with you, my love. It is time for the seasons to change.

I stood next to the tracks under the wooden porch of the station. William Craig, a tour guide with one of the many tour companies here, stood at the far end of the platform smoking, wrapped in a blue plaid quilted jacket, a muskrat fur hat. I waved politely. He blew a plume of smoke into the air, nodded in my direction. The platform was covered in a layer of thick snow. The lines too. The wooden sleepers could not be seen, but the steel tracks shone resolutely. Icicles hung from the porch above my head. I heard the crunching of William's boots as he shifted his feet. Any moment now, we would hear the sound of the approaching train transmitted through the very tracks that carried it along as though they were eager to announce what they had made possible. William flicked the end of his cigarette into the snow. A red glow sizzled and extinguished. He exhaled the last drag from his lungs. A door banged inside the station. I heard myself cough. The tracks rang with the vibration of the train. The station master took his position along them. A drop slid down the outer surface of an icicle to arrest at its tip. It pulsed as though breathing, threatened to let go. The train slowly and noisily made its way towards us. Esther would be looking out for me. She would see William first, and I wondered if, in his fur hat and quilted jacket, she would momentarily believe it was me. Or what if I did not recognize her? It was not an impossibility.

The drop finally broke free and fell to the ground. The train ground to a halt. William stepped forward. The doors opened and people disembarked. A young man with a backpack and camera cases. A group of men and women that William went to greet. An Indigenous woman and her son. A few more birders or wildflower enthusiasts. And Esther. Esther carrying a heavy suitcase in one hand and holding the open door with the other, carefully climbing down the steps. I rushed, there is no other word to describe it, to meet her. She smiled when she saw me, the weary smile of the tired traveler. She placed her suitcase on the snowy platform, and we embraced.

"Esther."

"Wade."

Churchill looks desolate in the morning. A barely noticeable inhabitation in the remote tundra on the edge of the Hudson Bay. A scattering of buildings roughly erected. Haphazard structures worn from the harsh climate in need of refurbishment. A few short miles of road with a distinct beginning and end. A small stretch of main street flanked by gravel. A tour office, a motel, a gift store, a café, a hardware and lumber store, an apartment building, a service station, all looking the worse for wear. Ancient gas pumps, rusted discarded components, empty crates, vehicles with potential for abandonment. The dull cloud cover, the snow-covered streets. The cracked paintwork, the faded signs.

What could I say to Esther, what promises had I made? I told her what I had already told her. There are only two months in the year when it doesn't snow. The temperatures reach minus forty degrees centigrade, minus fifty with wind chill. My house, our house, is nothing to write home about. She leaned her head in on my shoulder, and she closed her eyes. If she didn't open them, she didn't have to see anything. But this was not fair to Esther, she was tired that was all. A thousand miles of journey. A lifetime to arrive.

I drove her out by Gull Lake and Akudlik Marsh, the nesting area of the rare Ross's gull. We passed the airport and the polar bear jail, a converted military warehouse where troublesome bears that stray too close to the town were kept until they could be released later. I pointed out Miss Piggy, a C46 aircraft that lost air pressure in her left engine wing shortly after takeoff and clipped electricity lines to crash-land on the rocks where it has remained since. I showed her the dump where the great white bear was as likely to be seen as it was striding gracefully across a vast pristine ice range. The Aurora Domes where the northern lights had once been studied and where tourists now paid for the pleasure of seeing them in comfort. The Twin Golf Balls, two white domed dimpled structures that had housed radar antennae for the Rocket Range and were now privately owned. I drove slowly past Bird Cove and the wreck of *The Ithaca*, the wreck of my life with Tess, past the Rocket Range right up to our home.

I carried her suitcase up the laneway and opened the door. Esther stepped inside.

"It's not much," I apologized.

"It's more than enough." Esther put her arms around me and hugged me tightly. I held her awkwardly.

"You must be tired," I said, removing myself from her grasp. "You should rest." I carried her case through to the bedroom. A lacklustre light shone through the window. I put her suitcase down by the closet I had emptied for her. My own clothing I had placed in a chest of drawers by the door. My coats and jackets hung on hooks on the back door of the house. Clothing here was utilitarian. It kept out the winds and it kept out the cold.

Esther looked around at the empty walls, the bedside table, the lamp that rested on it, the chest of drawers, the closet, the worn green carpet on the floor, the window without curtains. "You might want to put curtains up," I acknowledged. "I never bothered. There is no one else around for miles." She walked to the window, looked out. The view was bleak. The brown tufts of sedge and grass showing through the snow, the dull concrete and metal of the rocket range in the distance, the few scrubby trees, small and thin due to the wind and permafrost. Esther sat down on the edge of the bed. She pulled off her fur-lined boots and rubbed at her toes beneath her wool stockings. She wore her coat yet, and I wore my jacket. This was to be our bedroom now, but we did not have the words for that.

"You rest up." I nodded and left the room, closing the door quietly.

Throughout the rest of the morning, I kept the stove burning. The gaps in the cloud cover opened up further, melted apart. I heard the whirr of a helicopter overhead. A science research group perhaps, or Conservation Officers. In wintertime, I have seen their helicopters fly above the frozen tundra with a large net hanging below carrying a tranquilized bear out onto the thick ice of the Hudson Bay to awaken later. Most times the bears moved on in search of seal, but occasionally they found their way back into town with no recollection of having left it in the first place.

That first night in bed with Esther, I held her close and told her of this. "Are we bears swinging in a net," she asked, "doped and at the whim of others?"

"We are creatures of survival," I replied. "We are at home in the wild."

✦

I brought Esther out to Bird Cove a few days after she arrived. It was early evening. The sky was covered in light grey clouds. Low winds blew in off the bay. The dark shadow of *The Ithaca* lay off to our left. Esther breathed the air in deeply. We picked our way across the icy rocks. I led her toward the shoreline to a section where the edge of the ice was low enough to step up on.

"Is it safe?" she asked.

"Yes, but not for long." I took her hand and we stepped out onto the snow-covered ice. Esther was wary and shuffled her feet along. I brought her out to where I usually drilled. Ice spread outwards as far as we could see. A cold chill rose up off it.

"We could walk all the way to the Arctic," I told her. "All the way up Hudson Bay to Baffin Island and Elsmere Island, out into the Arctic Ocean, the North Pole."

"We really could, couldn't we?" She looked out ahead of us as though it were a possibility.

I told her then for the first time of my weekly measurement of the ice thickness. Esther was enthralled, but she could not understand how I had not mentioned it to her before.

"I didn't really think about it, I suppose. It is just something I do."

She put her arm in mine. "I would have loved you sooner."

"I just bore a few holes, drop in a gauge for measurement. It is child's play."

"No, Wade," she disagreed, "it is anything but. You measure the freezing and thawing of our world, the depth of our winter. You bore within and determine whether the earth's surface will withstand our weight."

"I write figures on a standardized form."

"Wade, you are the guardian of us all."

Fifteen months after the ice gave way beneath Jack, I read the advertisement for the position on the notice board at work. It was the least I could do. If not I to drill into the ice and measure its depth, who then?

Esther accompanied me thereafter on all my trips. She dropped the gauge in the hole, read the measurement off it while I held it taut. She wrote the figures on the form in the cab of the truck. She was still cautious on the ice, but the measurements offered her increasing reassurance.

"One hundred and sixty-five," she called out into the cold morning, her breath gusting in front of her. A haze of mist rose from the surface of the cove, shimmered around us. "It is June, and the ice is one hundred and sixty-five centimetres thick. The sun is shining. I can barely see you, but I know you are there. The world is willing yet to hold us up." She reached out and touched my arm. "Will it ever let us down?"

I should have answered, yes. Yes, it will let us down as surely as this ice beneath our feet will melt and disappear.

Esther and I watched the ice continually, not just from the cove where we measured it but from the beaches and the port during our walks. As the shoreline warmed, a wide stretch of water opened along its edge. Snow melted and pooled on the ice. In winter, I explained to Esther, the ice thickness gradually increases, but in spring its decrease is rapid. The pools of water heated up hastening the melting process. The thin ice between the floes cracked and broke apart. The waves, the currents, the winds, the tides, all contributed to weaken it even further.

"As ice melts, it shrinks," I told her, "fractures itself, precipitates its own demise."

✦

Esther had, she told me, two men in her life before she met me. That was how she put it, *in her life*. She told me their names although I would have been as glad not to know of them. What advantage could it possibly hold? I do not need to know the names of the wildflowers to recognize their beauty. I did not need to know Jack's name to know I had done wrong. But Esther insisted on telling me.

She met Richard Kemp when she was twenty-five. For four years they had a relationship neither could depend on. He was as relieved as she was when she finally had the courage to break up with him. She met Paul Harding three years later. At the time she had thought she loved him, and he may genuinely have loved her. But whatever they had dissipated in time until every particle of their relationship was so far apart there was nothing discernible anymore. And that was it until I came along.

I did not mention Tess's name to her. I told her I had an involvement for a few years, *an involvement*, but that nothing came of it in the end. What could I say? I can hardly explain to myself what occurred between Tess and me. There was no relief in the end, no simple dissipation, there was a tragedy. There was an ending of lives.

✦

Throughout June, the ice got increasingly thinner. What had been 165 cm thick the week before was then 124 cm and then 78 cm. I no longer needed the second steel flight for measurement. By the last week in June, it was down to 33 cm. The sun shone warmly, the pools of water glistened. The snow turned to slush beneath our feet. By the first week in July, it had thinned to 15 cm. I would no longer permit Esther to stand out on the ice with me. She in turn was worried for my safety. The following week, I cleaned and oiled my auger, put it into storage. A few days later the icebreakers cleared a route through to the port, opened Churchill up to the outer world.

Once the ice had broken up and the shipping routes were free, the grain terminal resumed operation. The crops were harvested and transported to local grain elevators to be loaded aboard the trains which carried them here. My days were busy then, and Esther was left to her own devices. She needed other interests. In truth, I think she enjoyed the opportunity to be on her own. Esther, like me, had spent a long time without the constant company of another. She busied herself learning as much as she could about where she now lived. She was at a distinct disadvantage, she said. The people who had grown up here already knew everything they needed to know, already had that knowledge imparted to them, but she knew nothing. The least she could do was familiarize herself with her surroundings. So she learned the names of the birds which used Churchill as a migration route, the names of the wildflowers, the marine life. She learned all about the geography, the history of the region. She spent most of her days that first summer in the library or walking on the tundra and the coastal paths. I knew that sometimes she went down to the train station to watch people arrive and depart. Birders, photographers, students, backpackers.

In the evenings after work, I would often find Esther sitting outside our house reading. Inside, supper would be warming on the stove. Esther would ask me how my day was, and I would tell her no different than the one before. I would ask her then about her day, and she would proceed to tell me everything. Later, after eating, we would take a walk across the tundra or drive down to the shore.

On one of those evenings, on our way back from a shore walk, Esther suggested stopping off in town for a drink. "Something different," she said.

I hadn't been to a bar in twenty-five years or more. Shortly after Jack's death, I walked away from the company of others and settled into my solitude. But for Esther's sake, I agreed. I avoided The Churchill since it would hold too many memories and instead pulled in at The Port.

The lighting was as dull as ever and the décor sparse, as bleak as winter tundra. A few faded pictures of ice and polar bears hung on the wall. The bar was quiet. An elderly Inuit couple sat up at the counter drinking beer. A couple of young men I recognized from the grain terminal played the VLTs along the wall. A small group of research scientists sat at one table and a larger group of German tourists at another.

When Esther entered, everyone in the bar turned to look. What they saw I cannot tell. Esther's face was strong and direct. She was striking, tall. At five eleven an inch taller than I. Her thick brown hair, tied back, reached past her shoulders. She herself described it as frizzy. "Someday I will chop it all off." Her green cotton blouse, her long wool skirt, her ankle boots. And Esther, what did she see, a squalid bar, a homely place to talk and drink, a long distance a map's scale cannot itself explain? Perhaps she looked somewhere beyond where we were standing and wondered if there was a better location for her. I saw her glance at one of the pictures on the wall. A polar bear in mid-stride on a rough chunky surface of snow and ice with its head raised as though listening intently for some sound which would give him direction. To date, she had only witnessed the warmth and colour of the summer tundra. Her future was framed in that fading picture. She would raise her head, she would listen out.

One of the scientists greeted Esther as we walked past on our way to a table in the corner. It amazed me how many people she already knew. People she had met from her walks, or from shopping at the store, or borrowing books at the library. Esther dismissed it easily.

"They talk to me as they would talk to one of the tourists. They humour me. I have no doubt they think I will not last the winter."

The barman came over to see what we wanted to drink. Esther ordered a white wine, and I ordered a beer. I was also concerned that she would find the winter too harsh. She had no real idea of what she was letting herself in for.

"And will you?" I asked.

"That depends on you."

"I will do the best I can."

"I know you will." Esther held the stem of her glass like an icicle. "When the time comes, I want you to find me a polar bear and wrap me in its fur."

"Perhaps the polar bear will find you first." I immediately knew I had spoken aloud words that should never have been spoken at all, even in jest. I tried to apologize. But it was too late for that. I had troubled Esther in a way I had never intended.

"I dreamed about them again the other night. They were banging on our doors. Clambering across our roof. I don't know what it is." She pointed to the pictures on the wall, "See how beautiful they are."

"The beautiful are always to be feared."

"Are you afraid of me then?" she joked.

And I answered her honestly, "Yes, I believe I am."

That night in bed, I told Esther a story that Tom Fowler had told me years before. Tom was a trapper and had a log cabin further north where he used to trap Arctic fox. He had a dog team in those days, he said, just about everyone did. The dogs always barked excitedly when they returned to the cabin but this one time they barked louder and wilder than ever. He never locked the door, and he saw it then pushed open. Sometimes other trappers might come along, drop in for food or company, but he knew they would never leave the door open. He took his gun and walked around to the side of the cabin and looked in the window. He could hardly believe his eyes. There inside was a full grown polar bear up on its hind legs, its head just about touching the roof, knocking tin plates and cups off a shelf on the wall. A bag of flour was ripped apart on the floor, and Tom could see the white powder on the bear's black nose. He fired a shot up in the air, he said, and expected the bear to come hurrying out of the cabin. But instead the bear shook his head as if suffering some slight annoyance, then lowered itself gracefully onto all fours and walked slowly out. It never once looked in Tom's direction. It simply walked out the door and set off across the snow. Flour shook from its fur like a mist rising above him. "I have never felt so lonely," Tom said. "No way to explain it. I felt as though he had not simply walked out of my cabin but out of my life."

Esther if she ever left would leave like that. She would turn away from me, across the snow into the mist.

In the beginning, I was afraid that Esther would leave, but I was equally afraid that she would stay. Love and fear walk hand in hand. They are as perfect a couple as Esther and I. They may even look as unreasonable together.

✦

A few days after that visit to the bar, the first pods of Beluga whales appeared in the Churchill River estuary. I brought Esther out to Cape Merry at the mouth of the river to see them. A short gravel road led to the northern most tip of the cape. Across the mouth, on Eskimo point, a rocky peninsula, lay the remains of the Prince of Wales Fort built by the Hudson Bay Company to prevent an attack by the French. It was Esther who pointed it out to me as though I would have been unaware of its presence. It had been built in 1731, she told me. It had forty-two cannons and forty-foot thick walls, but none of this protected it when the time came. Comte de La Pérouse, with a fleet of three French ships, captured it anyway in 1782.

I told her she could probably get a job as a tour guide, and she answered that the main attraction in town was me. I told her to bring busloads of them to our home then. I would sit out front and they could take pictures of me. But Esther shook her head.

"I would have nothing to tell them," she said. "I know little about you, and there are no books on you anywhere I can read up on."

As part of the fort's defense, a gun powder magazine and a cannon battery were located at the Cape. Although Esther had read about them, she had not seen them before and was keen to explore. The winds had risen and the waves crashed in hard against the rocks. Herring gulls and jaegers swooped low at the edge of the shore. Rocks jutted from the ground. Small growths of plant life between them. The white topped water rose in small swells. And amongst them what at first seemed like more whitecaps breaking the surface.

"There!" I shouted to Esther pointing out into the water. "Look. There they are."

As many as forty or fifty white whales rose and dove, moved in on the tide towards the river mouth. Their ghostly bodies slipped through the waters like some pure unconscious knowledge released from the depths of the world.

"In the coming weeks, thousands more will follow."

Esther came over to join me. She put her arm around my waist. "I have read about these whales too, but nothing to prepare me for this." In all, Esther said, there were over twenty thousand whales in western Hudson Bay. Thousands of these summered in the estuary. Feeding, molting, mating, giving birth before the ice reformed and they returned north to the Arctic Ocean. "Imagine," she said, "if all of these whales, all twenty thousand of them, surfaced at once. It would be as if the bay had frozen over once more."

We watched the whales for at least an hour. Diving beneath the water, reappearing. The gush of spray from their blowholes. The waters of Hudson Bay splashing against and through their pale stout bodies. The breeze over the Cape. Strands of Esther's hair blowing freely. The ridge of rocks eroding invisibly before our very eyes. Esther and I were miniscule. A freak wave could suddenly lunge from the sea and take us back with it. We might never be missed.

CHAPTER 2

The log house was Esther's idea. "Something," she said, "to distinguish ourselves."

As if such a thing was necessary. And yet maybe she had a point, maybe all of us despite our shared lives and outcomes were seeking this, a moment of distinction. There was the house I had lived in for over twenty years. A small wooden house right here beside the rocket launch. But Esther shook her head.

"I do not mean to insult you, or the previous twenty years of your life, but I cannot live here in such a small house."

It did sound like an insult, but the truth is I am not a man to be easily insulted, besides she had given up much to move up here with me. Is a house too much to yield? Twenty years of your life?

At first she did not even want to build here. It was the rocket launch.

"Is this not a wilderness? We can build anywhere within it. No, not the rocket launch."

"Space," I said. "The greatest wilderness of all."

In time, she came to see this too. Despite our differences, we have much in common.

And so, we knocked my home to the barren ground. Burnt it piece by piece in the stove to keep us warm. Continue to burn it still. Burnt the frame of my small bed. That same bed Tess and I lay in together before she left, before the death of Jack Butan.

We had the logs brought in by train in early spring the year after Esther arrived. Seventeen hours from Thompson to here. The cold steel of the tracks. The driver stopping and stepping down in the dark to clear the drifts of snow away with a shovel. The stars twinkling above his head unnoticed. The pale greens and pinks of northern lights. His breath puffed out in bursts as he shoveled and tossed. The snow dispersing with the force of the wind. And meanwhile our logs snug together in the open freight wagon, light flakes settling on top of the wood, sinking in between the small crevices in the grain.

I went to the station to watch the logs arrive. The light just coming into being. A red burning edge of horizon. Cold wavering air. The bare stone platform, empty then. Different than bear season, whale season. Different than when the platforms throng with film crews, flower lovers, birders. Those with long hair and beards. Those with babies on their backs in modern versions of native cradle boards. Esther loves those moments. Many times, she comes to the station just to watch. It is an arrival, she has said, a confirmation that I am not alone.

That night after the logs had been transported from the train station to my old home, Esther and I stood out in the moonlight and looked at them piled on top of one another in one giant heap. A hill of wood. I closed the door to my house and turned out its outside light. I took Esther's hand and led her over to these huge tree trunks. Esther reached out her hand to one of the logs in front of her and ran her fingers along its rough surface. A half-moon shed its light, bestowed it upon us, just as though the shrill call of the snowy owl somewhere in the dark distance had been called for our ears alone.

"Did you hear that?"

I rubbed the back of her hand with my thumb. "I heard it."

Esther let go my hand and began to climb up on the wood.

"Be careful," I called.

She reached to the logs above her for support then stepped up on the nearest one to her foot.

"Come along," as she continued to climb.

I followed up after her. I felt the hard edge of the bark flake under my hands and feet. I warned Esther to test each log beneath her feet to make sure they were secure. It was too soon in our life together for one of the logs to suddenly give way beneath her foot, roll outwards, careening the other logs down on top of me, spilling Esther over the side, tumbling towards the ground.

I watched above me cautiously as we slowly climbed to the top. We were panting, at a loss for breath. We sat down on the logs and listened to the strained gasps of our bodies. Below us, the ground we had stood on. Esther shuffled closer and put her arm around my shoulder, her cheek against mine. Our chests pulsing in time. Out in front of us the occasional light of someone's distant house, the dark shadow of the rocket range with the tall metal launch rail reaching high into the moonlit sky.

Esther pointed the lights out to me. "Homes," she said squeezing my thigh. "For the first time since I moved here, I really feel at home. We are sitting right on top of it. I can feel its warmth beneath me." She took my hand in hers. "I feel as if we are on top of the world, that we have gone as far as it is humanly possible to go."

I showed her the range. "There are further possibilities yet," I promised. "This is just the beginning."

Esther turned and kissed me gently on the lips. She stroked my faced with her fingertips, pushed her mouth hard against mine. The black sky flickered with dots of light. A muted cry from some animal I could not distinguish as my arms held Esther tightly against me.

✦

Our house took three summers to build. Esther felt it was important to do as much of it as we could ourselves. Her grandparents had moved to Canada from Ireland. They had built their own log home without any prior knowledge. "When they moved here," she said, "they didn't even know anything about the land they were standing on, nothing of their environment. They were like the logs here on the tundra, they had to find their own way to fit in. We are like that too, you and I. We both need to find a new way to fit in. We will build this house ourselves. We will learn whatever it was my grandmother and grandfather learned. We will settle here, as the wood will settle over the years in our new home. We will sink through the weight of our lives together into this land."

Either that, I wished to tell her, or we will sink into the ground as Jack Butan did never to re-emerge.

"I am alone, and I am with you," Esther whispered to me one stormy night. The winds howled down our chimney, whined in anguish. The gusting snows beat at our window-panes. There was nothing visible of the outside world. Esther brushed her lips to my ear. The winter had come, the bears had arrived. Esther's fear gathered as thickly as the snows, hardened as strong as the ice. "What do I do if I meet one?" she softly asked. And I told her what an Inuit woman had told me many years before. "Take your clothes off while walking

27

slowly backwards. Do not look the bear in the eye. Lay down each item of clothing in front of you as you go. Bears are curious creatures and will inspect each one. Better to be naked and freezing than to be dead."

I ordered a peeling spud and drawknife at the hardware store. I picked them up two weeks later and carried them in through the front door of my old house. Esther stood in the kitchen with her back to me. Her long hair was tied midways down and hung six inches below her shoulders. Water splashed at her hands where she was washing dishes. Hands that had held my face in wonder, surprise and even anger. Hands cold as stone or warm as the water they now moved within. Her head turned slightly revealing the profile of her face. Esther, a woman whose life had opened up into mine, had slid into it as easily as the waves slid across the bay.

"Esther."

She turned from the sink. She smiled as she saw me. Shook her hands free of the water. Drops scattered around her. She rubbed at her forehead with the back of her arm.

"Wade."

She lifted a towel to dry her hands. Light slipped through the glass of the windowpane and spread across her. Illuminated her. A wisp of hair hung free across her face. I held the tools out to her like an offering.

She stepped forward across the kitchen floor and took them from me one in each hand. She balanced the peeling spud in her right hand, tested its weight.

"What does this do?"

"It pries the bark off."

Esther nodded and indicated towards the drawknife with its downward curving blade.

"And that?"

"It peels off what's left."

"Yes, of course it does." She placed the implements down on the kitchen table between the places set for our evening supper. "When do we start?"

"As soon as we have eaten."

Esther turned quickly to the stove where a beef casserole was simmering. "Well, let us eat then." She turned the stove off and lifted the pot with two dishcloths to avoid burning her fingers.

By day, I opened the gates on the bottom of the Hopper cars, allowed the trains to empty themselves of their grain, pouring, rushing, gushing into the receiving pits. The dust of the world filled our lives. I swallowed it, inhaled it through my nostrils, bore its brunt on my shoulders. By evening, outside with the logs, Esther and I took turns with the peeling spud and drawknife. Sliding the spud between the bark and the wood and prising away as much as possible, then shaving off the bark that remained with the drawknife. Esther loved the crackle of the dry bark snapping away revealing the smooth outer surface of the wood. "It was like cleaning away the crust of your living," she said.

Later in the dark, we nursed each other's cuts and blisters. Esther ran her bruised hands across the smooth flesh of my back and shoulders, brushed her lips gently against my cheek.

"This is what we must do to one another," she said. "We must strip the bark away, reveal what is underneath."

"It might take a lifetime," I warned.

"I would be disappointed if it took anything less."

Esther drew the design out on a napkin at Gypsy's Café. She wanted four rooms, she said. A living room, a kitchen/dining room, a bedroom, and a bathroom.

One bedroom was enough. Esther was in her late forties when I met her. "It is too late for children," she forewarned. "That is not a part of my future. The vicarious passage of my life has seen to that." She was saddened by this but resigned to it too. "I have no wish to look back. Up until I met you, it was the only direction I ever looked in. My whole life was lived with my eyes scouring my past while I walked back-wards into the future. And what I was scouring for were my mistakes of which I found plenty. You turned me around, so that I could see firmly ahead of me. We will have no children together. Do you think you can live with that?" All I wanted was to live with Esther, for her to close my eyes also to what occurred before we met.

I had spoken to Tom Fowler about the house. He lived in the flats now with a Cree woman but had lived and trapped all over northern Manitoba before settling in Churchill. It was he who told me what I would need to build a log home. He told me how the rooms could be square or rectangu-lar but since the logs joined at their ends, each room was self-contained. You could have a loft, but you could not have an enclosed room within a room without a stud wall. If you wanted another solid room, you had to build another adjoin-ing structure. I told Esther what Tom had said.

She drew quietly on the napkin. While she drew, I looked out on the gravel surface of Kelsey Boulevard, the service station across the way, the dilapidated pickups, the old yellow school bus which had been adapted for tours of the surrounding area, in so far as the few miles of road would permit tours. Esther finished her drawing and showed it to me. Two triangular boxes. "No false rooms," she said. "And no false lives." She pointed the first box out to me, a living room and upstairs bedroom. Then the next one, a kitchen, back hallway and an upstairs bathroom. Doors would connect one section to the other. I told her how we would have to build the structure whole first then later cut out the holes for the doors and windows.

Esther was delighted with this idea, delighted with the notion of living in an enclosed space before deciding where the light and exit should be.

"It is the way we should live our life after all," she said. "Living in the dark, searching the best way to see out, the best way to depart and return. For too long I have looked through windows of someone else's placement, I have walked through doors leading to where I did not want to go."

She folded the napkin snugly in her hand and in front of the diners leaned across and kissed me on the lips. I felt myself blush.

"Don't even worry about them," she said. "Soon they will be unable to see us, unable to find a way in."

Even though she was sitting back in her chair, I felt the pressure of her lips on mine still. I would have to tell her sometime that in order to get into our enclosed house in the first instance, we would have to select a doorway from the outside and cut it out irretrievably.

Esther met Marilyn while walking out by Goose Creek. She had gone out to look for sandhill cranes. Marilyn was looking for a particular wildflower. The creek was about six miles up the Churchill River. It was fished for Arctic grayling, northern pike and sea run trout.

Marilyn recognized Esther from around the town and introduced herself. She had come out to look for the One-Flowered Wintergreen, she said, a fairly widespread circumpolar sub-arctic species. Esther told me later how much she loved the language she spoke. "She is a fairly large woman, plump, and great in voice. She is certain of her opinions." *Moneses uniflora*. The Shy Maiden, the Wood Nymph. Marilyn was not shy. She was not a nymph. The herb's slender rootstalk crept upwards. The white flower on top hung its head low. Marilyn's head was held high.

That summer, she taught Esther as much as she could. She brought her to Sloop Cove, Akudlik, Cape Merry, Landing Lake, Bird Cove, Twin Lakes, Fort Prince of Wales, Launch Road, the coast road, townsite. There were flowers everywhere. You could not move but you stepped upon them. Esther was appalled. Even one footprint here in the tundra can last for hundreds of years.

"Good," I wanted to tell her. "We will survive."

On the way out that day from Goose Creek, they found Lapland Buttercup. *Ranunculus lapponicus*. Yellow Mountain Saxifrage. *Saxifraga aizoides*. Bog Laurel. *Kalmia polifolia*. Esther was intoxicated. She brought flower after flower into our home. At times of passion, she would occasionally speak the names of flowers. *Corallorhiza trifida*. *Spiranthes romanzoffiana*. *Menyanthes trifoliate*. *Myriophyllum exalbescens*. *Juniperus communis*. I opened up to her. I closed to the dark.

Once at the terminal, a few years after I arrived, I had slipped, fallen on a metal stairs. My arm and back hurt. I was immediately brought to the hospital, and Marilyn had treated me. Once I had seen her drunk at a party. She had hoisted her skirt in a way that nothing would be revealed. Esther would not get drunk. She would not hoist her skirt.

Marilyn eventually brought Jack into Esther's attention as though he was a wildflower she wished to preserve. The army base disappeared. The Dene disappeared. Someday Esther, you and I will disappear. Churchill itself will disappear as easily as Jack did.

I stepped on him. I wiped him out as though he had never existed.

✦

"It was a chance conversation," Esther told me. A few spoken words that could as easily have gone unheard. Is that not how it is, a life that could as easily go unlived?

It was early October, minus 5 degrees. The ice had yet to form. Esther had already lived here for seven years. She was having afternoon tea at Gypsy's Cafe with Marilyn. The wind whipped across the bay and down Kelsey Boulevard. It shook at the door as though seeking refuge. Marilyn's parka hung over the back of her chair. Her winter boots were crusted in snow. Esther wore her down-filled jacket. She squeezed her hands around her waist and felt the feathers inside. Wild fowl. It pleased Esther that she carried them with her throughout the cold. It was as though they had refused to migrate, she once said, had gone against their nature. The door opened and the wind rushed in, stung Esther's already reddened cheeks. At that very instant those words distanced themselves from whoever had spoken them, separated from whatever meaning they had possessed and hung there frozen in the cold air. *Jack Butan.*

That is all she heard. The door closed over. The words seemed to thaw and melt. They meant nothing to Esther, so she warmed her hands around her teacup and watched the steam rise. It was Marilyn who rescued them, imbued them with intent. She turned to see who had spoken your name, but the café was full. People hiding out from the cold.

She turned back to Esther, took a drink of her tea and said, "That is a name from the past."

Esther glanced up, considered if she should take her jacket off yet.

"I haven't heard mention of him in years, had quite forgotten all about him."

Marilyn held her cup off the table. She looked past Esther, through the window, out into the street, far past it to the open tundra into an altogether different time. From there, she told Esther what she remembered.

✦

What do I remember? I like to think I remember every last detail, every nuance, but I doubt it. The truth is I have done my best to submerge the events of that day just as Jack submerged beneath the ice and slipped from view. It is enough to live with the burden of my actions. I do not need to recall them to suffer their load.

That evening after I came in from yard work Esther was setting the table for supper. I walked over and from behind kissed the side of her neck. She placed a spoon down on the table. "You must be cold." The wind had not yielded all day. Esther took my coat from me and hung it up in the hallway. A pot bubbled on the stove. She filled our bowls with vegetable casserole and brought them to the table. "This will help warm you up."

She looked different although I could not tell what that difference was. Maybe an air of excitement as though she was the bearer of good news, as though something had occurred that allowed her to move here anew one more time. The winters are long here, and it is easy to forget to keep yourself busy. Sometimes I know Esther felt boredom creep in. Of late, she had seemed restless, but that evening an air of near calmness seemed to have lit upon her.

"What is it?"

I was prepared for any answer but the one she gave. My heart stopped. I do not say that in the way others have, as an expression, and I do not mean that my heart skipped a beat. It stopped. I am uncertain if I experienced a moment of my death, but I did not feel alive. Esther had stirred her casserole with her spoon to help cool it down. She had looked at me with patience in what must have been a time of great impatience to her. She had said his name. *It is Jack. Jack Butan.* I couldn't move. I had not one thought in my mind. In place of whatever I am, there was nothing.

Esther's eyes recorded this. "Wade," she said quietly.

It was this word, this articulation of my name that permitted me to live again. Esther killed me, and she brought me back to life.

"What's wrong?" She pushed her chair back and rose. She laid her spoon on the table and moved around to me. She stood at my side and placed her hand on my arm.

I have no answers to any of the questions Jack's death raises. For some time I tried. I kept to myself in the barren lands and spent my time seeking out those impossible responses. But only the punishing mixture of doubt, uncertainty, and guilt swept through me like an abrasive Arctic storm gouging and shredding at my humanity. For years I lived in utter despair. Eventually, in a desperate act of self-preservation, I learned to let it go. I gave up trying.

I felt Esther's hand on my arm. She no longer looked as though she was here for the first time but as though she had been here too long already.

"I am okay," I said, scarcely believing myself. I rubbed her hand with mine.

"I am sorry," she replied.

Esther let go of my arm and sat back down. She told me how Marilyn overheard the snippet of conversation. Heard the name Jack Butan. Marilyn told her how she had almost forgotten all about him. It must have been twenty years ago, after the army left. He had been quite a character, she said. Knew everyone and everyone knew him. He had worked in the port somewhere. In his early twenties. Always had a different lady on his arm. Then one day he simply disappeared. No one ever heard of him again. The police investigated but came up with nothing. His belongings were still in his apartment. Marilyn said that it was assumed he had gone out walking somewhere and had an accident of some type. These sort of things happen here. It would be easy for a body never to be found.

Esther told me all of this. I listened as though I was listening to an update on severe weather conditions. I chewed the vegetables in the casserole without tasting anything, chewed over every word she was saying.

"Marilyn said he was a friend of yours." Esther searched my face for anything that might be revealed.

I put my spoon down in my bowl, wiped my mouth with the back of my hand. "He was the closest friend I have ever had," I told her truthfully.

"I'm sorry," she said again. "I have upset you by bringing this up. It was wrong of me to do it in this way."

"Esther." I did not know what else to say. I felt the re-approach of those punishing arctic storms.

Esther finished her food and brought our bowls to the sink. I put both hands palm down on the tabletop and pushed myself up into standing. I held myself there, steadied myself then went to the back hall and got my jacket and my gloves and put them on. I put my hat on too and pulled my hood up over it, put on my boots, and opening the backdoor stepped outside into the dark and closed the door again. The winds howled around me. If you listened closely, you could hear any ghost you wished. I stayed by the doorway, looked into the blackness. The skin on my face tightened against the cold. I pulled my hood in closer around it. Jack was somewhere there, off in the distance, and although I could not see him, I knew he was making his way towards us. I was a fool to think that he would not return. A fool to think he had ever gone away.

The door opened behind me.

"Come in Wade. It's too cold out there." Esther shivered as she spoke.

I shook the snow off my boots and stepped back inside.

"Where did you meet him, Wade?"

The question that silently slipped from her mouth into mine when our lips first came together in praise of our own unlikely union. Where did I meet him, Esther? I met him in a place where the sun never sets, and I lost sight of him during a day that has never come to an end.

When I first saw Jack Butan, he was bent over a pool table at The Churchill Bar, his cue slightly raised, grey ash drifting softly onto the green beige from the cigarette hanging from his lips. The thud of a ball disappearing into a pocket. And then the inexplicable, a white ball traveling backwards towards the tip of his raised cue as though time was playing itself out in reverse. Jack, I learned, was capable of that. He dropped his cue level as the white ball came to a rest, and the ball once more propelled itself forwards like a comet through space. Jack's laughter, his sensuous grin. Swigging from a bottle and catching my eye. Later, I would be introduced, and I would speak my first words to him. I would tell him I had heard the call of a wolf on the wind that evening, and Jack would look at me as though he recognized the portent of my words. He bought me a beer and told me he had seen me around the port.

I had only been there a month at the time, having moved from Northern Alberta, and barely knew anyone. But most evenings after that we could be found there together, drinking beer, playing pool. Jack to the forefront. And, most nights, we would walk back to his apartment, where by now I resided, along the rocky road with the expanse of sky above with no discernible end. The wind blowing in off the bay, the churning waters.

Why the two of us, I will never know. And yet that is the way it was. Jack who knew everyone and me who did not even know myself. It took that first greeting, that first beer, and nothing more. He confided to me that initial night on our way home from the bar that the landscape here spooked him, the desolation, the bears that could not be seen.

"It is as though our lives are occurring in some other location," he said, "too far from anywhere to be witnessed."

"Is this such a bad thing?" I asked.

He merely shrugged. "I have no way of knowing."

As we walked, the sound of our footsteps sounded hollow on the empty road as though nothing existed within us. It was an August night but already the air was chillingly cold. The stars large and shimmering like molten silver. Our breaths in vapour ahead of us.

"Why did you come here?" Jack asked on another such night, his hands deep in his pants pockets. He glanced up at me sideways then looked ahead. Who knows what he saw?

"I came because I had nowhere better to go," I said. It was as truthful an answer as I could think of, but Jack just shook his head.

"Horseshit!" He looked at me again screwing up his forehead in something akin to disgust. "There are infinitely better places to go. The world is filled with them."

Water splashed onto the rocks along the shore, filled in their gaps momentarily before emptying away in loud exhalations. "What about you then?" I queried. Maybe he knew more about why I had gone there than I did myself, maybe he understood me better.

He took one hand from his pocket and trailed it through his dark hair, the pale reflection of his white fingers in the moonlight. He coughed as though something immovable was lodged in his throat. A small pebble spat from the heel of his boot.

"Like everyone else," he answered, "I was running away. *Am* running away."

"What are you running from?" I wondered if the obvious nature of this question would upset him, if he didn't expect, from me, something of more substance.

But he answered as though the question was substantial enough. "A happy life." He pulled out a cigarette, and tapped it on the packet as he walked, cupped his hand to shelter the blaze. He sucked in and blew out. "Is that not crazy?" He laughed loudly. His laugh carried in the air momentarily then seemed to slip out of earshot. He had already told me he had been brought up in Iowa where his family had a farm. Everything he knew about machinery he had learned the hard way there, he said. "Most people spend their lives searching out happiness, and I who have it handed to me on a plate can't get away from it fast enough." He dragged on his cigarette, looked puzzled by his own actions. "I had, maybe still have, a girlfriend there. Angie." He took another long drag then tossed the cigarette in front of him and stubbed it out on the road. He exhaled the smoke into the air. "She, I can honestly tell you, is very beautiful." He stopped and looked around. The water pressed to the shore, the tufted tundra, the rocky outcrops. "I can't see the beauty here. It eludes me." He exhaled loudly through his nose, rubbed at his lip. "What do you see?"

"Strangeness," I replied. "Whether that is beautiful or not I don't think I have been here long enough to know."

Jack nodded as though some part of what I said made sense to him. Something moved off to the right of us, hidden in the dark tundra. We both turned cautiously. A gull shrieked from the shoreline. I searched across the low vegetation for a shape. Something to indicate what animal might be out there. Some more movement and then the barking of a dog. We both laughed.

"There's plenty to run away from here too," I smiled.

"Our own shadows," Jack said. "Ultimately it is what we are all running from."

✦

I lay in bed that night unable to sleep. Esther, too, wondering no doubt what had occurred between us, why I would not speak to her. How could I tell her that I was unable to, that my words were frozen, trapped in another place? I could have said that I was waiting for Jack to return, Tess also. The creaking in the roof, the rattling at the door could just as easily have been the wind I suppose. And when I finally fell asleep if Jack was in my dreams, I did not remember it in the morning. There was no trace of him as though a light snow had fallen covering his trail.

Esther would have to hear something. I would tell her what I could, whatever words would surface.

I went outside to bring in wood. The winds had died down. The sky was clear. I felt numb. Whether it was the intense cold or the shock of his name off Esther's lips, I didn't know. I pulled my hat down over my ears and went to the wood pile, filled my arms with pieces of the front door, its wooden frame. The last time Tess had been at my house she left through that door never to walk through it again. Before the door closed, its frame was filled with her departure. I carried the wood in and laid it next to the stove. Esther was preparing breakfast in the kitchen. Oatmeal, eggs and bacon. I took off my gloves and hat and put them in the pockets of my jacket. I would take my coat off and hang it up. I would talk to Esther. As I turned around, I saw her standing in the kitchen doorway. She looked tired.

"Sit down. I will tell you about him."

Esther rubbed at her shoulder unbeknownst to herself. "We'll eat first." She reached her hands out. "I'll take your coat."

After breakfast, after the plates were cleared, Esther sat back down at the table. I washed my hands and joined her.

"I should have told you about him before. It was all such a long time ago."

"I didn't realize you were so close," Esther apologized. "It was careless of me to bring it up so nonchalantly."

"How would you know?"

"Marilyn mentioned that you knew him. I was curious, I suppose." Esther smoothed the sleeve of her blouse as though the creases could simply be brushed away. "It seemed strange that he just disappeared."

"It is strange. I have never got used to it." And that is the truth. His absence was always present. I clasped my hands together, felt the tremble within them as the thaw began. "Jack was one of the first people I met when I moved here. We hit it off straight away. Not that he had any shortage of friends, but there was something about us both that brought the best out in each other. He was the life and soul of the party. I was quiet, reserved. Opposite sides of the same coin. Four years

41

later, he disappeared." The shake in my hands spread upwards through my arms. "I don't think the police thought anything bad had happened to him. They felt he would just show up a short while later wondering what all of the fuss was about. It is not unusual for people to come and go up here. Nevertheless, they were urged on by a woman we both knew. She cared for Jack, convinced the police to search for him in case he had had an accident. They brought a helicopter in, scoured the tundra, searched along the coast. But it was the end of winter. They were frequently hampered by weather conditions. There were many days when they couldn't fly at all. The frozen over tundra, the winds, the snow. They gave up after a week. And that was that. Jack had gone, and he didn't return." A deep shudder ran through my whole body.

Esther listened quietly, intently, as though attending to words beyond the ones I had spoken. "What do you think happened?" she finally asked.

I sighed inwardly, tried to still the storm within. What had happened to Jack was something that had never been intended, something so out of the ordinary that it was barely credible it could occur in such a normal way. "He had an accident. That is what I believe."

Esther absorbed my response. I saw her chest rise and fall. She seemed to move forward in her chair.

"You think he is dead?"

"Yes. I think he is dead."

"And the woman, what did she think?"

"She thought he might have killed himself."

"Do you think that is possible?"

It would be too easy for me to say, yes, that I alone was not responsible for my actions. I have seen all manner of dead. A snowshoe hare frozen into the hard white snow, an Arctic fox caught in a metal trap, a ptarmigan with a hole through its breast, a whale cast up on the beach. Where does the living stop and the dying begin? I will answer that, it doesn't. They merge, unite until it is hard to distinguish one from the other.

"No, Esther, that is not possible."

Esther could not let it go. Jack's disappearance.

"Just because you believe he died does not mean that he did. His body was never found. He may have gone away for some reason you did not know about. No matter how close two people are, it does not mean that there are not things they choose to keep secret from one another."

I lay on our bed in the loft of our wood home, pillows propped at the back of my head. Esther spoke loudly from the adjoining bathroom through the open door. She was bathing, soaking her troubles away.

She could not understand how I was content to allow Jack to slip away like that. "He was your friend after all," she had said earlier in the day. "Surely you want to know precisely what became of him."

"Did you ever speak to his family?" she asked now. I heard the soft splash of the water. She was washing, cleaning away the grime of her day. She would dip her head back, immerse it beneath the water, and when she resurfaced her hands would join at her face and part to wipe the water from her eyes.

It felt to me as though I was sinking also. Every question she asked caused the pain of the past to rise within me and weigh me down.

"No, I never spoke to them myself. I only vaguely knew where they lived. The police contacted them I seem to remember."

"What did they say?"

The steam from the hot bath would have clouded across the mirror like frost. We were disappearing from each other's view.

"I don't recall. Possibly, I never knew."

I heard a louder splash as Esther rose from the bath. Water dripped from her body, slipped out of reach. She would step onto the bathmat and grasp for the towel. The bath water gurgled down the drain. Esther appeared at the door in her bathrobe. She dried her hair with a towel. "Perhaps he turned up there at some later point. You would never have known."

"Esther, he didn't."

Esther stopped drying her hair for a moment. "You don't know that." She came over and sat on the bed next to me. "I know this is hard for you, but I really think it would be for the best to find out what you can, to bring as much closure as possible."

"It is too late now. It all happened too long ago." How could I tell her how difficult it really was? How could I say to her what I could not say to myself?

"It is never too late." She gathered the wet towel up and brought it back to the bathroom.

Oh Esther, isn't it so, there are some truths that can never be known?

"He is dead," I said when she returned.

She looked at me. "I am forty-eight years old," she said, "and you are fifty-three. Together, our ages combined, we should be dead, but instead I have never felt more alive. I want to find Jack Butan for you, for both of us."

The steam in the bathroom dissipated, the mirror slowly cleared.

That is how it began. Esther's quest for Jack, for the truth about our lives together.

CHAPTER 3

We continued through that first spring and summer peeling the bark from the logs. Esther threw herself into the work, continuing at it even when I was working at the grain terminal. Thrusting the flat blade of the peeling spud under the corky outer layer that protected the living tree from water loss, and insect invasion, and bacterial and fungal infections. Forcing it from the now dead trunk. She scraped off the remainder with the drawknife. Sitting herself by the log, gripping the handles either side of the curved blade and using her feet for leverage pulled on the knife, drawing it down the log and scraping away the remaining bark.

Moving the logs was the hardest of all. I ordered a peavey, a long tool with a handle. It had a swing hook to roll the log into position, and a point on the end which was used like a pry bar to separate jammed logs from one another. It was hard and strenuous work, and we were learning as we went along. Each evening, Esther soaked away the aches in her back and put cream on her blisters. Despite the heavy nature of the work, she never complained. If anything, she seemed to enjoy it. She loved to look out at the large pile of logs, those that had been peeled clean and those we had still to do.

"We are building a trap," she said one evening after we had finished. I sat on the log we had just peeled and wiped the sweat from my forehead. "A trap that will capture us a true home of our own." She sighed and sat down next to me. She tugged at her skirt, looked up at the evening sky, the mellow light. Then she looked across to the rocket range, its dull shadow cast against the bright flowers of the tundra. "I wish I had been here when they were still launching the rockets. I would have liked to have seen them take off."

Despite all of the years I had lived there, I had only witnessed one launch myself, a research test on the ionosphere where the northern lights are formed. I watched it with Jack from the roof of my house. It was on an evening similar to that one with Esther. A clear sky, soft light. The greens and purples of the wispy tundra. The distant launch pad, the tall metal rail protruding high into the air. Behind it, the small, dwarfed trees.

"We don't know the half of it," Jack said lying flat out on the roof. He looked to the blue sky the rocket would later on propel itself through. "Ang liked to lie in the bed of my Dad's pickup and look up at the stars. She was corny that way. We'd drive out to the lake late in the evening. There was an old tarp in the back, and she'd spread it out for us. No fooling around now, she'd tell me. We're here for the stars." He still talked about her occasionally as though he had never really left her, as though he thought it possible she was waiting for him still.

Shortly afterwards, we saw the explosive flash of light and heard the thunderous roar as the sleek black rocket raced into the atmosphere, tore through the evening sky. Tess would tell me later how many of her people believed that the northern lights were their ancestors looking over them. What would they make of a rocket, she wondered, coming to disprove their existence? Sometimes we would lay a blanket on the cold ground and watch the pale greens and purples of their wavering light as though the tundra itself was reeling through the sky offering another possibility, more luminescent, less solid. And I wondered at those times if Jack had ever lain with Tess in this way too as he had lain in the back of the pickup with Ang.

The rockets were gone now, the range deserted, Jack nowhere in sight.

"We are building our home on permafrost," I warned Esther. "The rock and soil beneath us are permanently frozen. A soil formed by glaciers grinding across the land. Silt clays and sand. The top layer may freeze and thaw, reduce to slurry, but underneath the ice-age has never retreated."

I could tell Esther was secretly pleased, felt further north than she already was. She bent onto her hunkers before the logs, fingered the earth. I wondered if she understood the implications of what I was saying. I knew little of it myself.

"We need to get the foundations right or the ground will begin to heave beneath us, our house subside."

Esther tore away some moss as though looking for the ice beneath. "What do we have to do?"

"We have to talk to Joe Tyrell. He has helped build many of the homes here."

Esther, I think, hoped that we would do all of this ourselves. But it would be impossible. The weight of the logs alone saw to this. Even rolling them with our gloved hands or with the peavey was exhausting, and, at times, we were simply incapable of moving them at all. We did not possess the strength between us.

Joe told me he wouldn't be able to make it until the end of the summer, that now was his busiest time of the year, the only time he could get construction work done. Besides, he said, piles would have to be driven into the permafrost and freeze in place over the winter before any building could commence. Esther was disappointed. It wasn't that she wanted the house built over night. She was happy to watch the fallen trees be stripped and shaped, interconnected, built slowly upwards, but she was keen to move on with it. Not to have it too stunted in its growth by the climate, the conditions.

Joe came by in early September. It had rained for the two days previous, and the ground was muddy. I heard his truck pull in and went out to him. The rain had cleared the air, released the scent of the vegetation. Esther stood at the open door and watched.

He stomped his rubber boot into the muck. "That's what they call the active layer," he explained getting straight to business. "We need to get below that. The permafrost makes a great foundation as long as it doesn't thaw. Damn problem is the house. Changes the natural order of things. Shades the ground in summer keeping it cool and heats it up in winter with all that damn wood you're burning. Alters everything. The permafrost begins to thaw, loses its strength. Next thing you know you're living in a tilt-a-wheel."

He went to the back of his truck and took out a hammer and a long steel rod with a sharpened end. Esther and I had staked out the perimeter of the house with pegs and twine. Joe stepped over the twine and put the point of the rod into the ground. Then he drove it in with his hammer until it would go no further.

"Could be rock of course," he said. He hit it one more time with his hammer and listened to the sound it made. A dull clang. "Naw, that's ice for sure."

He stepped back out and returned the rod and hammer to his truck. "We need to keep the house up off the ground, allow for circulation, prevent heat flow. I'll bore some holes into the permafrost, put in some wooden piles, fill it in with some of this mucky stuff. Then all you have to do is sit tight and wait for winter to work its wonders."

He was back in the truck and almost out of there before I could thank him. He made no mention of when he would come back.

There are days that fool you, days so cold you are sure that winter has returned for the season. Then you wake up the next morning to a lengthy warm spell. The exact time of winter's arrival is near impossible to predict, but you can be assured of one thing, it will return. I woke early one morning in late September to a loud grating and screeching from outside. I looked out my window and there Joe was boring the holes. I was cold and tired and got back into bed to the warmth of Esther. I lay next to her and listened to the drill cut through the frozen soil. Esther stirred without really waking. I told her to go back to sleep. I must have dozed myself. When I looked out again, Joe was gone. The wooden piles stood out of the ground five feet in the air. I would awaken Esther to this. I would bring her to the window and show her. She would feel at peace. We would probably go back to bed then and drift off to sleep again. When we arose, it would surely be winter.

✦

Like Jack, Tess slid into my life as effortlessly as a breaking wave. It was September the eighteenth 1976. Minus 2 or minus 3 degrees. I was walking by Bird Cove. Flakes of snow drifted downwards like random thoughts. A half inch or so had already gathered on the ground, lodged between the rocks on the shore. It was sometime after six o'clock. I had finished work at the granary, got something to eat, and walked out to the cove. Few bears had been sighted so far, but, all the same, I knew I was taking something of a risk. The bears would gather in October and November waiting for the bay to freeze over to return to their frozen homes. The temperatures were already colder than usual. It was not unlikely that one may have strayed here early in its over eagerness to get back to the mainstay of its life. I stepped over the curved grey rocks humped like the backs of small whales, trod across the mix of snow and sand. The sky a solid mass of off-white cloud. The rippling grey of the water swept toward the shore.

Out in the bay to the west, the rusted wreck of *The Ithaca* lay abandoned, in the way it sometimes seemed to me that we were all abandoned in this remote location. I searched the rocks ahead of me carefully. A flock of gulls landed on the shore, lifted off and settled down again. I listened to the scrape of my shoes on the rocks, the bickering cries of the gulls. The gloomy freighter that never made it here but never got away either. Up ahead, I saw the figure. At first movement, I naturally thought of the polar bear, but of course Tess was no match for its size. A pink flush seeped through the cloud cover, the sun somewhere outside of this enclosed world. At my feet, a brilliant orange glow of lichen spread across the rocks. An icy gust bit at my cheeks. I inhaled the bitter cold air and walked over the gravel tightening my hands into the pockets of my jacket. The person continued to approach from the other side of the beach.

I recognized her as she neared. Her long black hair, her smooth dark skin, her generous eyes. She taught at the elementary school in town. I had often seen her around, but I had never had the opportunity to speak with her. Now, we were alone in this small cove off the great Hudson Bay, the vast waters that stretched to the Atlantic Ocean, to the Bering Sea. The gravel, the mounds of rock, the gatherings of snow, the sheltered sky, and beyond it the disappearing sun. Tess and I stopped at the same time. We stood not more than five feet apart. I had one foot resting on a low rock and one on the flat gravel. Tess's feet firmly planted on solid ground.

She greeted me and smiled. Her turquoise fleece jacket, her navy jeans. She brushed at some loose strands of hair blowing against her face. A red and orange fire extinguished at the horizon.

"Tess Cook." She held out her hand.

I took it in mine, felt its coldness before letting it go. "Wade Sinclair."

"I teach at the school." I nodded to indicate that I knew this much. "I come out here sometimes to clear my head. I love the children, but they are draining." She smiled again.

"The grain terminal," I said. "I come out here to clear the dust away. There, there is nothing to love." It was true. I did not dislike my job, but there was little to like about it either.

"I see you sometimes. You are a friend of Jack Butan."

Even then, everything was defined by him. "Yes, we are good friends. Do you know him?"

"I bump into him occasionally." She put her hands back into her jacket pockets. The sun had gone down. It was getting colder. "We should keep walking."

This is where we would part, is it not? When the wave would break and rush back out to sea, when the tern would turn and flap determinately against the breeze. Where walking away we would hear the small sounds of our departures echo on this barely habitable shore.

"Which way are you going?" she asked.

I told her how I had walked here from my house at the rocket range.

"It is a long way back. Walk with me to my car if you wish, and I will drive you home."

Tess parked outside my house. I opened the passenger door and thanked her for the lift. Outside, the low scrub of the tundra. Lichen, reindeer moss, stunted spruce and willow, sedges, heath. She inhaled the sub-arctic air. "Are you going to invite me in?"

I opened the storm door with the torn mosquito netting and the front door which had warped on its hinges and led her into the cold living room. She sat with her fleece jacket on while I lit the stove, her arms wrapped around her. I remembered our cold hands on the beach when we shook each other's, the cold air of her vehicle which did not have time to warm up during our drive back here. It was always that way between Tess and me. There was a coldness we could never get rid of no matter how much we tried. No matter how many fires we lit, how much clothes we wore, how close we held each other. We accepted it as something unavoidable. Something borne of the landscape we lived in, our shared environment. There were nights I held her under thick layers of blankets, the wood stove burning, our hearts, and still our bodies were cold to the touch.

That night in the living room, Tess sat on the couch while I sat across from her in an armchair, the stove between us. She talked about the school, the children. She asked me about my work at the grain terminal, whether I planned to stay.

"Nothing is certain," I told her, "but I see no reason to leave."

"When did you move here?"

"In '74."

"We were relocated the year before that." Tess turned to see if I understood what she was saying.

"You're Dene?" I had heard how the native Dene people had been relocated from Churchill to Tadoule Lake the year before I came.

"Yes. My family moved, but I stayed on."

Tess then telling me something of her life, and I telling her something of mine. I made tea, and we drank in its warmth as the evening darkened outside. She eventually rose from the couch and said she should leave.

"I have school in the morning." She zipped up her jacket.

We went outside. Tess opened the door of her car, slid into her seat, and started up the engine. I bent my head inwards as though I might kiss her cheek, but instead I advised her to drive safely. I stood back to allow her to close the door. She reached for the handle, gently pulled it towards her.

I asked Jack about Tess soon after I first met her. We were walking down by the port. The terminal had closed for the winter although the water had yet to freeze. Jack pulled his hat down over his ears. We passed by the tall workhouse of the terminal where the bins were kept for gathering and weighing the grain. Normally, you had to shout to be heard. The trains coming and going, the flow of the grain into the receiving pits, the conveyor belts, the metal storage bins filling and emptying, transfer belts, elevating equipment, the galleries that transferred the grain to the ships. Noise on top of noise. But walking with Jack that day there was nothing to be heard as though everything had already frozen over. The huge concrete building stood empty. Gulls flew in and landed on its roof. The harbour was still. A lone fishing boat was tied up at the dock. The water in the bay was relatively calm. A steady roll of low waves. We walked down onto the stony beach.

"So Tess Cook," Jack said and winked over at me.

"Tess Cook," I said back. I shrugged. "I met her out at Bird Cove. We got talking. She mentioned she knew you."

"I kissed her," Jack said.

His words were slight, but they weighed heavily on me nevertheless. I thought he would be smiling when I looked up at him, but instead he squeezed his lips together resignedly.

"It was down at the Churchill Bar. I had had a beer or two too many. Someone had introduced us earlier in the night. We had talked a while, and then I went to play pool. Later on I bumped into her again. We talked some more." Jack shook his head. "I have no idea what I was saying, but Tess was laughing. I guess she looked pretty. She stopped laughing and stood there looking at me, smiling. I leaned in and kissed her."

He looked at me, gauging my reaction.

"What did she do?" The small waves broke, washed in over the stones then drained away.

"She told me a gentleman would ask permission first, and I told her she was living in the wrong part of the world if it was gentlemen she was seeking."

I had to laugh. Jack was like that. He would tell you something that would stop you in your tracks, and then he would tell you something more that would cause you to laugh, make you almost believe that what you had heard was of no real consequence.

Jack had kissed Tess. He simply leaned over and kissed her.

He stopped suddenly, bent down and picked up a stone, cast it into the water. I followed its flight, watched it dip, splash lightly and disappear. Jack was not going to tell me anything more. I would have to pry it from him. Like the stone, Jack's words often sunk without a trace.

"What did she say to that?"

Jack stooped down on his hunkers, scanned the bay as though his answer lay out there. "Wade," he eventually said, "I won't lie to you. She said nothing. She left the kiss there as though I might come back for it any time I wanted." He peered up at me. I made no response. "Tell me now," he continued, "did you kiss her?"

I felt silly standing so tall above him, yet I didn't want to stoop down. "I talked to her Jack, nothing more than that."

"There's no such thing," he said. "When you talk to someone there's always something more." He rose up before me.

At times, the cold suddenly gets into your bones, a wayward breeze, a momentary chill. It is hard then to lose yourself of it. You can pull your jacket around you, blow into your hands, but it is of no use. That is the way I felt then. As though Jack when he stood up had displaced a wave of cold air that infiltrated my body.

"I'm starting to feel the cold," I told him.

Jack nodded. "The wind is picking up."

We both took a last look at the bay. Jack said something I didn't hear properly. He had already turned around and was walking back towards the port. I had not kissed Tess. I had listened to her as I listened then to the slosh of the water sliding through the stones.

✦

Early the following spring, with the piles frozen in place, we began cutting the peeled logs. Esther measured them out, and I made the cuts with a chainsaw I borrowed from an old work friend of mine. "Get a feel for your machine," he advised me. "Start it up and get used to how it responds to the throttle. Take a boxer's stance. Stand with your left foot forward and your right foot back. When the bottom of the chainsaw bar makes contact with the log, it'll pull you towards it, and when the top makes contact, it'll push you away. If you're not ready for either, you'll get knocked on your ass. Bend your knees as you pivot the saw and always think about where the saw will exit. You don't want to cut your leg off. And bear in mind, it's heavier than you think and gets heavier the longer you hold it. You wouldn't carry a bowling ball around for hours on end." He showed me the kickback zone and how to cut to avoid the saw sticking in the down cut when the downward force caused the log to close up on the chain. "Fill any open areas under the log with wood to take the tension off," he explained. "It's just like using a sawhorse, without having to lift the tree off the ground. You're using the natural contours of the land instead."

I took it slow, cutting as he had shown me. The labouring noise of the engine, the noxious smell of the fuel overpowering the sweet aroma of the wood chips. It was arduous work but in an odd way not dissimilar from drilling through the ice, the same sense of pressure and tension in the body and in the surface being cut into. I even had augers stick when the ice chips built up too much behind them.

Esther would not be left out and insisted on learning how to use the saw also.

"I did not come this far," she said, "to simply observe. I came to take part in the workings of this world."

So I showed her how to use it as I had been shown, and Esther cut what she could cut safely until her energy was expended.

I cut notches at the ends of the logs, so they could interlock, with an axe and finished them off with an adze, a tool similar to an axe but with its arched blade perpendicular to the handle, swinging both of the tools crudely, chipping roughly into the wood.

Later, with Joe's help, we tied chains around the logs and began raising and lowering them into place with his backhoe. They were interlocked in a square, one set at a time. Esther and I did our best to manoeuvre them as they swung in the air using our gloved hands and the long peavey. The work was slow and tiring. I wondered if Esther would give up, suggest we hire more people. But Esther never yielded. The house was a test, I knew that. A test that would confirm if she had made the right decision or not in coming north with me.

By the approach of winter, we had the main floor set in place. The work came to an end to accommodate the earth's turn away from the sun. The temperature dropped, the waters froze, and the ice thickened. I bored my holes, measured and recorded the depths of winter in my book. Like the earth, Esther and I turned, but not away from one another. In the cold, we reached for each other. We held our bodies close and shared between us whatever warmth we had.

The following summer we built the lofts and raised the roof. Even Esther acknowledged then that we needed help. We hired four enthusiastic labourers and constructed a summer like no other. Each day, Esther watched our home growing like a shrub she had planted.

Eventually, with the walls completed, we cut out the front door. Esther was the first to step inside. She beamed. She walked throughout the unfinished structure.

"Wade," she called.

"I am here."

"Wade, come into the kitchen, your dinner is ready. Wade, sit down in the living room. I will get you a cup of tea. Wade, I am tired, let us go upstairs."

The windows still had to be cut, the walls still had to be chinked, the floors and ceilings installed. There were stairs to be built, doors and windows to be put in place. Plumbing and wiring fitted. We would spend this winter dreaming of the next winter.

CHAPTER 4

The next time I saw Tess she was standing with her students on the beach across from the school. It was late July. It had been a year since we had met at Bird Cove. The waters had frozen over and melted again. You would think this length of time impossible in a town of so few people. In a town where there was nowhere else to go.

It was as if the very act of our meeting had caused us both to disappear. Oh, I knew that Tess was still here, living, breathing, going about the routines of her life as I went about mine, but I could not see her. And she in turn, I surmised, could not see me. I would watch out on my way to and from work. I would search the tables at the bars I sometimes drank at. I would look in the aisles at the store. I would be extra vigilant on my walks along the shore. I might have thought that she had gone away, relocated like the rest of her people, but Jack sporadically confirmed that this was not the case. "I saw your Tess," he would begin. "Did you kiss her?" my response. Perhaps he had seen her on the street, or at someone's house or at the café drinking coffee. He had talked to her but forgot to mention me. "She must be avoiding you," the way he would end his tale.

I could have gone to the school where she taught. Indeed I had often considered this option. I could have walked down the corridor to her classroom and peered in through the glass window on the door. But if I had done, I would surely have seen the children sitting at their tables staring to the top of the class where no one stood. I sometimes wondered if I had somehow managed to absorb her spirit and she mine.

It took a beached white whale for us both to reappear. I heard about the beaching from Gus the foreman at work and had walked down to see it on my morning break.

"Tess," I said lowly when I noticed her by the water's edge as I crossed the dunes. My word must have caught on a gentle breeze and have been carried to her ears because at that moment she turned from the children and looked in my direction. She smiled, and even from that distance the whiteness of her teeth showed as though another whale had beached between her lips.

I walked over the dunes and down onto the gravel. Apart from Tess and the children, about twenty other people were gathered around the whale pouring water from the bay onto its huge body. It looked at least fifteen feet long. A thick white teardrop of blubber stranded on a vast bed of stone. Water from the tides lapped against its tail, teased it. Its broad flippers, stout neck, and surprisingly small head.

"Is it dead?"

Tess shook her head. "Not yet. And you, you are alive too."

Not yet, I wanted to reply. The loud chatter of the children, their laughter. The crunching of gravel beneath their feet. "Do you know what happened?"

"There are those who say it swam too close to the shore when chasing its prey and got stranded when the tides went out. Others say it was escaping killer whales."

"And what do you think?"

Tess pushed her hair back behind her ear, took the hand of one of her children, a small dark-haired girl no more than ten years old. Tess's eyes turned to the whale's small head. I followed her stare. Its blowhole, its little eyes, its wide mouth which almost seemed to be smiling. It looked serene, completely at ease.

"I think it flew here," she said. "I think it has something to say." She laughed self-consciously. Her hair escaped her ear, and she pushed it back in place.

"Will it fly away?"

"That depends on whether we listen to it or not."

A conservation officer nearby spoke into her radio. The static from it crackled and hissed in the air. A gull teetered on the small stones along the shore. A helicopter flew overhead drowning out the static, circled and flew off again.

"I better get the children back to class."

Tess was saying goodbye again. She would walk away with the children, holding the young girl's hand. And as she walked, she would start to fade until she was no longer there, and the girl was alone.

"Tess, I would like to hear what it has to say."

Tess smiled. The girl tugged on her hand. "Meet me after supper if you can."

"What time?"

"Eight thirty. The White Bear Café."

She gathered up the children and walked back along the beach towards the school. I held her in my sight.

After work, I stopped by the beach again to see how the whale rescue was progressing. All day long, I had heard reports of their efforts. Over fifty people, I was told, had gathered to form a chain passing buckets along to keep the whale covered in sea water. They were waiting for the tides to come in to begin the process of refloating it. It was hoped then to pull it out to sea using fishing boats, cables and nets.

When I got to the beach, the tides were already coming in. The lower half of the whale's body was covered in water. Three boats were in place. Members of a search and rescue crew floated by the whale in an inflatable dinghy. Others were gathered around the whale up to their waists in water trying to attach nets and a harness to it. Although the waters were reasonably calm, they were having trouble keeping their balance. Lifeguards stood nearby at the ready. The dinghy bounced over the small waves. Those on the boats watched on, waiting for the go ahead. I stayed with the other onlookers for about three quarters of an hour, but I couldn't see any great progress being made and decided to go home for something to eat before meeting up with Tess.

I sat by the window in the café where I could see Tess approach. The coffee steamed in the mug between my hands. It was quiet at this time of the evening. Only a few tables were occupied. All talk was of the whale. How they would get it back in the water, how much longer it had left to live. Outside, two scraggy dogs sniffed at each other. A red rusted pickup drove by. Dust blew off the sides of the wide street. The back door opened then banged shut.

Before Tess, there was no one in my life. When Jack and I shared an apartment together, he would often bring a young woman home from whatever bar we had been drinking in. I would let them walk ahead. Jack with his arm around her shoulder, her with her arm around his waist. Talking and laughing and kissing. Inside Jack would light a cigarette while I would boil the kettle for tea. We'd sit a while, drinking tea, chatting then I would go to my room, and Jack and whoever he was with would go to his.

"I need to share myself around," he would say. "It is the only fair thing to do."

I sometimes wondered if he was missing Angie, the girl he had left behind. But Jack would only tell you there was no time for regrets of any sort in this life. That it was far too short for that.

If only he had known how short his would be. If only he had known how much time I would spend regretting that.

"I am not like you," I would tell him. "Women do not look at me in the same way. Nor I them."

Jack would shrug and smile. "Don't give up."

I took a drink of coffee, looked down the café to where the door had banged, then glanced out the window. Tess was walking up the road. The two dogs yapped at her heels. Someone at a table behind me dropped a spoon on the floor. One of the dogs relieved itself against a wooden crate. Then the door opened and Tess walked in. She looked around and saw me. I half-rose to greet her. She smiled, pulled a chair out from the table. She took off her jacket and hung it on the back of her chair and sat down across from me. She wore a navy sweater and jeans. Her hair was tied back. The owner's daughter came over to take her order. Tess said hello and asked for tea. The girl nodded, walked away.

"I taught her once," Tess said. "Three or four years ago. She dropped out to work here. She was needed. That is how it goes."

I turned my mug between my fingers, wondered what to say.

"I dropped out myself, stayed at home to help my mother. There were six children. I was the eldest."

"But you went back?"

"I was one of the lucky ones. Neither my mother nor father drank. I don't know how they escaped, but they did. Someone from the church helped us out a lot, persuaded me to go back to school. Said I could be of more help to my family there.

They were right. With their help, I even got to college. I had to move to Winnipeg which wasn't easy. It was during this time that the Dene people here decided to move to Tadoule Lake."

The young girl came back a few minutes later with a small pot of tea and a cup and saucer. She placed it in front of Tess. Tess thanked her and poured out the tea.

"How come you came back here?"

Tess toyed with her spoon, stirred in some milk. "Maybe I'll go to Tadoule Lake soon, but I felt then I owed it to the people who had helped me here." She put her spoon down and took a drink of tea as though she didn't want to talk much more about it.

"Well I am glad you did." I shifted uncomfortably in my chair.

Tess said nothing. Chairs scratched along the wooden floor as two elderly men got up to leave.

"I went to see the whale again," I said changing the subject.

"Me too," she admitted. "After school and again before coming here."

"Have they managed to pull it out yet?"

Tess shook her head. "One of the nets had broken and a cable had twisted. The tide was going out. There was talk they might have to leave it until morning." She wiped her lips with a napkin. I wondered if I were to lean over right now and kiss them if she would disappear forever.

After our tea and coffee, Tess and I walked through the town past the Catholic Church and the Eskimo Museum, past the school she taught at, and crossed over to the dunes. The tides were going out, and the wind had picked up. Small waves washed in and out through the gravel bed. The sun bled across the sky, orange and red. The faint outline of the pale moon. Gulls drifted on the air currents. Everyone was gone.

The whale lay in about a foot of water. Someone had rigged up a pump which continued to spray its large body with water. Tess linked her arm through mine, walked me to the shore, and together we bent our heads to listen.

✦

For three days the boats tugged at the harness and cables, trying to pull the whale out into the water. A strong northerly wind didn't make the rescue attempt any easier. Each day, crowds gathered to watch and help, but the whale refused to move. Tess and I watched together. I think we both felt as though the whale was ours alone, that it had beached solely for us, to share some knowledge from the depth that only we would be privy too.

At no point did Tess think it could be saved. That night after we bent our heads to listen, after we heard whatever it was we were meant to hear, Tess told me that the whale now had no option but to die.

Midways through the third day, a marine biologist who had flown in to aid with the rescue announced that the whale was dead. All morning, he had been warning that its body temperature was rising and threatening to shut down its vital organs. In the end, we were told the whale, without the water's support, had been killed by the weight of its own body. It had put too much pressure on its internal organs.

Tess looked relieved. Some of the Inuit community had already sought permission to salvage what they could of it. When the boats were gone, and the cables and harness and nets removed, Elders from the community held a ceremony around the whale, then they began the process of dissecting the body. Almost as many people came to watch the whale being cut apart as did the attempt to refloat its living body.

The swells of the last few days abated. The waters stilled as though offering their respects. An air of calmness had replaced the frantic efforts, the loud calls of the rescuers, the muffled sounds of the boats, the engines, the breaking waves, the strong hum of the pump pouring water over the whale, the snap of the chains.

Tess insisted I watch as a group of women cut off the flippers and tail.

"I'm not sure I am going to like this," I told her.

"I'll hold your hand if you like," she said.

"I would like that very much."

Tess took my hand in hers, not the touch of our cold handshake at Bird Cove but the intertwining of our fingers, the fragile warmth of my palm touching hers.

The Inuit men made cuts about a foot apart along the body of our whale. The knives sliced into the skin and blubber, removed it from the flesh. It was handed to a group of young men and women who cut it into chunks and placed them in plastic tubs. We watched as the flesh was torn from the huge backbone, as the ribs were broken off exposing the internal organs that the whale's own body had caused to malfunction. The liver, the heart, and the tenderloins, all cut away for consumption. The remaining organs were thrown into a bucket for dog food. The skin, the meat and blubber, the organs were carried away leaving the skeletal remains behind which were washed clean by the lapping tides. The smell of the whale's inner life released to the evening air to spread across the beach and dunes, drift above the roofs of the town, float across Hudson Bay, past the estuary where the remaining Belugas would surface and inhale the odour of their own mortality.

Tess invited me home for supper. She lived opposite the school in a house provided by the school division. We stepped inside the hallway and walked towards the back into the kitchen.

"I share with Eloise," she said pointing to a coat hanging up on the back of the kitchen door. "She teaches grade one. She's probably upstairs preparing for class tomorrow."

The kitchen was small, but it held Tess and I. Tess took her own jacket off, hung it beside Eloise's. She went to the refrigerator and looked in.

"Can I help?" I asked taking my jacket off also. There was no more room on the door, so I draped it over one of the chairs.

"You have helped greatly already." Tess held the door of the refrigerator open, looked earnestly at me.

To have stepped forward then, to have rubbed my fingers across her cheek.

"I have pork chops, potatoes." She reached in and took out the meat. "Sit down, there is little to do."

I sat and watched as she placed the chops on the pan and boiled the potatoes, opened a can of peas. She moved from the table to the stove as the food cooked, talked about school-work, placed plates and cutlery on the table. It was only when we were both sitting down eating that the whale returned.

"We should be eating him now, not this," she said pointing to her plate. "His flesh, his heart."

"Would you? I don't know if I could."

"Growing up, we eat a lot of wild foods. Yes, I would eat a whale."

"But would you eat that whale?"

"More than any other one." Tess paused. "I have heard tales of Beluga hunts in the past, but I remember little about what I was told. I know they will share the meat out amongst their community, first to the Elders. They will eat what they can and dry the rest. Some will be stored in jars in oil

66

they have made from the blubber. Nothing goes to waste. Tomorrow they will return for the teeth and bones to use in carvings."

I looked at Tess as she spoke, her flesh, her bones. Tomorrow I wondered what would either of us return for, what would we find?

Eloise appeared in the kitchen shortly after we had finished supper. She said hello when she saw me. I had seen her around before but had never known her name. Tess introduced us.

"I cooked supper," she told Eloise. "I didn't want to disturb you from your work. It's warming in the oven."

Eloise thanked her, went to the sink and washed her hands.

"Wade is a friend of Jack's," Tess said catching me off guard.

Eloise looked over her shoulder at us. "That sorry bastard. I should have washed my hands of him a long time ago."

I was taken by surprise. Obviously, from what she said, they had been seeing each other in some sort of way, but I knew nothing about it. Jack, of course, rarely told me about his girlfriends, and unless I met them I didn't ask. When I first moved up and we shared a place together, I couldn't help but know them, but since I had moved into my own home I didn't know who he was seeing if anyone at all.

"He stood her up last night," Tess explained. "Arranged to meet her at The Churchill Bar but never showed."

Eloise dried her hands. She brought her food over from the oven, got a knife and fork and sat down between us.

"I hate him," she said. "I honestly think I hate him."

"He's a horse's ass," I said. "I tell him that all the time.

Both Tess and Eloise laughed.

"So what are you going to do about him this time?"

Eloise pointed her fork at her. "Not what you think," she answered over a mouthful of food. She finished what she was eating. "Besides I don't want to talk about him. He gives me indigestion."

"Topic dropped." Tess stood up to clear away our dishes.

"Over a steep cliff," Eloise added. She ate some more food, swallowed it down. "I heard the whale died."

Tess nodded. "Yes, this afternoon. It has already been stripped clean."

"Story of this place." Eloise put her fork and knife down on her plate, sighed. "Oh God, I want out of here. She pushed her plate away as though she had lost her appetite. "How long have you been here?" she suddenly asked me.

"Three years."

"Don't you absolutely hate it?"

"Not really," I said. "I like it here. I came to get away. It has provided me with that."

"I came here two years ago. I was just out of college and couldn't get any other job. Worst choice of my life. No, let me take that back, Jack Butan was the worst choice of my life."

"I am not sure you have any choice with Jack. It seems to me that he chooses you not the other way around."

"No truer word was spoken," Eloise agreed.

Tess washed the dishes, put them on the rack to dry. "I'd like to take a walk. "What about you Wade, Eloise?"

Eloise refused. She had too much work to do. Work she should have done the night before instead of wasting her time in The Churchill.

Tess and I got our jackets. I said goodbye to Eloise, told her it was great to have met her.

"As for Jack...." I threw my arms up in the air.

"I know," she said. "Horse's ass."

68

Outside the light was fading fast. The moon had risen, a rich creamy yellow. Tess took my hand and led me across the street towards the beach.

"You can't keep away."

"It has me besotted."

"I could say it is just a whale."

"And you would be right."

We walked back over the path through the dunes, down towards the shore. The huge empty skeleton glowed brightly under the light of the moon. We walked across the gravel towards it. The tide was out. It had left the whale behind forever. Tess let go of me and walked up to its remains. She rubbed her hand along its large spine, across its neck vertebrae and over its skull. She patted its head as she would a young child. The remnants of the broken ribs jutted down. Tess stooped and climbed inside the whale. She crawled around from his tail to his mouth. The she sat down and waved for me to follow her in. We sat side by side on the damp gravel, our knees drawn up to our chests, and looked out through the jagged ribs at the world we had left behind.

"When we, the Dene, were moved here, my mother told me, we felt swallowed up. Swallowed up by the Inuit, the Cree, the White man, swallowed up by the bear and seal we did not know how to hunt, by the caribou we were forced to leave behind. We were swallowed up in a town we did not know how to survive in. We were swallowed up by the government, swallowed up by food vouchers, swallowed up by alcohol, and swallowed up by despair." Tess wrapped her arms tightly around her legs. "For a while I thought I had escaped all that, but now I don't know." She looked immensely sad, and I did not know why. Then she turned to me. "What about you, Mr. Sinclair, what are you swallowed up by?"

"Don't laugh when I say this," I said, "but I believe I am swallowed up by you."

Tess smiled as though some small burden had been taken off her shoulders. "In a moment," she said, "the moon will disappear, and when it does I want you to kiss me."

I looked to the moon and the clear sky that surrounded it. Both Tess and I waited drenched in the moon's reflected glow. I listened to our breathing as though it were the breathing of the whales. For a moment, it seemed as if the earth lurched, as though we were diving deep beneath the waves. I reached over with my fingers and very gently lowered Tess's eyelids shut, and as my own eyes closed over the moon was gone, and our lips touched together like water and shore.

I hadn't seen Jack since the whale beached. Although we both worked at the port, it was easy to go days without bumping into one another. But that morning of all mornings, we were, I suppose, ordained to meet. I was heading towards the grain terminal to begin my shift. A ship had just arrived from England and was soon to be loaded with wheat. Jack had an errand to run back in town before he helped with the loading. He smiled as he saw me approach, his hands in his pants' pockets.

"Sinclair," he called, "where have you been hiding out?"

"I could ask you the same question." I replied.

Jack pulled out a packet of cigarettes and lit one. "You know the problem?" he said. "This place is too big for us. We need to move somewhere else, somewhere less crowded."

"What would you do for women friends then?" I asked.

Somebody yelled from down at the port. The screech of a conveyor belt, the loud clanging of metal.

Jack blew smoke in the air. "Mail order, I suppose."

"They'd never keep up with the demand."

Jack roared laughing. Behind him the huge cargo ship was moving into position alongside the pier where the grain could be fed into the ship's hold.

"I met one of your less ardent admirers yesterday," I told him.

"Now who would that be? The line is usually not short."

The ship scraped along the edge of the pier. One of the front-end loaders used to clear residual grain from the storage sheds drove by. Both Jack and I waved up at Willy Bergan, the driver.

"Eloise Thiessen."

Jack threw his half-smoked cigarette to the ground, stubbed it out with his foot. "What did she tell you?"

"Just how you stood her up at The Churchill."

"It wasn't intentional." He looked down at the remains of his cigarette, scratched the stubble on the side of his face. "I forgot. I was tired and lay down after work to rest for a while. I clean forgot. She was gone by the time I got there."

"She didn't think it was too clean at all."

Jack genuinely looked guilty. "I've been meaning to call her."

"You probably should," I advised.

Jack looked back at the ship. "I'll be in worse trouble if I forget about the ship. I'll talk to you later. Come by The Churchill about nine."

"Okay," I said. "Don't forget."

Jack muttered something and began to walk in the direction of town. I turned to the entrance of the terminal. Suddenly I heard him call after me.

"Hey!" He had stopped a little bit up the road. He looked puzzled. "Since when do you know Eloise?" Then a smile grew across his face. "You've been spending time with Tess!"

I pointed to my watch. "We both better get going." I reached for the metal handle on the door.

"You're already going," he said. "There's no stopping you now."

I turned towards the terminal door and opened it in front of me.

I would have preferred to have seen Tess that night rather than Jack, but I didn't want to rush things, and I sensed that she didn't either. I had left the night before saying I would call her, and she said she wasn't too hard to find. But nothing could be further from the truth. A woman like Tess was the hardest thing in the world to find.

Jack was, as usual, playing pool when I got there. I walked through the smoky bar over to the pool table. Pete Magnusson was bent over the table taking a shot. Jack nodded but said nothing so that Pete wouldn't be disturbed. The blue ball rattled the top pocket but didn't go in.

"Tough luck," I said.

"It's more than luck you need playing this shark." Pete lifted his glass from the table beside them.

"Get yourself a drink," Jack said. "You can play the winner."

I went to the counter and ordered a beer. The bar was quiet enough, only ten or so customers spread out around the tables. The television above the counter was turned on to a hockey game. Wally, the owner, handed me the beer and told me we had been on the news. The whale and all, he said.

"We'll be famous yet," I told him.

"In the meantime, I'm not getting any younger."

I paid him for the beer and went back to Jack and Pete. Jack had a shot lined up, easy enough into the side pocket. He sank it and the next one a long shot up the table. He was onto the black now. Unlikely to lose. He named his pocket and slotted it in.

"Good game," Pete said. He finished off his drink and handed his cue to me. "I have to be off." He put his jacket on and left.

"Do you want to play?" Jack asked.

"Maybe afterwards. I wouldn't mind resting my feet. I've been on them all day long."

We left our cues on the pool table and sat down.

"So you and Tess," Jack said lighting up a cigarette.

"You and Eloise." I played with a beer mat I found on the table.

"Probably not anymore." Jack took a long pull, blew out the smoke.

"Have you been seeing her long?"

"A few weeks." He flicked his ash into the ashtray. "And Tess?"

"It hasn't been like that," I said. "I hadn't seen her since last year, as you know. But then I met her at the beach the day the whale washed in."

"I see," Jack said as though there was something imperfect with my story, something he didn't quite believe.

I heard a roar from the crowd on the television. Someone must have scored. A few heads looked up from the tables to see what had happened.

"You should call Eloise," I told him. "Let her have her say. I don't think she has given up on you just yet."

Jack grinned. "I suppose."

"She doesn't sound too happy here."

"I probably haven't helped there either. She has committed to one more year, but I think she'll leave after that."

"What about you, how long do you intend staying?" When I first came here I hadn't thought too much about it. I figured I'd stay a while, earn some money and worry about that later. I needed a break from family. Something different from what had gone before. Churchill seemed to offer that.

"I might die here."

Those were Jack's words then, and they of course have come back to haunt us all. Like so many who had come before us and so many who would come after, Jack had been attracted here by the ruthless lure of the north. Some magnetic pull that satisfied an innate base instinct. Despite the trappings, we were all primitives at heart. All fugitives from our uncomfortable selves.

Jack swirled the rest of his drink in his glass. "Eloise reminds me too much of Ang." He watched the liquid settle, drank it down. "I left because of her. I cared too much. There had to be something more than getting out of high school and falling in love. You can't just settle for that."

"It may be more than most have." I tapped the edge of the beer mat on the tabletop.

"It may be all they ever have." Jack picked up his glass. "I need one more." He excused himself and went to the bar.

Everything always came back to Ang. Jack knew it as much as I did. He ordered his drink, chatted to Wally a while. He came back with one for me as well.

"Here," he said. "Thirst. That's what it's all about."

We clinked glasses and drank to our health.

"I should tell you," Jack said holding his glass in front of him like an offering, "I went out with Eloise first as a way of getting to know Tess better."

I was about to take a drink but stopped myself. I put my glass down. "Jack, I hardly know her."

"I know that. I hardly know Eloise. Have I told you about my dream?"

I shook my head.

"It's wintertime. I am walking across the tundra. I don't know why. It is not something important. I am up to my ankles in snow. The shrubs poke their shriveled heads out. It is a vast empty space. I am feeling alone. I see something in the distance, a presence. I walk towards it. There is nothing there. Then it begins to take shape. A form emerging from the surrounding whiteness. A great bear. I am mesmerised. Nothing can prevent me from walking towards it. Even when I know it is going to kill me."

How could I possibly have known then that the dream would return? Who could have predicted that? Not I who was privy to its contents, nor Esther. Esther who knew nothing about it at all, but who nevertheless had exactly the same dream so many years later. It seems we cannot run away from the things which surround us. They travel with us. They bring us home. Jack did not run far enough away from Ang. And later, he did not run far enough away from Tess.

I told Jack I wasn't very good at interpreting dreams.

"I wouldn't believe you even if you did." He lit up another cigarette. "I've had it a half a dozen times or more. It's become like these things," he waved the cigarette between his fingers, "a bad habit."

Another roar from the television. The door to the Gents banged shut.

"Let's have that game of pool," I said. "It's time you met your match."

For a while at least, it seemed that Jack had met his match in Eloise. In all our time together, I had never seen him so keen about anyone. It seemed logical that we would end up meeting each other at Tess and Eloise's house, but we never did. In truth, I suspected that Jack was avoiding any such meeting. Eloise spent all her time at his apartment not at hers. Tess too preferred to visit my house. "Living in the town is convenient," she said, "but better to live on the tundra proper where there are no other houses around."

I called in some evenings on the way home from my shift for a cup of tea. Tess was always busy with school work, so I wouldn't stay too long. Occasionally we'd go for a walk along the shore depending on the sort of day Tess had. The temperatures were getting cooler, the days shorter. Winter was nearing. The waters were cooling down. The whales had given birth to their young. They had left together heading for the Arctic Ocean. The polar bears were heading north from James Bay following along the coast of Hudson Bay looking for an early freeze. The snow geese were on their way to Texas and the Mississippi Valley. Tess and I were migrating towards an unknown destination.

"Where did you come from Wade Sinclair?"

"I blew in on a northern breeze."

Sometimes it seemed as if Tess and I were like that. Aspects of the weather determined by climatic conditions we had no control over. Carried along by currents. We drifted up against one another, and we merged in the way of vapour.

CHAPTER 5

We finished our house in the summer of 1998. While the floors, ceilings and stairs were being installed, Esther and I chinked the wood to get rid of the gaps and create a seal from the external elements, the rain, the snow, the sleet, and ice. It would provide insulation and prevent water from pooling too and rotting the wood. Esther wanted to do it the old-fashioned way with mud, but Joe convinced her to use fiberglass and foam. The wood would shrink and swell with the changing weather, he warned. The chinking needed to be flexible. Esther hadn't thought about this before she said, our house shrinking and swelling, almost as if it were breathing in and out.

It was a tedious and time-consuming task, but Esther took to it as if her very life depended on it. The logs had to be cleaned of any surface level dirt. The chinking came in five-gallon pails, and Esther and I applied it with trowels. Meanwhile the doors and windows were installed, the plumbing and wiring completed. Our house was built. We had built it.

"Who would think such a thing was possible?" Esther said on that final evening after Joe and the other workmen had left. She looked across the treeless tundra. The sun was setting in a clouded sky. Our house grew from the ground like a tightly packed forest.

It was already the end of July, and Esther wanted to wait to move in with the first fall of snow. "It will be our refuge," she said. "A sanctuary from the extremes."

As it happened, it didn't snow until September the tenth. Esther and I were waiting. Each morning, she would wake up and go to the window. She listened avidly to the radio for each weather forecast. Throughout the day she would look to the sky, examine the clouds.

We lay together in bed one morning discussing our move. When it was completed, Joe was to return to tear down the old structure. Whatever wood we could salvage, we would keep and burn. Everything else, he would take away. The tundra beneath would be reclaimed.

"Our new house too," I told Esther. "Someday the tun--dra will reclaim that space. It is a temporary refuge at best."

"That's good enough for now." She pulled the blankets up to her chin. She shivered. "I can feel it coming," she said smiling. The wrinkles on her forehead. The crow's lines at the edges of her eyes. I looked into those eyes, the pupils, the green irises, and I could have sworn I saw snow fall across them.

"I love you," I told her.

Esther took her hand from beneath the covers, stroked my lips with the tips of her fingers. "That is a temporary refuge too," she may have whispered.

I kissed the tips of her fingers. The lids of her eyes closed. The snow melted and slid down her cheeks. I took her in my arms and held her against me. I listened to the winds of our breathing.

"I was lucky to meet you Wade."

"We were both lucky."

"Remember, we are a rare pair of Ross's gulls." She flushed pink. She opened her eyes and looked out through the window. "There," she said.

The white flakes fell.

The house was everything Esther had hoped for. The wood floors, the log walls, the loft, the high beams. The only reason she would leave it was to come back in. She would look outside at the ice and snow covered lands and listen to the winds seeking out a crevice to slip through. "We are safe here. We have winter leashed."

My old house lay in a heap in the back. Joe had pulled it apart with his backhoe and chains. Ripped the supports away, tore it to pieces.

He offered to let me drive. "It will do you good," he said. "Better than any of those wacky therapies."

But I couldn't do it. I could barely stand to watch. All I could see was Jack, and Tess, and I. The three of us inside desperately trying to hold the house together while it came tumbling down around us.

The first few days after we moved in, I couldn't sleep at night. It was a beautiful home, a marked improvement on my old one, but it held so little of my life.

"How did you sleep?' I would ask Esther. And she would reply, "I slept like a log."

Outside, the winds increased carrying the intense cold of the bay in towards us. They blew the falling snow into a frenzy. If we were to look beyond our window, we would have seen nothing. A white void as though we alone were the only people in existence. If we were to step outside, clothed as we were, we would have died. Instead we sheltered beneath the bedcovers. Our stove burned the last two planks of wood from my old kitchen floor. It was relentless in its destruction.

The heat kept us warm. Esther lay her body on top of mine, and I sank into the mattress under her weight. Our log house creaked under duress. Somewhere a bear was braced against the wind treading across the frozen ground. The snow blew hard on his downturned head. He was following the path of his hunger. The waters of Hudson Bay beat against the underside of the ice. They had trapped themselves in. The hollow boom of their plight fought to be heard.

Esther pressed against my chest and spoke of the ice age. She told me how the weight of the glaciers depressed the land here, pushed it down as her weight pushed down on me. The ocean waters flooded in, she said, over three hundred kilometres from the current coastline. Seven thousand years later, the land is still rising back up. There are lines along the coast, stripes of sandy material showing a succession of beach ridges during the stages of its rebound. Esther rubbed her fingers across my forehead as though tracing the lines evident there too. Later she eased herself off my body and lay next to me. She looked to see how long it took for me to rise back up again.

Outside the winds persisted. Frostbite, amputation, death. Snow silently walked across our property. It blew in wild from beyond, and then it walked. Sometimes it strolled like an old man, lay down at our door.

"There are no paths until you dig them." That's what I told her.

Esther listened to the howl as the wind found an opening. "There is always a way in," she replied.

Once more, I knew that I loved her.

The bears, that winter Esther and I moved into our house, were more plentiful than ever. Throughout October, hundreds arrived waiting for the ice on the bay to freeze to begin their northward journey. Many times, it seemed that the ice would extend far enough for them to set out, but each time a strong southerly wind blew the shore ice out into the bay. They prowled the tundra impatiently foraging through the snow and ice, the rock and gravel, the clumps of lichen and sedges. Stalking the shoreline, hunting out solid ice. The sun rose and set. The bears' coats glimmered white, and yellow, and pink, and orange. The brittle ice spread across the bay in a similar display of colour.

Bears wandered brazenly through the streets of the town, rummaged at the dump for food. People reinforced their doors, left nail-studded boards outside their houses, slept with their guns. Tranquilised bears were carted away, airlifted to the North Knife River. Taken in large steel traps to the Polar Bear Jail, a discarded Air Base hangar.

Esther no longer slept well. She heard bears at the doors and windows. She heard them on the roof. She woke up to find one in the bed beside her only to wake up again and find it was a dream. Now she didn't dare leave the house.

"I told you it was our refuge."

It began to feel like a jail.

A snowstorm blew through, and the bears disappeared from sight. Invisible, they lowered their heads and stooped their shoulders, braced themselves against the gusting winds. One bear reappeared inside the shelter of an airline depot eating large stocks of food waiting to be airlifted north. Another startled a group of native boys on their way home from the bar. It surprised them in an alleyway. They felt sure they had reached the end of their road, but the bear was as drunk as they were, they later swore. It barely glanced at them but stumbled off down the alley in a haze teetering on its four unsteady feet. In the confusion of the storm, a group of three bears sought to make their escape and set out cautiously across the thin ice. They were no more than twenty feet from shore when the ice gave way. The bears instinctively dropped and spread-eagled themselves to distribute their weight, but the ice, nevertheless, cracked further. Bears along the shore lifted their heads, listened in the dark to the sharp retorts of the breaking ice, the splash of the bodies into the freezing water, before hunkering down once more, scarcely noticing the return of the three who had swum and waded back to shore. A team of sled dogs tethered outside were slaughtered as they sheltered in the blinding snow. The pitched barking, the wild fury as they yanked at their chains and spun in circles. Until, dog by dog, the barking stopped, the chains hung limp, and they all lay perfectly still.

In their dens south of town, three mothers gave early birth to cubs. Small down-covered creatures no larger than a squirrel. Their eyes still closed as sightless they crouched in against their mothers for warmth. Beyond the cloud-covered sky, the northern lights ignited unseen in the ionosphere. Ursus Major and Minor blinked unnoticeably.

"I see a bear in the sky," Esther said standing at the bedroom window.

"Impossible," I replied.

"I see it," she insisted. She wrapped her blanket tightly around her.

"Come to bed, Esther."

"It has wings."

"Fly into my arms."

The following day, the storm passed over. Northern winds which had brought low temperatures and flash-freezing blew ice into the shore, carpeted it with snow. The bay froze over in days. A solid white landmass as far as the eye could see. Endless icefields. The bears departed without so much as a goodbye.

I brought Esther out to Cape Churchill to watch them go. But it was already too late. They had merged into the white ice and snow, were no longer distinguishable, may never have been there at all.

✦

Esther said she was doing it for me. She was going to find Jack. She was going to bring him back to me. I could have told her not to. But I did not. I said nothing. Not a word. How could I tell her that he would be our undoing as he had been the undoing between Tess and me?

She came in the front door, the cold wind at her back. She closed the door quickly, pulled off her gloves and hat. Her down-filled jacket, her boots. Our old bedroom wall burned hot in the stove next to where I was sitting reading the paper. Her cheeks were ruddy, her hair askew. She put the large envelope she carried on the living room table then put away her things. She pulled on a woolen sweater and placed her feet in her slippers. She retrieved the envelope and sat in the armchair next to mine. The wood crackled, split. Esther smiled over at me. I put the newspaper down on my lap.

"You must be cold," I said.

"Beginning to warm up." Her hands were joined across the yellow envelope. She seemed to be considering what it was she should do next. I pushed back in my chair. Tugged at my sleeve.

"A polar bear was sighted on the beach in town."

"You need to be careful when you are out," I advised unnecessarily.

"They have a trap in place." She lifted the envelope as if testing its weight. "I was at the library." Esther spent a lot of time there. Reading local history books, books on birds, flowers. "I was looking through their archives. They have some of the old newspapers on microfiche. I found this." She opened the envelope and took out two sheets of paper. She handed them to me. Transcriptions she had made. "They are about Jack," she continued, "when he went missing."

The papers shook in my hands. I felt my stomach heave. I looked at the top sheet, but my eyes were unable to focus on her handwriting. I coughed, closed my eyes momentarily. I felt the urge to stand up, walk from the room. Esther was watching me. I felt the heat of the stove on my legs. I looked at the paper again, the heading she had written down. LOCAL MAN MISSING. May 23, 1978. And below it the rest of the article. "The RCMP reported today that Jack Butan, age 25, has been missing for several days. Mr. Butan had been living in the area since 1972. He works with the Port of Churchill and has been described as being of average build, 5 feet 11 inches in height, 170 pounds, black wavy hair. Anyone who has any knowledge of his whereabouts should contact the police as soon as possible."

What could I have told them? The truth. Even I do not know what the truth is. Why did I do what I did? Why do the polar bears come here instead of somewhere else? They come, Esther tells me, on account of the tides, the currents, the winds, the temperatures all of which combine to form ice more quickly. They come because the coastline of Hudson Bay takes a sharp turn east at Churchill forming a hook which protrudes into the bay, and this hook captures ice from the north which is blown south by the strong October winds. They come because the water is shallow in the hook and accentuates ice formation. They come because it is the easiest place to depart from. I did what I did because of all the variables. I did what I did because I knew of nowhere else to go.

The second brief article was from *The Winnipeg Free Press* a week later. "Jack Butan, a resident of Churchill, Manitoba, has been missing from his home of Churchill for over a week. Foul play is not suspected at this time."

That was it. Jack's disappearance from the face of this earth was worth no more than a few lines of print. It is no wonder his breath was so easily extinguished.

I could tell Esther the dreadful facts of that dreadful day, but what truth would that reveal? I did not want to lose her. I had lost too much already. I put the papers down alongside my newspaper and looked back up at Esther. She continued to watch me closely.

"It is 1978 still," I told her. "I never left that year. I grew older, but I remained there."

Esther rose from her armchair and came to me, kissed my forehead. "I will return you to the present," she promised. She lifted the papers, returned them to her envelope, went upstairs. I opened the door of the stove, threw a few pieces of wood inside. Wood that had witnessed Esther and I together in our old bedroom that had witnessed Tess too. Outside the temperatures continued to drop. The stars came and went.

Esther pressed Marilyn to tell her all she could remember. Marilyn told her it was such a long time ago. Another lifetime. She sat with Esther here in our home, while the floor Jack had slept upon burned in the stove. Was he sitting there with them, sipping from his whiskey and listening to what was being said about him? Did he attempt to interrupt, to right their wrongs, to tell them they were talking of a different Jack Butan, or was he happy to hear about who he might have been, the person he had now become?

Marilyn drank tea, heard his heavy breathing, mistook it for the wind in the stove chimney. Esther heard the light clink of his glass as he returned it to the arm of his chair, confused it with the rattle of the storm window.

Marilyn put her cup back on the saucer, admired to herself the dried flowers Esther had framed on the wooden walls. The purple Alpine Fireweed. The Yellow Tundra Rose. The pink Trailing Azalea. The blue Star Gentian.

"Jack Butan came here," she said, "the way so many do, without any notice. The way you did yourself." She smiled across at Esther. Esther may even have blushed. "Wade never told anyone about you before you arrived."

"I know," Esther said.

Who would I have told? I knew many people here, spent portions of my time in their company, but since Jack and Tess, right up until Esther, there had been no one else I felt close to. I met Esther, and she moved up here. There had been no long courtship, no great emotional turmoil, just an unexpected love of real significance.

Marilyn's father had been stationed here in the early days of the army base. She had been born here, had lived here all her life.

"I'd see him around," she told Esther. " Some of my girl-friends talked about him. Some probably even went out with him. He intrigued us, I guess. He seemed certain of where he was going as though he had his whole life plotted out in front of him. He had the pick of every one of us. You asked me the other day if I had ever gone out with him. I probably would have if he had asked. But even then I was overweight, not too much, but, as I say, Jack had the pick of us." Marilyn looked to the flowers again. Esther said it was as though Marilyn was searching the tundra itself for memories, some details of her past she had forgotten. She shook her head. "It's amazing how little you remember. I couldn't even tell you if I ever spoke to him. I knew he wouldn't be interested in me, and so I stopped paying attention. I remember his wavy black hair, his loose smile, his carefree laugh." She stopped, shrugged. "What can I tell you about him, Esther, when I barely remember myself?"

Esther felt the urge to go around the table to her, the same urge she said she felt towards me that night she disclosed what Marilyn had told her about Jack in Gypsy's. In my case, she acted upon it, but, in Marilyn's, she stayed where she was. Marilyn was merely telling the truth, a truth not often heard, a truth few were capable of uttering. Indeed, Esther said, Marilyn looked as though she had surprised herself. And then she had shrugged again.

"There must be a photograph of him somewhere. Some of the girls from back then, the few that are left. Some of the boys he worked with."

"I'd like to see him," Esther said to her.

Not see the picture, but Jack himself. Esther wanted to see him. And what would he have seen in her? If he had seen all that I had, and if that had promised more for his future than his past thus far, would he have loved her, and would he have blinded himself in that love? And Esther, would she have been taken in by him? Would she have been on the verge of letting go?

"Look at this." Esther held the photograph under the lamp. The dull yellow light of the lamp brightened across Jack's face as though the moon had slipped free of the clouds and revealed him in the shadows. He stepped out to greet me, and I almost said hello.

I took the photograph from Esther, held it out in front of me. Jack stood in front of The Eskimo Museum with his arm around some girl. A cigarette dangling from the corner of his mouth, a beaming smile. A fur collared jacket, a gloved hand, his windswept hair, the smoke from his cigarette hanging in front of his mouth like a breath captured forever in an instant. The girl smiled too, but no smoke as though her breath had escaped her or he had taken it away. I heard him laugh, the loud laughter that drew everyone in. And then he turned and walked away, his arm around her yet.

I handed the photograph back to Esther. "He's gone," I told her. My heart thumped out the hollowness of his absence

"No," she replied. "He's here still. He never went away."

Esther had needed to put a face to him. "If I am to find him, I must know who I am looking for."

She truly believed she could do this, find Jack. A name that escaped across the crowded air of a small café. She wanted to know him in the same way that she wanted to know the names of all the wildflowers, all the details of our weather, every ebb and flow of the Hudson Bay. But like the water rushing to shore, she had no idea what it might wash in. I should have put an end to it there and then, but there is no holding back the tide. We would stand on the shore together, and it would rise above our ankles and where it would stop we did not know. The truth is, I wanted to know what had really happened as much as Esther did. The extent of my culpability. I had been carried along on the currents of that day for far too long.

The photograph belonged to a friend of Marilyn's. Nicole Fairfield. Esther went to meet her.

"I don't remember the year," Nicole said. She put the photograph on the table beside the couch as if you could do this, pick up and put down portions of your life. "Nineteen seventy-three maybe."

Before my time.

"We were together during freeze-up. A brief time. I was infatuated. The temperatures were dropping, and he told me he needed to hold me closer for warmth." Nicole laughed. "The colder it got, the tighter he held on. I thought that maybe we would make it through the winter and beyond. Slush formed in the bay, Jack and I laughed like never before. Large plates of ice began to wash into the shore, we went everywhere together. New ice began to form between the plates, Jack rang to say he couldn't make it. I awoke early and took a morning stroll. The bay was frozen completely. When I saw Jack that evening, he started to apologize. I shushed him. I knew what was coming, and I didn't want to hear it." Nicole picked the photo up again, took another look at how things were. "I can't remember who took the photograph. In fact, I don't remember it being taken at all. If it wasn't so glaringly obvious, I would insist it wasn't me, some other girl Jack knew back then."

"What do you think happened to him?" Esther asked her.

Nicole stood up, put the photograph away in a drawer and closed it. She turned back to Esther. "We never knew."

"But what do you think?"

Nicole sat back down. Esther said she looked lost as though she did not know where she was in her own home.

"I think he fell through the ice. He was last seen walking out past the shipwreck. It had been a warmer spring than usual. Break-up came early that year, I remember. The ice on the lakes would have been fragile in parts. Some thought he might have done it on purpose."

"Why?"

"A woman."

"What woman?"

"I don't know. It was careless talk. We have little else to do up here sometimes." Nicole fidgeted with the sleeve of her cardigan. "I don't know why he left me," she continued. "It is not that there was anything much between us. I knew it was not serious. But I don't know why he left at that time. We seemed to be having a good time together. He seemed happy in my company, and I was happy in his. It wasn't such a big thing. I got over it soon enough, over the disappointment in myself. Until Marilyn asked me if I had a photo of him, I had clean forgotten all about him. I dare say most everyone has."

Nicole said she didn't remember much about their time together, where they went or what they talked about. She remembered him holding her. That was all. "It was a bitterly cold winter," she laughed.

Jack, all of the winters have been bitterly cold ever since.

CHAPTER 6

"I have brought you a present." It was minus 18, mid-November, the month of the heaviest snowfall. The bay was still open, but freeze-up would not be far away. The sun rose after seven and set before five. The winds were high. Tess had brought me a present.

She shook the snow from her boots. It was five thirty in the evening. I took her boots, her gloves, and jacket and placed them in front of the stove. I took the gift I was offered. I weighed it in my hand then opened it slowly. The wrapping came away, a small white seal dipped and dove in the palm of my hand.

"One of the children at school." Tess paused. "Her mother carved it."

"Bone?"

"Our whale. From its neck."

The seal swam into the space between us, dissolved it. Our lips touched.

From that November until just before the death of Jack, Tess and I swam together. We slipped in off the rocks, washed in on shore. We moved beneath the ice, came up for air. Made holes in the frozen cover as the seals do for breathing. Agloos, the favoured hunting spots of bear.

Shortly before his death, we rose from the depths and stuck our heads above the ice, and Jack was there waiting.

Eloise arrived home one night unexpectedly. She had intimated to Tess that she would be spending the night with Jack. Instead the key turned in the door and it opened inwards. Snow that had drifted against it spilled into the hallway. A window rattled with the draft. Tess and I sat on the couch together. We had turned the light off to watch the new quarter of the moon. Tess jumped.

"It is only the wind," I said.

The door slammed shut.

"It is Eloise."

Tess stood up quickly, turned on the light. The moon vanished. The door to the living room opened and Eloise entered. She looked distraught. Tess went to her, and Eloise put her arms around her, allowed her tears to fall. She saw me and gathered herself. "You were right, he is a horse's ass."

And then we could laugh. We could open our mouths and release something from inside of us disguised as mirth.

"He is a good man too." I should have spoken those words but they faltered on my lips, fell backwards, drowned.

Tess took Eloise and sat her down on the couch. "Wade, will make you hot chocolate, and we will talk."

I went to the kitchen and put on the milk to boil. By the time I brought in the steaming mugs, Eloise was laughing. Tess was just being herself.

Why Jack decided to tell Eloise about Ang I did not know. And yet, on so many occasions, I have wanted to tell Esther about Tess. What occurred I cannot say for certain. Eloise related little to Tess or me. But it is not unreasonable to surmise that they would have had a few drinks at The Churchill and then have gone back to Jack's. Eloise hardly smoked before she met him, but, in his presence, she would not have been able to resist his offers. They were just lighting up. The moon would have been present, but neither of them observed it. They stood in the kitchen. Jack moved them to the front room. He closed the curtains, removed the outer world. He sat down beside her on the couch. Eloise smiled at him. The drinks had made her feel even more loving than usual.

"I love you, Jack," she told him.

And Jack balked, recoiled into a time Eloise was not privy to. She must have known the pointlessness, the sheer futility, the destruction of the question she was then to ask. "Do you love me, Jack?"

Four months and no more. The rest of both of their lives to come. Do you love me, Jack?

"I thought I loved Ang."

Jack did not think he loved Ang. He thought that he was still in love with her. But take this from me, Jack did not love Ang. He was mistaken not in his belief but in his annunciation. Jack loved Tess. True and simple. And that love clouded all else.

✦

The first night Tess stayed over at my house we both slept the sleep of the dead. We had gone for a walk along the shore. It was early December. Minus 20 degrees. The ice was barely 10 centimetres thick but strong enough to support the weight of the bears who were already venturing out. We kept a cautious eye out for them. The snow had drifted in heaps across the ice, and on the shore it came up above the ankles of our boots. We were well wrapped up. The sun set shortly after four. We watched it sink. A pink hue filtered through the thick clouds.

"There." Tess pointed.

Out on the snow and ice-covered bay, a young bear traversed the uneven surface, struggling as it walked along. Its hind legs occasionally breaking through the thin ice, and the bear collapsing on its haunches. We watched it persevere through the blowing snow.

"There is our lesson," Tess said. "We can go now."

We walked back to the truck and drove back to my house. The evening darkened as we talked and drank our tea. The winds picked up, blew in sharply off the bay. It was too dangerous to drive her home.

"Let's give it a while," I suggested. "It might die down." But the winds gave no sign of abating. Increased in strength if anything, gusted at high speeds.

At nine o'clock, she walked to the window, folded her arms. She spoke into the darkness. "I will have to stay."

"Yes. You will."

We sat in chairs by the stove and listened to the winds that kept us together. We said little occupied as we were in thought. Then, of a sudden, Tess rose. As unexpectedly as the winds in the first place. She drifted to my chair and laid her hand on my shoulder. I looked up into her face.

"We are adults," she said. "Young as we are, we are grown adults."

"I feel like a child," I told her.

"I know, but we are adults." She took her hand from my shoulder and offered it to me. I took it in mine. She led me then from my chair, led me up the stairs, and led me into my own bedroom. She led me to my bed. And in the darkened room, she undressed and climbed in beside me. And then, Tess stayed.

I awoke before sunrise. A drowsy light entered through the window. It lingered over Tess and me. Tess breathed heavily in her sleep. The warmth of her body next to mine. I could reach out and touch the bare skin of her shoulder. I could stroke her long black hair. A thick blanket of off-white cloud covered the sky. I felt calm, at peace. The storm from the night before had abated. I lay next to Tess and looked about my room. I hardly recognized it. Something had occurred in the night to alter it. Tess shifted in her sleep, turned towards me. I could scarcely recognize her either. Despite the dull light of morning, I could see her more clearly than ever. Her forehead, her eyes, her nose, her mouth, her chin.

It was already past seven. She would have to get up soon to teach. The snow would have drifted with the winds, swept in mounds across my path, heaped against the walls and door. I would have to dig her out, let go this woman I had newly discovered.

I lay there beside her without moving. Lay there until she stirred, murmured something I could not understand. Her lips moved and sound escaped once more.

"What is it, Tess?" She had spoken more clearly but still I did not understand what she was saying.

Tess opened her eyes. She seemed surprised to see me there.

"Wade," she said softly.

"Tess."

We were a fingertip away. Her breath on my face and mine on hers.

"You were speaking," I told her.

"When?"

"As you woke."

"What did I say."

"I don't know. I could not understand you."

"Dene. I was speaking Dene."

"What were you saying?"

Tess shrugged. "I don't know. I did not hear myself. If I did, I still would not know. I have forgotten what little I knew. We never really spoke it in our house. Even as a young girl, I used to do that, however, speak Dene in my sleep."

She looked like a little girl then, a younger Tess dreaming of the future.

"I may have said good morning."

"You may have said goodbye."

Tess touched my face with her hand. "Good morning."

"The storm has stopped," I could have told her.

"I know," she would have replied.

"The snow will have drifted."

"I can feel it pushed up against us."

"I will have to dig us out."

"You will lead us further in."

She took her hand away. I went to the window and looked down. Waves of snow four feet high spread across the lane and yard, had crashed against my door in an eight-foot swell. I went back to my bed and got in under the covers. Tess reached for me, and I was there waiting.

Esther occasionally brought Jack's name up, would wait for my response lest I could be drawn in further.

"Do you think Nicole is right, that Jack may have disappeared on account of a woman?"

We had come to Bird Cove to measure the ice. The bears were gone. They had departed the second week of November. A flash freeze and, in days, their heavy bodies were leaving their prints behind, trudging across the vast icefields towards the Arctic. The tourists left soon afterwards by plane and train, cramped together, heading in the opposite direction.

We stepped across the snow and ice, protrusions of rock. The frozen bay washed in over the steel grey granite shoreline in peaks two to three feet high. A scarlet glow diffused through the thick blue grey clouds, reflected off the ice, slid along its fiery surface to the horizon. Our breaths froze in the air in front of us tinged with sunset. Further north, a migration of crimson bears.

"There were many women in his life."

"But if Nicole is in any way right, this one must have been important to him. Surely you would have known." Esther stopped, walked right up to the edge of the cove, pulled away long shards of frazil ice. Snapped off parts of the Arctic Ocean as though she held sway. The ice melted in her gloved hands from the warmth of her body, returned to the earth as water. Through the clouds, a tangerine flush as the sun sunk lower.

"I don't know that I knew anything about him at all," I confided. "I don't remember what we spoke about. Like his cigarettes or our beers, our conversation was for consumption, used up with little thought."

"So he never mentioned any one woman who may have meant a lot to him?"

Esther was half-turned, dividing her attention between the ice and shore, between me and the infinite beyond.

I stepped up on the ice with my auger, held my hand out for Esther's, helped her up, and told her about Ang. It would be easy to say that the truth is hidden or concealed in some deliberate fashion, but what little I know of life does not convince me of this. The truth is there for all of us to see, it is a matter of knowing where to look. It would have been a falsehood to have owned up to Jack's death, a lie to have said that Tess was the cause of it. And so, I said nothing. Nothing to the authorities back then and nothing to Esther. She would have looked in all the wrong places if I had. Like the ice on the bay, the truth of what happened to Jack is out there extending as far as the eye can see. And like the ice, it is thick. You could walk on it, and it would not give way. But look in the wrong direction, and you will miss the obvious, step instead upon a thin stretch which will crack and break. You will slip into the freezing water, grasp at the edges with numbing fingers, see it for what it really is as you disappear beneath it.

I connected the flight of the auger to the brace, attached the cutting bit, pushed it through the snow until it hit the hard surface. I leaned into it and started drilling as though I could bore away my guilt.

"There was someone named Ang. Angie." Esther looked to the dying sun, the pale wan remnants. The cold penetrated through the soles of my boots. "It was before he moved up here. They met at high school, believed they were in love. Jack, I think was afraid of his life occurring too swiftly. He thought if he stayed, they would most probably end up married soon after, children, a home. He wanted more than that. There was a whole world out there to explore. He was from somewhere in Iowa. His family had a small farm. I'm not sure where he heard about Churchill. He came up, I know, shortly after the army had moved out, got a job straight away with the port. Churchill was far enough away, he thought, different enough, to slow his life down, to give him the chance to explore it."

A light breeze blew in off the bay. Esther listened keenly. "And Ang?"

I turned the handle of the brace slowly, the tool twisting, grinding its way through the solid mass. "Although Jack told me he left her behind, I really think he brought her with him. Maybe that is why he had no need to go back home before."

"Before?" Esther stood next to me her arms wrapped around her body.

"The Christmas before his disappearance was the first time he had gone back home. He must have been here six years at that stage. In the beginning, I think he was afraid he would see Ang and be unable to leave her again. Later on, he was afraid he would find out she was no longer there for him. It was easier to stay here and keep Ang with him in whatever way he wanted her to be."

"What happened that time he went home?"

"Ang was in a steady relationship. Whatever place Jack had occupied had been settled by someone else. I think she loved him still. He just had wandered too far away. When he went back, it was by then too late."

"Do we keep making the same mistakes all our lives?"

"We have rectified ours, have we not?"

Esther put her hand on my shoulder. "I would like to think so."

Esther was right. There was no way of knowing for certain. As Jack had turned to Tess in place of Ang, perhaps I also had turned to Esther in place of Tess.

I drilled until I felt the give of the tool as it broke through to water. I removed the auger and dropped the gauge through the hole in the ice. Esther knelt to take the measurement: 32 cm already.

Esther and I gathered wood from the small shed at the back of our house. Walls, roofs, floors, doorways that had been neatly stacked for the winter. Snow had blown through the gap at the bottom of the door and was heaped at the entrance way. Our prints were in it still.

"Perhaps he went back to Ang. Maybe they are sitting on a sofa somewhere together wondering how it was that their children grew up so quickly."

"I am sure the police would have checked all that out," I said.

"They might not even have been aware of her."

"They'd have spoken to his family. Someone would have checked."

Esther dropped a piece of wood she was carrying and stooped to pick it up again. "You would think so, but I wonder."

My arms were full. I stepped out of the shed into the open. Esther followed after me. I kicked the door of the shed shut. The snow was about eight inches high. It was early afternoon. Thin white clouds stretched from one end of the sky to the other. A house sparrow landed on an aluminium bucket that had blown over in the wind.

"There will be no happy ending," I warned her.

"You don't know that," she insisted.

"Yes, I do."

"What do you know?"

I carried the wood over to the back door of the house and laid it against the wall. Esther put her wood down beside mine. I sat down on the back step. Esther had swept it down earlier in the day, cleared the snow off it. She sat down next to me. We looked into our back yard. There was nothing to define its boundaries. It was as if the whole tundra was ours. I placed my gloved hands on the knees of my jeans, breathed in the fresh air. Esther's elbow bumped against me accidentally.

"It was a clear spring morning. The ice had not broken. Against the blue sky, a sudden snowstorm. Large white flakes which failed to fall. A distant shrieking. The snow geese returned. Tens of thousands floating on a warm southerly breeze. This I know."

Esther laid her gloved hand on my leg, its brown leather exterior and its rabbit fur interior.

"The ice reflected the blue of the morning. A pale cool blue covering the landscape. The sound of water dripping.

The fragile edges of frazzle ice tinkling. The crisp chill of the air. The smell of coffee in Jack's small kitchen."

I placed my hand on top of Esther's. The house sparrow spread its wings and took flight.

"You miss him still, don't you?" She turned her face towards mine. She looked tired.

"I don't know what happened," I said. "One moment he was there, and the next he had disappeared." That was indeed the truth, the facts of what occurred before me. What do I know? I know, I raised my clenched hand in anger, as others have done before. I know, I did that.

Esther pushed hair from her eyes, looked past me now. The sparrow was gone. The metal bucket glittered in the sun. The wind started to pick up. It bit at our faces.

"We should go inside." Esther stood up and opened the door, stooped to gather her wood.

If we waited long enough, would the sparrow return, fly in through the open door?

CHAPTER 7

Esther slept soundly beside me. It was five thirty, the December sun had yet to rise. I lay in bed for another forty-five minutes but could not get back to sleep. My mind was on Jack. Esther was persistent. She had asked Marilyn if she could recall the names of the police officers from back then, if any of them still remained here. She could as easily have asked me, but out of consideration, I presume, she did not. Nevertheless, she kept me informed. She did not want to do anything behind my back. Marilyn remembered the sergeant, Ross Loewen. I did too. She couldn't recall the other officers. Most only stayed a few years then moved back south. Loewen had left some years after Jack disappeared. Marilyn had no idea where he was now. The person to talk to, she told Esther, was Janice Palichuk. She had worked in the detachment office forever. Esther told me last night that she was going to drop in on her today.

While she slept, I dressed and went downstairs. I got my coat, gloves and hat, put on my boots and stepped out into the still dark morning. I unplugged my pickup, started it up, turned on the heater and waited for the engine to warm up. I scraped just enough ice off the windscreen so that I could see out, got back in, and drove to Bird Cove.

The pickup bounced over the icy road. The suspension creaked. The sky began to lighten as I drove. What would Janice know? What would she remember?

I remembered that Sergeant Loewen and one of the officers named Terry had called to my house to talk to me after Jack was reported missing. Tess had made the report. Jack had failed to return to his apartment that evening and night. She assumed he had gone out with one of his friends and stayed over, but by the following afternoon she got concerned. She waited all that day and most of the next. Later that evening, she arrived at my door. She was distraught. She had not slept well the night before. She was worried enough to call on me.

I heard the knock on the door. It was around four thirty in the evening. I too had not slept the night before nor the one before that either although it felt as though I were asleep, living in an indecipherable dream. Jack falling down and I falling after him, an endless plummet. I walked to the door half-expecting to see the sergeant there, and if he had been, I believe I would have told him whatever he needed to know. But when I opened the door it was Tess. Standing there in a light rain jacket, her sweater and jeans. She looked in shock. At first, I thought it might have been my appearance that caused this state.

But Tess simply said, "Jack has not come back for two nights."

How quickly our feelings dissolve and solidify in some other fashion. I did not even know if I would be permitted to ask her in. So we stood there at the door, the entrance way between us.

"Did you have a fight?" God forgive me, but that was my response.

"I would not be here if we had."

It was then she asked if she could come in.

"It is too late for that," I could have said, but instead I stepped back and made room for her to enter. We went into the kitchen and sat at the table across from one another.

"I am very worried," she said. "I think something must have happened."

My breathing lurched like a bird in a storm. The tremor in my hands, the fighting pulse of its small heart.

"It's Jack," I said, "you know him, he could be back at any moment." The words seemed to speak themselves, surprise my ears as much as hers.

"We were to have supper ..." And then she stopped. "You haven't seen him?" she asked, regaining her composure.

I shook my head.

Tess let a breath escape. Her hands were spread on the table, holding on. "I had to know. I didn't think it likely."

"I'll make us tea." I went to the sink and filled the kettle. I tried to think of what I should say or do. Tess was crying at the table. And Jack was gone. My mind reeled as it had been reeling for the last few days.

I put the kettle on the stove to boil. "What can I do?"

"I am not asking you to do anything," Tess replied crossly. She wiped at her tears. "If it were possible not to have come here, I would not have come."

"I know that." The flame licked at the bottom of the kettle. "We will take my truck and look for him after the tea." It was all I could think to say.

Tess did not disagree. Jack was missing, and Tess and I would sit at my table and drink tea. I would even have wiped away her tears if I could. Instead I excused myself and went to the bathroom, threw up in the sink. I washed my face and dried it, stared at myself in the mirror. I would have to get through this somehow. I would have to go back out to Tess and bring her to look for him.

Tess left her car at my house and drove with me in my pickup. We followed the road back past Bird Cove, the Golf Balls, the dump, the airport, the polar bear jail, out past the port, all the way to Cape Merry where the road ran out. We stopped off along the way at any of the places it was possible Jack would go to. We got out and walked. What were we looking for? Jack aimlessly ambling along having lost track of time? Or Jack lying face down on the ice and snow unmoving? His beaver hat, his fur lined jacket? His body floating in a break in the ice?

I could have brought her to him there and then. I could have led her straight to where he rested beneath the ice.

It was barely minus five and yet the cold took root in my bones. My flesh prickled into goose bumps. There on Bird Cove, the site of our meeting, she looked at *The Ithaca* stranded in the ice in the way I believe Eloise looked at the grain ship the night Jack told her he was going home for Christmas. Did she wonder if Jack had walked out to the steamship across the fragile ice? Was he there yet at the wheelhouse sailing into unfamiliar frozen lands?

We walked in silence. The ice had warmed at the edge of the shore. Meltwater dripped steadily onto the gravel below. Pools gathered on the surface. Whatever we were searching for, we did not find. There was no trace of Jack anywhere, nothing to say he had been here. After looking out along Cape Merry and the Churchill River, we returned to town. We checked back at his apartment. Afterwards I accompanied her into every bar, every store, as she asked after him to no avail. Jack had not been seen anywhere.

I drove her back to my house to collect her car. I did not ask her in, and we did not say goodbye. If Jack did not show by eight thirty, she said, she would report him missing. And so it was. By eight thirty Jack had not shown, and Tess rang the police.

✦

A mist rose off the ice. Esther would awaken and wonder where I was. I parked my pickup at Bird Cove. A pale yellow circle of light in the white sky where the sun had just risen. I pulled the collar of my jacket up around my neck and tightened my hat over my ears. I left my auger in the truck and walked to the shore where the ice spilled over, a foot and a half high. I clambered up on top of it and walked out into the mist. That was all it took. A few steps and I was no longer there. I walked straight ahead unable to see where I was going, following the pale yellow glow. The water beat at the underside of the ice, boomed in the air around me. The hollow sound of emptiness.

Esther would wait for me to return. By mid-morning, some concern would register. By early afternoon, she would be truly worried. She would wander in and out, look for my truck. Evening would slowly pass. She would wish we had installed a phone, that she had another vehicle. She would contemplate walking out to the road and hitching a ride into town, but what if I returned in the meantime? And so Esther would wait and worry. She would wait all night. She would wish she had gone into town earlier, and she would wonder if she should still go. But the night would deter her. By morning when I still had not returned, she would seek a lift into town. She would go to the police.

✦

The day after Tess reported Jack missing Sergeant Loewen and another officer, Terry, called upon me. I had only managed a couple of hours sleep and could hardly function. I tried to shut out the events of that day, but they would jump back at me suddenly, flash before my eyes or sit in the base of my stomach, infiltrate my hands and legs, reduce them to trembling wrecks. I would alter between shivering and sweating. My mind would reel. Like Tess, I was waiting for Jack to return, and, like Tess, I knew he was not coming back. I retched at the bathroom sink, but, unable to eat, there was nothing to come forth.

I brought them both into my living room. I was afraid to offer them tea in case they should notice the shake in my hands. The sergeant and I knew one another from incidents at work and other general occasions. He sat on the couch, the officer sat in one of the armchairs, and I sat in the other.

"No sign of him?" I began.

The sergeant shook his head. A light snow had been falling. Flakes fell from his jacket, cascaded inside my home, across my couch and coffee table, down onto the floor.

"The teacher told me you hadn't seen him either."

"Tess?"

The sergeant nodded. "Miss Cook. Tess."

"She told me she saw him last Saturday, but I haven't seen him in almost two weeks."

"Oddest place," the sergeant said, "you think you couldn't miss seeing someone around here and yet a month could go by."

"I haven't been into town much recently. A few provisions, that's about all."

The sergeant folded his arms, sat back in the couch. "He's probably fine. These things happen all the time." The young officer sat with his legs folded. He had nothing to add at this point. He was about my own age, twenty-three, twenty-four. I wondered if he knew Jack, if he drank with him, played pool. "Of course," the sergeant continued, "an accident could have occurred. These things happen all the time too."

I worked hard not to tighten my grip on the arms of the chair. "Tess is very worried," I said. "I am concerned too. She expected him back that day. He gave no indication that he would not return."

"How well do you know Miss Cook?" he asked, methodically.

"We were in a relationship, but it didn't work out."

The sergeant nodded. "You were a good friend of Jack Butan's?"

"Probably his best friend."

"But you haven't seen him in two weeks." The officer leaned in, repeated what the sergeant had just said.

"It is like you said," I replied looking to the sergeant, "a month could go by without seeing someone."

"And how well did Miss Cook know Butan?" The officer continued his questioning.

I looked to where the flakes of snow had fallen from the sergeant's jacket, but they had already melted, were gone. I felt the need to cough, to clear my throat, but thought it could easily be misinterpreted as some form of guilt.

"We were all friends. Jack used to go out with Tess's house mate, Eloise, before she left."

I wondered how much of this they already knew. What had they asked Tess and what had she told them?

"And when did this Eloise leave?"

I looked back at the officer, tried to appear calm. "March. Spring Break. She said she was going home for the week, but she never came back." I could feel the bones in my fingers tense up, the pulse of the blood in the veins on the backs of my hands.

"Now, why was that do you think?"

"She didn't like it up here. She was planning to leave at the end of the year, but I think she couldn't take it any longer."

"Cabin fever?"

"That, and things weren't going as smoothly between Jack and her. Only for him she probably wouldn't have stayed any of this school year at all."

The officer continued to lean forward. "What happened?" He sounded more aggressive than curious.

"Jack was not as serious about her as she was about him."

"So you and Miss Cook, and Jack Butan and this Eloise, not exactly the most successful of relationships? Hmm?" He leaned back in his chair now as though something decisive had been discerned. Something relevant to their investigation.

"Not exactly," I agreed. "Maybe it didn't help us all being so close."

"Was Mr. Butan upset about the situation?" the sergeant interrupted.

"Somewhat," I said. "He felt bad about the way it ended."

"Do you think he might have gone to see her?" He spoke quietly almost reverently.

"I don't know. I would not have thought so, but I suppose it could happen."

"So where is she now?"

"She went home to Quebec. The school would have her records."

"Was there anything else going on with Mr. Butan that you were aware of?"

"I don't think he did anything to harm himself if that's what you mean." I felt agitated. I needed to dispel any unsavoury rumours that might arise.

Sergeant Loewen stood up abruptly. "Well thank you for your time, Wade." He indicated for the officer to depart. "I expect he'll turn up. In any case we have a helicopter going out this afternoon to take a look." The officer got to his feet. He seemed reluctant to go.

I thanked both of them and walked them to the door. Light snow whirled through the air as randomly as my thoughts. I said goodbye and watched them leave.

After they had gone, I shaved and took a bath. I watched the snow through the bathroom window. It was coming down heavier now. For the umpteenth time I tried to reconcile my thoughts. The officer may have been suspicious or simply doing his job. The sergeant had looked as though he expected Jack to walk into the room at any moment wiping snow from his shoulders.

The dense steam of the hot bathwater filled my bathroom like snow. I lay back and felt it land on my hair and on my damp skin. Watched it fall down around me thickly, drift into heaps on my bathroom floor, built up around me as though it might contain me forever.

✦

The mist lifted. I was an hour's journey out onto the ice. Exposed. Esther would have risen by now, have seen the empty side of my bed. She would be in her robe in the kitchen filling the kettle, making tea. She would look out and see the light snow, feel excited about her visit to Janice later.

The sun had disappeared behind a thick ridge of clouds. I stood in a six inch covering of snow, the hard ridged ice beneath my boots. I could scarcely see the shore. The thick snow and ice lapped at the edges of the sky. I inhaled the clean shrill air. A light sprinkling of snow began to fall, sparkling with sunlight. I turned around to return to shore just as the wind picked up and the snowfall began to increase. The wind whipped at my face. All I had was a small woolen hat. I would have needed my balaclava. I proceeded with my eyes half-closed to keep out the snow. Within ten minutes, the winds had increased with such speed that I could not see before me. I walked forwards hoping that I was moving in the right direction. I had lived here long enough to know better than to head out so carelessly as I had done. The bitter chill penetrated my gloves and boots. My fingers and toes felt painfully cold. I wriggled them constantly to keep the blood flowing. It was not the first time I had been caught in a blizzard, but it was the first time I had been so far from shore, so uncertain of my surroundings. Snow gusted in around my feet and legs slowing me down. I could as easily have been walking upwards off the ground as moving forwards. The wind called into my ears, told terrible tales of painful arctic deaths. Men, women and children caught in the same sudden squalls. I clapped my hands together to warm them, and the winds howled louder as though I were praising their efforts, urging them on. In the dark at night beneath the ice, is not the sound I hear the hands of the dead applauding their own demise?

I lost track of time or maybe just lost use for it. I was disoriented, being guided solely by the wind that threatened my very life. It has been that way since the day of Jack's death, perhaps even before. I have wandered blindly through a blizzard using the forces of destruction to feel my way to safety. The blow that sent him to his death sent me to mine. There in the blinding blizzard the truth was clear to see. I had done more wrong in my life than I could ever undo. Even then as the wind surged, lifted me clean off my feet, I shuddered under the burden of my being. I left the ground as easily as Jack sank towards it.

✦

Esther drove into town the next morning. The blizzard the day before had prevented her from calling on Janice. It had passed over, but snow continued to drift over the roads making driving difficult and dangerous. After my experience on the ice the day before, I had wanted Esther to wait until the winds died down completely, but Esther couldn't wait any longer.

"Drive carefully," I urged.

Esther kissed me goodbye. She walked to the truck and unplugged it. Snow rose to her waist, threatened to swallow her up completely. She got in and started up the engine. Thick fumes billowed from the exhaust pipe. She sat with the engine idling to warm it up. I watched her from the doorway. Wisps of hair escaped from the front of her hat. She brushed at her nose as though to wipe a drop of melted snow away. She set out even as the snow blew against the windscreen making it hard to see, as it heaped in banks across the road in front of her. She was leaving and I was staying. She was searching. I had already given up hope.

Strangely in those days after Jack's death, I had more moments of deep calm than I did of panic. As though I too had entered another world, one somewhere in between living and dying. I didn't truly believe that he was gone. In fact, he seemed more present than ever. I could almost believe he had gone to see Eloise or returned home to win over Ang. I rose, I slept, I ate, I dreamed. I did not distinguish between day and night. And then amidst this calm some coarse recognition would filter through, and I was filled with dread. I could scarcely control my body and my mind broke loose. I had killed him, had I not? And I had allowed his body to disappear. I had gone so far into that uninhabitable place I would never find my way back.

I called to the school the following day, but Tess was not there. She had taken sick leave. I wondered if she would be at Jack's apartment waiting, but I decided to try her house on the way past. She answered the door quickly as though she had been listening for a knock.

"Oh," she said. She walked back to her living room, but she left the door open for me.

I closed it behind me. She lay back on the couch, a pillow beneath her head, a blanket at her feet. It looked as though she had slept there the night before.

"How are you?" I asked.

"Lost," Tess answered. She looked exhausted. "I feel the way my people must have felt when they disembarked from the military plane. I know it is unfair to say this, but it feels as though you and Jack have led me here then cast me out to fend for myself."

I felt the force of her words, their bruising impact. "He may turn up yet."

"As you have returned?" Tess closed over her eyes as though to block me out.

"I just wanted to see that you were okay."

"But instead you see that I am not okay. What did you expect?"

"Tess, this is hard on me too."

"Did you hear the helicopter?"

Yesterday afternoon circling overhead. Looking down on us all. And again this morning.

"Yes, I did."

"It has revealed nothing that we did not know previously."

I told her about the sergeant calling over, how he said that these sorts of things often happen, that Jack might still be okay.

"You don't believe that," Tess opened her eyes, seemed disappointed by what she saw.

How could I? And yet Tess as I spoke, I almost did believe in it. I almost believed in all the words that were to follow.

"There was an officer with him. I think he thought Jack might have gone back to see Eloise. It's possible."

"Do you really think that's likely?" Tess was still angry with me. So much had happened in such a short space of time. This was not the environment for a quick succession of events. Everything moved so slowly here. Time was of less consequence. Long periods of day and night, long winters, large expanses of terrain. Tess's forgiveness would come as slowly if it ever came at all. Perhaps we were all in too big of a hurry. "Should we contact Eloise?" she asked.

What could I answer? I could tell her there was no point, that Jack was not there with her. But maybe this was the way it was meant to be. Maybe we were meant to contact her, tell her Jack was missing, feared dead. Maybe our mutual sadness would pull us all together in a way we were unable to in Jack's lifetime.

The whirr of the helicopter's engine spread above us. Tess looked instinctively to the ceiling. She pulled her blanket up over her, seemed to no longer need an answer to her question. "I want you to leave," she said.

"I know that."

"Don't begin," she warned. "Now is not the time."

I left her lying on the couch. I opened the door to her house and stepped out into the light. The helicopter hovered over the beach, where the whale had washed in, then flew out into the bay.

✦

Esther climbed the steps to the RCMP office. She pushed open the door and entered. She walked over to the reception counter and rang the bell. Janice looked up from a desk to the side of the counter.

"Esther?" she enquired.

Esther nodded and said hello as Janice stood up and came over to her. "Sorry about yesterday."

Janice leaned on the counter. "I didn't expect to see you today either with these winds."

An officer passed by the back of the counter, left some papers on Janice's desk.

Janice looked back at her desk briefly. "I'll be about another hour," she told Esther.

"That's okay."

Janice suggested meeting at the café in the complex. Esther told her she looked forward to it, said she would spend the time before in the library there.

While she waited for Janice, she sat at one of the tables in the library reading about Jens Munck's failed expedition in search of the Northwest Passage in 1619, of the winter he and his crew spent on the west peninsula of the Churchill River. Sixty-one out of sixty-four of the crew died of scurvy and the cold. Munck and two others survived and somehow managed to sail back on their own to Europe after break-up.

Jack will rise yet, will he not? He will claw his way back to the surface, return home.

Janice joined Esther at her table. Like Esther, she selected the homemade vegetable soup. Steam rose from their bowls. Esther had rung Janice from Marilyn's some days before to arrange their meeting. She hadn't mentioned what it concerned, just that she wanted to ask her about some of the officers who worked here before. Janice was used to questions about the early days of the detachment and assumed that Esther was working on some local history project.

Janice's father had moved to Churchill in 1952 when she was five, she told Esther. He was a radio operator. For most of the time he was on watch keeping duties. Three eight-hour dog-watches from four in the afternoon to midnight, three middle-watches from midnight to eight in the morning, and three day-watches from eight until four in the afternoon. This was followed by 72 hours off. These watches were kept all year round. If the weather was too bad for their replacements to get there, they had to stay on duty. It was tough, but he never complained that Janice remembered. When the station closed, he was redeployed to Ottawa. But I was already working here and didn't want to leave, she said smiling. I had met someone. He worked as a mechanic on the base.

Esther told Janice about me then. How she had come to see the wildflowers but had found me instead.

"You have that new log house out by the rocket launch," Janice said.

"That's right."

And then Janice cast judgment on me. "We thought he would be alone for the rest of his life. He seemed such a solitary man."

Esther may have smiled at Janice's comment, but she recognized the truth of it. Instead of acknowledging this, she asked, "Are we not all solitary people? Is it not the nature of our design?"

Janice did not answer immediately. An Inuit mother and child passed by their table. The hot soup cooled. A large embroidered hanging of a seal and a native hunter with a harpoon hung on the wall opposite them.

"My husband was killed in a snowmobile accident, six years ago next January. I do not feel it is in my nature to be alone."

Esther lowered her eyes momentarily. "I am sorry. I do not think I would feel it either if, God forbid, anything were to happen to Wade."

The Inuit child screamed from the other side of the café, cried loudly. Her mother held her hand and spoke to her, but the crying did not stop. Janice drank some of her soup. Esther noticed a second hanging on a separate wall. In this one, the harpoon had been thrown by the hunter, and it pierced the neck of the seal. Out in the parking lot, snow built up in the back of the pickup, on the roof and hood. Back at our house, I shoveled snow to clear a path to the door. I hoped Esther had made it to town safely. I worried about what she would hear.

In the circumstances, Esther wasn't sure if it was the right time to bring up Jack, but Janice asked how she might help her, and she felt obliged to answer. She told her how a friend of mine had disappeared twenty-five years before and that she was trying to find out what she could about it. She said she knew that there was a Sergeant Ross Loewen stationed here at the time and wondered if Janice had any idea where he was now or any of the other officers involved in the investigation at the time. Janice asked for my friend's name.

"Jack Butan," Esther replied.

"It rings a bell," Janice said, 'but off the top of my head I can't recall the incident." She held her full spoon less than two inches from her mouth and gazed back into the past only to find nothing there. She ate her soup and replaced her spoon in the bowl. "I remember Ross well. He must have been around almost twelve years. That's a long time for here. Most of them just come on rotation, a short tour before going somewhere else. Ross liked it here. Many of the other officers can be quite intolerant of the native people because of the drinking and domestic violence, but Ross was never like that. He felt sorry for their situation. You only meet the ones with troubles he used to tell his men. Don't make assumptions based on that."

"What year did he leave?"

"Oh my goodness," Janice tapped her fingers on the table-top. "It must have been '85, '86. I'm not sure."

"Do you know where he went?"

Janice shook her head. "I know he went down south at first, probably Winnipeg, but it wouldn't surprise me if he moved back north again. He used to talk of going to the Yukon."

"Who else was here at that time, do you remember?"

Janice stirred her soup. "Terry Mitchell." She laughed. "I remember him. He was always full of fun, devilment. Who else?" She shook her head. "How do we forget these things? Oh yes, Duncan Walker."

"I was hoping I might be able to talk to some of them, see if they remembered anything about Jack, if they discovered anything that might help us understand what happened."

Janice said she'd see what she could find out. She wanted to know more about him, and Esther passed on what little she knew.

"Isn't it terrible?' Janice said, "I can't remember him at all. You would think something like that would stick in your memory. But then there have been so many tragedies, it's hard to keep up with them all. You wouldn't want to know the half of the things that have happened around here."

"How do you cope with it?" Esther asked.

"By observing the routines of work. Until it happens to yourself of course." Janice looked tearful.

Esther felt bad for bringing all of this up. The dead do not come back to life no matter how hard we try. We simply make them die all over again. Esther was stitching him into a tapestry. I held the harpoon while he lay on the ice. She would hang it in this town complex for everyone to see.

They finished their soup without talking, then Janice said that she better get back to work. She told Esther to call her the following week. In the meantime, she would find out what she could.

Esther walked out into a gale. It would be impossible to drive in it. So she went back to the library to wait it out.

Esther waited out the storm with Samuel Hearne, three Chipewyan and two Cree men on the shores of the Seal River. They all huddled together inside a single wrap around tent made from moose hide with snow packed around the outside. They set up nets through the ice for pike and trout, awaited better weather to walk towards the Barren Grounds in search of the Coppermine River. By June, they were headed north towards Shoal Lake and the timberline. By the end of the month, they made it to the Barren Grounds, due north along the ninety-third meridian, a hundred miles from the nearest trees.

Esther checked outside, but the snow continued to blow. She returned to Hearne and his men, late July 1770, already too late to head further north. They made camp for the winter.

Esther got home around four thirty, the winds having died down sufficiently for her to travel. She reluctantly left Hearne before his third expedition having followed his two failed ones. In her search for Jack, Esther felt kinship with these explorers. The quest for the Northwest Passage, the Coppermine River, the Strait of Anián. She was ready to walk hundreds of miles in a treeless waste, a ravaged land of rock and stone, scrubby willow and stunted spears of grass, through thousands of square miles of permafrost, where the earth is frozen forever to depths of hundreds of feet, a place unfit for habitation where food is scarce and at best to be avoided by human life.

Perhaps, she would fail in her search for Jack. Perhaps, she would discover instead the barren wastes of my ground. I know that she wished I would accompany her on her journey, but before she even set out, I had failed her. The truth is that I did not possess the courage. How could I say this to her, she who feared the bears more than anything yet moved here to be with me?

There was an Inuit story I told Esther shortly after she arrived. I told it to help dispel her fear. And, many times after, she would ask me to tell it again. She listened so intently always as I recounted how a young Inuit hunter set out walking alongside his small sled and three dogs to hunt for seal. He crossed the frozen water seeking an agloo to wait next to for a seal to appear. He would kill it then with his harpoon. The strong winds made it difficult to see, and the hunter struggled against the blowing snow. He turned his head to the side and covered his face with his parka. He walked forwards slowly. The dogs pushed ahead. When he looked up again, the thick flakes of snow seemed to shape themselves before his eyes. The young hunter stopped and peered into the whiteness. Ahead of him, appeared three large white bears. They roamed one after another on the ice on all fours, their stout bodies, their thick paws, their small erect ears, their black tipped snouts.

The young hunter had never killed a bear before. To do so now would give him prestige amongst his people. The bear was the most powerful and most dangerous of all Arctic animals. The boy knew it would take all his strength and maybe more. If he managed to catch up with any of the bears, the fight would be hazardous. He would have to take on the great strength of this almighty creature with his harpoon alone at close distance. The boy considered the possibility of his own death. But what he had seen was surely a sign, and the boy knew he had no option but to follow and hunt down the bear. If he was successful in killing it with his harpoon, the bear's spirit would remain in the tip of his harpoon for days. When he returned, the death rituals would have to be observed. He would have to take off all of his outer clothing before entering his icy home. For a whole month, he could not eat of the meat or blubber of the bear. The soul of the bear was very dangerous during the days it remained in the harpoon's tip. If offended, the soul could transform into an evil spirit bringing illness and great danger. The skin would have to be taken with the skull intact and hung outside the igloo by the nostrils. Its spleen, bladder, tongue and genitals would be hung together inside with offerings. As long as this death taboo was being observed, no man or woman's work could be done.

The boy jumped onto his sled and hurried the dogs, following the tracks of the disappearing bears. For three days and three nights, he gave chase without rest. Early on the fourth morning, the boy looked up into the northern sky and watched a dervish dance of light, sweeps of swirling greens and purples and white as the aurora borealis filled the heavens. The winds abated and the snow settled. Up ahead, he saw an igloo bathed in the northern lights. The tracks of the bears led to the door. The boy brought his dogs to rest and climbed down off his sled. A great calm descended upon him as he reached beneath his furs for his harpoon. He took it in his hand and slowly made his way to the entrance of the igloo. The boy crouched down and peered inside to where a fire was lit. At first, the light blinded the boy so he could not see, but gradually his vision returned. Around the fire talking and laughing sat three human male figures and beside them on the floor the white fur coats they had removed.

Esther liked to believe that this old myth was possible, that the bears could become human by removing their fur coats and become bears again by putting them back on. I would sometimes put my parka on and peer through the fur-lined hood.

"I am a bear," I would say. "You have all and nothing to fear from me."

One evening she wrestled me to the ground, raised her hand as though it bore a harpoon within it and fought me to my death. She took off her outer clothing, removed my fur and hung it on the door outside. Then she laid offerings at my feet until my soul left the tip of her harpoon and only the good spirits remained.

✦

That morning in the blizzard on the ice off Bird Cove, when my body lifted with the forces of the winds and carried me through the air like a great Snowy owl, I truly thought that my time had come. The Arctic currents carried me away from the shore. There was no turning around, no going back. As I drifted further and further away, I too saw the snowflakes cluster, take shape. The team of white, black and red-brown Eskimo dogs, the sled and the polar bear sitting astride it. Their frantic yelps biting into the air. Trotting easily across the ice and snow through the white veil towards me. I thought they had come to carry me on the last stages of my journey. The team pulled up alongside me. The white-haired lead dog sat on its haunches and observed me, squinted through the slanting snow down its nose at my plight. I had fallen on my hands and knees. The bear got up from its sled and stood up on its hind legs. It walked towards me. I awaited my fate. It walked right up to me and stared down. Its large white paws swooped towards me. I closed my eyes. My eyelashes froze together. The bear lifted me in its arms and carried me to the sled where it lay me down and covered me. The loud yelps as the dogs tore into motion once more.

Later the bear took off its white fur parka and trousers, transformed into a human and accepted Esther's offering of tea. I sat in my chair by the stove wrapped in a blanket recovering from the cold. Afterwards the bear put its fur back on and stepped out again into the storm.

CHAPTER 8

The port was closed for the winter. Jack and I sat in The White Bear Café drinking coffee. A bitterly cold wind chased through the streets. A snowmobile sped past the window. A truck skidded on the ice as it tried to park at the hardware store opposite. Eloise had told Jack about Tess staying over with me. He said, winking at me, that she told him Tess and I had gone for a walk and got caught in the storm, built an igloo and sheltered there for the night.

That was when he informed me of his plan to go home for Christmas. His parents weren't getting any younger, he said. I felt certain the news Eloise had given to him about Tess and I had influenced his decision to go. I told him he was probably making a good choice, and Jack looked at me as if I was complicit in some conspiracy. It was obvious he needed to see Ang again, find out if there was anything left between them.

"Are you staying?" he asked.

I had been here two Christmases already. Like Jack, I had yet to go home. My relationship with my parents was strained. There was little to encourage me.

"Yes, I'm staying," I said.

Although Jack had expected nothing less, he seemed disappointed with my reply.

"Do you love her?" He sprung it upon me. His cup to his lips, steam rising from his mouth like anger.

"Ah now Jack, it's early days for that," I said. "We hardly know each other yet."

"You seem to know her well enough."

I looked outside. A dog, some husky crossbreed, ran helplessly after a snowmobile. "I like her. That is for certain. Unlike you Jack, I don't know anything about love."

"Maybe you should talk to Eloise about that, she would put you straight." Jack put down his cup, smiled in a tired way. "Will you spend Christmas with Tess?"

"I don't know. Perhaps she will go to see her family." She hadn't mentioned Christmas to me at all. "What about Eloise?"

"She thinks I am staying. She plans to spend it with me."

"You'll have to tell her."

The door opened and a strong gust of wind blew in. Leo Mitchell from the water treatment plant came in and pushed the door shut. He nodded at Jack in passing. Leo pulled off his gloves and threw them down on the table beside us. He drew down the hood of his parka, unzipped it.

"Frickin' cold." He spoke to anyone who would listen. He turned back to Jack. "What do you say, Jack?"

"No brass monkeys out and about, that's for sure."

Leo laughed harshly. "Damn plant froze up. Some bloody underground pipe. Thought we were going to have to shut the water down. I have been out in the freezing cold all day. Digging this way and that."

"Did you solve the problem?"

Leo hung his coat over the back of his chair and sat down heavily. "Not me. Bloody water started flowing again of its own accord."

"Temperamental."

Leo called out for coffee. "Don't see you around so much."

"Keeping busy," Jack said. "You know how it is."

Leo laughed loudly again. "Damn sure I do. She got a name, or did you even bother to ask?"

Jack laughed along. "I've been meaning to. I'll get around to it one of these days."

Leo shook his head. "You young ones."

Leo was probably in his early forties, twenty years or so older than us. I had met him once or twice with Jack but didn't really know him.

"Speaking of young ones," Jack said, "how's Lena?"

Leo pulled at his nose. "Hard to say. Spends more time with her relatives than she does with me. I don't know the half of what goes on. But you know, we weather the storm."

Jack told me later that Leo had married an Inuit woman ten years his junior. He met her on a drinking binge. The first person ever to out-drink him, he said, how could you not love her? They kept meeting up in bars, kept getting drunk together, falling into bed. Her brother came up to him eventually and told Leo it was time he married her, told him he had no option, that it was an old Inuit custom. They had drunk and slept together their allowance. Now they must marry, otherwise it would be disrespectful to Lena, and then he, her brother, would be obliged to hunt Leo down. So he married her in the Inuit way, no ceremony. Lena came to live in his house, they began a life together.

Leo got his coffee, turned his attention to someone else he knew.

"I know I have to tell her," Jack said turning back to me. "I had to make up my mind about going home before I could say anything. No sense bringing it up if I decided not to go in the end. She knows about Ang. She'll only assume the worst."

"That was a long time ago. Why should she assume anything?"

"You're right. Yet it's what we do, make assumptions, second guess each other. We don't know any other way to relate. It's why we're so lousy at it." He drank down the cold dregs of his coffee. "Tess isn't going home for Christmas."

"How do you know?"

"Eloise told me. She doesn't get along with her family, or maybe it's that they don't get along with her."

Tess had never mentioned this to me. "I didn't know."

"I didn't think so." Jack looked at his empty cup. "It's okay, what do you know about me, or I about you? All those years with Ang and I didn't learn a thing."

"You make us sound pitiful."

"That's the rosy picture."

It was true. In all our talk, Jack and I never really mentioned our pasts, nor our futures. Our whole lives back then it seemed were happening in the present alone.

But since the day of Jack's death, that came to an end. The past absorbed the present. Then Esther came to Churchill to live with me. She moved in and we began a life together without ceremony. And now, it appeared, the future was in peril.

This part I have to imagine too. Jack surely had to tell Eloise he was going home for Christmas, but how he told her or what occurred I do not know. If Jack told me what happened, I cannot now remember. Eloise, in turn, would surely have told Tess, but I do not recall Tess telling me about that either, and so I am left to my imagination. There are so many parts of our lives we know nothing about, so little faith we can place in memory. It is no wonder we tell so little about ourselves to others.

In my telling of it, Jack and Eloise are walking home from The Churchill Bar. It is December 12, eleven fifteen at night. It is -32 degrees. The ice is 63 cm thick. They are walking back to Jack's apartment across from the port. The road is slippery. Along the edges, the snow has accumulated to a depth of a foot. The sky is clear of clouds. The stars look close enough for Eloise to touch if she were to sit on Jack's shoulders. The moon is a sliver, an orange sliver. Eloise's breath smells of vodka and love. Jack reeks of smoke and beer. An Arctic hare runs down an alley unseen. The engines of vehicles cough and start. Driver and passenger doors bang shut. Jack wears a beaver hat and his fur collared jacket. Eloise, a lined wool jacket and a knitted hat pulled down over her ears which lets in the wind. They both wear heavy gloves and warm winter boots. Jack's arm lies across Eloise's shoulder as though there was nowhere else in the world he could place it.

Despite Eloise's cold ears, she feels warm inside from the alcohol, from Jack's arm, his presence. They pass the closed buildings on Kelsey Boulevard, hear a human roar from one of the side streets. Dogs compete in barking loudest and shrillest. A pickup truck sits on blocks, its wheels missing. The street is wide and empty. They follow the bend in the road towards the grain terminal. Jack is lost in thought. Eloise is twittering on unheard. Jack stops then on the road, the frozen harbour in the background. A ship that failed to get away in time is caught in the ice. A yellow star falls across the sky. Eloise wonders why Jack has stopped. She thinks he is going to kiss her. Instead Jack pulls away. He stands on the icy road. The tall looming grain terminal, the long galleries to load the ships.

"I'm going home for Christmas," he says. He speaks quietly. Eloise has to strain to hear him.

"What?" she asks. By this time, the words have reached her ears, but Eloise needs to absorb what he has said.

Jack repeats himself. Eloise feels cold all of a sudden. She feels like the large ship, trapped by the pressure all around her. "But I thought you said you were staying, that you never went home. I decided to stay for that reason."

Jack too feels trapped. "I'm sorry."

"I told my family I wouldn't be coming home. They have made other arrangements now. They are to spend Christmas with friends of theirs." Eloise looks back to the dark ship, the space in the sky where the star had been before its fall. Jack, for his part, scuffs at the ice with the toe of his boot. He thinks of the occasion when he told Ang he was leaving. Eloise bangs on his chest with her fist almost as if she is knocking to see if there is anyone in there. "Do you have to go?"

"Yes," Jack answers. "I do."

Life with Jack will always be like this Eloise knows. She should tell him now that they are finished, but Jack pulls her to him, and they kiss. He throws her a lifeline, and Eloise takes it tentatively. This is her last year here for certain. By next Christmas, Churchill will be but a distant memory, Jack too.

✦

Esther called in on Janice again towards the end of the following week. Janice, she said, looked pleased to see her. They arranged to meet for lunch once more. Esther went back to the library. She was determined to guide Hearne to the object of his quest.

She set out with him on his third expedition. Within weeks, they were facing starvation and the unenviable decision whether to press on further into the barren wasteland in the hope of finding food, a deer or ptarmigan or lake with fish, or to return back to the fort at Churchill. Esther urged him to press on. She would not have, she told me later, if she had known that they were heading into Eskimo territory with Chipewyan guides, bitter enemies. They left the tree-line behind and have entered the bare rock of the tundra where the Chipewyans discovered the Eskimo camp twelve miles downstream and massacred them in their sleep. Men, women, and children. She would, she said, like Hearne weep about it for the rest of her life. None of it was worth the discovery of the Coppermine River, the disproof of the famed Northwest Passage.

Is it ever worth the outcome? That surely is the question. And yet, I urge Esther on in the same way.

Esther and Janice met once again at the café in the complex. It was close to Christmas and decorations hung from the ceiling and walls. A Christmas tree stood in the open area across from the café. Esther ordered a tuna sandwich. Janice ordered spaghetti and meatballs. She brought a yellow manila envelope along with her which she placed on the table. Jack's absence sat between them, brought them together. Janice asked how she liked it here. She wondered how Churchill must seem to someone who had not grown up in it. Esther answered as honestly as she could.

"Even without Wade, I think I could stay."

"I did not know how I would manage without Eb," Janice confided. "It is certainly not easy, but I do. I never knew how much a part of our family this place could be."

Esther asked if she had children.

"Just one," she replied. "He left to go to college in Montreal and only comes back to visit. I do not see him often enough. He missed the death of his father. He missed his funeral. The weather was too bad for the plane to fly."

"I bring out the sadness in you," Esther apologized.

"That is not a bad thing," Janice said. "In many ways, I am grateful for it." She pushed the envelope in Esther's direction. "It's a copy of everything we have on the case. Please don't mention it to anyone. I would lose my job."

Esther shook her head. "Don't do this."

"It is already done. No one will know as long as you say nothing. Please."

It was the please that convinced Esther. She thanked her and took the envelope.

"I looked into it that day we met." Janice took a drink of water. "I remember him now, Jack Butan. Funny how it all comes back. He walked out into the tundra and did not return."

"Do you think that is what happened?"

"Yes, I do." She looked up from her plate, took in the café, the space beyond. "I was already married to Eb by then. I thought I had reached my life's end, and I was glad. How little we know."

Esther ran her fingers over the envelope as though reading its contents. "Did you find out anything about the officers involved?"

"The names and current phone numbers for two of them, Ross Loewen and Duncan Walker, are in the envelope. Terry Mitchell seems to have disappeared off the face of the earth."

"It'll soon be Christmas," Esther said changing the subject.

Janice nodded. "Eb never much cared for it. He thought it would be better if it only came every two years." She laughed a little. "Mark, that's my son, is coming home. There's that to look forward to." She pushed her plate away leaving half her meal uneaten. "I don't seem to have the same appetite I used to. Maybe that's not such a bad thing." She patted her stomach.

Esther thought that Janice could do with putting on some weight but didn't know her well enough to say this.

"What about you and Wade, do you celebrate Christmas?"

"The usual," Esther replied. "We buy each other gifts, eat turkey if we can get it, put up a few decorations. Nothing too much."

"Will you have anyone visiting?"

"Neither Wade nor I keep much contact with our families. I think we've grown too used to each other. Neither of us are very good in company anymore."

"That's why a lot of people come here," Janice said. "That's its attraction."

"I think you're right. Wade and I are at our happiest walking by the shore or on the tundra or sitting by our stove. It took me a long time to find that, and I don't want to let it go."

When Janice left to go back to work, Esther watched her leave, watched the sadness in her gait, the loneliness that trailed after her.

Esther went to our bedroom to read the contents of the envelope. I busied myself in the shed, did some minor maintenance work on the generator, some general tidying. It is hard to know what I was feeling. At times, an anxious gnawing worked its way deep into the pit of my stomach in the way I had heard of animals chewing off their own foot to free themselves from traps. Other times, I seemed to be floating outside of myself with a sense that Esther's enquiry would eventually restore peace or upend everything once and for all.

I dug out the Christmas lights and decorations. It was a cold but windless day, mid-afternoon. I strung the lights around the porch. I heard the sound of an engine in the distance and looked up. A half-ton pulled in at the rocket launch.

Occasionally, some people came out to look at the launch, part of the tour we gave people around here.

I had seen the envelope in Esther's hand. I knew it wasn't mail as it was not addressed. Janice had given her something. After all these years, I have to assume I was not seen with Jack on that day or seen close to where he was last observed. At the time, when I existed in that dreamy netherworld, I half-expected that someone would say they had seen me with him. That I would be quizzed about my whereabouts on that day. And I honestly did not know what I would say. I could deny it. Claim it must have been someone else. It is easy to mistake people in these parts with jackets, toques, balaclavas, scarves. Other times, I thought I should have reported Jack's death. Accidents happen so easily. But I thought it better to let Jack go. And now Esther it seems is digging up his remains.

The initial feelings of panic, unease and despair dissipated far more quickly than would be believed possible. Somehow, I learned to live with the horror of it all. The search was called off quickly since it was a fruitless one. Sergeant Loewen, I think, believed Jack fell through the ice, got carried away by the currents, washed in on some inaccessible shore. Perhaps, he is there yet. Bones that sweep in and out with the tides as though he continues to swim for safety and is constantly being pulled back. Tess thought that Jack took his own life, and she blamed herself for this. There were those who thought he had faked his death, walked out of one life into another to avoid his responsibilities. Eloise may even have chosen to believe this. She who carried his baby and, perhaps, carries the brunt of him still. Was there anyone who thought he was killed by another? There may well have been. For years, I thought I saw each and every inhabitant stare at me with that very thought in their mind. And so I retreated to this house, avoided the town as much as possible. I continued with my work. I bought supplies. But I no longer drank in the bars or socialized in any way. Not until Esther.

At first my co-workers felt sorry for me, sorry for how I turned in on myself from the loss of Jack. They would often ask me to stop in for a drink on my way home from work or suggest a game of pool, but in time they gave up, let me sink into myself completely.

The evening light began to dim. I called in to Esther, and she came out to watch as I turned on the lights. A string of reds, greens, yellows, and blues flickered along the porch. Snow on the windowsills and across the roof. Smoke from the stove poured through the chimney. The strong odour of burning wood. Esther wrapped her arms around herself. Her brown hair sparkled. The tip of her nose reddened in the cold. The truck at the launch started up and pulled away. The noise of the engine carried in the cold air. Esther and I looked up. The twin beam of the headlights spread across the back road, escaped across the frozen tundra.

"Who was that?" Esther asked.

"Probably just another visitor taking a look at the site."

The noise of the engine faded away.

"You still haven't brought me there."

I had promised her I would find out who had the keys and seek permission to take a look. I had never been inside it myself even when it was in use. Esther asked me one time about the launch I had seen from my home, and I had tried to describe it in such a way that she could feel that she had partially been a witness to it herself. I told her about going up on the roof, but I had not said who it was I had gone up with. I simply said I had been up there with a friend. Now as I looked to the darkening sky over the tall launch pad I could almost see the explosive flash, hear the deafening take-off, the long thin rocket slicing through the sky, piercing through Jack's wounded heart.

"It was Jack," I said. Esther turned and looked. The Christmas lights reflected in the snow at her feet. The reds, greens, yellows, and blues bleeding into the icy crystals. "That time I went up on the roof to watch the rocket launch, it was Jack I went up there with."

Esther shivered, held onto herself tightly. "I often wondered who it was. You seemed so secretive about it that I assumed it was the woman you had once mentioned."

She looked at me plaintively. Her hair hung loose around her face. The cold was soaking through her. I had not been able to bring myself to tell her about Tess. I mentioned her vaguely when she had told me about the other men she had relationships with, but I had not mentioned her name as I had not mentioned Jack's. I was afraid to. Afraid of how Esther would react, afraid of how it might affect the two of us.

I took Esther's arm. Her lips were set together thinly. They were almost blue. "We should go inside."

I walked with her into the warm house, closed the door on the lights outside. Esther sat by the stove while I made us tea.

"I would like to know about her," she said when I came back in.

I supposed I owed it to her since she had told me about the other men she had known. But she had, in fact, told me little about them since I had not wanted to hear. I knew that things had not worked out for her with them, and that she truly believed our relationship was as good as it got. But could I say the same of Tess? I had never got the opportunity to find out how it would end, whether my love would disappear, disintegrate, flourish. I did not know how to respond to Esther, how to say I did not want to tell her.

Esther read my silence. "Sometime I would like to know." She took a drink of her tea. "I met Janice today."

"Did she have any information for you?"

"She gave me a copy of the police investigation. Some contact numbers. She took a risk doing it. She said she could lose her job if they found out."

There was little I knew about Janice. I remembered her husband, Eb Wiebe. He had been killed in a snowmobile accident some years back. A quiet man, but he could get violent when he was drunk. I often wondered how it must be for Janice to have to see him being brought into the station or to arrive in for work the next morning knowing he was waiting in the cell.

"She seems keen to help," Esther said. "I think it has something to do with losing her husband. He was killed in an accident."

I nodded to let her know I was aware of this.

"Did you know him?"

"Not really." I did not tell her about his violent behaviour. There are some things best kept hidden. "They found Eb's snowmobile first. The water was so cold the underwater rescue team could only search for limited periods of time. It took two days before he was located under the ice."

"That must have been hard on Janice. She must have hoped that he had managed somehow to get out of the water and was waiting nearby to be rescued." Then she asked me if that was what it was like for me when Jack went missing, the long wait, the uncertainty of what had occurred. "You would have had to hope too that he was still alive out there somewhere."

Strangely I did. I sometimes heard a sound and imagined that Jack was walking up my lane or standing at my door, that somehow he had cheated death and had come back. "I knew he was dead," I said, "but, yes, there were moments of futile hope. Those were the worst, knowing that hope was unfounded. Janice would have known that too."

"She had her husband's death confirmed," Esther said. "You didn't have Jack's. That must be worse still."

"Jack is dead, Esther."

"You don't know that for sure."

Walking home afterwards on that dreadful day, the same thought had struck me. What if he wasn't dead, if he could be rescued still? And yet I kept moving forwards swiftly although I did look back occasionally as if I would find him there behind me following in my tracks.

"What did the report of the investigation say?" I hadn't seen her copy of it anywhere nor had I seen the transcripts of the newspaper articles or the photograph of Jack since she first showed them to me. Esther must have been making a file of her own on him. An attempt to gather up the various pieces of his life and to organize them in a way that made sense, in a way Jack himself could never have done when he was alive.

"I'm not sure how to read the report. It could be saying nothing, or perhaps it adds up to something I cannot yet grasp."

All I had to do was ask Esther and she would give it to me. But I didn't need pieces of paper to know what I had done.

"Who's Tess Cook?"

The question caught me off-guard. Of course, Tess would be mentioned. It was she who had contacted the police after all. I hesitated before replying. "Tess was a friend of Jack's. She was the first to realize he was missing."

"Were they close?"

"Towards the end, I think they were."

"Were they in love?"

Oh Esther, I am as uncertain of this as I am sure of his death. Did love strike them like I struck Jack? Was it as unexpected and as deadly?

"I think Jack thought he loved her."

"And Tess?"

"She did not know what to think."

"Where is she now?"

"I don't know. She left to go back to her family after Jack's disappearance. I did not keep contact with her."

Esther looked deep into her cup, seemed to taste her words before she uttered them. "Did you know her well?"

I swallowed mine. "I barely knew her at all."

"Is it possible that she is the woman Nicole mentioned and not Ang?"

"Nicole is wrong. Jack did not do it on purpose."

She said nothing in response. We sat in silence. The stove hissed, seemed to encourage our quietness. Then Esther told me that the interview I gave to the police was mentioned in the report too.

"What did I say?" Despite the dreamy nature of those times if I had to, I think I could have remembered every word. They would spill out of me again as they had the day they were spoken.

"The report said little," Esther replied. "That you hadn't seen him for a few weeks, that you did not know where he was."

I had spoken to the police of Tess, of our failed relationship. I wondered if that was included. If so, then Esther would know that I had not been truthful in my earlier response. She went on to recount more of the information from the report. Nothing in her countenance suggested that she was disappointed with me, that I had let down her trust. There were details concerning the weather, how it hampered the search, how the winds had prevented the helicopter from flying for some of the days, how the drifting snow had covered up any tracks he might have made. Someone, she could not remember the name, had reported possibly sighting Jack heading away from the town past Bird Cove on the day of his disappearance. Many people from the town had been interviewed, but Esther did not recognize any of the names. They had little to add other than speculation, she said. His parents too had been contacted, but they had not heard from him in months.

"That was the gist of it." She sounded despondent. She had the names and numbers for the Sergeant at the time and one of the officers, she said, but she didn't know if there was any point in contacting them.

"Probably not after all these years," I concurred. "Whatever they knew is most likely in the report already."

"I'm sure you're right." She stood up. "We should get supper." She walked over, laid her hands on my shoulders. "I'm sorry I couldn't find out anything more."

"I am content with what I already know." I might have said, I am afraid of what you will discover.

I wondered if this was as far as Esther was going to take this. I hoped so. All the same, I felt troubled by the report, anxious that my denial of Tess was a mistake, that we were mentioned in it together. Already the truth begets a lie. One act of secrecy creates another. I would rise from my chair to assist Esther in the kitchen. We would labour together unawares of the workings of each other's minds.

Esther went into town a few days later to pick up some groceries. I watched the truck drive away. The thick imprint it made in the snow, the red taillights that shrank into the distance. I was still worried about the report Janice had given her, that it would reveal I had been concealing the true nature of my relationship with Tess. I didn't think that Esther was deliberately hiding it from me. Janice had given it to her confidentially, and I assumed she was simply being cautious. Nevertheless, I would have to search for it, snoop around my own home. It felt wrong, as though I was prying into the private corners of Esther's life and not the other way around.

I began in our bedroom. I stood outside the door, turned the handle and opened it. The room looked and felt different. The bed we shared was perfectly made up as though closed off from use. The curtains were pulled looking out into the larger world. The log walls and hardwood floor, the woven rug. I looked in the drawer in her bedside table. A novel she had borrowed from the library, a magazine on wildlife, a capped pen. I walked over to the chest of drawers by the wall where she kept some of her clothing. I caught sight of myself in the mirror and barely recognized what I was seeing. I half-expected to see my younger self. A man nearing his mid-twenties. Instead I saw the glut of years that, like Jack, had mysteriously disappeared. The years I had killed off. I turned my back on myself and opened the top drawer. I carefully probed through Esther's neatly folded blouses trying not to disturb anything. I closed the drawer and opened the next one down. Her woolen and fleece sweaters. The third drawer opened to her underclothing, and I hesitated. Although Esther was not prudish, I was not accustomed to seeing such an exposure of delicate cloth. I gently lifted and replaced her garments but found nothing there either. The last drawer contained her stockings and tee shirts which I sifted lightly through.

I opened the closet where her skirts and pants hung, her jackets. Her shoes were arranged in pairs on the floor. On the shelf above the railing, I saw her various hats and scarves. It was there my fingers found the envelope. I felt it but did not withdraw it immediately. Instead I went over to the window. I cannot say that I was consciously checking to see that she had not turned around for some reason and was returning home, but I looked along the space where I knew the road to be. There were no vehicles in sight. Occasional spurts of wind blew gasps of snow upwards. I looked to the flat horizon. I would reach in and remove those equally flat white sheets of paper, the black print-like tracks left behind. Tracks that Esther was following, tracks I may have made. I went back to the closet and took down, with trembling fingers, the envelope, sat on the edge of the bed, breathed in, and removed the contents. The picture, the transcripts, the case file, and the contact information for the police.

I looked again at Jack outside the Eskimo Museum with his arm around Nicole Fairfield. Windswept and carefree. Who could have known where those winds would blow him? I put the photo, transcripts and contact information aside and scanned quickly through the report for my name. I found the section dealing with my interview. I looked for Tess beside me, but she was absent. There was nothing included about our relationship. I felt a huge surge of relief. I took a breath and then slowly read the report through from the beginning. It described Jack's disappearance but could draw no conclusions. Afterwards, I put everything back in the envelope as I had found them and replaced the envelope on the shelf beneath the hats and scarves. I closed the closet door over and went downstairs. Although I felt relieved about Tess, I was ill at ease at over the stealth that had crept between Esther and me. I should have told her about Tess from the beginning. I should have held nothing back.

Esther arrived home mid-afternoon. I helped her carry in the bags of groceries. When Esther initially moved up here, she had hoped we might be able to obtain our own wild food. I think she wished I would spend some time with Tom Fowler, the old trapper I knew, who had given us the initial advice on our log home, learn how to trap from him, how to bring home the meat and furs. In my younger days, I had often thought about this too, whether I should learn to hunt and trap. For whatever reason, lack of time or real lack of interest, I never did learn. Now, I no longer wanted to. "It is more a romantic idea than a practical one," I told her. "Life up here has little room for romance." "You romanced me," she replied. "That," I declared, "was a practical decision."

We put away the groceries. The tinned foods, the frozen meats, the processed goods. We saved the plastic grocery bags to store our garbage.

Not telling what had occurred to Jack was the most practical decision I have made in my life, but it was not a good decision. To this day, I do not know which one would have been better.

CHAPTER 9

December is the darkest month. With barely six hours of light, we could not see what happened without him. At Christmas, Tess and Eloise and I fought over turkey bones, we fought over gravy, we fought over his absence. It was as though we had left and he had stayed. That whole Christmas, he swirled around us like the northern lights. Every bite we ate was a bite he did not. We were incomplete without him.

Even yet, he is missed in a similar fashion.

Jack returned early in the New Year. Eloise met him at the station. Tess told me that he lifted Eloise off her feet and swung her around. Their breaths lingered in the air long after they had both departed.

He came to see me a few days after his return and handed me the bottle of Jack Daniels. "A souvenir." He shrugged off his coat and made himself at home. We closed the door tightly and sat around the stove, the bottle between us, a glass in our hands. I asked about his trip home.

"It was always going to be a mistake," he said stretching his feet out in front of him, crossing them at their ankles. "Nevertheless, I am glad I made it."

We drank our whiskeys, soaked in as much heat as possible.

"Your parents?"

"As well as could be expected. They made me remember why I left. We need these reminders from time to time."

"And Ang?" As simple as that. A question that slipped off my tongue with unburdened ease.

"Ang." Jack wiped his lips with his forefinger. He shook his head. "I didn't go to see her. Didn't feel the urge to in the end."

He looked across at me as if wondering what I would make of him.

"And there wasn't any snow this winter either." I raised my eyebrows as though I had made my mind up about him a long time before.

Jack laughed hard, poured us both stiff ones. "Ang," he said sighing, "put the A, N, G in angel." He rested his glass on the arm of his chair. "I lost her the moment I walked out on her. I knew it at the time. But once again, I needed a reminder. Warren Baldwin. Vaguely remember him, a grade or two above us. Never in our lives at the time, but now he is completely in hers. She says they have no plans. 'I never got over the hurt, she told me, when you left, but I got over you.'"

"I'm sorry," I said.

"Wade, I had to leave. It was not a mistake."

"What was it then?"

"The randomness of a life."

Jack did not sound sad. He sounded resigned. And I thought he was probably right.

"And Eloise?"

"Oh shit, Wade." He laughed, reached for his glass. "I'm in over my head."

"She's a good sort. She's pretty. She's head over heels for you."

"Which doesn't make her very smart."

We both laughed. I got up and threw a log into the stove. The burst of heat as the stove door opened.

"I shouldn't have let it go this far," he said. "I don't quite know how to stop it. I am not sure I want to."

"Why bother then?"

"She asked me if I loved her. And I told her I thought I loved Ang. But the real answer to her question is no. I don't love her. I like being with her. We have lots of fun. She is pretty. She is more than a good sort. But I am nowhere near being in love with her."

"Love grows on you," I said half-heartedly.

"Warts grow on you, Wade. Love is just there."

Do you love Tess? I could have asked him there and then. But I knew, as Eloise had, the pointlessness, the sheer futility, the destruction that would follow.

"I don't want to hurt her, but neither am I ready to let her go just yet." Jack kicked his boots off, settled in for the night. Outside flakes of snow twinkled in the moonlight like a smothering of tiny falling stars.

"I don't think it can harm either of you to stay together a while."

The light flickered. The fire in the stove crackled. Jack shifted in his chair. The legs creaked unsteadily. "This time it will be me who remains, she who leaves."

"Maybe things will work out, and you'll convince her to stay."

"I would hardly call that things working out." Jack sounded angry but not with me.

"And if Ang had been waiting for you all those years?"

"Then she would have put the A,N,G in strange." He forced a smile, tipped some whiskey into his mouth. "I don't know. Who can go back into time like that? Even if she was willing to move up here with me, it would seem as though all those years in between had been wasted ones." He turned and looked at me face on. He looked troubled. "That's the thing, Wade, I have never wanted to waste my years. That's why I left home, it's why I left Ang, and it's why I should leave Eloise."

I can still see the troubled look on his face. Every time I think of Jack, I think of how he looked at me almost as though was begging me not to allow him to waste his years.

The days began to lengthen, but Jack returned to a prolonged stretch of cold. The temperatures did not rise above minus 35 degrees for almost three weeks. With the strong and bitter Arctic winds blowing through incessantly, it was all we could do to prevent our blood from freezing. On many days, it was simply too cold to go outside. Minus 50 with wind chill.

For that long cruel month, Ang was everywhere he looked. She swept across him, chilled him to the bone. He had barely placed his feet on the platform that day at the station when Ang stepped lightly down off the train behind him. She watched as he lifted Eloise off her feet, slipped her arm in his as they walked home together. She sat at his breakfast table, she stood by his sink, she entered and left with every opening of his door, she sat hogging the heat in his small living room, she crawled into his bed. She shouted at him, and she covered her ears when he tried to respond. She belittled Eloise in front of him, and she belittled him in turn. Jack went out for walks in dangerously cold conditions in an attempt to drive her away, and he drank more beer and whiskey than he could handle to block her from his mind. Eloise suffered the brunt of it. She returned to Tess in tears.

"You have to do something," Tess told me. "He is your friend after all."

"I am doing all I can." And I really believed I was. I believed that it all would pass. That the weather would begin to warm and Jack would thaw. That Ang would melt into the background. I had persuaded him not to give up on Eloise just yet. I had given him my home when he had to escape his own.

"Well, it's not enough."

He started to come between us then, between Tess and me. Like Ang, he filled the space where our love ought to have been.

The sharp winds of January finally stalled. Eloise asked Jack if it would be better if they stopped seeing each other. He told her that going home had unsettled him, but that it had now passed. The days would continue to lengthen and brighten. He asked her not to give up on him. Eloise against her better judgment acquiesced. Still, she told Tess that he was becoming more and more distant.

"I sometimes think he does not recognize that I am there at all. I am talking and he cannot hear me."

"Reach out to him," Tess advised. "Stay as close to him as you can."

Alone with me, Tess admitted that he was probably already lost to Eloise. We sat at the table, the evening dishes emptied of food. It was twilight, minus twenty-five degrees outside. The small shrubs poked their heads out of the snow, shivered on the tundra, trembled with the light wind. Snow gathered on the windowsills, heaped against the panes.

"She never had him in the first place, she knew that," I told her. "But despite his treatment of her, he needs her right now."

Tess looked at me as though wondering if I believed what I had said. She joined me most evenings for supper now. Sometimes she stayed over. But if she had work to do for school or if she felt Eloise needed her, she would go home. Those nights she stayed, we sat by the stove and talked or bundled up and went for a walk outside. Later we would go to bed.

Tess called me over to the window one of those evenings and told me to be quiet. A three-quarter moon lit up the snow covered ground. White drifts rose and fell like waves. She pointed towards a post from a broken down fence. An Arctic fox sat on its hind legs barely noticeable in the snow, its black nose and dark narrow eyes defining its presence. Its dense white coat fluffed outwards. The small tufts of its ears. It lowered its front legs and lay down. It seemed to be looking right at us. I put my arms around Tess' waist, nuzzled the side of my face to hers.

"What would your grandmother have said about that?" I asked. "Would she take it as a sign?"

The fox opened its large wide mouth and yawned. The pink fleshy inside, the sharp white teeth.

"She would have said it was telling us it was late, that it was time for sleep," she laughed.

But neither of us moved. We watched the fox in the moonlight until it lowered its face and covered its nose with its tail, closed its eyes and faded from sight.

Later in our chairs by the stove I asked her why she hadn't gone to visit her family for Christmas. Tess curled her feet in under her.

"It's a little late to be asking that, don't you think?"

"I didn't know how to ask before."

Tess folded her arms around her waist. "You don't know much about me, do you?"

"Tell me," I said.

She stared at the rug in front of the stove, the pile of wood. "I told you when the government forced my people to relocate here they really didn't know how to survive. Mostly they had hunted caribou in the past. They didn't know how to live in a town, live without the caribou. A military plane arrived for the people at Duck Lake. They took what belongings they could. Then the plane dropped them on the shores of the Churchill River. For years they lived in tents and tar shacks before flimsy cabins were finally built beside the cemetery. Camp 10 it was called. People had no jobs, no way to survive other than welfare. Alcohol was suddenly available to them and people quickly turned to it. They traded their food vouchers for alcohol, and when food ran out people scavenged at the dump. Everyone did it. It was like a social gathering. Domestic violence became a common way of life. Beatings and rape. Depression and despair. Starvation. In ten years, almost a hundred people died of unnatural causes. Drownings, fights, hit and runs, house fires. They froze to death. My parents were one of the very few who did not drink. But the rest of the family wasn't so lucky. My uncle drowned while fishing with his brother. It was not clear if it was an accident or not. My cousins were raped by members of their own family. My sister had a baby boy at fourteen. She committed suicide three years after the birth. The boy grew up with Fetal Alcohol Syndrome. I have two brothers. One drinks too much, the other is lost to drugs. All of those my parents forgive, but they do not forgive me for going to college, abandoning them." She looked up, tightened her hold on herself. "Now you know me."

I wondered if the fox was out there still. I liked to think it had come on Tess's behalf, was here to protect her. She sat in the chair wrapped into herself. I didn't know what to say.

"I probably should have stayed," she said. "They needed my help. It was selfish of me to leave."

"No," I said. "It wasn't selfish, someone has to break the cycle. It is right that you left to go to college. You can help far more in that way."

"That's what I thought, but now I no longer know. It was too much for my parents without me. The community supports had broken down. My grandmother died in my first year away. By the time I came back, they had all moved to Tadoule Lake in an attempt to return to the wilderness, a return to our survival skills. My grandmother would have been proud of the decision. But no one was proud of mine. I had deserted them. I told you before that the reason I returned here instead of Tadoule Lake was because I owed it to the people here who had helped me leave and get my training, but as you can see that has little to do with it."

"But you did come back here. You could have stayed in the city."

Tess shook her head. "No, unlike the others I learned how to survive here, but I never learned how to survive in the city."

"But you did survive it."

"I kept by myself, stuck with the old ways."

The wind howled outside, wailed in the stove pipe. My old house creaked with age. Everyone was alone up here it seemed. Jack, Eloise, Tess, me. In a bleak frozen world so sparse in life, where despite our solitariness, each one of us was dependent on the other for survival.

"Have you visited your family?"

"Once, shortly after I returned from the city. I wasn't well received. I haven't gone back. Besides it's not easy. There is winter access only when the rivers are frozen. It is too expensive to fly."

"How have your people managed, have the old ways come back?"

"The new old ways have come back. The drinking, the fighting, the abuse, the unnatural deaths. They have no running water, poor housing. Too many generations had passed. They had hoped to survive through hunting and fishing, but the younger people knew nothing of that wilderness. They have now entered a wilderness of their own, and they don't know how to survive that either."

Tess sat up, unfolded her arms. The fire spat. She stood up, walked to the window. I went over and stood beside her looking out into the moonlit night. There was no sign of the fox I hoped had been sent to look out for Tess. A light sprinkling of snow fell and fluttered in the wind. And then from out of the blank whiteness, the two dark ovals of the eyes and the round black snub of the nose. A blink and the eyes were closed again, and the tail flicked back in front of his mouth and nose. I turned to Tess and saw the look of wonder on her face.

"I think I love you," I said.

"Yes," she agreed, "I think you do."

We lay in bed later unable to sleep.

"Wade," Tess quietly called.

"Yes."

"I have been thinking that maybe I should go to Tadoule Lake over Spring Break. Would you come with me if I did?"

I was surprised by her request. "Are you sure I would not be more of a hindrance than a help?"

"It would be nice to have your company, your support."

"I am White. It was people like me who forced your people to leave their home in the first place."

"No," Tess said turning to reach for me, "those people were nothing like you."

I held onto her and hoped she was right.

✦

I drove into town on the snow-packed road, past the granary ponds, the elevator, out to Jack's apartment across from the wharf. It was ten o'clock in the morning. Grey clouds covered the sky. They were thick and full and seemed to press down on top of us. Snow was ridged out in the harbour. A tall metal crane stood next to the dark bulk of the ship still frozen in. I pulled in at the duplex where he lived and climbed the snowy steps leading to his porch. A cat mewed beneath them. I rang Jack's bell and waited. There was no reply, so I rang again. An upstairs window opened and Jack stuck his head out. His hair was tousled. He looked half-asleep.

"Be with you in a moment."

Jack opened the door a short while later. He had a jacket thrown on over his pyjamas. "Have you nothing better to be doing?" he asked, showing me in. The cat scampered past our legs into the hallway. Jack led me up the stairs. The stairway was dark, uninviting. We walked through his living room into the kitchen. The living room was sparse. A couch, two armchairs, a small coffee table, a lamp. The walls were bare. Jack put on the kettle.

"You really should move out," I told him. The dishes were piled in the sink from the night before.

He rubbed his eyes, yawned. "What, like you, out in the sticks? No thank you. I prefer to be here in the thick of things."

Jack liked being close to his work. No more than a ten-minute walk even in the worst of weather.

"Are you alone?" I thought I better check.

"Of course I'm alone. Eloise has work."

"This is Jack Butan we're talking about."

Jack got out a jar of instant coffee from the cupboard above the sink. "I'm a changed man."

"So Eloise seems to think."

"Now what's that supposed to mean?" He leaned up against the counter, waited on my response.

"Oh nothing," I tried to brush it off.

"You don't get away that lightly."

I walked into the living room and looked out the window at the harbour. From behind the grain terminal, a snowmobile cut across the ice out towards the bay. Jack came to the doorway. "I'm doing the best I can."

"I know that."

He went back into the kitchen returning a few minutes later with two mugs of coffee. A pickup drove past. Even with the window shut, I could hear the loud rasp of its exhaust. Like everything else here, it looked on its last legs. Jack handed me a mug. He hadn't bothered to take his jacket off. "It's Ang," he said settling down on his couch.

"It's always been Ang." The snowmobile was but a dot. I watched it fade into oblivion.

"I was a fool," Jack said. "But I wouldn't have known how to be anything else. Anyway, it's all in the past. I just have to reconcile myself to it."

I sat down in an armchair across from him. "Eloise is finding it hard. She feels you are distant."

Jack crossed his ankles. "I am back home with Ang half the time. I suppose, I'll have to do better. The funny thing is, I don't really believe it would have worked out between us, but the only way to have known for certain was to have tried."

"Maybe you did. Maybe coming here was the end of your attempt."

"Could be," he acknowledged. "I'm over the worst anyway. I don't feel as sorry for myself anymore."

"Good," I said, "since the reason I called over was to see if you'd like a night out. The four of us."

Jack put his mug down on the table. "Tess?"

"Tess, Eloise. All of us."

We had never gone out together before. In fact, the four of us had never even met up together once. Sometimes, I saw Eloise when I was visiting Tess, but Jack never went to their apartment. He always met Eloise at his. It may have been a deliberate act on all our parts. It was Tess who had made the suggestion to me a few days before. She thought it would be good for Eloise to be with Jack in company. "They've been too serious of late," she reasoned. "Maybe if they could just have a night of fun, things would improve." I hoped Tess was right. It would be good if it worked out. I didn't like that our relationships kept Jack and I apart. I missed his company. I missed the laughter.

Jack lowered himself back down. "Why not?" He yawned again. "Where would we go?"

"The hotel has music tonight. We could have a bite to eat, a few drinks, dance."

"Okay then," he said. "Have you spoken to Tess yet?"

"I'll leave a message for her and Eloise at the school."

"What if she doesn't want to go?"

"Why wouldn't she, a rare evening out with the great Jack Butan, who would want to miss that?"

"You're right," he said. "I wouldn't miss it myself."

I left the message for Tess on my way home and arranged to meet her later.

Tess answered the door promptly when I called that evening. She was flustered. "You should have checked with me," she said before I was hardly in the door. "I have papers to grade, lessons to plan."

"I thought this was what you wanted."

She walked upstairs to her bedroom brushing at her long hair as she went. "Yes, but you should have checked first if tonight suited or not." I followed up the stairs after her. "You shouldn't take my time for granted." Her brush caught in woven strands of hair. "Here," she said handing the brush to me. "Make yourself useful."

I brushed from the top of her dark black hair downwards. Past her shoulders, her shoulder blades, across the curve of her spine, down to the small of her back. "We don't have to go."

"Yes, we do. You have arranged it with Jack. It would not be right to let him down now." The brush snagged in a tangle of hair and tugged her head downwards. Tess winced. I apologized. "You are enjoying it all the same, aren't you?" she said sounding a little less cross.

"It wasn't my intention to take your time for granted," I told her

"I know." She turned around and took the brush from me. "Thank you for brushing my hair." She kissed the side of my forehead. "I want to go also. It will just leave me behind in my work. I don't like that. It makes me feel as though I am letting the children down, and I have seen too much of that in my time." She unbuttoned her blouse and took it off, unzipped her jeans and pushed them down her legs.

I had spent little time in this room of hers and felt intrusive. I thought to avert my eyes, but instead the unfamiliarity of my surroundings made me look at her anew.

"You are very beautiful."

Tess had opened her closet and was reaching inside. "Don't try to charm your way out of it."

"I mean it."

She reached in and took out a mid-length blue cotton print dress. She unzipped the back of it and stepped into it. She asked me to zip it up for her. I had never seen her in a dress before. Like everyone else around here, she dressed for the weather. She spun around suddenly after I finished. Her long black hair swept around her like an arm, like someone pulling her away from me.

"Now what do you think?"

"I think I spoke too soon. Beautiful does not do you justice."

"Wade Sinclair!"

I wanted to reach out and swing her around as her hair had swept around her or as Jack had swept Eloise off her feet, but much to my regret I did not. Instead we walked down the stairs together and waited for Eloise. She too had dressed for the occasion. A gold satin blouse, a short green skirt.

"I feel underdressed," I said.

"Never too little, Wade," Eloise grinned. And Tess, I believe, blushed.

Despite their parkas, even the short journey to my truck was too severe for Tess and Eloise.

"My legs are freezing," Eloise squealed.

"Never mind," I teased, "Jack will warm you up."

Tess squirmed on the cold leatherette seats. "Turn the heat on Wade."

Eloise giggled. The thick clouds continued to hang over us. It was already dark. The streetlights reflected on the snowy roads. Pickups drove past, their lights a glare in our eyes. The closed offices and stores. Dogs. People unrecognizable in their winter clothing. The empty alleyways. The wide streets. Snow was packed on the roofs of the buildings, heaped up against walls and signposts. The windscreen fogged over. I turned on the wipers. They juddered as they broke free from a thick film of ice and scratched across the window. I was lucky they had not frozen tighter or they would have broken off completely. Eloise pulled her coat around her stockinged legs. Tess rubbed her hands up and down hers. What are we doing? I could have asked and not one of us would have been able to answer.

I pulled in at the back of the hotel. Sergeant Loewen was parked near the exit with his lights on. An elderly native man coughed a white plume of illness before opening the door and slipping inside. I parked the truck and turned off the lights. The three of us sat there a moment in the warmth of the cab. Tess and Eloise were avoiding the cold outside, and I a cold of a different kind, one I could not decipher. A truck roared past. A light went on momentarily at the side of the hotel then flickered off. The truck cooled down almost immediately, and I opened the door. Tess and Eloise jumped down onto the snow, ran for the door. Ross Loewen glanced over at me, waved. I nodded. It struck me then that I liked Churchill. I could not say I was unhappy here, especially since I had met Tess. I had made it my home, and although it was early days, I had a feeling I would not leave. Sometimes though it felt as though the cold had taken its toll. Words had a chill to them, gestures an awkward momentum. It seemed as if we each looked upon each other with envy, as though everyone else had somehow managed to make a better life for themselves.

I hurried after Tess and Eloise. In under the Exit sign as though I was already leaving. The loud chatter in the bar, instruments tuning up, ceramic plates hitting wood. The plentiful supply of warmth that rushed at you down the corridor, fooling you with its presence as it rushed to depart. Jack stood at the bar with his arm around Eloise talking to Tess. They were all laughing.

"Hey Sinclair," he called throwing his arm around Tess's waist, "didn't you come with anyone?"

I shrugged nonchalantly. "They became too much of a burden, I had to let them go."

Jack's laugh that would haunt me to my grave. "What are you having?" Eloise and Tess already taken care of. Tess took Jack's hand away.

"The usual."

Jack called for my beer, and I pushed in beside them at the bar.

I was happy to see Jack in such good form. Tess and I rarely went to bars together. She didn't drink alcohol as far as I knew. I assumed it had to do with her family circumstances. She had an orange juice in her hand. Eloise may have had a soda of some sort, but I imagined it was mixed with something stronger. Jack, like myself, was predominantly a beer drinker. Neither of us drank to excess. We enjoyed our beers, occasionally our whiskey, but we tended to keep it to that. Jack pulled on his cigarette, offered one to Eloise. She looked a little embarrassed as she took one from him.

"Tess?" He offered his packet to her.

I wanted to refuse on her behalf, lay claim.

She shook her head. "Can we sit down?"

We found a table mid-ways down the bar. Tess and Eloise took their jackets off.

"Watch out," Jack called out from behind his cigarette looking at the way they had dressed up for the night, "wildlife can get hunted around here."

Eloise thumped his shoulder playfully. Tess smiled. Jack looked at me, raised his bottle. "The band is about to start up. We should probably order our food."

I looked around the smoky room. Approximately twenty people sat at tables or at the bar. The band was setting up in the corner. Guitars, a drum set, mics, and amps.

"Who are they?" I asked.

"The Clementines." Jack began to sing. "...oh my darling, oh my darling, oh my darling Clementine..."

Tess and Eloise laughed infectiously.

"I hope you're not laughing at my singing," he said feigning annoyance.

"God forbid," Tess responded. Jack looked at her in a way I cannot explain, and Tess received that look in a way equally inexplicable.

Jack and I ordered steak sandwiches and fries. Eloise a plate of scampi and Tess Arctic char. Eloise looked so happy. Her demands from life were not high. An evening such as this could satisfy the most of them. That night, I know Eloise believed she loved Jack, and I knew that I loved Tess. We danced to "The Tennessee Waltz" in front of the makeshift stage. Tess's hand in mine, my other hand at her back and hers on my shoulder, our faces touching. I was only too aware of the words, but I held her as if I would never let her go, and I thought it possible that she might hold me in the same way. *I was dancing with my darling to the Tennessee Waltz when an old friend I happened to see. Introduced him to my loved one and while they were waltzing, my friend stole my sweetheart from me.* It was later that Jack asked Tess for the pleasure of this dance, and how could I interfere? Eloise stood up and took my hand, leading me to the floor also. The tall lanky singer sang Hank William's *Cold Cold Heart*. It is possible to say those songs were fated, but I have never believed that. It was bad luck, pure and simple. Smoke rose from the ashtrays. A twang of guitar, the steady beat of the drum. Two other couples danced alongside. One of the men was drunk, stumbled in his girlfriend's arms. An elderly couple waltzed perfectly across the floor. Eloise smiled. We held each other at a slight distance. I tried not to look at them. Their hands touching each other's bodies. The band picked up the tempo. We stayed on the floor. Jack and Tess, Eloise and I. Twirling our partners. The flow of air through Eloise's skirt, Tess's dress. Eloise's short hair, Tess's long and unbridled. The set came to an end and Eloise and I sat down. I expected Jack and Tess to follow, but they stayed for one more dance. Eloise said something. I took my eyes from them. I asked Eloise to repeat what she had said. She was looking to the dance floor also. She had lit up one of Jack's cigarettes. Smoke trailed upwards from her fingers.

"He's going to leave me, isn't he?" She looked to my face searching for the truth.

"I really don't know. You both seem happy together tonight."

Eloise drew on her cigarette, took a drink from her glass. "Seem. That's the problem." She stubbed out the cigarette she had started. "I wish we could be more like you and Tess."

"Is Tess happy with me?"

Eloise looked incredulous. "Is it not obvious?"

I took a drink of beer, glanced to Tess and Jack. He was swinging her around. She was laughing.

"Yes, I suppose it is. But is that enough?"

"It would be enough for me for Jack to be happy with me." She reached over and put her hand on my wrist. "Tess needs you. She was too immersed in her work before you came along, still can be. It was a way of not having to deal with her past, I think, the way things went with her family. She rarely went anywhere. Meeting you was the best thing that ever happened to her." Eloise took her hand away, sat back. "I often asked her why she didn't go out with some of the men here. She said she hadn't the time to get involved. She has made time for you, Wade."

Eloise could have no idea how important her words were for me. I began to believe that we would make it together after all. It is easy to delude ourselves. It is not a complicated act.

Tess and Jack came back to the table out of breath.

"You're too much for me," she panted and flopped into her chair. "He's all yours," she said to Eloise.

Jack took a drink, lit up a cigarette. He tilted his head back and blew smoke upwards. "You're quite the dancer, nevertheless. Must have been all those pow wows when you were growing up."

I had thought his comment might upset her, but Tess only laughed. "What would you know?"

"Not a lot, Tess. That's for sure." The fun seemed to go out of his voice. I wondered if Ang had stepped into the room, was pulling over a chair. There was no place for her here tonight.

"A drink, Jack?" I offered quickly seeing his near empty bottle.

"Only one?" he joked, as the door quietly shut behind her.

The band stopped playing at ten thirty.

"The mine's shut down," Jack said.

We sat around and talked for a while more, then Tess said she had better get back before it got too late altogether. Jack and Eloise said they'd wait for one more. Eloise was going to stay with Jack for the night. I drove Tess back to her house. She kissed me on the cheek.

"Thank you," she said. "I am sorry for being angry earlier. I had a wonderful night."

She hurried from my pickup into her house. Her bare legs, her inadequate shoes. I sat and waited until the light came on in her living room. Then I pulled away.

CHAPTER 10

I didn't see Tess until three days later. Usually she came by my house after she finished teaching. An evening might go by without her if she was busy but rarely more than that. I could have called into the school, but I was afraid that my arrival would be unwelcome. I knew I was being unreasonable. Jack had kissed her once a long time back, and she had not responded. They had danced together on the dance floor as Eloise and I had. Eloise herself had told me how much I meant to Tess. Still, I was afraid that I would lose her to him. Afraid of the strength of my own love.

Tess, I reasoned, was most probably busy with school work, would come by when she was able. And sure enough she turned up on that third evening, knocked on my door around five o'clock.

"I've been watching for you." I stepped back to let her in.

Tess shook the snow off her boots and entered. She had brought a chicken with her which we roasted in the oven with potatoes. I boiled up carrots and broccoli, made gravy from the juices of the chicken. She made no mention of the days that had passed since we last saw one another. After dinner, we sat at the table and played cards.

"Have you thought about what I asked, about coming to Tadoule Lake with me?" Tess asked as she dealt out our hands.

I had thought about it constantly since. "If that is what you want?"

"It is. I do not think I could go there alone."

"Have you said anything to your family yet?"

Tess shook her head "I am afraid they will tell me not to come." She threw her cards on the table. For the first time since I had known her, I saw her cry.

"Tess." I went around the table to her. She leaned in against me.

"It will be okay. You'll go back and talk things through with them. They are missing you as much as you miss them."

"I hope so." She wiped at her tears. "I don't know how to live my life."

"There are none of us who know how to live our lives. We all make it up as we go along."

"Does everyone get it so wrong?"

"You are doing nothing wrong, Tess."

"What about us? Are we doing the right thing?"

"I have never done anything more right in my life."

She squeezed my hand. "You are a good man, Wade. It is just that so many other things have turned out badly."

"Shh," I whispered. "Nothing could have turned out better than this."

Esther and I had little need for Christmas, could as easily have let it pass us by. Nevertheless we exchanged small gifts that morning, and Esther cooked a pleasant meal. We walked it off afterwards at Bird Cove. She insisted on bringing the auger to measure the ice. It was her way of celebrating, she said, her spiritual ritual. After all these years together, she still came with me as often as she could. It was bitterly cold, and my fingers ached inside my gloves. The drill stuck in the ice. I could barely twist it free. Esther urged me on. The tool eventually cut through to the water. I removed the drill and Esther measured. "Eighty-nine centimetres," she said. The ice was getting thicker by the day. Esther, as ever, looked pleased by this, comforted.

We measured through the month of January: 95, 102, 106. By the time Esther made contact with Loewen in late January, the ice was 114 cm thick. Having heard nothing since her last meeting with Janice, I had half-hoped that she had given up on contacting him.

Loewen told Esther that he remembered the case clearly but could not discuss it as it was a confidential matter. Esther asked him if he ever thought about it now, and he replied that truthfully, he didn't. It was but one of many. There are those who think of it every day, she said, whose personal torment has remained confidential also. She wasn't speaking to him as Sergeant Loewen but as someone unofficial who might have some thoughts as to what happened to Jack Butan, a son to some, a friend to others. Loewen asked her what her connection to Jack was, and Esther told him. She asked him if he remembered me, Wade Sinclair, and he said he did. He told her he'd have to think about it, and he'd call her back via Marilyn.

If I had not already known what had happened to Jack, I would have been deeply upset by the lack of interest the police showed in him. As it was, I was relieved they did not pursue it vigorously. Loewen seemed to have begun his investigation with his mind already made up. We are even more inconsequential than we realize. Churchill did not come to a halt when Jack disappeared. The grain terminal did not come grinding to a stop. The ships were not frozen in port.

We flow through this world as the millions of grains of seed flow through the spouts on the galleries into the ships' holds, as the tens of thousands that miss their mark and are lost or swept away.

Marilyn called on Esther in early February to tell her that Loewen had phoned. She was to phone him back that evening. Esther was like a child all day she was so excited. She could scarcely focus on a single task.

"Remember," I advised her, "he may have nothing to tell you."

"I know that," she said, but this knowledge did nothing to dampen her mood.

I too found it difficult to treat the day as normal. It was not excitement I was experiencing but anxious anticipation. What if Loewen knew more than I had realized? In those vague days after Jack's death, I did not suffer the guilt of my actions as intensely as I deserved. Nor have I since felt sufficient remorse, and that, I regret far more. When I raised my arm to strike him, and when he fell through the ice, I walked away from him as he had walked away from Ang and his baby. But he did not leave them for dead as I left him.

Esther took my truck that evening. She started the engine. Initially, it growled in the low minus thirty temperatures as though it might resist her touch, but then it yielded to her will. Already the light was starting to fade. I stood in the house we had built together, this dead forest we had planted in the bare tundra. I looked at the chinked walls, the sheen of the stained wood, the clean hardwood floors, the loft above. I would have liked to have gone to the door then and opened it to Tess, invited her in. "This is the life I now inhabit," I could have told her. I would have liked to sit her by the stove she had so often sat by to warm her body, and I would have liked to have led her up the wooden stairs to the bedroom above.

"Look, Tess," I could say. "I have done all of this for you."
I would lay her down. I would lie beside her, and I would
never rise again.

Instead I walked into the kitchen for a glass of water.
What was to become of Esther and me? Before Jack walked
into her life, I thought that we would stay together forever,
but I could no longer be certain of that. I could lose her to
him as easily as I had lost Tess. Perhaps, it was no more than
I deserved.

I never learned who it was spoke his name in Gypsy's Café
that day Esther heard it for the first time, and I am inclined
to believe no one there did, that it slipped through on the
wind and found the ears it was searching for. It may even
have escaped with my own breath, glided above the curve of
my tongue, have emerged from the gasp of my open mouth.

I sat back in the armchair by the stove and drank the clear
water. I stayed there for over an hour and a half waiting for
Esther to return. What if she never did, if Loewen told her
something that caused her to reconsider her relationship with
me? She might disappear, and I would never see her again.
I took fright suddenly, stood up and began to pace the room.
I looked out the window for the lights of the truck, but there
were none to be seen. Surely Loewen would have interviewed
me again if he had any suspicions. If I had been seen with Jack
that day, Loewen would have followed up on it back then. He
knew nothing. I began to perspire with the heat of the room.
I opened the front door to let in some cold air. A trail of snow
blew in, pure white ashes. I closed the door again and watched
them melt. I went into the kitchen and sat down. I folded my
arms on the table and rested my forehead on them. I would
have to stop Esther somehow, persuade her not to continue
with her investigations. I could tell her that I did indeed know
what had happened, that Jack had found out about the baby,

that he left abruptly not wanting to be found. Surely that would satisfy her, would bring this to an end.

I heard the door of the truck being slammed shut, and, a few moments later, Esther entered. She wiped her boots and shut the door. I raised my head. She would hang up her jacket and put away her hat and gloves. She would come to find me then. Confront me with what she knew.

"Esther?"

Esther came into the kitchen. She was flushed. Her hair windswept. She looked at me then went to the sink and filled the kettle.

"Is everything okay?"

"Look," she held her hands out in front of her, "I'm shaking."

My heart pounded. Esther leaned her back against the counter. She looked at the backs of her hands as though she had just noticed how wrinkled they had become. She smoothed the front of her skirt. "I almost went off the road."

"Where?" My thoughts lost traction too, what was Esther telling me?

"Just past Bird Cove where the road bends. I hit a snow drift. The truck skidded. I turned the wheel just before it went off the side, and the truck righted itself." She folded her arms and held herself tightly. "Nothing much would have happened in any case. All I would have done was get stuck in the snow and have to walk the rest of the way, and yet I am shaking all over."

"It's the surprise," I said, "the unexpected."

"I should be able to cope with it. I chose to live here. If I can't even manage that..." She went to the cupboard and got out the tea and the teapot. "I disappoint myself." She poured water from the kettle into the teapot to warm it. "Do you ever do that, do you ever disappoint yourself?"

I wondered where this was leading. I could have held my hands out in front of me and have shown her the same trembling that most likely would never stop. "I am a constant source of disappointment to myself," I told her. "I have never been anything less."

Esther took two mugs from the drying rack, and although they were already dry she still wiped them with the tea cloth. "You could have left here any time you wanted," she said, "why did you stay?"

After Jack and after Tess, I thought to go, to begin over again. But such a thing, I knew, was not possible. There was no way that Jack's death could be an end to anything. Some people might even say it was a beginning, but this was not possible either. Jack's death, and my hand in it, was a part of my life. I could not live it out of me. It was there forever. And so I stayed. And somehow, I continued on.

"I could think of nowhere better to live," I answered Esther, and that was as much a part of the truth as any other explanation.

Esther started to cry. I went to her, and I held her to me. "What is it?"

"I got scared. For a moment I thought I was going to die."

The kettle began to boil. Esther pulled herself away, unplugged the kettle and made the tea. "Go inside, I'll bring it in."

I went in and sat in my chair and waited for her. She came in a short while later. She seemed more composed. She handed me my tea and sat down.

"I spoke with Loewen," she said after a few moments.

"What did he say?" I waited on her answer with trepidation.

Esther took a drink and swallowed. "He said he had thought about what I had asked. He knew you and Jack were very close at the time, and although he shouldn't really speak to me about the case, he had decided that he would. Everything he told me, he said, was in strictest confidence. I told him I understood. In any case, he said, there was little he could tell me that wasn't already known. He said that at the time they considered a number of possibilities. That Jack had simply gone away for a few days without telling anyone. These things happen all the time. Or that he had left for good without telling anyone. That he had an accident. He was last reported being seen out near Bird's Cove. The ice was thin that year, and something could easily have happened. Perhaps he committed suicide, or maybe he was murdered. He was a bit of a ladies' man. One of the other officers wondered if a jealous husband or partner had a run in with him, but that was mere speculation. Loewen didn't consider it likely at all. The main problem with the case was that there was no real evidence apart from the reported sighting. But even that, he said, given how people are dressed up for the weather, could easily have been a case of mistaken identity. There was no evidence that Jack was depressed or particularly unhappy. No reports of arguments with anyone. He had been to work as usual. People remembered that he was his normal self, full of life, full of fun. He hadn't left by plane, and no one could recall him having taken the train either. Loewen said they conducted a helicopter search of the area, but that there was no sign of him. He said that there had been a lot of snow, and that if he had been out walking his tracks would have been covered over. There really was little for them to go on. In the end, they came to the conclusion that he most likely had an accident. The one thing he did find out he said was that he had broken up with a girlfriend of his some months before, and she had left Churchill. He said that in itself was nothing unusual, but when he tracked her down, as a matter of course, it turned out she was pregnant. She claimed she hadn't told

Jack however, and she herself hadn't been back to Churchill since she left. So he said that he didn't really think this had any bearing on his disappearance."

"Jack fell through the ice," I told her. "I have always known that."

Esther looked at me solemnly. "We don't know that." She took a drink of tea. "Was it Tess who got pregnant?"

No, Esther, not Tess. And yet, could I say this for certain? Tess left shortly afterwards, would I ever have known?

"No. It was someone else. Eloise Thiessen. They had split up before Tess and Jack got close."

"Did Jack know she was pregnant?"

"She never told him." That much was true.

"Did you?"

"Tess told me."

"How did she know?"

"Eloise and Tess were friends. They both taught at the school. They shared a house together."

"Loewen was right, it seems," Esther said, "Jack was a bit of a ladies' man." She seemed let down.

"It is more complicated than it appears," I said by way of his defence.

Esther put her mug down on the floor, curled her legs in underneath her. "It does not seem to me that it could get much more complicated at all."

"Do not think badly of him," I urged. "Nothing that occurred was intended in that way."

"Which matters most," Esther asked, "our intentions or their consequences?"

Time, Esther, will answer us that, will it not?

✦

We never got another chance for all of us to go out together again. Within two weeks of that night, Jack told Eloise that he thought it would be for the better if they stopped seeing one another. Tess told me about it the following day. Eloise was devastated. I do not know the details of how it occurred, but, to this day, I can see it in my mind.

Jack is sitting with Eloise in his truck across from Sloop's Cove. Eloise had heard that a mother bear was spotted there with her three cubs. The bears have made the long arduous journey there from a denning area forty miles south of town where the cubs were born. They are tired and hungry and looking for food before setting out on the ice to follow the bears that left in November.

The engine is running and the heater is on, but there is no sign of the bears. Eloise wonders if they have left already. Jack lights up a cigarette and looks out at the frozen river. He hears Eloise talking, but his mind is elsewhere. He pulls open the ashtray compartment and stubs out his half-smoked cigarette.

"Eloise," he begins. He wants to touch her as he speaks but feels that he shouldn't. She is looking for the bears and mutters a response. "Eloise." He repeats her name. She is afraid to turn her head in case she will miss them. She has never seen a bear cub before. "This is important."

Eloise hears the change of tone in his voice. Before her head has turned in his direction, she already knows what he is about to say.

"I know," she says. Trails of snow rise and drift across the river.

Jack hears it in her voice too, sees it in her face. "I'm sorry."

Eloise feels her chest tighten. She finds it hard to breathe.

"I wish I could say that I love you," Jack says, "but I can't. It would be wrong to continue."

Eloise looks back to the ice. Despite the heat in the cab, the cold seeps through her as though she is standing alone on the river. She feels like asking Jack for directions out of here. She doesn't want to cry. She had gone into this with her eyes open. It had always been meant as a diversion, but somehow it had become much more serious than that.

Jack watches her and sees that she is lost. He feels like a guide who led someone out into a remote place and abandoned that person there with no way back to her now.

Jack looks to his left. The mother and cubs are almost camouflaged. They pick their way carefully through the deep snow.

"Look," he says. And Eloise sees them too. The mother and cubs stop. They stand close together, one after the other and extend their heads and neck outwards in a straight line with their backs, and with the black tips of their outstretched noses they sniff the scent in the air.

"They have found us," Eloise speaks in a hushed voice.

Jack and Eloise sit there and watch the bears as the day proceeds, as the passing moments of their finite lives spend themselves quietly unnoticed.

Tess drove out the following evening to tell me what had occurred.

"I need to get back to Eloise," she said soon after. "I just called in case Jack might like your company."

I found him later in the bar playing pool by himself.

"What has you in here this time of the evening, Sinclair?" he asked shaking his head. "You're slipping into the lowlife."

"The best place to find you," I told him.

Jack laughed. "Pull up a cue."

I got myself a drink, and we played a game. Jack broke and potted a half ball. We were both playing well and after about ten minutes it all came down to the black ball. It was my shot first. The black lay against the cushion. I decided to try and cross it into the middle pocket. I hit it perfectly and in it went.

"It's been that sort of week," Jack said. He went over to sit at the table his bottle was resting on.

"So I hear," I told him as I sat down.

"Am I the louse of the century?"

"Something like that," I answered.

"How's Eloise?"

"How do you think?"

Jack closed his eyes briefly and winced. "It's for the good in the long run." He looked at me to see if I agreed.

"I know."

"What did Tess say?"

"She told me you might need company."

He smiled, looked pleasantly surprised. "You're one lucky man."

"I know it."

"I should probably never have let it go this far," he said. "That was my mistake."

"You needed each other," I reminded him.

"I know Eloise thinks it has something to do with me going home at Christmas. Ang and all that. But even if I hadn't, it wouldn't have made a difference."

"She probably knows that."

"I'd like to think so, but I'm not sure."

"Why did you decide to tell her now?"

Jack shrugged. "I've been thinking about it since that night at the hotel. The night of the Clementines."

"It was a fun night."

"It was. That was part of the problem. Eloise had too good a time. I felt as though I was making a promise I couldn't fulfill."

I hear some loud laughter from one of the tables.

"I need a beer," Jack stood and went to the bar.

I wondered if I should tell him what Eloise had said at the hotel. How she asked if he was going to leave her. Would it ease his mind or just make matters worse?

Jack carried two bottles of beer back. He handed me one and sat down. "It wasn't just the good time that night," he stopped to take a drink before continuing, "it was Tess too."

I know how Eloise must have felt, that tightening of the chest, that sense of cold, that difficulty with words.

"Tess?"

"Dancing with her. It reminded me of times before Eloise. I began to miss them."

He was speaking a simple truth. That was all.

He laughed. "I told you about the time I kissed her, long before you and her started going out. Things had become too serious in my life, and I wasn't ready for it. I saw that that night. At least not with Eloise."

If not Eloise, who then? What was it he had said about Tess's reaction to his kiss, that she had said nothing, left the kiss there as though he might come back for it any time he wanted?

"And Ang?"

"I'm finally through with her. It's time to move forward. The world's my oyster, right?"

"Move on from here?"

"Maybe." Jack looked ahead as though he were staring at the dark of late evening through the window. "I never planned to stay here. It was an escape. Now I don't know. Sometimes it feels more like a confinement."

"Where would you go?"

"I have no idea. I haven't given it any serious consideration."

Although I would dearly miss him if he left, the thought of his going provided some solace. I took a drink and decided to divulge to Jack what Eloise had said. "I don't know if I should be telling you or not, but that night at The Clementines when you were dancing with Tess ..."

Jack, you wondered what I was going to say next. You cocked your head towards me in a mix of worry and interest. You rubbed at your bottom lip tentatively. I wanted to stop then, leave it like that. Leave you wondering what it was you perhaps should not be told. Let you live the rest of your life in that state of unknowing. I wanted to take Tess far away and leave you here at this table wondering.

"...Eloise asked me if you were going to leave her."

Jack looked relieved. "What did you answer?"

"I told her a lie. I told her I didn't know."

"Sometimes," Jack said, "I think none of us have a notion what is happening inside of ourselves, other times it seems that we are completely transparent. If only she hadn't fallen in love."

"She'll get over you," I told him, "in time. As you have gotten over Ang."

Perhaps it was cruel of me to add this. Perhaps it was just what he needed to hear.

"Go ahead, tell me, I am a horse's ass, am I not?"

"Yes you are Jack Butan. You are the original horse's ass."

I stopped by Tess's house on the way home. It was snowing lightly. Tire tracks ran the length of the street. A dog stopped at a lamp post and peed leaving a yellow patch amongst the whiteness. Flakes fell upon the dog's dark coat. Tess took my jacket and brought me in to the living room. Eloise sat on the couch reading a magazine. Her eyes were red from crying. She looked up and said hello when she saw me. Tess sat down beside her. I sat in an armchair opposite them. The room seemed colder than usual as though the heating had been turned down. The paintings on the walls, all by Indigenous painters, Cree, Dene, Inuit, looked so familiar to me now that I barely saw them.

"I can smell the bar," Tess said teasingly.

Eloise put her magazine down on the table.

"Yes. I called in on Jack."

Eloise did not speak, but I knew she wanted to hear everything.

"He feels bad," I told them. "But I know he thinks he has made the right decision."

Eloise held her hands in her lap. She looked like she might cry again at any moment. "I have made a fool of myself."

Tess looked at me, silently asked for help.

"No you haven't. I have never seen him as content with anyone else. He really cared for you. There is nothing foolish about that."

"I didn't mean to fall in love with him," she said. "It just seemed to happen. I hoped it could happen to him too."

"Perhaps, it didn't, but you were right to try."

"Someday, I might believe that."

Tess made hot chocolate, and we talked for a while about anything but Jack. I knew I could not stay the night, that it would be too hard on Eloise, so after a while I said I'd better be off.

Tess showed me to the door.

"Thank you for stopping by." She hugged me, and I put my arms around her.

"Will she be okay?" I asked after we had let each other go.

"She needed to hear what you had to say. It will take a little while, that's all."

Don't you ever leave me Tess, I wanted to say, but instead I wished her good night and left her behind also.

CHAPTER 11

Esther noticed two more vehicles at the rocket range. "It's getting ridiculously busy here," she joked. "We may have to move somewhere quieter."

The trucks arrived around eight in the morning. By mid-afternoon, they still had not left. I stood outside the door looking across the flat snow-covered distance. At the range itself, clusters of short pine trees were the only growth visible. The sky was clear, blue. Esther came out to join me.

"What are they doing here?"

"Photographers," I suggested.

"It feels like an intrusion," she said. "I have come to think of all this land here as being our own.

We stood in the cold in the shelter of our log house, warm inside our clothing. Esther took my hand in hers.

"Marilyn is lonely," she said, after a moment, turning herself towards me and her attention away from the rocket range. "Even my friendship is not enough for her."

I felt the softness of Esther's palm against mine, our intertwined fingers clasping against the cold. "It is hard living up here alone." I had done it long enough myself.

"She needs the company of a man. She told me this herself. But she has never found anyone. She substituted her beloved wildflowers for a male companion, I think."

"Has she thought about leaving?"

"She loves her flowers too much."

"Before you came, I convinced myself that I loved the loneliness."

"I was no less lonesome." She looked absently into the territory she had claimed as her own.

"We are not the same Esther, but we are not so different."

She smiled a resigned smile. "I think she had a thing for Jack once."

"Marilyn?"

Esther nodded. "She has never said anything directly, but I sense it sometimes."

"She may have been one of a long line."

"She would know that too. She would imagine she was the one right at the end. Or more correctly, she would think she had no right being in that line at all."

"That is sad."

"Yes, it is. We have that within us, that capacity for sadness."

"I have vague recollections of her back then. She worked at the hospital, a nurse. I have told you this before."

"Yes. She has told me about her time there too before her position was cut. There is a shortage of nursing staff now. She could still go back, but she won't. Pride, I think."

The sound of an engine starting up carried across to us. We looked back over at the range. One of the trucks drove away. The other started up soon afterwards and left us on our own.

Esther had asked Loewen about the other police officer, Duncan Walker. Loewen told her that Walker, as best he remembered, had not been involved in the investigation. Terry Mitchell had worked with him on it. She asked him if he knew where Terry Mitchell was now, but Loewen said he hadn't seen him for many years. He had been working in

Toronto last he heard of him. Loewen added that Mitchell wouldn't know any more about it than he did. Except I knew that he did. He knew about Ang and the baby, about Jack deserting them both.

Esther wrote down all that Loewen had told her. She sat at our kitchen table with what little light the day provided and hoped she had left nothing out, some small detail perhaps that was the key to it all.

✦

I met Terry Mitchell again in The Churchill Bar about a month after Jack's death, before I began to hide myself away. He was off duty, a plaid shirt rolled at the sleeves, jeans, a thick moustache. Although I didn't know him well, I knew he was considered a bit of a character. There was no shortage of them around here. He was standing at the counter drinking when I went up to order.

"Wade Sinclair," he greeted me.

I nodded hello, tried to remain calm.

He rested his elbow on the counter. "No sign of your pal?"

I shook my head.

"Strange business. Neither hide nor hair of him."

I was glad when my drink arrived. I swallowed a large mouthful to settle myself.

"What do you think?" he asked.

"What do you mean?" I stood there nervously.

He pulled at his moustache. "What do you think happened to him?"

"I really don't know."

"Well damn it Wade, I don't know either, but I have my thoughts." He spoke lowly so that others would not hear. "I'm off duty right now. I'm entitled to my opinions."

"So what do you think?" I held my bottle by its neck, had another drink. A cascade of noise surged up the bar. The afternoon shift from the terminal had just got off. The door banged noisily. I worked with many of them but rarely drank with any. I had always preferred the company of Jack.

"I sort of knew him," Terry said. "In a roundabout fashion. He started going out with a girlfriend of mine after we had split up. I had been seeing her for over a year. Then she split up with me and started going out with him shortly afterwards. If you asked me, I'd say she started going out with him before splitting up. Son of a bitch stole her away from me. I'd meet them every so often. Susan, that was her name, would always stop to talk. You have to up here. Hard to avoid it. Anyway she introduced me to Butan, so we'd have a few words. I still liked her, didn't want to get on her bad side. Then I met him in here one night. We played pool together. It was very strange. Anyway, he proposed a bet, and I told him I'd play him for Susan. He laughed so hard. I told him I meant it. This is as true as I am standing here. "But she's finished with you," he said, "even if you were to beat me." "Here's the deal," I told him. "You win, you get to keep Susan. I'll even be godfather to your children. I win, you break up with her." Butan looked bemused, but that look soon changed. "I ran your name through our database, found out some very interesting things about you, things Susan might find of interest also." Terry leaned in real close to me. "This is between ourselves," he said. "I'm off-duty remember. Besides you were his friend, he's probably told you all about it."

I said nothing, kept to my drink. I was beginning to feel its effects. Jack was my friend and he had told me nothing. We are not who we say we are. We are not even remotely close.

Terry went on with his story. "So we played our game of pool. It was a close fought game. We tossed to break. I won. I broke and potted a full-ball. Two more to follow. Then I was in a tight spot and played a safety. Not safe enough for your friend, Jack. Sank an impossible half-ball. Another after that, and set two more up with his next shot. I scraped one in, tried to cross a ball and missed. Jack sank a tough cut into the corner pocket. He still had the two he had set up earlier, but he left them alone. Tried a tricky angle into the middle pocket and didn't make it. It left me open and I got two more. I only had one left. It was covered by one of his balls. I tried to swerve the white around but clipped his giving him two shots. He had three balls left. He set the remaining ball up next to a corner pocket. All three were for the taking. One, two. The third one was left and then an easy black. I almost handed him the game. But somehow he got the angle wrong with the white ball and both balls jammed in the pocket then bounced free. I couldn't believe my luck. I had a straight forward shot to the top pocket, followed by the black for the game. We shook on it. A deal's a deal, he said. And sure enough, true to his word, he broke up with Susan the next day. I'd see him around after that, but he tried to keep his distance. I was happy to let him."

"In an off-duty sort of way," I said feeling more confident now, "what did you find in your database?"

"He didn't tell you?" He watched me, measured up my response.

"How do I know until you tell me?"

"Fair enough," he said. He ordered a beer, asked me what I was having. "I'll tell you what," he said while waiting for them. "I'll play you for it."

"Pool?"

"No, women's water polo! Pool, of course."

"Remind me," I said, "what are we playing for?"

"You win, I tell you what was in our database about him. I win, you tell me what you think happened to him. No horseshit. You tell me what you know or think you know. This is off the record. No matter what you tell me it will never come back to you. A deal?"

He held out his large hand. I had to know what Jack had never trusted me to tell, so I took his hand and shook it. Our beers arrived.

"Deal." We stood by the pool table and waited for the game being played to finish.

"What happened to Susan?"

"I tried to get her to go back out with me, but she would have none of it. She was a nurse at the hospital. Left about eight months later. That's how the story goes up here."

I tried to recall a Susan in Jack's life but couldn't. Even Jack probably couldn't keep track of them all.

The game finished a few minutes later. One of the young men started to set the balls up again. Terry stepped forward and laid his hand on the table on top of the green cloth.

"Sorry folks," he said, "but I'm commandeering the table." He winked at them. "Police business."

The two young men looked at one another. One shrugged his head. The other placed his cue against the table. They headed off in the direction of the bar. Terry set the balls up, took out a coin and tossed it, catching it in the palm of his hand and turning it over onto the back of his other hand.

"You call," he said.

"Heads."

He took his hand off and looked at the coin. "Tails." He slid the coin into his pocket before I could even see it. "In that case, I'll break."

I played every shot as though my life depended on it. Jack had taught me most of them. Terry got off to a good start, but I soon caught up. He was a good player, but I knew I was better. I put him in a few awkward positions, forced him to make some mistakes. It didn't take too long to finish the game.

"I've got to hand it to you," Terry said. He grabbed his bottle. "Come on." He nodded his head towards a table in the corner next to the window. He folded his arms on the table in front of him. I sat down opposite him. It was nine thirty at night and still bright outside. A light snow fell so softly it appeared as though it might never reach the ground. The temperature teetered near zero degrees.

"How well did you know Jack Butan?"

"I thought I already answered those questions at my house."

"You did. But that was at your house. This is here at the bar, an altogether different kettle of fish. The thing I've learned, Wade, from my few years up here is that the law works differently here. It adapts to its environment much as we have to. So I'll ask again, how well did you know Jack Butan?"

"He was one of the first people I met when I moved here just over three years ago."

"'Bout the same time as myself," Terry interrupted.

"He was my best friend here. I thought I knew him reasonably well. As well as anyone else here."

"How well did he know you?"

"About the same. I guess we didn't talk too much about our past. He had a girlfriend from high school that he left behind. I think he still loved her. Most of what we shared were the times we spent together. Even his girlfriends here, I didn't know the half of them."

"I have to say, I didn't like him, but of course I was biased. I ran a check on him for the hell of it. I suppose I wanted to know what Susan was letting herself in for. I was jealous too naturally and wanted to see if I could find something to have a hold over him. To tell the truth I didn't expect much." He paused to take a drink, wiped his moustache. "He came up from the States, Iowa."

"That's right." Although the bar was noisy, I was so focused on what he was saying I could barely hear any outer distraction.

"Two parking violations, one charge of underage drinking. And then, bingo, one missing person's report. It appears he bailed out on that high school sweetheart of his. Left her *and* Jack Junior in the lurch." Terry raised his eyebrows, seemed to ask what I made of that.

I didn't quite know what to make of it. Keeping it quiet all those years. Jack walking out not just on Ang but on his baby. I wondered what had really happened at Christmas when he had gone home, if he had gone home at all.

"I didn't know," I said.

"That was the way Jack wanted to keep it. Swapped Susan for the opportunity to keep it hidden."

"You never reported him?"

Terry shrugged. "Why would I? He was old enough to make his own decisions. I don't approve of what he did, but the way I saw it, it was his life. Besides we had a deal."

"He let you win that game." I thought I ought to tell him.

"How do you know?"

"Jack wouldn't have got the angle wrong. He'd never have missed an easy black like that."

"You think so?"

"I'm sure."

"Why would he do that? He could have stayed with Susan. I'd have kept my mouth shut."

"Maybe he didn't trust you."

"What are you saying, Sinclair, that I'm not a man of my word?"

"That he'd still be going out with her and you'd still be upset. He might have figured that it made more sense to let you get what you wanted."

Terry took a long drink. "Who knows?" He squinted at me. "So why did you not let me win, let me get what I wanted?"

"I wanted to hear about Jack more."

"So what do you know about his disappearance?"

"That wasn't the deal."

"Maybe, I'm not a man of my word."

However little I thought I knew Jack now, I knew Terry even less. I decided to give him the information he needed.

"Okay," I said, "I'll tell you what I know."

Terry straightened up in his chair. "Go ahead." Spoken as though he were in the station.

"You remember that time Sergeant Loewen and you came by my house, I mentioned a woman, Eloise, who Jack had recently broken up with. She was a teacher, went home for Spring Break and didn't come back."

Terry nodded.

"Well, it turns out she was pregnant too."

"Jack?"

"Yes."

Tess only told me after Jack had disappeared. Eloise hadn't wanted anyone to know. She hadn't told Jack, hadn't made up her mind if she was going to keep it or not.

"Did Jack know?"

"I know she didn't tell him."

Terry folded his arms and sat back. "There seems to be a pattern developing, does there not?"

"I don't think he'd just disappear."

"Would you have thought he would high-tail it out of town when his girlfriend from high school got in trouble?"

"No, I don't suppose so."

"It beats my other theory anyway."

"Which is?"

"That he stole one too many ladies."

"What do you mean?"

Terry folded his arms behind his head. "I mean that someone didn't solve their grievance over a game of pool."

What did he actually mean? I didn't think he could know about what had happened with Tess unless she had told him something about it. Despite the alcohol in my system, I felt my arm twitch involuntarily, my chest strain. Terry watched me closely. I said nothing.

He finally unfolded his arms, sat forwards and slapped the table lightly. "Anyway, I've taken up enough of your time." He stood up. "Who knows, maybe someday we'll walk back in here, and we'll see him over at the table playing pool."

"He might ask for a rematch," I said.

Terry laughed, headed back to his place at the counter.

The end of February turned cold. For over a week, the temperature, before wind-chill, hovered around -40. The ice was 153 cm thick. Esther and I had enough provisions and only ventured out to bring in wood. For the want of something to do, I started telling her stories from my early days up here. Gradually Jack began to intrude. He sat in amongst us and regaled us with his tales. We burned the last of the floorboards and the last of the kitchen walls. We drank tea. We ate stew and bean casserole. The winds beat at the shutters. The cold threatened to freeze the water in the pipes. We barricaded ourselves in, had him for company.

Esther laughed at our tails of high jinx. On one occasion she turned on the radio, tuned it in to Celtic music from

Newfoundland and dragged me up to dance across the floor.

"Tell me more," she'd say, and I'd start up again.

Jack and I down at the bar, drinking too much, losing our way home. Jack and I ice-fishing on the bay, drilling with a hand auger for almost an hour before hitting rock not having gone far enough out on the ice. Jack and I sitting on the roof watching the rocket. Jack's lady friends. Jack sleeping on the very floor we were burning. Jack this and Jack that.

It took the winds to die down and the temperatures to rise before we were free of him. It took the month of March to arrive, that same month I had gone to Tadoule Lake with Tess twenty-five years previously, two months before Jack fell off the face of the earth.

I opened the door March the third, mid-morning, a calm day, minus 27 degrees. The sky was a mix of cloud and open blue patches, thawed out lakes amidst the frozen ground. I looked up into it, and I might even have seen him rise from the edge of one of those lakes, brushing at his shoulders, sending showers of water dripping down.

Esther walked out and looked up too, and I knew she saw him also. She kissed my cheek.

"It's still cold," she said, "close over the door."

I closed it and left Jack on the other side. I went into the kitchen, returned to Esther.

✦

Tess drove Eloise to the airport. It was the third week in March. School had closed for Spring Break. They parked and made their way to the terminal. Eloise carried a small suitcase. They kicked through the snow as they walked. The air was harsh on their cheeks and nostrils.

Eloise had long since exhausted herself of tears. She had seen Jack four times since they broke up, each time unintentionally. The first two times they acknowledged each other with courteous gestures. On the third occasion, they stopped and spoke. They stood on the street outside the hardware store. Jack asked her how she was, and Eloise told him she had been better. Jack told her she was looking well, and Eloise thanked him for his lies. The next time they met was a week before she left. She saw him in the grocery store. Eloise may have already made up her mind not to return. She had said nothing to Tess about it but may have wanted to tell Jack to see his reaction. But instead she was chirpy, told him some story from her day teaching like she would have done in the past. Both Jack and she laughed, and Eloise felt better than she had for a very long time. She almost kissed him goodbye.

Eloise bought her ticket and sat with Tess in the waiting room amongst the other passengers. A few smiled or laughed but most looked anxious. No journey here was undertaken lightly. The cold air blowing in from outside was tense with departure. Eloise and Tess spoke little. They heard the announcement over the speakers that boarding was commencing and both stood up together. They hugged. Tess wished Eloise a safe journey and said she'd see her soon, little knowing that nothing could be further from the truth.

The following day, Tess and I flew to Thompson and from there to Tadoule Lake. Tess was nervous. She preferred to keep her feet firmly on the ground, she said. We took-off and ascended sharply into the thick white snow clouds. The small plane bumped and lurched upwards. The engine roared through the small cabin. We had to talk loudly to be heard. Outside the window the dull grey clouds through which nothing was visible. The plane was tossed to one side. A baby down the back started to cry. I could see clear into the pilot and co-pilot's cabin. Lights flashed. Something beeped. An elderly woman opposite us with long grey pigtails looked terrified. Tess gripped my arm tightly.

"It's okay," I reassured her. "We're just passing through the clouds."

It was cold. Tess huddled in her jacket. "We should never have come. We have no business being up here. In the past, we would have used dogs and sleds."

"In the past, it would have taken many months."

"We are in too big a rush," Tess replied. "We cannot even tell where we are going. Our people used to find their way by telling stories. They'd find some feature in the landscape in the direction they needed to go and move towards it. If they needed to turn, they'd find another feature and so on until they reached their destination. Then they'd link all the features in a story to remember their way. The White people were amazed at them when they first arrived. They would look out at this bare landscape with no apparent trails, no sense of direction. They couldn't understand how we could just set out walking for weeks on end and arrive at the place we wanted to be."

"I wish we had a story like that."

"Perhaps, we do. Maybe, we just have not been told it yet."

"Maybe, this week we will hear it."

Tess looked at me anxiously. "Remember, I don't even speak the language."

We landed in Thompson early that afternoon, changed planes and travelled on to Tadoule Lake. Tess had called her brother and asked him to meet her at the airport. She hoped he would remember, was worried he wouldn't on account of his drink problem. She looked apprehensively out the window. "It isn't my home. I don't even remember Duck Bay.

Churchill is the best I've got." She turned from the window, seemed to survey me as you would survey the landscape from on high. "Will you stay in Churchill?"

"I have no plans to leave."

"Neither had my people."

Tess remained silent for the rest of the journey. We met with some turbulence on our descent, and she held my arm once more. Visibility was poor. The pilot made an attempt at landing at the small airstrip but pulled up sharply before touching down. Tess looked at me in dismay. We circled round and approached the runway again. This time the wheels touched down. The aircraft shuddered hard before coming to a stop. The co-pilot opened the door and people stood up to leave. I stepped out into the small aisle and stood back to make room for Tess. She squeezed through in front of me. It was snowing outside. A brisk wind blew into our faces as we made our way down the metal stairway. The steps were slippery. I warned Tess to be careful of them.

We followed the people ahead of us across the gravel runway towards the small airport terminal. Heavy drops of snow beat down upon us. The sky was dark and the day dour. I hoped for Tess's sake that her brother would be waiting. Someone drove out with an open trailer to collect our baggage. A high chain metal fence ran around the edge of the runway and terminal.

"It feels like we are in a prison," Tess said, her head bent low against the wind.

She was right, I thought. It felt as though we were walking into a trap, one we could have as easily avoided. We followed through the open door into the airport building. A tiled room with an unmanned counter and chairs where some people sat waiting to board the next plane. Others gathered to greet the passengers who had just arrived.

Tess shook her head. "He's not here." We walked out front into the small parking area. Tess looked through the line of trucks. "I knew it," she said.

We went over to the side of the building where our bags were to be collected. I watched the luggage being loaded from the plane onto the trailer. The truck and trailer drove back across the gravel. Two men got out and began unloading the bags. People reached in quickly and grabbed their own. I got Tess's for her and my own shortly afterwards. The snow fell harder. I could feel my cheeks burn with the wind. Tess pulled up the hood of her parka.

"Now what?" she asked.

"I guess we'll have to walk."

"In this wind." She was clearly annoyed.

We picked up our bags and set off through the car park towards the road. A plane's engine roared into life behind us. The departing passengers would soon board and the plane take-off, disappear into the clouds taking one more route of escape away. We bent our heads low against the blowing snow and walked out onto the frozen gravel road. Between the sound of the plane's engine and the strong wind neither of us heard the pickup pull in behind us. We were startled by the loud beep of the horn and looked behind. The window rolled down and a man stuck his head out.

"Tess," he called.

I saw Tess smile as she walked back. She opened the passenger door and got in. I got in beside her and closed the door. A stale smell of beer lingered in the cab. The man beamed over.

"Hey, sister."

Tess leaned across and kissed him on the cheek. "Peter."

He put the truck into gear and drove on. He didn't say anything to me. He didn't even look my way, and Tess did not introduce me either almost as though I wasn't there. He looked tall and thin, his face pock marked. He had short straight black hair. I put my bag at my feet. Tess carried hers on her lap. The wipers wiped furiously at the falling snow. I couldn't see the road ahead of us. I hoped Peter was still in command of his driving.

"You in trouble?"

"No!"

"So what brings you back here?"

Tess shrugged. "I don't know really. I wanted to see you all. I am not sure what Mum and Dad will think, if they will even agree to see me."

"Might not," Peter said. "They don't mention you much."

"And you?"

"I'm here, am I not?"

"You are," Tess smiled at him again. "How's John?"

"Oh, he's in bad shape. They had him at the treatment centre for a while, but he left that. We haven't seen him in a few months. We think he's in Winnipeg."

"Mum and Dad?"

"Much the same, I guess. Not getting younger." He pulled out a packet of cigarettes and lit up. "You still don't smoke I suppose?"

Tess shook her head. "You drinking any less?"

Peter laughed loudly, coughed on the smoke from his cigarette. "Well, you haven't changed. That one thing's for sure." The pickup bounced over some ruts in the road. The cab filled with smoke. "Where d'you want to go? Go see the old ones? Come back to my place?"

"Who's there with you?"

"You remember Shelley Disain?"

Tess nodded.

"She moved in . . . eighteen months ago? Brought two kids with her. Beth, Cyrus."

"What age are they?

Peter shook his head. "Oh, they're young. Just little ones really. They're okay I suppose. Don't listen to me much."

"Like you listened to Dad?"

Peter laughed again. "We'll go see the old ones later." He turned left, drove past a group of houses. Tess stared ahead through the snow swept windscreen. Peter stopped a few minutes later. "We're here." He opened his door and got out. I opened the passenger door, took my bag and stepped down. Tess handed me her bag and climbed down beside me. A cluster of small houses surrounded us. A few pickups parked at odd angles. Peter banged the door of his truck shut. He tossed his cigarette into the snow and went around the back. Tess and I followed after him. A low black dog, some crossbreed I couldn't distinguish, ran towards him and barked excitedly.

"Shut up Yap!" He pushed the dog aside and opened the back door.

Tess patted Yap on his head as she passed. I could hear fighting from the children inside, loud music on the radio. We passed through a small kitchen into the living room. The two children who looked about eight and six were shouting and pushing at one another. A woman I assumed was Shelley looked to be asleep on the sofa. A small wood stove burned in the corner. The red chequered curtains were pulled across on the window leaving the room dark.

Peter pulled the young boy away from his sister. "Go somewhere else to fight." He pushed him towards the door. The boy and girl ran from the room slamming the door behind them. "Shelley!" He shook the woman by her shoulder. "Wake up. Tess is here." He smiled over at Tess. "We had a bit of a late night."

Three empty glasses sat next to an overflowing ashtray on the low table by the sofa. Peter shook Shelley again and she opened her eyes. "What's up?" she asked straightening up.

"Tess is here."

Tess put her bag down beside her and held out her hand. Shelley took it looking bleary eyed. "You look the same," she said taking her hand away again, running it through her dark curly hair.

"It's good to see you Shelley," Tess said. She sat down on a wooden chair beside the table. Peter went back out into the kitchen. I saw another chair by the wall, set my bag down and brought the chair over next to Tess. Peter came back in with a bottle of whiskey and two more glasses. He put the glasses down on the table and opened the bottle. He poured himself and Shelley a large shot.

"Care for one?" he asked Tess.

Tess, who I had never known to drink, accepted it. He poured her a small one, then poured another large one and handed it to me. I had come into view at last. Shelley rubbed at her eyes and took a drink. The children were still shouting. Peter coughed and lit up another cigarette. No one seemed to know what to say. Tess sipped her whiskey. The radio played country gospel music. Then Tess started to cry. She wiped at her eyes and sniffled.

"I'm sorry," she said.

Peter nodded. "Cheap whiskey, it's all we can get up here. I cry over it all the time."

Tess laughed between her tears.

"You should move here," Shelley said abruptly. "They are always short of teachers at the school. Get these young White kids coming up straight out of diapers, just so's they can get a job, make some northern money. Lucky if they last the season."

Peter agreed. "Yeah. There'd be work for you if you wanted."

Tess brushed her hair from the sides of her face. "I've thought about it. I didn't feel I was welcome much anymore."

Peter shrugged, took a drink. "Story of our life. Didn't stop anyone of us before."

"This is different. I am not wanted by my own parents."

Peter and Shelley said nothing. One of the children laughed loudly from some other room. "We'll go see them tomorrow," Peter said after a few moments. "I am not sure they will let me through the door either."

He made Tess smile again.

Peter and Shelley drank through the evening. Tess made tea for her and me. She eventually told them she was tired and Shelley told her she could have the children's room. They would sleep with her and Peter, she said. She told her which room it was. Tess thanked her. She took her bag and stood up. She nodded at me to go with her. I thanked Peter for the whiskey earlier and went out with Tess.

The children's room was small and untidy. The bed had not been made up. I helped her clean up and fix up the bed. She pulled the curtain open. The snowfall had eased. A smattering of flakes drifted down. We faced out onto a small snow covered yard and just beyond it another house. I heard a dog bark and assumed it was Yap.

Tess sat down on the edge of the bed.

"Are you okay?" I asked.

"I don't know how I am," she answered. "It's good to see Peter again, but it's not good to see him killing himself. He and Shelley, they are not good for each other. But, at least, he seems happy enough."

"That has to count for something." I sat down beside her and put my arm around her shoulder.

"Thanks for coming." She kissed my cheek. "I couldn't have done this on my own." She lay back on the bed on top of the covers. I lay next to her. She closed her eyes. "Let us try and dream of caribou," she said. "Let us pretend they are returning."

CHAPTER 12

Tess did not dream of caribou that night.

"They must have taken a different route. When my people were first relocated to North Knife River they were told that the caribou would pass by there, but instead the caribou passed them by. We have spent our life in search of caribou, and once we knew how to find them."

She looked deeply unhappy.

"It's still not too late." I stroked the side of her face. I had found what I was looking for, and yet I too was plagued with inexplicable distress.

"I will go to see my parents today, and I have no idea if they will wish to see me or not. Now, who can I blame for that?"

"Blame is too easy," I said. "Who can ever fully understand the purpose of their actions?"

She smiled faintly at me as though she recognized the truth in my words but could not embrace it.

There was no sign of Peter or Shelley nor of the children when we got up. The empty whiskey bottle lay on its side on the table. The radio still played. Despite the cold, Tess opened the window to let out the smell of alcohol and smoke. She shivered into her sweater. "I'll make breakfast."

Tess went into the kitchen and searched through the cupboards and the refrigerator. She shook her head in dismay.

Some canned food, beers, hardened cheese, sour milk, and stale bread.

"We need to do some shopping," she said.

We got our jackets and went out into the back yard. Yap ran over and Tess rubbed him. "There boy." He began to follow us, but she turned around and told him to stay. He dropped his head and turned away.

"I am impressed," I told her.

"You ought to be scared," she replied.

We walked around the side of the house grateful for the lack of wind and headed towards the town. A pickup drove past, but otherwise there was no one to be seen. To our left, motor boats were pulled up on the shore of the frozen lake. We followed the dirt road into town. We eventually located a small store. It was almost as bare as Peter's cupboards. Tess bought bread, tinned ham, powdered eggs, tinned tomatoes and frozen sausages. She brought them to the counter where a middle-aged Dene woman sat behind the till.

"Hello Ida."

The woman looked up. Her dark greying hair was tied in a ponytail. Her light brown skin was taut and wrinkled. "Tess Cook. Oh my, oh my." The woman stood looking at her.

"It is good to see you," Tess said.

"It has been a long while. I heard you were down in Winnipeg, at a big school there."

"I am back in Churchill now. I am just visiting here for a few days."

The woman shook her head. "You should have stayed in the city."

"I didn't know how to," Tess told her.

The woman began to ring in the cost of the goods on the till.

"How are Nancy and Rosanne?" Tess looked in her pocket for her purse.

The woman sighed. "Aye, aye. They drink too much, get pregnant too often." She looked up at Tess again. "You always did so well. I don't know where we went wrong."

Tess paid what she owed.

"Come by and visit," the woman said. "The girls would like to see you."

"I'll try to," Tess said. "Tell them I said hello."

On the way back, Tess told me she had been good friends with Nancy and Rosanne when she was younger. Then they dropped out of school and she didn't see them so much after that. "I am not sure I want to see what they have become," she said. "I have seen too much of it already."

We walked down to the lake. A few small dilapidated looking docks were frozen into the ice. I brushed the snow off the bottom of an upturned boat and sat down. Further out on the lake, a man was boring through the ice to fish, his skidoo parked beside him. A dog scrambled over the rocks. Behind us the small town with its snow laden roofs and its snow laden sky, a heavy burden weighing it down. Tess and I sat by the lake without speaking. The dog did not bark, and the fisherman could not be heard. We inhabited the silence and felt the better for it.

Peter smelled the ham and eggs in his deep stupor. He rose, pulled on jeans and a tee shirt and came out to the kitchen. He nodded to us, opened the refrigerator and got himself a can of beer. He burped loudly. Tess put some scrambled eggs and ham on a plate for him.

"Sister," he said by way of thanks. He scooped a mound of eggs up on his fork and stuffed it into his mouth.

"Where are the children?"

He talked through his full mouth. "Gone to Shelley's mother's house. She came over after you went to sleep."

"And Shelley?"

"She's there too." He took a slice of bread and buttered it, cut some ham, placed it on top of the bread and ate it, washed it down with beer. "We'll go see the old ones when we've eaten. Better to face them on a full stomach."

"You didn't tell them I was coming did you?" Tess put her knife and fork down, pushed her empty plate away.

"I haven't seen them since you wrote." He wiped his mouth with the back of his hand. "I don't see too much of them really. They don't like Shelley."

"Why not?"

"They think she's a bad influence." Both he and Tess laughed hard.

After we were all finished, Peter suggested we get ready to go. He went back to his room, and Tess and I went to get our jackets. She looked concerned.

"Tell me again it will be okay."

I squeezed her shoulder lightly. "It will be just fine."

Peter drove past the band office and community centre. He turned left away from the lake heading out of town. He drove for another ten minutes then pulled in at a small wooden house set back from the road. Smoke spewed from the chimney.

"The last time I came, they barely acknowledged me," Tess said. "Dad told me I was a disgrace not staying with the family. He told me I had forgotten my place."

Peter opened his door. "Come on, Sister. None of us remember our place. Some of us never had one." He jumped out onto the snow. We got out after him. He walked in the front door and into a small parlour. There was no one there. Tess looked around her nervously.

"Where are you hiding?" Peter called.

"Peter?" A woman's voice sounded from further back.

"That's Mom," Tess whispered.

We could hear her movement as she came to look for Peter. Peter winked over at Tess. She attempted a smile. The door to the parlour was half open. Tess's Mom pushed it open wide.

"Peter ..." she began but stopped when she saw Tess. "Tess."

"Hello Mom."

They stood facing each other. Her Mom looked older than she could possibly be. Her hair was short and grey. She was small, thin looking. Tess finally went over and hugged her.

Her mother took her embrace then stepped back. She turned to Peter. "Did you invite her?"

"She invited herself. Turned up like a bad penny."

"What will your father say?"

"Where is he?"

"He's not feeling too well. He went to bed."

"What's the matter?" Tess asked.

Her mother looked at her. "Now you ask." She said she needed to sit down. She sat at the table, held her face in her hands. She looked as though she might cry. Tess went over and sat down across from her. Peter left the room presumably to go see his father. I stayed where I was by the door.

"Who's that?" Tess's mother asked her about me.

"Wade Sinclair. He's a friend of mine."

I went over to her and held out my hand. "I am pleased to meet you."

Tess's mother looked at me briefly. "You shouldn't have come without telling us," she told Tess.

"I was afraid you would tell me not to."

"I would have." She took her hands away from her face, placed them on top of one another on the table. I moved back towards the door. "What did you come here for?"

"To see my family."

"You left your family a long time ago."

"That's not fair," Tess said. "I went to college because I thought it would help us all. I didn't leave anyone."

"And what help has it been?"

"Please mother."

Her mother lowered her voice a little. "If you had to come, you should have come alone."

Tess did not respond. "I'd like to go see Dad," she said after a short while.

"He's not well. Maybe you should come back tomorrow."

Tess stood up. She walked behind her mother, kissed the top of her head. "I'll just look in on him. Talk to Wade."

She smiled over at me as she left the room. Her mother stared down at her hands. I tried to think of something to say. I looked around the room. A wooden cabinet with a few black and white framed photographs propped up on it. A couch with a blanket thrown over the back. A painting of a sunset. The table and chairs where her mother sat.

"How do you know my daughter?" She looked at me disapprovingly.

"I work at the grain terminal in Churchill. We met."

"Why did you come here?"

"Tess asked me to."

"Our family is none of your business," she said. She stood up from her chair but did not move from the table. "I have lost all my children. Something has happened in this world that I do not understand. You have no right to be in my house."

"I am sorry."

"No, you're not." She went over to the cabinet and lifted up one of the photographs. She brought it over and showed it to me. It was a picture of a young woman with two boys and a girl. "That is my other daughter," she said pointing to the girl. "She is dead. That boy is dead. That other boy may as well be if he isn't already."

"It can't be easy," I said.

She replaced the photograph on the cabinet. "Do you drink?"

"Sometimes."

"Go then, take my other son Peter, drink with him and fill him with alcohol. Do not stop until his life is taken too."

"I would do nothing to harm Tess," I told her.

"It is too late for that."

I heard footsteps in the hall. I hoped Tess was coming back. Instead Peter came into the room.

"He's not looking too bad," he said. "Maybe even a little less grumpy than usual."

"Mind your manners," his mother warned him.

"Tess?" I inquired.

"Hammer and tongs," he answered. He took out a cigarette and lit it. "We should make some coffee." He proceeded into the kitchen. I walked after him. He filled the kettle and put it on to boil. He leaned against the sink and smoked on his cigarette.

"Should I not have come?"

He blew smoke in my direction. "That's not for me to say."

"Your mother said so."

"She would also say that Tess should not have come. Sometimes, she wonders what I am doing here."

"Tess wanted me to."

"Who's talking about me now behind my back?" Tess walked in. I hoped her meeting with her father had gone reasonably okay.

The kettle boiled. Peter made coffee for everyone and brought one down to his father.

"Are you alright?" I asked after he had gone.

"He's as stubborn as ever, but it's still nice to see him."

We went back into the parlour with the coffees. Tess and her mother made hesitant small talk. We stayed another hour or so and then went back to Peter's house.

✦

The following day, Tess borrowed Peter's snowmobile and drove us out of town. It took a little while to start up. The engine roared deafeningly. I sat behind Tess and held onto her waist. We quickly picked up speed. Clouds of snow gusted behind us. Tess drove along the lake. The town raced away from us. Tess had seemed subdued the evening before. I wondered if she was angry too, if this was a way of burning some of it off. She might keep going as far as the snowmobile could across the frozen barrens until finally we ran out of fuel and were stranded with no reasonable way of returning to safety. It did not seem implausible. She bumped up over the bank back onto land. The visor of my helmet steamed over with my breath. I wondered if Tess could even see or if she was riding blindly ahead. I shouted at her to ask if she knew where we were going, but my voice was whisked away by the swift passage of air. I looked back. The town was out of sight. She drove for about half an hour before slowing down.

"Where are we?" I shouted again.

Tess shouted back something I couldn't hear. She slowed even more then came to a halt and turned off the engine. She pulled off her helmet and got off the snowmobile. I took my helmet off and asked her once more if she knew where we were.

"In the middle of nowhere. There is nothing as far as you can see. Who could ever believe there was life up here, and who here could ever imagine there was life anywhere else?"

The snow and ice extended all around us. The only tracks our own. "Are you glad you came?"

Tess shook her long hair free from her jacket. It was like a live animal we might yet need to feed off. "Yes, I am. They did not tell me to leave."

"Your mother does not think I should be here."

"Wait until my father sees you," she laughed. "They are still very upset and disappointed with me, but it does not seem as intense as the previous time."

"They will have missed you."

"Yes I think you are right. There is still a long way to go however."

"We do better on longer journeys than short ones."

"Do you think so?"

"If you go astray on a short journey, you may never find the path back, but on a long journey there is always the chance of meeting up with the way again."

Tess brushed her hair back. She smiled then kissed my cold cheek. "I could love you, Wade."

And I thought if there was anywhere that this might be possible, it would be there and then with the frozen earth, the impenetrable sky, and the dearth of life other than Tess and me.

✦

"This is why you shouldn't have come here," her mother told Tess when she was saying her goodbyes. Her father stood up and left the room. Peter drove us to the airport. He was drunk. He kept telling Tess how much he missed her. Tess told him to keep his eyes on the road. The trip had gone about as well as Tess could have hoped for. Tess and I stayed at Peter's and called on her parents every day. Each day they told her there was no need to come the next, but Tess knew they didn't mean it.

Tess was quiet on the journey home. Part of this was due to her fear of flying but most had to do with her departure. She had left her family yet again.

"They were happy to see you," I told her.

"They tried hard not to show it."

"They would have preferred if I wasn't there."

"I would not have preferred it. Peter seemed comfortable with you around."

"He hardly said a word to me."

"He would have told you if he didn't like you. He would not have let you stay in his home."

"What would you have done then?"

"Thrown you the scraps."

I would have settled for the scraps. I would have been content to feed on those.

CHAPTER 13

Esther felt like eating out. We drove to the Traders Table restaurant and parked outside the old wooden saloon-styled building. A few of the tables were occupied but by no one Esther or I knew.

"Tourist season must have started early," I whispered.

"Time for you and I to go into hibernation then," Esther replied.

We took a table at the back and looked at the menu. Esther wanted to eat wild meat. So we both ordered the caribou steaks.

"I feel like I am on vacation." Esther reached back and released her hair from the clasp. She shook it free then tied it back up again. In all the years I had known her, I had seldom seen her with her hair down. She wore a green corduroy blouse, a long black skirt. I had never seen her wear pants either.

"You look lovely," I told her.

"Why, Mr. Sinclair!" she joked. She took my hand and held it. "Should we order wine?"

"Maybe we ought to." I called the waitress over and ordered a bottle of house red. She said she'd be right back. She looked in her early twenties, the same age Tess was when I met her.

"We could be somewhere other than here," Esther said.

"Do you want to be?"

She shook her head. "I have found my place in the world."

"Despite the bears."

"Yes, despite them. I am still afraid, but now I have room for my fear."

The wine arrived. I poured us each a glass and toasted Esther. "To our place in the world."

We clinked glasses and drank to it.

"Who would ever have thought I would end up here?"

"Who would ever have thought I would end up with you?"

Esther put down her glass. "Janice once described you as a solitary man. She said that everyone thought you would be alone for the rest of your life."

"There is no one more surprised than I."

"If I hadn't come on that excursion?"

"Then everyone would have been right."

"We are lucky then. Or was it fated?"

If I were to believe in fate, then I would have to believe that I was fated to end Jack's life, that I could not even prevent it if I tried. It would absolve me of all guilt would it not?

"We are lucky at the very least."

Esther swirled the wine in her glass slowly, stared into it. Then she looked up at me. "I'd like to have met Tess."

I was caught off-guard and felt myself blush. I hoped Esther didn't notice. "Why?"

"I have heard so little about her, and yet she seems so important to Jack."

"He barely knew her."

"But you said they were friends, that he loved her."

"I said he thought he loved her."

"But still, they were friends."

"For a while, but I don't think he really knew her that well."

Esther stared at me as though she doubted what I was saying.

"All I mean is that they only got close towards the end of his life. The Tess he thought he loved may never have existed at all." I washed down my words with wine.

"I'd still like to have met her." Esther twisted the stem of her glass between her fingers. "You said she went back to her family after Jack went missing. Where did they live?"

"Tadoule Lake. She was Dene."

Esther looked from her glass to me. "Hearne's guides were Dene, Chipewyan. They led him through the barren grounds."

"Tess was a teacher, so I suppose she was a guide of sorts too."

"Do you think she could still be there?"

"I suppose she could." This was until then the unspoken truth. In any of the intervening years, I could have retraced our journey, looked for Tess. Instead, I stayed where I was, kept to the paths I knew.

"Maybe, I should try to contact her."

Esther looked serious. I could think of nothing I would desire less.

"There would be little point," I insisted. "She could tell you nothing more."

"All the same."

"Tess held herself somewhat responsible for his vanishing. It would not be wise to drag it all up again."

"Why would she feel that?"

"The confusion between their feelings for each other."

"It is I who am confused."

"Well damn it Esther, I don't understand it either." I snapped out my response without thought. Esther looked hurt. "I'm sorry." I shook my head in dismay.

"No," Esther said, "it is I who should be sorry. All I have ever wanted was to learn for you the truth. It might lessen the burden both for you and Tess."

"It might make it worse." I should probably never had said it, but now it was said.

"I have a feeling he is still alive." Esther placed her glass in front of her. "I can't explain it, but I really believe I can find him for you."

Esther, I should have said, it is entirely possible that we all live in a world of illusion, that we deliberately avoid the truth to make our passage palatable. Jack is dead. He is as dead as death makes possible. And I killed him. Do not ask me if I intended to or not, since I do not know.

"Esther, he's dead."

"You don't know that any more than I know he is alive."

Esther I killed him.

"The police would have found him."

"They gave up. They barely investigated at all. Look Wade, he may well be dead, but it is not an absolute. It is just an assumption that the police were content to go along with. Stranger things have happened."

I lost Tess, and I met you.

"Do you want me to stop?" Esther looked at me seriously.

I took a drink of wine. It had been so long since I had a drink that I was already beginning to feel its effects.

Yes, I want you to stop.

"I don't know, Esther. I am not sure it is for me to decide."

"We are helpless, are we not?"

"We are," I agreed.

Esther smiled, reached for my face. "God, I love you." Could there be anything more helpless than that?

The door to the restaurant opened. Marilyn walked in. She immediately saw us and came over to our table.

"Well, well," she said, "if it isn't the two lovebirds. What brings you here?"

"A whim," Esther replied. "And you?"

"Oh, I often come here. It's a chance to get out, take my company elsewhere."

Esther asked if she wanted to join us. Marilyn said she would only be interrupting, but Esther assured her she wouldn't. "Would she Wade?"

"Not at all," I said. Truthfully, I would have preferred to be with Esther alone, but I would always prefer that.

"Well, if you're sure." Marilyn took off her jacket, pulled out a chair and sat down beside Esther. "It's good to see you out together."

"It's nice to be out. I was just telling Wade it was like being on vacation."

"I rarely see you around." Marilyn looked my way.

"When the terminal's open," I said, "otherwise I avoid town."

"What about you?" she asked Esther. "Would you like to live closer to town?"

"I have lived close to towns all my life. I came here to escape that. Besides it's not exactly far away."

"I couldn't manage it," Marilyn said. "I love it here, but I need to be around people. Too much loneliness in this world if you ask me."

"Why not move somewhere bigger then?"

"I have thought about it. But I am afraid that the bigger it gets the lonelier it will get too."

Esther called the waitress over to bring another wine glass for Marilyn. Marilyn ordered her food without even looking at the menu.

"We never really knew one another, did we?" she said to me after the waitress left.

"You treated me at the hospital once, a minor accident at work."

"I don't remember. I see too many people. I used to see you around with your friend Jack. After he ..."

And then she faltered. For twenty-five years Jack was gone, but somehow now he had returned. His name was on many lips, and it was Esther who helped place it there.

Marilyn did not know what to say. Her words had run ahead of her. She could see them clearly but did not know how to catch up with them.

"Jack took me out of myself," I responded. "His zest was infectious. Without him I returned to my old self."

The waitress returned with our food and the glass for Marilyn. She poured Marilyn some wine.

"What do you think he would be doing if he were around today?"

Esther I think would have stopped her, prevented her words from losing themselves, setting out. But it was too late. You first had to see Jack dead to know there was no way back to life.

"He would still be at the bar playing pool. He would have looked at himself and hated what he saw."

"Can I tell you something?" Marilyn took a drink of wine before continuing, "I sometimes look at myself in a similar manner."

"Wade and I have been lucky," Esther said. "We got a late chance."

Marilyn looked immensely sad. "Perhaps, then it was better he went the way he did."

"If it were possible, I would prefer to be at the table with him, chalking my cue, convincing him that he had made all the right choices."

"Don't mind me," Marilyn said. "I am feeling sorry for myself. It is that time in my life. You don't deserve this on your special night out."

Esther put her hand on Marilyn's arm. "It has been wonderful meeting you here."

"Maybe, it's just the wine," Marilyn laughed.

"Maybe, we need a whole lot more."

Esther and Marilyn were tipsy. I had not drunk too much and offered to drive Marilyn home. Esther would not hear of it. Marilyn would spend the night with us. She would prove to her that the town was not all it was said to be. On the way home, Esther told her about all the comings and goings at the rocket range.

Outside the truck window, the night sky, pockets of stars, a hint of a moon. The unending spread of white that refused to reflect its light. A darkness inexplicable by day.

"Haven't you heard?" Marilyn asked.

"What?"

"It's all over town. They are planning another rocket launch."

"When?"

Marilyn had no idea. "It's just a plan. It may not ever happen. They have talked about redeveloping the facility before and nothing came of it."

Esther could not contain her excitement. "It is all I have ever wanted to see." She turned to me in the dark cab. I caught her gleaming smile. "Right over our house, think of it."

"Let us hope for the best," I said. "We always seem to be on the cusp of something. Military bases, rocket launches, tourism, melting ice caps. That's the latest. Global warming which may drive the polar bears to extinction, wreak havoc with the climate, melt the ice caps, unlock passages and extend the shipping season. The ice melt they say will open up an Arctic bridge, a regular shipping lane from Russia to Churchill. A far shorter shipping route than from Europe to North America. We'll become the gateway to the world."

"Thin ice," Esther smiled. "It will be our saving."

"What do you think, Wade," Marilyn asked, "you measure it, is the ice thinning?"

By the very second, I might have replied.

"That's what we should do," Esther interrupted excitedly. "Let's stop at Bird Cove and measure it for Marilyn."

"I'm sure Marilyn doesn't want to."

But Marilyn disagreed. "I think I'd like to. I've heard Esther talk about it often."

So at Bird Cove, I turned in on the gravel road leading towards the shore. I went as far down it as I could, then parked. I took my auger and we got out, followed the trail to the shore. We picked our way carefully over the rocks. The snow crunched under us. There was barely enough light to see.

"We should have brought a flashlight," I said.

"I'm glad we didn't." Esther gripped my upper arm lightly for support. "We see too much of this place. It's time to feel it too. Shh, listen."

We stopped and listened for what Esther had heard. The slow creak of the straining ice. The low boom of the water beneath it. We continued on down to the shore. The creaking and booming increased in volume.

"It's alive," Esther said. "Warning us against something."

"You'll put the fear of God into me if you don't stop," Marilyn whispered.

"I just think we have ignored it for far too long. The noise of our living blocks it out."

Marilyn turned to me. "Can you make her stop?"

"I can't make her do anything."

"You made me fall in love with you." Esther squeezed where she gripped my arm.

"I did nothing of the sort. I would have persuaded you against it if I thought you would listen."

"It's like I said, the noise of our living blocks it out."

The wine and occasion had made her perky. The dark frozen air made her behaviour seem brittle, fragile. I led both of them out onto the ice and set up the auger.

"*The Ithaca* is out there," Esther said, "but I can't see it."

"Have you ever been on it?" Marilyn asked out of the shadows.

"I am afraid to," Esther admitted.

It was the case. Esther would never walk with me out to its ruins. Although no one perished upon her, she felt she would be stepping too closely to the dead. She who chased after Jack with reckless abandon.

"It was not the Munck expedition of 1619, wintering off-shore with the loss of sixty-one lives," I would often remind her. But, for Esther, it may as well have been. She would have run from the whale too. She would not have entered its body.

"It reminds me too much of myself," she told Marilyn. "Before Wade, I was stranded too, helpless against the incoming and outgoing tides."

"But Wade rescued you."

"Yes, he sailed me safely back to port."

Munck and the other two surviving members of crew, against the odds, making it back home to Europe.

I found a suitable location and began to drill into the ice.

"One summer, after the sun had set," Marilyn told us, "I went out there. A moonless night. Not unlike tonight but warmer. I stood on the deck, an hour before the tides came in.

215

There was no one else around, no lights of approaching vehicles. I don't know quite what came over me, but I undressed there on board. I left my clothes beside the mast. I walked to the prow, pointlessly naked. As you know my body is large. I am not proud of it, but that night it felt ideal. I was the perfect fit."

"I couldn't do it," Esther said. "I could never undress in such a situation."

Ask Wade, she might have added if it were to sound less vulgar. But yes, even yet Esther felt embarrassment undressing in front of me. The act of unclothing was not for her a simple task.

Midways through my drilling, a loud rumbling echoed from beneath the ice and then a tremendous thud resounded.

Marilyn jumped. Esther gripped my arm tightly, "Who is it?" she demanded to know.

As if we needed an answer.

CHAPTER 14

Eloise phoned Tess the last evening of Spring Break. Tess and I had returned from Tadoule Lake the day before. Tess spent that night with me then went back to her own house the following noon. She had expected Eloise to be already there. Eloise did not call until shortly after six o'clock. She said hello to Tess, and Tess asked her if she had been delayed.

"Tess ..."

"Yes." Tess knew something serious was to come. The phone crackled, and she told me later it sounded like the crackle of wood burning outside on a cold winter's night.

"Tess ..."

"Yes, Eloise."

"I'm not coming back."

The crackle disappeared as though the flames had been suddenly extinguished, the wood too damp to stay alight.

"Are you sure?"

"Yes."

"And the school?"

"I haven't told them. I'll call tomorrow. I suppose they'll be furious with me for leaving them in the lurch."

Tess told her not to worry about that. "Is it Jack?"

Eloise started to cry. "I was never happy there anyway even before him. You know that."

"I know."

"Tess, I'm pregnant."

There are some things, Tess said, impossible to foretell despite the obviousness of their forthcoming.

"Jack?"

"Of course."

"Does anyone else know?"

"Only you."

"What are you going to do?"

"I don't know."

"How long have you known?"

"I have been wondering for a few weeks." She paused. Tess heard her swallow. "The ridiculous thing," she continued, "is that it was the night we all went out together. I knew that night he was going to leave me. I should not have gone home with him." She cried so that she could no longer speak.

Tess comforted her and when Eloise had recovered she told Tess she would call her again soon. "Don't do anything rash," Tess advised.

Eloise said goodbye and put the phone down.

Tess hadn't even thought to ask if Jack knew.

What would you have done, Jack, if you did know? Would you have accepted the situation and tried to get back together with Eloise, or would you have done what you did with Ang, desert her and the child? Or maybe you would have done what the Inuit did in the past with their unwanted babies, leave it out in the cold to die.

Tess was unsettled for weeks after she got back from Tadoule Lake. She did not say it directly, but I knew she was thinking of moving there to be with her family. I sometimes wonder if she brought me along just so I would know what it was like if I was to consider going there with her. Peter's drinking worried her a lot. And although her father had not been too ill, she was concerned about his health.

She didn't tell me about Eloise until she phoned her again a few weeks later to say she was keeping the baby but not to tell Jack.

Tess arrived at my door and asked me to take her for a walk. "I've been cooped up in school all day."

It was mid-April, no less than − 5 degrees outside. The sun shone brightly. We drove out to Goose Creek. I parked and we walked down towards the Churchill River. The snow was soft beneath our feet. The short willow and spruce were in abundance sprouting from the ground. Tess pointed out two pure white ptarmigans over by a clump of spruce. Our movements startled them and they rose together into the air.

"It is Eloise and her baby," she said, "taking flight." I looked at her in surprise. "She is expecting Jack's child."

I was stunned. Ahead of me the frozen river, its hidden undercurrents. "She told you this?"

"Yes."

"And Jack?"

"He doesn't know."

"Is she going to tell him?"

"I don't think so."

The snow glistened with the light of the sun. A snowshoe hare ran across the frozen river. "She ought to."

"I know," Tess agreed. "I have told her that."

The hare stopped suddenly and doubled back, its long loping stride. "For such flat open country, this life of ours takes a lot of turns."

"If I told you I was pregnant?" Tess turned to await my reaction.

I thought for a moment she was telling me that. My stomach churned. I was not ready yet for that development in our relationship. "Are you?"

"If I was?"

"I would be scared."

"What would you do?"

"I would love you both."

"I know you would." Tess looked to where the ptarmigan had landed and breathed out deeply. "Eloise should have met you instead."

"What do you mean?"

"I mean, I am very fortunate."

"What would you do?"

"I have been thinking about that. I would tell you, but then I would leave you." She did not hide her face from me. She was resigned to her decision. "I'm sorry."

"Why would you leave?"

"We are not ready for a child. It would ask too much of us. It would stretch what we have too thinly."

"Even though I would be the father."

"Even though."

Maybe, I should have walked away then. Perhaps what we had was already stretched too thin, like the ice was doomed to fracture, melt away. Instead, I stood there unable to move. Tess came over and took my hand.

"It is not the case. I am not pregnant. I am walking towards you and not away."

But although she took my hand, she did walk away. For a while, I walked alongside.

It was five in the morning. Dawn. Tess lay beside me in bed. She would rise soon and leave. Her dark hair, the lustre of her skin. She had folded her clothing across my chair. She had carried her body to mine.

She wondered if we should tell Jack about the baby. Eloise might never forgive her, but she thought it only proper that he should know.

"It would be best to convince Eloise of that," I told her.

"I have tried, but her mind seems made up." She turned in the bed to face me. "You tell him."

"Okay."

Tess laid her hand on my hip. "Do you mean it?"

"Yes, I'll tell him if you think it is for the best."

"I do." She moved her hand along my stomach and chest. "Remember the whale?"

"Of course."

"We climbed inside." Her fingers traced my ribs.

"Yes. I remember the moon. Creamy yellow."

"I have climbed inside you, have I not?" Her face serene, her brown eyes searching.

"You have, Tess, and I see no way out."

She bent her head, kissed my shoulder. The moon appeared before me, gigantic in my small room. "Wade."

"Yes, Tess."

As the moon waned and the tides receded.

✦

Janice resurrected Terry Mitchell. She called Marilyn who of course called upon Esther. She made some enquiries, followed up some leads. She conducted an investigation, I concluded to Esther. We were preparing for bed. The lamp light was dull in the room.

"If that is how you put it." Esther emerged from the bathroom. She tightened her bathrobe around her. "He was easy to talk to. He remembered you."

"Where is he?"

"He took advantage of early retirement. He is a carpenter outside of Calgary."

"What did he remember about me?"

Esther faltered. In our life together Esther did not falter. She was as sure as the God-given winter.

"He said you were a suspect."

The ground gave way beneath me as the lake and river ice yield to the overbearing weight of water, as the body of the whale gives way beneath its own weight.

"A suspect?"

Esther laughed, sat down on the bed to comb her hair. "It is ridiculous is it not? I told him so. I told him you were his best friend. He said this was what made him suspicious. He suspected that you knew more about his disappearance than you let on."

"Why would he think that? They barely asked me anything about Jack at the time." I was sinking slowly below the surface. I struggled to speak.

"He said that it was only his opinion, that the sergeant was convinced it was an accident. He said he didn't believe that. He thought it most likely that Jack had planned it all, had heard about the baby and absconded. He wondered if I knew about the baby and I told him I did."

I excused myself, went into the bathroom to wash and brush my teeth. I looked at myself in the mirror above the sink. My face was pale. I held my hands in front of me. They shook noticeably as they had taken a habit of doing.

"Did he say why he did not think it was an accident?" I called out.

"I asked him that. He said it was a warm spring and the ice was particularly thin, that everyone knew that. He didn't think that Jack would be fool enough to take unreasonable chances."

I filled the sink with warm water. "Accidents are not always the result of unreasonable chances."

"I know that. He seemed a bit unreasonable himself. He even said Jack could have been killed deliberately."

"I suppose these things could have happened. But they seem a bit far-fetched. Why would anyone kill Jack?"

"He said Jack was not above stealing someone's girl. That was how he put it. But this is the odd part, he said Jack had stolen a girlfriend of his once, that some people wouldn't forgive that sort of thing."

"I think I remember hearing something about that," I told her drying my hands and face. "Why do you say it is odd?"

Esther came to the bathroom door. "Don't you think it's odd that he said someone might have killed Jack because he stole their girl, and then he says that Jack stole his girlfriend?"

I watched her from the mirror, felt myself float upwards towards the surface once more as though a lifeline had been thrown to me. "What are you suggesting?"

"I'm not suggesting anything. I just think it is odd."

"Terry Mitchell didn't kill him."

Esther tidied up the towel I had been using, looked embarrassed. She folded the towel, hung it on the rail. She looked at me, tried to smile then went back out into the bedroom. I brushed my teeth, rinsed my mouth. Esther was in bed reading. I turned down the covers and got in beside her.

"I wonder why he left the police force?" she asked placing the book down on the covers.

"It's a tough job. Long hours, nights, a lot of stress."

"I suppose." But Esther didn't sound convinced.

"There is no great mystery here."

"You are most probably correct. But that does not rule it out." She sat up against the pillows. "I think Terry Mitchell killed him. I am undoubtedly wrong, but that is what I think."

"You are wrong Esther."

"It is what I think."

Esther awoke bright and early in the morning. She shook me awake. The sun had yet to rise. I stumbled from my sleep.

"What is it?"

"I had another thought."

I wiped sleep from my eyes, yawned.

"Maybe Jack did fake his death. You said Tess went back to her family soon after, but maybe she didn't. Maybe they had a plan. She might have joined up with him, be living out their lives somewhere else."

She was animated, enthused.

"Maybe she killed him," I said sarcastically. Immediately feeling the sharp edge of my words cut inwards.

Esther sat out on the edge of the bed. "Do you think so?"

"No," I told her. "I do not think so."

She slipped her feet in her slippers and stood up. "You don't know, none of us do. There is nothing we can rule out."

I watched the drift of her nightgown against her body. "Esther, let it go."

"Is my quest for Jack offending you?" Esther pulled on her dressing gown, sat down on the edge of the bed.

"No, I am not offended, the opposite in fact. I am just afraid you expect too much from your search. It is possible you will find a Jack that does not meet your expectations."

"I have no expectations."

There were few words she could have spoken less truthful than that.

✦

Marilyn took on a greater role in our life. I vied with her for Esther's attention. Esther, I believe, felt indebted to her, and, in a non-judgmental way, she felt sorry for her too. In some ways, I resented the interference. In others, it seemed a respite. I thought maybe it would take Esther's mind off Jack. For that, I forgave her seemingly constant presence in our home, but instead it proved the reverse. What Esther could not say to me she said to her. Although it was only March, Marilyn spoke frequently of winter coming to a close, the advent of spring and summer, wildflowers. I measured the ice with Esther and her. It continued to thicken, 163, 170, 173, as though defying Marilyn's optimism.

They went for long walks together at Bird Cove, Cape Merry, Sloop's Cove. They talked about Jack, about Tess, about Eloise, Terry Mitchell, and me. Marilyn strangely did not remember Tess. Nor did she recall Eloise. She was fascinated nevertheless by the details Esther unearthed. She encouraged her further on. It was Marilyn who had urged her to call Terry. He liked to speak his mind, she recalled. If there is anything to tell, he'll tell it.

Their feet pressed through the snow as they walked in conversation. The winds whipped in over the bay or lay close to the ground. Their breaths frosted over in front of them.

Marilyn remembered Susan, the woman Terry said Jack had stolen from him. She was a nurse in the hospital. He met her, Marilyn said, bringing drunks into emergency that had got into fights. You'd hear him coming before the drunks. "Feeding time," he'd shout as he approached the nurse's counter. He was rough with the people he brought in and openly made fun of them, but he made the nurses laugh. He livened up the long nights. We all enjoyed seeing him. Susan most of all. It didn't take long for us to notice. She seemed to have a special smile she saved for him. They went out a long time together. Marilyn did not recall how or when they broke up. Terry usually got one of the other officers to bring the injured in after that. Or if he did have to come himself, he was a lot more subdued.

I did not ask Esther if she had mentioned her suspicions about Terry to Marilyn for fear it would encourage her to do just this if she had not already. And so I didn't know, but I imagined Esther would halt in her stride by the shore and point out a Pine Grosbeak to Marilyn. The sky a cobalt blue. Then Marilyn would stop also and together they would watch the bird fly overhead. Esther would lightly cough. She would follow the flight of the bird a moment longer then turn to look at Marilyn.

"I know this sounds silly," she would say, "but I sometimes wonder if Terry Mitchell killed Jack Butan."

Marilyn would look at her in complete surprise. A wisp of cirrus cloud above. "Why would you think that?"

Esther would tell her her reasons. Common sense could then prevail. Marilyn could tell her that she was reading too much into a few hasty sentences, that Terry was not capable of such a deed. And Esther could pause for thought.

"Talk to Janice. She might know more about Susan and Terry Mitchell's relationship. What have you got to lose?"

They would continue their walk, and Esther would step ever closer towards the edge.

April was mild, the temperatures hovered around minus ten degrees. The sun rose at six and set at nine. The ice thickness remained steady, in the low 170s. I worked on cutting up the remaining wood from my old house. The bedroom, bathroom and roof. I stacked it up neatly in the shed. I was standing outside the shed one morning nursing a blister on the side of my forefinger. Esther came out of the house. She was dressed for leaving.

"Janice?" I might have asked, but I didn't.

"I'll see you when you get back," she called over.

I nodded. With the regularity of her comings and goings, as she attempted to resolve the mystery of Jack's disappearance, my initial anxiety had given way to a resigned calmness. How quickly consistency reduces the extraordinary to the mundane.

They met at Gypsy's. It was busy, but they managed to get a table by themselves close to the window. A yellow tour bus passed by, an old adapted school bus. Cutlery banged on the tabletops. Chair legs scraped on the floor. Janice seemed glad to see Esther as though she didn't have company often enough. She asked her if she had contacted Terry, and Esther said she had.

"A carpenter," Janice said when she told her. "It is a world of endless surprises."

Esther wasn't ready to talk about him just yet, so she asked Janice how she was doing. It struck her then, she told me later, that she seemed to attract lonely people. Janice, Marilyn.

Me. I could have added.

"I am doing well," Janice said. She smirked, blushed even. She lowered her voice, leaned in towards Esther. "I was asked out on a date. Could you ever believe it? It is like I said, it is a world of endless surprises."

"Did you accept?" Esther likewise whispering.

"Of course not." Janice pushed her fork in and out of her food. "It felt good to be asked though. At times, after Eb died I thought my life was over too. I am not ready to spend time with another man, but it gives me hope for the future. My son Mark wants me to move to Montreal where he is at college.

He will finish soon and plans to work there. My life is here, I told him. Whatever little is left of it."

"Good for you," Esther said.

Janice settled back in her chair. She said a strange thing then Esther said. She said she envied Esther and me. Esther asked her what she meant.

Janice put her fork down although she had barely eaten anything. "I didn't love Eb." She looked close to tears. A fine morning mist rose over the roads off the bay. "I did like him. We got on well together, and when he died, I could not bear to be without him. But, in my heart, I have always known I did not love him."

Esther did not know what to say. She was dumbfounded. Oddly, she felt as though a part of her fell away. A part she said she might never recover. "I barely know her." Esther looked lost when she told me this. "It was not Janice. I did not so much feel for her but for what she had told me." Janice had spoken some great truth that had somehow been obscured from Esther's view. She had revealed a void all around us Esther had previously filled with distortions.

Janice told Esther that Eb did love her though. That love, she said, was what held them together most. "Even though I did not love him, I would never have left him. Even if I had wanted to, his love for me would have prevented it. I do not have it in me to do that to anyone."

"She was right to be envious," I told her. "You and I are blessed."

Esther cried hard as though to fill the void with tears.

Later in bed with the dark of night falling all around us, she told me what Janice had said about Eb. There was a prolonged silence after Janice's confession, she said, as though her words were seeking absolution. Then she and Esther resumed eating. When they were finished, they ordered coffee and oatmeal cookies. Esther asked Janice then if she remembered Susan.

Janice laughed. "It all comes back. I shouldn't laugh, but she somehow managed to keep him on a leash. Terry was a lively one. A lot of fun, but a bit unpredictable. He fell hard for Susan. She was a good influence on him. Ross Loewen, the sergeant, had a hard time I think with Terry. He was a good police officer, but tended to follow his own set of laws. Unconventional, I suppose is how you might put it."

"Do you remember when she broke up with him?"

"Yes, that appeared to hit him hard. He didn't talk about it though."

"He seemed to think Jack Butan had something to do with that. He told me Jack had stolen Susan from him."

Janice dipped her cookie into her coffee and took a bite. "I seem to remember hearing that she was seeing someone else shortly after. I know it upset him too. Maybe it was Jack. I had forgotten that."

Esther placed her cup down on her saucer, felt the bones in her wrist. "I need to ask you something."

"What is it?" Janice heard the unease in Esther's voice.

"Would he be the sort to seek revenge, do you think?"

"Terry?"

Esther nodded.

"Revenge on Jack?" Janice's voice now filled with unease.

"I know," Esther said, "it is unfair of me to ask."

"Do you think he had something to do with his disappearance?"

Esther rubbed her forehead. She felt embarrassed. "I don't know what to think. Terry suggested that someone might have killed Jack because he stole their girlfriend. It was just a comment, but it made me wonder if he had been upset with Jack on account of Susan."

"Terry really liked Susan. If he thought Jack had stolen her from him, I am sure he would be upset. He might even have wanted to get back at Jack in some way. But I can't believe for a moment he would kill him."

"But could he be right?" Esther wondered. "Could someone else have been upset enough to do Jack harm?"

"Of course it is possible. But Terry would often jump to conclusions like that."

"Is it any different than reaching the conclusion that Jack had some sort of accident without any proof?"

Janice fidgeted with her spoon. "There is something." Esther waited for Janice to continue, noticed Janice's wedding ring was missing, saw a pale indentation where it used to be. "There was a bit of trouble one time when Terry got too rough with a man he had detained. The man claimed Terry had assaulted him, hit him across the side of the head, and knocked him against the desk to the floor. He suffered a few broken ribs. Terry said it was the man who had tried to attack him and was just protecting himself when the man lost his balance and fell over. Sergeant Loewen convinced the man not to file a complaint, told him it would only make matters worse for him. But I don't think he believed Terry. Occasionally, he'd push some of the other prisoners around." Janice stopped. "I still don't think he would have harmed Jack Butan. Most of those prisoners were drunk. It was his way of keeping them under control. People handle things in different ways. God knows I often wanted to hit Eb when he was drunk. I could have hit him most when he drove his skidoo through the ice. I still feel that way sometimes." She looked at Esther as though waiting for admonishment. "You shouldn't have to hear any of this," she said after a moment.

"It's okay," Esther told her. "I am sure I would feel the same way."

Janice looked at her with something approaching jealousy. "I am sure you wouldn't."

That night, Esther dreamt the dream of Jack. The same dream he had told me about in the bar just after I found out about his relationship with Eloise.

"I had another one." We lay in the drowsiness of waking. Esther's hair tousled across the pillow.

"More bears?"

"It is still winter. I am walking through deep snow across the open tundra. I am alone. Then from out of the distance I see someone approach. I walk towards the person, am driven to by need, the overwhelming sense of loneliness. The figure disappears, and I am all alone again. I search frantically in all directions, and finally I see the figure again. As I grow closer to it, I recognize that it is not a person after all, but a large bear. And although I am fearful, I cannot stop walking towards it." Esther stopped, faltered in her telling of the dream.

"What is it?' I asked.

"The bear was going to kill me, Wade. I knew that, and yet I could not stop myself from walking to meet it."

Esther, my beloved, I am watching every step you take.

Esther pursued Terry Mitchell. She pursued the idea of his involvement as Hearne might have pursued the Coppermine River, the famed Northwest Passage. I could have dispelled the myth, but that would require revealing the truth.

"I expect he was forced out of his position," she said one morning over breakfast. The sun had risen yellow in the sky.

A mist wandered outside the window. The tundra appeared and disappeared before our eyes. "That would explain why he is now a carpenter."

I wiped the yolk of my egg off the plate with a slice of bread. "It's probably like he said, he took early retirement. Made his hobby his business. Lots of people do that." I bit into the yolk stained bread.

Esther shook her head. "Janice was surprised when I mentioned carpentry as though it was not an interest of his."

"That was a long time ago, Esther. What could Janice or any of us know about his life now?"

Esther cut the fat off her bacon. Behind her head, the mist swept past like the tides.

"I remember him," I told her. "He didn't do it."

Esther wiped at her lips with a paper napkin. "Perhaps he didn't. But none of us can say for certain that he didn't. Who knows what a person might do? Very often, it is the people we least expect."

"Is Terry Mitchell the person you least expect?" I was tempting fate now. Sometimes I thought that this was what I needed, for Esther to answer what I could not. To tell me what it was I had really done on that desperate day.

"Hardly, since I do not know him."

"Esther, you are looking in the wrong direction." I took another slice of bread and wiped my plate clean. "Terry came to me after the investigation was closed. Or rather I met him at the bar, and he started talking to me."

Esther listened intently.

"He told me about Susan. He told me about his theory that Jack might have been killed, how someone might have been aggrieved at him."

"Why did you not tell me this?"

"You did not ask."

"Why would I ask? I didn't think you wanted to talk about it. You rarely talk about your time here with Jack or what happened after he disappeared."

And just like that, the unspoken was finally spoken. The clink of my knife and fork as I laid them down on my plate. "You are right. I did not want to talk about these things before."

"You wanted to forget?"

I shook my head. "I will never forget. I did not speak about them before I met you because I had no one to talk to."

"But now you have me. You have had me for years, and you have never said anything. I know so little of your life."

It is like a fall of snow, my life. It falls upon me and covers me entirely, then melts and falls again. When it melts I am laid bare. "Sometimes it seems to me that when we speak about things, the words distort the truth more than memory itself. I have been silent in order to remember."

"So why tell me about Terry now?"

"In your search, Esther, you will never find Jack, you will only find me. You are drawing words from me."

In my silence, I had found a way to live with myself, a way to endure. If Esther were to draw the words from me or if she found a way to speak them in my place, to utter the savagery of my living, could she then live with me? Or I, could I ultimately live with myself?

"Am I making everything worse?" Esther looked close to tears, but it was I who would be the first to weep.

✦

That night I agreed to tell Jack about his baby, Tess told me what I already knew. She was thinking of moving to be with her family. We had made love, and were soothed by our bodies, but my mind reeled.

"Not straight away," she said. "But I feel the time will soon be right."

"You will leave."

Tess curled up in my arm. "I will arrive."

My fingers trailed along her bare shoulder. "What then?"

"Wade, you could leave me in the morning. I have no way of knowing. I have to consider other people. My family came close to leaving me. I can claim them back. They do need me, and I know I need them."

"And me?"

Tess put her arm across my stomach, rested her hand on my chest, the rising pulse of my heart. "My feelings for you are very deep. I do not know where they are leading to yet."

"You know, I love you."

"Would you come with me then?" She looked up from my shoulder.

"And if your feelings lead you in the opposite direction?"

"It would be a chance we would have to take?"

"What would I do there? All I know is the terminal, the ships."

Tess smiled at me. "That is the least of your knowledge. Believe me, there would be no shortage of things for you to do."

Our hushed breathing in an otherwise silent room. Tess in the crook of my arm, her head on my shoulder. *Would you come with me then?* The unanswered question on which that silence hung.

CHAPTER 15

By the second week in May, the ice began to thin. The sun shone brightly down, and a yellow haze shimmered above the frozen cove. Snow Buntings gathered for their journey north. "One hundred and fifty-two centimetres," Esther read. The ice was eighteen centimetres thinner than the week before. She smiled at me. Winter was coming to a close. The ice would give way, and a few weeks later the gooseberry bushes would blossom. Marilyn and Esther would talk of lingonberries, crowberries, dewberries and cloudberries. Insects would cram their entire life cycle into a few months of sunshine. Voraciously hungry for flesh and blood and nectar. Ships, ice-breakers, would break through the ice floes, driving their sloping bows through the ice pack, opening up the shipping lanes. But before that, Jack would have to die. He would have to walk out on the melting tundra and yield up his life.

✦

"How well did you know Tess?"

Surely, we had not been over this ground before. Had we somehow lost our sense of direction, or had Esther missed some sign the first time around?

"We were friends. Sometimes, I think, I barely knew her at all."

"Do you think he could have killed himself on account of her?"

"Jack didn't kill himself."

"It happens."

"Please, Esther."

"I intend to find her."

The white sliver of an Arctic tern, a wan bone knife, the sharp point of a frosted icicle. My heart froze over. Tess may even have reached in and grabbed it.

"Why?" I asked.

"She was close to Jack before he disappeared. Perhaps, she knows something which might help."

"I spoke to her after Jack disappeared. She was as mystified as everyone else."

"All the same," Esther said.

There was more to it than this, I knew. Esther wanted to meet Tess. To meet the only woman that Jack truly loved. A woman he had disappeared for. I wondered if she thought that through Tess she could make Jack reappear. For if there was anyone she wanted to meet more than Tess, it was Jack himself.

"She may not appreciate it," I said as warning. "It may be best to leave well enough alone."

Esther nodded to show she understood this, but I could see she was prepared to take the chance, suffer the consequences. And then that particular day did not so much end as become suspended, and how we made it to the next I do not know.

Esther stopped by Marilyn's a few days later. She took the truck I had driven Tess in on so many occasions. She may even have smelled the lingering aroma of her presence. She would have looked out the window anticipating the open waters moving to and fro, the tide line littered with drying kelp, the lyme grass and sandwort growing in the sand, the Arctic daisies peering from the crevices in the rocks. They would have sat a while in Marilyn's living room discussing Arctic Dryas, miniature orchids, sweet vetch. And Marilyn may have mentioned the common butterwort and how it caught and digested insects on its sticky leaves.

Then Esther would have asked to use Marilyn's phone.

"Who today?" Marilyn might have asked.

"Tess," Esther would have said in a quiet reverential tone, and Marilyn would have nodded knowingly, a willing accomplice.

Esther told me later how easy it all had been. I who could not decide between Esther finding Tess or Tess having disappeared like all before her.

She had gone to the library before calling on Marilyn and got the telephone directory for Tadoule Lake. She looked in it for Tess Cook, but she wasn't listed. There were a lot of numbers for Cook however, and she wrote them all down. At Marilyn's, she called the first one and said she was looking for Tess Cook but wasn't sure if she had the right number. "A young woman told me I didn't," she said, "but she gave me the number I needed. It all took less than a minute."

A minute. Tess disappeared from my life for twenty-five years and in less than a minute she returned. I had been filling the kettle at the sink. I stalled, frozen where I was. Like an ice-breaker unable to push its way through the thick pack ice.

"Are you alright?" Esther leaned against the countertop watching me.

"Heartburn. It will pass in a moment." I tried to regain my composure.

"You look pale. Perhaps you should sit down."

I managed to finish filling the kettle, plugged it in, and walked slowly to the kitchen table. Esther had found Tess. What else was I about to hear? There was nothing in Esther's countenance to give me any indication. Twenty-five years. The life Tess had lived in that time. The other men she had encountered. Would it be too much to hope that she had found no one else? No one to replace Jack. No one to replace me.

"Did you call her?"

"Yes." Esther wiped her palms along the sides of her skirt. "But, at first, she wasn't there."

At first. A build-up of broken ice pushed back hard against the bow.

"I sat with Marilyn a while, an hour or so, and tried again," Esther continued. "This time a young boy answered the phone. I asked for Tess, and he went to get her."

A young boy. In that instant, Tess was a mother. A mature woman walking through her home towards the answered phone. So many times, I could have succumbed to my desires and have done what Esther finally did. I could have sought Tess out. But Tess had gone, and I had not followed. I don't think I could have borne to be rejected yet again. And thus I allowed the days to pass, to fall over themselves one by one until they stacked so high I could scarcely see Tess behind them. And now, she is out in front, and we are all walking towards her.

Tess lifted the phone and said hello.

Tess Cook? Esther asked.

Yes, she replied.

Her voice sounded soft like muskeg, Esther said.

"I told her my name. I told her I was living in Churchill. I told her I was living with you, Wade."

I held onto the sides of the table with my hands. I could easily begin to fall. I heard the water in the kettle boil, a gusting wind. It blew through my kitchen. It blew across the tabletop and swept over my face. It pushed against me hard, and I leaned into it to take its brunt. Esther was speaking, but I could hardly hear.

"Pardon?" I tried to look up at her, to see her face, but the wind caused my eyes to water, so that I could not see Esther at all but instead the tragic face of Tess.

"I told her I knew she had been a friend of yours and Jack Butan's, and I asked her if she would mind if I asked a few questions about Jack."

Why do you need to know anything about Jack Butan? Tess asked in reply.

I would like to know what happened to him, Esther said. I would like for Wade to finally know.

Tess was quiet. It is possible the world had stopped. Who are you? she eventually inquired.

I am Wade's friend, Esther told her. I love him.

Esther walked over and unplugged the kettle, made the tea. The winds blew themselves out. The ice gave way. My fingers were white from the tightness of my grip. Esther was moving somewhere in the kitchen, things were occurring, actions were being carried out. Tess was passing by my door. She was sauntering in and out. The beat of a heart goes unnoticed for the overwhelming majority of a life, but occasionally it springs into being, pulses as though it might burst as if seeking proof of its own existence. Close to Jack's, near the Granary Ponds, Jack and I once found a Lesser Yellowlegs hurt on the rocks. One of its tall thin legs had somehow broken. Jack picked it up and cupped it in his hands. His thumb rested on the bird's small heart. It beat rapidly against the pulse of Jack's own blood. "I feel so helpless," Jack said at that moment, and I have felt that helpless ever since.

Tess told Esther she did not know how to respond to her, and Esther said she understood this perfectly. She said there was another long silence between them, and then Tess spoke again. The moist give of the muskeg beneath the weight of their bodies.

I cannot speak about this over the phone, she said. Although it may not be easy, I think we should meet.

After the winds and after the blizzards, the hushed calm is to be welcomed. After the waves crash heavily onto the shore, the still waters provide respite. After a death, there are other lives to be lived. Tess thought that Esther and she should meet. When no one was looking, I should quietly begin to walk and silently slip away.

Tess suggested meeting in Thompson, a mid-way point of sorts. It avoided either of them having to make so great a journey. Esther agreed, and asked when she could get there. She told Tess, she herself was flexible with her time. Tess said she could make it in three weekends' time. If it went any longer than that, she said, she could not guarantee she would go through with it. Even as it is, she told Esther, I might put down the phone and you might never hear from me again.

It's important, Esther said.

I'll be there, Tess said seeking to assure herself as much as Esther.

✦

I would have to tell Esther the truth about Tess and me. But how could I expect her to understand why I had not told her before now?

Esther, when Tess left me she took everything with her. It was as though she had never been there. All I remember is her absence. Although you could not have known it, you were right that we should build a new house, and I was right to burn the old one. Who would have thought such absence could burn so well?

For days, I pondered how to tell her. I looked out the window at the glare of white, the hoar frost, the rising ground of the tundra. Those days were getting warmer, longer. I took in the chopped up roof of my old house and burnt a hole above me. The ground beneath my feet had already turned to ashes. There were no walls left to contain me.

Esther, I have not been entirely honest.

I rose at dawn, around five o'clock in the morning, and went for walks across the tundra. It was barely minus ten or eleven degrees. I hoped, I think, to find the answer somewhere out there.

Esther, there is something about Tess I have left out.

The creak of the packed ice and frozen vetch as I walked across the snow towards the rising sun. Straight ahead past the dwarf willow and sedge to the yellow ochre of the morning sky. The haze of my exhaled breath.

Esther, I loved her.

The small mounds and hollows. The endless world. I walked for miles. Walking until our house was but a shadow. Something indistinguishable. I was alone. A solitary human being stalking the cold earth in search of anything approaching comprehension. My error it seemed was in discovering another. Man seeks out loneliness not company, I am convinced of this. But we stumble upon another and, recklessly, believe they can provide some element of solution while in truth they add to the conundrum.

Esther, as I stumbled upon you, I stumbled upon another.

Returning from my walk one of those mornings, I heard the sound of distant but approaching vehicles. I felt angry. I was no longer alone. The invisible road now existed. And when I turned to my left, the rocket range which had never been more than a head's turn away would be revealed. The brightening day caused the headlights to pale, but I could see them approaching nevertheless. Three vehicles drove in a convoy. The engines got louder. I walked towards the launch. The sharp crunching of my footsteps. The rocket range grew in front of me. The metal launch rail rose towards the cloudy sky. Two trucks and a car compressing trails of snow and ice pulled up outside the gate. I was still a distance off. Someone got out to unlock the gate and opened it inwards, then got back in the truck and all three vehicles drove through. Shortly the sound of doors opening and closing and a barrage of loud talk made its way back to me. No one came back to shut the gate.

It took another twenty minutes or so through the heavy snow to approach the buildings. I stepped inside the open gate and looked around. It was the closest I had ever got to the launch itself. There was no sign of the people from the vehicles. I assumed they were either in the launch area or in the launch centre across from it. I was trespassing. Here in this land where the great white bear roam free, where seas freeze, and where the earth never thaws. I walked further into this tall metal-fenced enclosure. The buildings looked at best in disrepair and at worst dilapidated, flimsy, makeshift. It was hard to believe that thousands of rockets had propelled themselves upwards and had gotten safely away.

The car and trucks were parked just ahead of me. A massive hill of gravel was covered in snow to my left. I have no idea how far I would have gone if someone had not come out of the launch centre at that moment in time. He stood at the door and lit up a cigarette. It took him a little while to see me. He pulled the cigarette from his mouth and immediately walked in my direction. I continued to walk in his.

"Hey," he called as we approached each other. He waved me off with the hand that held his cigarette. "You can't be here."

I kept walking towards him. Patches of blue sky poured through the clouds behind his head unfazed by the metal fencing.

"This is a restricted area."

We stopped about six feet from each other. I didn't recognize him. He took a drag on his cigarette, blew out smoke.

"Sorry," he said, "I'm going to have to ask you to leave."

I walked right up to him and held out my hand. "My name's Wade Sinclair. I live in the house nearest to the range. I heard your trucks."

He looked at my hand and reluctantly shook it. "The way it is, Mr. Sinclair, the range is off limits at the moment. We're doing some work here."

"I know. You're going to fire a rocket over my home." He wondered how he should take this. "Is it possible I could have a look around? In all my time here, and I have been here over twenty-five years, I have never seen the inside of this place. I have lived beside it. I have seen rockets blast from it. I have got up as far as its gates but no further."

"I'm sure someone could arrange to take you around sometime," he said. "But that really wouldn't be up to me. I'm just contracted in to do some work. It's going to be a busy day." He took a few more drags on his cigarette then threw it into the snow and stubbed it out with the toe of his boot. "I'll walk with you to the gate. It really ought to have been locked."

I looked at the tall corrugated fence surrounding us. It looked like a prison except the prisoners were on the outside free to roam as far as they were physically able. The remainder, those who weren't prisoners, were confined in here sending rockets into a space they would never enter.

"Where are you from?" I asked as we walked back.

"Guelph, Ontario."

"What do you do?"

"Check the equipment, make sure it is still safe to use."

We were almost to the gate. "And is it?"

"I've got a lot more testing to do, but we're pretty hopeful it is."

The cold air was drawn into our bodies and then released.

"Do you know when the launch is planned for?"

"Well, I should think your house is safe for a while yet." He smiled and led me through the gate. "Strange place you've chosen to live in," he said as he pulled the gate over.

"No stranger than anywhere else when you get to know it."

"If you say so." He closed the gate, locked it behind him.

I was on the outside now, back where I belonged.

Esther was baking bread in the kitchen when I got back. I kicked the snow off my boots and left them just inside the door. I pulled off my jacket and gloves. She was at the table kneading the dough. Her hands coated in flour. Specks of flour dotted her hair as though she had been out in the snow. I sat at the table and told her about being over at the rocket range.

"You probably should not have gone in." She wiped her forehead with her arm.

"I'd like to go back."

Esther rolled out the dough, put it on a baking tray, and placed it in the oven. She wiped the table down and washed her hands at the sink. "I am looking forward to the rocket. I have never seen anything like that in my life before." She cleaned her hands in the towel.

"Very few people ever have."

Esther laughed. "We're the chosen few." She wiped flour stains from her skirt, came up behind me and put her arms around me. "Were you in love with her?" She must have felt the heave of my stomach and chest. My hands rested on the table in front of me. They looked strangely old.

"Yes, I was."

Esther brought her face to mine. Her hair brushed against my cheek. "You should have told me. I would have understood. You are entitled to have loved. So many of us have loved so little."

"Is that why you want to meet her?"

"It is not only that."

"Perhaps you shouldn't."

"She still might have something she can tell us about Jack. Something she could never have told you." Her face turned slightly that our lips were almost touching. Her words were leaving her mouth and entering mine. Our breaths were shared. "Did Jack steal her from you?"

"Did I kill him?"

Esther pulled back. "Oh Wade." She started to cry. She shook her head swiftly. "I never asked you that." Tears fell down her cheeks. She started to back out of the room. "I can't believe you think I would."

She walked through the door and up the stairs to our bedroom.

"Don't follow me," she might have called over her shoulder.

Esther stayed in our room all morning. I took the bread from the oven when it was ready. I felt her arms around me still, her hands on my stomach, her breath escaping into mine.

But Esther I did. I killed Jack. As God is my witness.

I heard a sharp crying from overhead. The noise grew louder. I walked to the window. A thin line of geese flew beneath the dark clouds of the hemmed in sky. I heard the floor creak above. Esther had heard them too and was watching from our window. It was the sign she had been waiting for. Winter was coming to an end.

I cut us both a slice of Esther's warm bread and buttered it generously then carried it upstairs on a plate. I knocked on my own bedroom door and entered. Esther stood by the window. The geese were visible off to the north. She leaned against the sill, did not turn around.

"You heard them," I said. "Year after year, they never give up on us." I brought the plate with the bread to her. "Don't give up on me, Esther. It is you I love now."

A tear escaped her eye. The geese were no longer in sight, but they were not gone. We sat on the bed and ate the bread she had baked. The soft white duvet on the bed beneath us. The gleaming wooden floor. The clear panes of glass and everything else beyond.

"I know you would never have harmed him."

"I know you would never think that way."

Esther wiped a crumb from her upper lip. "There are times, despite our ages, I wish we had tried for a baby. Perhaps, I should not have ruled it out."

"We have done nothing wrong," I assured her. "We are doing the best we are able. This process of living is not an easy task."

"We are dying, Wade. You said it yourself, you are getting old."

"Well then Esther, there is nothing wrong in the way we are going about our deaths. We have to believe in that."

Esther placed the plate on the bedside table and stretched herself out on the bed. "If Jack had not taken her from you, what then?"

"I did not say he had."

"Did he?"

"Maybe Tess can answer that. What I thought was occurring might never have occurred at all."

Her body sunk in the duvet. It gathered up around her as though she could disappear within it. I lowered myself upon her, my body reaching into hers. I tried to speak.

"Shh!"

Her mouth hungry for mine. Her face cradled in my hands. Her arms around me. She lowered her hands along my back, and I cupped the soft flesh of her shoulders. We were carried along on the waves.

Oh, Tess, I might have murmured.

And she, unable to prevent her release, may have murmured back, Oh, Jack.

Then the tides washed in, and everything, but everything, was swept away.

CHAPTER 16

It was bright by four in the morning. During the day the temperatures rose above zero. The ice thickness measured at 120 cm. Esther kept track of the geese. The stove did not need to burn so often. With no concern on our part, the wood was getting low. The ponds would soon open for waterfowl. The migrants would return. The Purple Saxifrage was on the verge of blooming. Esther would board the train and take it to Tess. And Tess would take a dog team across the barrens and meet with her, trade.

Since the knowledge of my relationship with Tess had come into the open, something had changed between Esther and me. We seemed closer than ever, and I hoped it was for the better. It was like trekking for days through the bush to finally break through the tree line and emerge into bare land. I hoped in our arduous journey we had not stumbled upon desolation.

Unlike her quest for Jack, she did not want me to tell her anything about Tess. "Let me discover her for myself," she simply said.

She did ask about a photograph one evening. The gate was down on the pickup and we were both sitting on the back. We had no need for gloves or hats. Our jackets were open. "Just so that I might recognize her when we meet."

"There are no photographs. We never thought to take any."
Tess was engrained within me as I wished I was engrained within her too.

The sky was pale grey with streaks of darkness, but the evening was bright. The unseen sun would not descend until ten thirty. There were large depressions in the mounds of gathered snow where melting had already begun. Hard frozen beads on the thin branches of willow.

"Do you miss her?"

The world revolved, and I felt it. The sun did not descend, we rose, turned away from it. I have never wanted to lie to Esther. I have tried to answer her questions as fairly as I could. Yes, I had lied about my relationship with Tess, whether to protect her or me or both of us I am unsure. But in everything else I have attempted to tell her what she has asked. Did I miss Tess?

"Yes."

Esther must have felt the shifting world too. She must have felt its spin, and her inability to make it stand still. She must have felt the ice melting beneath her feet. I turned from the pale grey sky to Esther's pale grey face, her streaks of darkness too.

"I am sorry," I said.

"No," her lips parted, her brow slightly furrowed. "I would be saddened if you had not."

"It was a very long time ago. It in no way alters my love for you."

"Perhaps it shaped it." Her hands gripped the edge of the truck, the creases in her fingers, the ridges of vein.

"Maybe you shouldn't go."

"It is too late now." She leaned forward, looked to the ground her feet did not touch. "I would always be wondering."

The waters wash in off the bay and everything is altered. The rocks, the pebbles, the grains of sand. Nothing remains unchanged. Tess would wash against Esther in the same way. The tides carried the whale in but were unable to carry it back out. The sheer weight of its body caused its own death. The waters as much a part of the whale as its inner organs. When Tess and I climbed inside the whale, I know now that we were seeking shelter, that we never do anything else.

We sat there, side by side, on the back of my old pickup, its rusted exterior, a small crack in the rear window, the house we had built behind us, the rest of the world in front, flat and white, stifling growth. Both of us holding on.

I brought Esther to the train station. We stopped on the way to measure the ice. It had melted fast since she and Tess had arranged their meeting. It was only 64 cm thick. I couldn't remember when it had been this thin this early.

"It won't hold us up much longer," I warned.

We drove on to the station, parked and went inside. Esther carried a small ancient suitcase. She stood in line at the ticket office, placed her case on the floor.

"Remember when you met me here the morning I arrived to stay?"

"This will be the first time we have been apart since then. It feels as though you are leaving me."

Esther took my arm, kissed my cheek. "You know I'm not."

It was Saturday. Esther would return on Tuesday morning. She had booked into a B&B and was being picked up at the station by the owners. The next morning she would meet Tess. They arranged to meet at the small zoo just out of town. "It was either that or the Nickel mine," Esther said, "deep beneath the surface of the earth." I could think of no better place to have chosen.

Esther bought her ticket. The train was already on the platform. "Don't wait with me. I am not good at departures." She lowered her forehead, and I kissed her upon it. She smiled and boarded the train. She waved from the window and then was gone from sight.

I drove straight to Bird Cove. *The Ithaca* rigid in the ice seemed to be observing me. A white Willow Ptarmigan pecked amongst the rocks. Tess's cold hand here the first time I met her. What had happened in between? Esther, now, somewhere out on the tundra headed towards her. Me alone once more.

✦

Esther got a taxi to the zoo. She arrived at five minutes to twelve and waited. When the next taxi pulled up, she already knew who it was.

"Tess?" Esther held out her hand, and Tess shook it.

I wondered if it felt cold to the touch, if it chilled them both to the bone.

They paid their entrance fee and went in. Lynx, polar bear, Arctic fox, snowy owl, grey wolf, seal. All caged in. Tess, Dene Woman. And Esther, White Explorer.

They ordered coffee in the small café.

"I don't know what I am doing here," Tess said.

"Nor I," Esther agreed.

For a while they sat in silence, then Tess spoke again.

"How is Wade?"

"He's good."

"Is he still working at the terminal?"

Their coffee arrived.

Esther told her I was, and Tess smiled. She took a drink of her coffee.

"What do you know about me?"

"I know Wade loved you but little else."

"And now he has found another love."

Esther nodded. "Yes, we are very happy."

There was another awkward silence. They drank coffee. A young woman and her daughter came in, sat down at an empty table.

Tess, once more, was the first to speak.

"What do you want to know about Jack?"

"I want to know what happened to him."

"Why?"

Esther could not even explain it to herself. "It feels important to me, important for Wade, important for Wade and me."

"Has Wade talked much about him?"

"Not at all. I only discovered about his disappearance by accident. It was then I talked to Wade about him, but he would tell me little. That's when I decided to try and find out what occurred. I think if Wade discovers what really happened, it might help him to get over it."

"I don't know what I can tell you," Tess said. "Wade already knows everything I do."

"But he's not telling me." Esther was almost pleading.

Tess looked at Esther, took all of her in. Her brown hair, her solid face, her firm strong body. "It is not easy to talk about," she said. "I have never mentioned it to anyone since I left Churchill. I moved to Tadoule Lake to be with my family, but I have never told any of them about Jack." She looked at Esther's hands resting on the table. Long and thin. Hands you would long to hold.

"Did you know Wade came with me to Tadoule Lake shortly before I made my decision to move there?"

Esther told her she didn't.

"I was afraid to go on my own. My parents had distanced me when I chose to go to college in Winnipeg instead of following them to Tadoule Lake. They had moved there from Churchill. After college, I returned to Churchill. I didn't have the courage to face them. It is strange, but it was Wade, I believe, who gave me the courage in the end. The time we spent together made me feel more secure in myself. I still, to this day, don't know if I loved Wade or not, but he loved me, and I hadn't felt loved for such a long time. I decided to confront my parents and like Wade, I offered up my love uncertain if it would be returned or not. When I decided to go back after Jack's death, after Wade and I were no longer together, nobody mentioned him although he had been there with me before. Not even my brother who Wade and I stayed with. They never asked anything about my life without them. It was the compromise I suppose. I would return to them as though I had never left. As though Wade, and Jack, did not and never had existed. When you rang, it was the first time I had heard Jack's name in over twenty years."

"Is that why you're here?"

"It could be. Maybe, it's to do with Wade too. Maybe, I just need to hear that he is doing fine." Tess paused, looked into the past. "Wade thought that something happened between Jack and me. He really seemed to believe it. He resented me for it, and he resented Jack. And I resented him for thinking such a thing. We were young. We hadn't lived enough to know how to deal with our feelings."

"Do we ever live long enough for that?" Esther asked her.

"Eventually, I think we do. Do you know about Eloise?"

Esther nodded. "Jack's baby."

"Yes. I felt sorry for Jack. Just as I was uncertain about my feelings for Wade, he was uncertain about his for Eloise. I thought he should know about the baby, but Eloise had made me promise not to tell. I wanted Wade to tell him. We argued over that. It was silly really. I felt he was letting me down, letting Jack down too. It was more than that of course. What I was really angry about was that he wouldn't move with me to Tadoule Lake. By that time, I had made my mind up to go back to my family. I can't say now I blame Wade for not wanting to make that move. Even then, I knew it was a lot to ask. Nevertheless, I was upset about it. After we argued, I decided I would go to Jack and tell him myself even if it meant going back on my word to Eloise. I went to Jack to help him, but instead it was Jack who helped me. When I got to his apartment I started crying. I didn't tell him what our argument was about, I couldn't. He said it would blow over. Wade loves you, he said. He'll come looking for you. I should, of course, have gone to Wade, but I thought it was up to him to come to me first. When he still hadn't called after a few days, I was even more upset. I called in sick to work and went to see Jack again. I was in a terrible state. A while later, Wade arrived at the door. Jack went down to talk to him. He didn't say anything about me being there, but Wade knew. He got the wrong idea I think. We didn't see each other after that until Jack went missing. By that time, things had gone too far." Tess stopped. Esther saw tears in her eyes. She offered her a tissue. Tess wiped her eyes. "I left him. That's what happened no matter how I dress it up."

"Do you have regrets?"

Tess squeezed the damp tissue tightly in her hand. "What am I supposed to say?"

"If you still have regrets about leaving Wade."

Tess looked resigned to her response. "I made the biggest mistake of my life in leaving him. I have never met anyone who comes within his range."

Esther regretted having asked her. She had heard, perhaps, what she wanted to hear, nevertheless she knew she should not have put Tess into this position. She could not imagine anything sadder than that which Tess had just spoken.

It is not too late, she desperately wanted to reply but was unable to.

"You are a fortunate woman," Tess told Esther. "Don't ever make the mistake I did." Esther at a loss for words. Tess filling her silence. "Jack may have thought he loved me too."

"Wade seems to think so."

"Wade also thought I returned this love to Jack, but he was mistaken." Tess rolled the tissue in her fist. "I think Jack may even have given up Eloise on account of his feelings for me. I really only got to know him after I called on him the time of my argument with Wade. We became close in that short time. He saw how much Wade meant to me, and he realized that he and I would be friends and nothing more. Despite this, he helped me through that tough time, and he was determined that Wade and I would get back together. That day he went missing, he had planned to call on Wade, to try and sort things out."

"But he didn't go to Wade?"

"In the end, I think it was too much for him." She released the tissue from her grip and looked to Esther. "In the end, I killed him."

Esther looked at Tess aghast.

"If I had not gone to him, Jack could have loved me from a distance. He could have believed that anything was possible. Instead I went to him, and Jack knew the futility of his feelings. I don't think Jack had an accident. I think he took his own life, and it was my fault that he did."

Esther regained her composure and told Tess that she should not think this way, that Jack seemed stronger in spirit than that.

"You didn't even know him," Tess reminded her. "You can have no idea what he was like."

"I am sorry," she said. "You are right."

Tess reached across and took Esther's hand. "I didn't mean to sound angry."

Esther felt her touch. Tess's flesh on hers. She felt a strange surge of comfort. She looked into Tess's eyes, thought she saw Jack pass through them.

"I never told him about the baby in the end."

"Why?"

Tess took her hand away. Esther felt at a loss. "In the beginning, I was too upset about Wade, and then I was concerned about Jack's feelings for me. I thought they would prove a distraction. I decided to wait until he was reconciled to my feelings too. I had intended to tell him that same day after he had returned from seeing Wade. That baby could have saved him."

It was Esther now who reached for Tess, who offered Tess her hand, and at that exact moment the grey wolf must surely have howled in his cage and the great snowy owl spread its enormous wings. A plate of ice on some lake must have cracked and shattered, and a body buried in the deep rise and fall.

Esther and Tess took a taxi back to the small hotel Tess was staying at. On the way there, Tess told her that although she had been wary of meeting her initially she was glad now that she had. Esther said she felt the same.

"I am so happy Wade has met someone like you. I let him down badly."

"You can't blame yourself for that," Esther told her. "You did what you thought was best. Is that not the most we are capable of?"

"I met someone else about ten years ago. I thought maybe things could work out for us. Before that, I measured everyone against Wade, and they did not come near. My mother scolded me, told me I was too fussy. "For someone who has gone to college," she said, "you seem to have no idea of how this world works. You should have moved here with us from the start. You would be married now, have children. I would be a grandmother many times over." She was so happy when I met William. He was Dene, a hunting and fishing guide. He flew a sea plane. I had never liked flying, and he helped me overcome that fear. He would take me up in the plane when I first met him. "You have no reason to be afraid," he would tell me, "there is nowhere I cannot land this. The land is so flat. There are no trees, nothing to hit." I grew to love that plane. I loved looking down on our small community from on high, seeing its place in the world. When you are on the ground, living your daily life, the houses, the stores, the school, all the buildings and the people around them seem to comprise your world. Then you fly up in the air and the true importance of events and circumstances become apparent. I often wish I could have flown high above Wade and I, high above Jack, high above Eloise. I wish we all could have, have looked down upon ourselves and seen us for what we truly were. William would take me up at night. Flying amongst the stars, the bright holes of light in the surrounding blackness. The roar of the engine reminding you that you were only up there by the grace of some all-forgiving god. Some nights, that was all there was, the blackness and the pricks of light. Other times, the moon would cast its light below as we glided across the frozen lake, the flat icy ground. Returning eventually to the few lights of the town like stars that had somehow got misplaced, a small portion of the heavens that had fallen to earth and we had claimed as our own. I loved that plane more than William unfortunately. We were together six years. We had a boy. He is six years old now."

Esther sat next to her in the back of the taxi and listened gratefully to her tale. "Is that the boy who answered the phone?"

"Yes." Tess spoke absently. She was still up there in the air, far away from where they sat. Perhaps, Esther thought, she was looking down on herself and Esther trying to understand what was really occurring.

"What's his name?"

Tess flew low above the tops of the trees in this boreal land, glimpsing the silver glint of lakes and rivers below, the dull grey of the granite rock loping amongst the forest, and then the large open section stripped of trees, the rivers of soft concrete pouring into the land, the metal rebars sprouting from the ground like young shoots, the rising hills of wood frame and sidings. She flew over the tops of roofs, down towards the hotel.

"Jack."

She brought him back to life. Tess, his Tess. She did not search out his body and resuscitate it. She gave birth to him anew. She gave him a second chance.

The taxi pulled up at the hotel. It was late afternoon. Tess was to return home the following day. "We have much to talk about yet," she told Esther. "There is a bar across from here. They have music playing later. I don't normally drink, but we could go there for something to eat, dance a while, if you like. I am in need of entertainment."

And Esther who could take or leave bars too could think of no more suitable way to take her leave from Tess. She said she would go back to her bed and breakfast first to freshen up. Tess said it was hardly worth her while and offered the use of her room instead, and Esther gratefully accepted.

The room was comfortable and spacious. An ensuite bathroom, a large double bed, a dressing table, bedside locker, television, built-in closet, a small circular table and two soft chairs. Tess took their jackets and hung them in the closet. She sat on the edge of the bed and took off her boots. Esther wandered to the window. It looked out onto the car park, a small mall opposite.

"This is the first time I have left Churchill since moving there."

Tess placed her boots in the bottom of the closet. "I have not been outside of Tadoule Lake either."

Esther turned around in amazement. "How long has that been?"

"Over twenty years."

"Why is that?"

"I had no reason to leave before now." She closed the closet door. "How long have you been in Churchill?"

"Seven years."

"It becomes ten and soon after twenty." Tess sat back on the bed. "We are more similar than I might have thought."

Esther sat on one of the chairs by the table, loosened her boots and pushed them off, gazed into the space between Tess and her, Tess lay out on the bed and stared at the ceiling.

"When Wade opened the door, his heart must have lifted. He must have thought I had returned. And then when he registered what he was seeing his heart must have sunk again never to come back up. I asked if Jack had been there, and he said no. I told him he was missing. Did you have a row? he asked. I told him that Jack and I were merely supporting each other in a time of need. All I wanted was for Wade to help me find Jack, but instead Wade thought he heard me asking him to bring Jack and me back together. And as he died inside, he said yes."

Through her tears and through the ever decreasing distance between them Esther felt Tess's sadness. The tides of her tears ebbed and flowed, and Esther floated upon them, drifted across to Tess, washed up beside her and, once again, clasped her cold hand for comfort.

"We looked for him everywhere. Throughout the town, the trails, the beaches, the land and the frozen water. But Jack whose presence had never been felt more forcefully was not to be found. I departed from Wade, and we never spoke again."

Esther and Tess felt the pulse of each other's blood in the palms of their hands and listened to the perfect rhythm of their breathing. Sleep fell so gently it came and went unnoticed.

Esther heard the shower running. The bed beneath her seemed to be carrying her somewhere undetermined. She felt as though she really were floating in a building without foundations. The flow of water stopped abruptly. Esther heard Tess step from the shower. She felt the cold tiles on the soles of her own feet, the drops of water on her skin, the heavy weight of the bathrobe falling upon her shoulders and wrapping around her waist, the hasty rub of the towel through her hair. The bathroom door opened and Tess came out. She rubbed at her wet hair, smiled over at Esther.

"I am all the better for that," she said.

"What time is it?" Esther asked.

"It's almost seven."

Esther rose and asked if it would be okay to shower also.

"Of course," Tess replied. "There are plenty of fresh towels inside."

Esther closed the bathroom door after her and undressed. She looked at herself in the mirror. One year did indeed beget the next. She would step into the shower, and the water would fall. So why did everything seem so uncertain? Why when she looked in the mirror did she expect to see Tess's face there?

Tess and Esther entered the bar together. They couldn't ever remember seeing a bar so large.

"It's like a warehouse," Tess laughed, "where drunks are stored."

They found an empty table and sat down. Loud country music played on the jukebox. Pitchers, glasses and bottles banged down on the tabletops. VLTs sang out annoyingly. Across from them, a long shiny counter ran half the length of the room. Deer and moose heads hung on the wall. Antlers, trophy fish, steel traps, snowshoes, hockey pennants. Posters of scantily clad women advertising beer. In the corner, a large flashing square that served as a dance floor and behind it the stage, the speakers and amplifiers.

The bar was filled with what Esther assumed were the miners and their wives and girlfriends. A whole world of plaid shirts and jeans, long hair and beards. The women in shirts and jeans too, bleached blond hair, heavy make-up. A large girl, eighteen or so, came to ask what they wanted to drink and if they needed to see a menu. Tess asked what beers they had. The girl listed them out and told them what was on special. They ordered the special asked for the food menu.

Tess looked down through it after the girl was gone. "There's nothing healthy on it whatsoever," she warned Esther.

"We didn't come here for our health," Esther replied.

In the end, they decided to share a pizza. The girl came back with their drinks and took their order.

Tess raised her glass to Esther. "To Wade."

Esther tipped her glass in response, "And Jack."

At that point in time, Tess must have seen the pool table at the back of the bar. She must have seen the dark wavy hair on the pool player, and, for one brief moment, she must have believed that it was him.

As they drank from their beer and waited on their food, Esther told Tess the details of her first trip to Churchill to see the birds and wildflowers and how she had met me. She spoke of the letters we had written to each other, and the chance we had taken on each other. Tess seemed riveted by her story. Their food arrived. They ordered another drink, and then they talked again. They talked as though their lives depended on it. Esther told Tess how she filled in her time walking, watching birds, drying flowers, reading. She told her of the house we had built together, the logs we had brought in by train. And Tess told Esther about her job teaching in Tadoule Lake, about her son Jack, how she had split up with William after she learned he had other women in some of the places he flew hunters and fishermen to. A cook at one of the lodges, and somewhere else a sister of a guide he sometimes worked with. She told Esther about her sister who had committed suicide, her brother Peter and his drinking, and her other brother who was a recovering drug addict. She had finally managed to get him into rehab, she said. He had his ups and downs, but eventually he managed to go clean. He has been clean for five years now, but it is a struggle every day.

While they were talking, the band came in and set up their equipment. Two men came over to Tess and Esther's table and asked if they could join them. Tess told the men they were expecting company. One of the men asked if the company they were expecting was them, and Tess replied, unfortunately not. The men stayed talking for a few more minutes then left. Tess and Esther laughed together after they had gone.

"Should we be ashamed of ourselves?" Esther asked filling up their glasses.

"I'm a single woman," Tess said. "You're the shameful one."

Esther felt the drink going to her head, but she was enjoying herself. Tess too felt light-headed. She looked at Esther, saw what I, Wade, would see in her. She smiled to herself.

The band had been playing for a while before Tess suggested they dance. Esther stood up uneasily on her feet. They walked past the tables to the dance floor at the back of the room and stepped onto the bright flashing lights to join the other dancers.

"I think I have forgotten how to dance," Esther shouted to Tess above the loud music.

"Me too," Tess shouted back. "It has been a long time."

How long, I wonder, Tess? Since that night you danced with Jack, when Eloise and I watched you both and knew we had lost you. Oh yes, Tess, Eloise knew it too. Is he going to leave me? she asked. And although she told me that she wished Jack and she could be more like me and you, although she told me how much I meant to you, she too knew what was about to occur, was already occurring before our eyes.

Esther would try to recall later what occurred before her own eyes. She remembered dancing. She remembered looking to the beams on the roof and seeing a deer watching Tess and her. One of the traps on the wall may have sprung. The music slowed down. The people danced around her. Tess moved lazily in front, the sway of her long dark hair, the lights that reflected off her gleaming white teeth. Esther's feet felt heavy as though she were wearing snowshoes, trudging through deep snow, a low blowing wind. Her eyes lost focus. Falling snow interrupted her vision. Tess somewhere in the blizzard ahead. Esther lifted her feet clumsily unsure now if she was moving towards Tess or if Tess was moving towards her. Edging forwards blindly, aware of the dangers but unable to stop, until out of the haze of snow they stood face to face in front of one another, not Tess but Jack. And as the winds swept past, and the moist flakes settled upon the lids of their eyes, Esther had no way of knowing if what was happening actually occurred, if their lips really pressed together, if what she felt was real.

CHAPTER 17

Tess and I fought. We argued over my silence. My refusal to tell Jack what I had said I would.

"I can't tell him," I tried to explain. We walked down to the port. The large grain ship was frozen in yet, but the snow and ice would start to melt. The ships would come and go again. "He seems so content."

"Content?" Tess walked ahead of me. The huge terminal behind, the wide open bay in front. Hoar frost covered the twigs and needles of small willow and spruce alongside us on the shore. A vee of geese angled through the white sky. I had not answered Tess's question yet, whether I would go with her to Tadoule Lake or not. I had not mentioned it since. I wanted to be with Tess, but I was unsure how much further I was prepared to move into this remote land. How much, therefore, could I claim to love her after all?

"Look," I said, "the geese are back."

"But Eloise is not."

"If I tell him, what then?" I caught up with her, put my hand on her shoulder. She stopped walking. "Eloise may refuse to see him, even talk to him. It could make matters worse."

"You told me you would tell him. You said he ought to know."

"I still think he ought to know, but it has got to come from Eloise."

Tess was disappointed, angry. "We discussed this already. She won't tell him."

"Why is it so important to you? Why do you care so much whether Jack knows or not?"

"Because he's your friend."

"Precisely, he's my friend. You barely know him."

Tess pulled away so that my hand fell from her shoulder. "He deserves a better friend than you." She turned around briskly and walked back towards the terminal.

I started to walk after her, but Tess looked over her shoulder. "Don't follow me."

I stopped and watched her walk away.

You cannot believe how quickly the ice can disappear, how a large bay can be filled one day and practically emptied the next. How quickly something so vast can disappear from your life. Tess walked past the door of the grain terminal, the door I would enter and leave. She walked back towards the town. The geese cried. The ice groaned. I stood where I had stopped as though motion was not an option. The tracks of her footsteps in the snow. I could have followed them all the way to Jack's door. I could have followed them into his small apartment, all the way into his living room, all the way into his arms.

I do not know what happened after she left. I can only imagine. Tess angry not just with me, but with Eloise, with her brother Peter, her lost brother, her dead sister, her parents, her family, her people, angry with her whole life. Pressing hard on the doorbell determined to tell him the truth. But instead when he answers she starts to cry, to sob intensely. Jack brings her upstairs to his apartment, seeks to comfort her, to find out what is wrong. She stands in his living room convulsing and Jack puts his arms around her, holds her close and quietly says, Shh. His face is next to hers, and he strokes her hair. They stand together like that for a length of immeasurable time. Tess crying, Jack stroking. Then Tess, her sobbing having ceased, raises her head a little. Jack wipes her tears from her cheeks with the front of his bent forefinger, and they look at each other in a way that neither has seen before. The brushing together of their lips is but a moment away.

That night, I hardly slept. My mind wandered as though it were lost. It stumbled along paths shin-deep in snow. It raced through dark alleys, and paced empty streets. It left all reason behind. The crumpled sheets and flattened pillows Tess had once lain on. I searched her out until morning but found no trace of the woman I had known.

She did not call that day nor the next. I should have told Jack about Eloise. I had given her my word. I drove into town the next morning. Tess would already be at the school. I determined to call on Jack and tell him. I would meet Tess during her lunch. I would apologize and explain that Jack now knew. It might not be enough to rescue whatever had slipped away, but at least I could try.

The morning was dull. The windscreen frosted easily. I directed the heat towards it. My feet were cold. A few pick-ups, a handful of people out on the streets well wrapped up. I slowed to allow a drunken man to cross. I drove past the school. Tess would be teaching. I drove down Selkirk Avenue and along Kelsey Boulevard out towards the Granary Ponds. Morning was usually a good time to get Jack. To my left, the port, the bay, where Tess and I had been, where she had walked out on me. I turned off for Jack's apartment, parked in front and rang the bell. A cold wind blew in from the bay. I turned away from it. I heard footsteps on the stairs inside. The door opened. Jack seemed surprised to see me there.

"Wade." He stood at the entrance, the open door behind him.

"It's cold out. Can I come in?"

He scratched his head, lowered his voice. "It's probably not the best time."

"I see." I stood back. "You have company."

"That's it." He shivered. "You're right it is cold. Do you want to call back later?"

"Okay." I was about to say goodbye, about to turn away when the full import of his words descended upon me. "Is it Tess?"

Jack stood there unsure what to say, telling me all I needed to know. "She was upset," he finally said. "That's all."

I sighed, looked to the ground. I didn't know what to do in fact, or what to say.

"It would be best if you came back later."

At times, a flake of snow appears to fall from out of nowhere. Flutters from the heavens. It is possible you might not even notice it. But there and then, I saw one fall. I saw it drift past my nose, land on the tip of my boot. I do not remember leaving, but, for certain, I was gone.

The steel tracks cut through the tundra, sliced through the ice and snow. The weight of the passing train pressed down as the weight of the passing glaciers once did. The rocks, sedges, dwarf willow fleeting past in the dawn light. Esther had awoken. She had felt a hand on her shoulder shaking her, but when she opened her eyes there was no one there. The seat opposite her was empty. She felt an ache in her neck. In the rows of seats behind her, people were sprawled out in a heavy stupor.

She remembered her dreams. Jack and Tess crashing through the disintegrating ice. Esther cornered on a beach by an approaching white bear. Jack and I running breathlessly through blinding snow. Specks of glimmering snow flew past the window of the train. Strips of dark cloud lay low in the sky. Esther allowed her eyes to close over once more.

She had asked Tess about Terry Mitchell, if she remembered him at all. And Tess had confessed she had once accompanied him to a community social. He was all hands, she said. The long and short arm of the law. She could not remember Susan, too many comings and goings. She hadn't known anything about Terry and her or Jack's involvement. Why do you ask? she wondered.

Esther told her how she had spoken to Terry, and how he was not completely satisfied with the official conclusion. She asked Tess then if it was okay to talk about the day of Jack's disappearance.

"I have not been back to that day for many years," Tess told her. "I have stayed away as you might stay away from someone you hate or someone you love too much."

But she told Esther that since their meeting she had already made the journey back. "It was a Saturday," Tess said. "I called in on Jack for coffee. I was lonely. Eloise was gone, and Wade was gone. I called too early. Jack was still in bed. He got up to let me in. I remember he told me I was a sight to behold. With his hair askew and his sweater hastily pulled on over his pyjama top, I told him he was a sight to behold too. We laughed, and it made me feel a little better. "Wade has still not contacted me," I said. That was when he shook his head, berated us. He said he'd have to call on Wade and put an end

269

to this nonsense. I asked him not to, argued that it was up to Wade and I. He just rolled his eyes, said if it was up to Wade and I, we'd be waiting a long time indeed. I stayed with him until lunchtime. We had something light to eat, then I got up to go. I had school work to prepare, and Jack said he needed to get cigarettes. "Drop by later," he said, "when your work's done. We'll have supper together." I promised I would. "I'll be waiting," he replied. I walked with him uptown. We said goodbye, and I went home.

I worked on my lessons all afternoon then rested up a while. I was still feeling lonely and sad, but in truth it pleased me to be meeting Jack for supper. Talking with him seemed to cheer me up, make the circumstances more palatable. It was about seven by the time I got there. I rang his doorbell, but he didn't answer. I sat on the step and waited for over an hour, but there was no sign of him, so I went home. At first, I was angry thinking he had let me down just as it felt to me Wade had let me down, but I realized later that we really hadn't planned any particular time. Jack might easily have gone out again and have returned after I left. So the next morning I called over again, but there was still no reply. I assumed he had met up with somebody the day before and forgot all about our plan. He may even have called on Wade, as he had said he might, and have stayed the night with him. It would not be the first time. I knew that Jack had forgotten a previous arrangement with Eloise. I tried again later that evening and the following morning before going to work. By now, I was beside myself with worry. That evening after school he was still not back. I decided to call on Wade." Tess started crying again. "Wade had not seen him of course. None of us ever did again."

Esther's tears were just as real. Jack walked into Esther's life in the way he walked out of ours. He had stepped right up to her on the dance floor with Tess had he not, and leaned in and placed a kiss on her lips as he had once placed a kiss on Tess's?

On the train back, Esther looked at the empty seat opposite her. She saw Jack sitting there. He smiled at her, ran his fingers through his hair. Then he glanced out the window and looked towards the rising sun. Esther smiled. She was bringing him home. She would swear he stepped down off the train at Churchill station. He strolled unnoticed through the groups of birders arriving for the early season. The last she saw of him, he entered the building, and then he was gone.

✦

I met Esther early Tuesday morning. She stepped off the train. I went to greet her and took her suitcase from her. She did not look different. But my kiss had been washed from her forehead, that much I knew. She put her arms around me, and we embraced.

I drove her home, and Esther went to bed. While she slept, I tidied the kitchen and swept the floors. I prepared a light lunch for when she awoke. Then I waited until Esther dreamed herself awake.

She came down the staircase in her dressing gown, her hair straggly from her lying down. We went into the kitchen for the food I had prepared. Esther sat down.

"It is good to be home," she said.

"It is good to have you home."

I had been at a loss without her. Had I roused myself from Bird Cove in all that time? If I had I did not remember. I remember the bay thawing and freezing over again. I remember *The Ithaca* sailing away and returning. And I remember dying and somehow coming back to life.

"How was your trip?"

Esther chewed before replying. "I am glad I made it."

We finished our food in silence. Esther thanked me for it. "I am unsure how we should talk about this," she said.

"Perhaps we should walk?" I suggested.

"We could go to bed."

Upstairs, Esther pulled the curtain. She closed the door. We undressed in the darkened room, climbed beneath the covers. We lay side by side on our backs.

"I have missed you."

"I have not lived since you left."

"But I did come back."

"Yes, you did."

"Pretend something," she said. We remained unmoving, stared upwards at the ceiling. "Pretend I never went."

"You were here all the time."

Esther reached across and took my hand, held it beneath the bedclothes. I felt her fingers, her soft palm, not warm as usual but strangely cold. "There are structures," I told her, "built during the fur-trading years that did not have foundations, that rode the permafrost."

"What are you saying?"

"I am saying those buildings could move around, drift across the frozen earth."

"Be here one moment and gone the next?"

"You could go to sleep next to the frozen bay and awake far from water in a northern land so remote it could never be accessed again."

"You could wake on the frozen sea could you not, move with the vast ice floes?"

"You might never be in one place."

"Are we moving, Wade?"

"Can you not feel it?"

"I can."

"If you were to look outside the window, everything would be a blur. A whirl of white and grey. Listen."

We both lay there and listened, and we heard it. The sound of us moving through air.

"It is like breathing," Esther said.

"Breathe then."

We breathed together and moved through this distant land. Across the shores of ice and rock, across the frozen earth, the treeless terrain.

"I met her," you whispered.

Once, I met her too.

✦

"Come back later," Jack had said, but I did not come back at all. I did not try to contact Tess, nor did she try to contact me. If Tess had knocked on my door, I would have welcomed her with open arms. But it was Jack's open arms she had fallen into now. The day after I left Jack's apartment, a snow storm blew in that lasted for three days. I piled wood next to the stove in the living room and barricaded myself in. Tess should have been teaching when I called, but instead she was with Jack. I listened to the winds howl, felt the drifting snow push up against me. I burned wood as one would burn passion. I could not bear to think of them together. I knew in my heart I would lose her to him. His first kiss saw to that. He leaned in, and Tess was his. Then later he held her close on the dance floor and all of our fates were sealed.

The snow blew in heaps against the sides of the house, up past the windows and above the roof until I was covered in completely, buried in a grave of my own making. I tossed and turned, the unsettled sleep of the ill-at-peace dead.

I lived for weeks in the warmth of my anger. My mind fumed with possibility. I thought I saw Jack and Tess constantly. Hand in hand by the port. His arm around her shoulder at Sloop's Cove. His lips on the lobe of her ear in the dark of his room. I reluctantly ate and slept. I waited for Tess to come, to tell me I had been mistaken, or ask for my forgiveness, to offer apology. Countless times, I went to the window expecting to see her approach. I rose in the night and listened for her knock on the door. I stopped sleeping in my bed. I could not withstand the pressure of her presence bearing down on me. What sleep I managed was filled with dream. Tess, Jack. Me. I hurt relentlessly. I avoided going to town lest I should see either of them or worse still, see them both together. I lived off a low supply of stocks. Endless times in the beginning I had thought to call upon Tess, to beg her return, but I couldn't bear the prospect of her refusal.

As the temperatures rose, as water dripped from my roof, as Tess's memory flooded my mind, I grew desperate and knew no way to calm my agitation. I would walk for hours on the wet snow towards some pale bland horizon. The cold granite pushing its way to the surface. I tried to walk Tess's shadow off me. I sought to put great distance between myself and Jack. But every time I reached a point of exhaustion where I knew it was impossible and all I could do was turn around and return.

On one such day late June, when I turned around, I found Jack standing there. Motionless in the chilly white expanse. I stopped in my tracks. Jack's hands were in his jacket's pockets, his windswept appearance on this otherwise breez-eless day. The years we had known each other filled the space between us. At what point in a friendship does love for another human being intervene? We could look around and as far as we could see was the immensity of our world, an open landscape from which there was no escape. The snow-covered vegetation at our feet, the small source of life.

"Hello Wade."

Jack's words crisp in the cool air.

"Hello." I could not bring myself to speak his name.

He took his hands from his pockets, ran one through his hair as though to confirm his identity. He pulled out a cigarette and lit it up. "I need to talk to you."

I watched the smoke rise, the red flicker of the ash. "How did you get here?"

"I walked."

"It is a long walk, Jack." His name finally released itself from within. It was over seventeen kilometres from town. It would have taken him most of the afternoon to get here.

"I went for a walk out towards Akudlik Marsh. I decided to keep going."

"Why?"

"It's like I said, Wade, I needed to talk to you."

We both resumed walking. Jack moved slowly to allow me to catch up. We headed back in the direction of my house.

That was it. That was the beginning of another long walk. Past my home, past the rocket range, past where the tundra tours now start, all the way to the watchtower at Gordon Point. A walk he never came back from. But I somehow made it home although to this day I do not know how.

Esther, we will take a walk out there someday soon. We will follow the path Jack and I took. We will take it to its end.

On that day, Jack and I walked slowly as though both of us were somehow seeking to prolong what little time we had left together. At first, we said nothing. We walked in silence. He pulled on his cigarette reducing it with every inward breath until it was extinguished. The disappearing smoke and his exhalations indistinguishable from one another. Although he must have been tired, he walked as though every step was his first.

As we passed the rocket range, he recalled the night we had sat on the roof of my house and watched the launch together. "The rocket must have come down," he said, "but it is forever in my mind high up there in the air just far enough away that it cannot be seen."

The anger I had felt towards Jack was somehow contained in his presence. As if its energy had been spent in its launch. "Were our lives any different back then?"

"From our vantage point on the roof, they may have seemed so," he replied. "In a way, they are just far enough distant to appear untouchable, but like the rocket we must all fall to the earth in the end."

"Why did you take Tess from me?" I couldn't even look him in the face. I looked to the ground, the flakes of snow I crushed in my passing.

"I didn't take her Wade. She came to me."

At night, I hear sounds that are audible throughout the day but nevertheless escape my ears. There are distractions. In the few moments after Jack's response, I heard a cacophony. I heard the pleading of ice as it tore apart. I heard the plaintive cries of individual crystals as they warmed and melted into molecules of water. I heard the moans of departing snows.

Even yet if it was possible, he would deny those words, but I clearly heard them. "She came to me, Wade. I did not take her."

"Wade, she was upset. You had argued. Eloise had gone. She could think of no one else to go to."

"And you took her in."

"I could not leave her outside. I could not turn her away. If it were the other way around, Wade, if Eloise had called on you, would you have closed your door?"

"But Eloise did not call, she did not come to me."

"I couldn't turn her away."

In the weeks since Tess had left me for Jack, I had heard other sounds too. I heard the sounds of my body. I heard it rasp and creak. I heard it grate. I heard the scrape and the grinding of my heart. Its pitiful din deafened me.

"Can you tell me you did not take her in your arms?"

"I comforted her." The path we followed was laid down by whom? Our footsteps would take a lifetime to heal. "She wants you back. That's what I came to tell you."

I soaked in his words. We walked deep in the silence, our hands thrust in our pockets, our breaths ahead of us. We walked amongst the small shrubs and trees. We walked over the protrusions of rock. He had walked that great distance for this. Or had he walked for something more? Had he walked along the edge of the bay, the shore of our northern land, to face the frozen waters, to bellow into the emptiness?

It was then they came like a winter storm. Tens of thousands of snow geese filled the sky above us. *She doesn't love you Wade. She wants you back, but she does not need you.* Were these not the words that grew wings and circled above your head, swooped at my ears?

"Did she send you to tell me this?"

"No. I was afraid she would try to stop me."

A mass of shrieking snow clouds threatening to open up.

"She could have come to me any time. I was waiting."

And we waited too. Waited for the white sky to fly away, and when it did, we pushed on across the tundra heading back to that great bay. Jack kicked his way through a drift of snow. "She was waiting too."

Tiredness threatened to overcome me. I felt my legs weaken with each trudging step. Jack looked strong, as though he could walk indefinitely. He was walking back to claim her. He would leave me far behind. I would falter, and he would walk from my sight. I struggled to keep up. The snow built up against me. Jack strode on through. The wind held me back, thrust Jack forward.

"I love her," I may have shouted.

She does not love you.

"I will gladly go back."

I tell you, you are not welcome.

"She doesn't love you, Jack."

She fell into my arms.

Jack may not have said a single word. Or if he spoke, his words were lost to my ears. Lost in a blizzard of thought.

I had fallen behind. I struggled to hear what it was Jack had to say. Onwards across the tundra. I fought to keep up. I left each step behind me in the thick snow. He seemed in a hurry to reach the water. I heard his voice constantly in my head. He was speaking, was he not, of his love for her, how vast it was, how abundant with life it had become and how empty my love was by comparison. Speaking incessantly, surely, of Tess's love for him. Tormenting me with his barely audible words which somehow resounded in my head. He did not appear to hear my cries, my fierce appeals, begging him to cease.

He walked in great strides as though he had claimed this territory as his own. Was I to seek permission to even lumber in his tracks? Amongst the dwarfed trees, he seemed enormous, colossal. I followed after him mile after mile. I sweated beneath my clothes from the effort, the heat of the day. The snow was wet. The sky now a dome of pale grey. There up ahead, Gordon Point. The Hudson Bay. Jack seemed invigorated by it. He smiled back at me triumphantly, reached it before me and took it all in before my arrival. Pools of melt water had already gathered on its frozen surface. A steady drip of water off the thick edge of ice overflowing on the harsh grey rock. He stood on a rise of rock elevated above the ice on the bay. I dared to step up beside him.

"Look."

I followed his gaze and saw what he observed. The warm spring air mingled with the near freezing air above the ice, producing large heaving swells. Wave after wave broke across the ice. As light refracted through the waves, misty whirls rose up out of them, swirled across the bay. Before our eyes they took form. A group of three pale white bears standing on their hind legs. They moved together, passed through each other, turning in slow ritual. Wading through the sea of churning air. More and more bears emerged from the waves until the bay was filled with bears all standing aloft, moving and turning. As I watched, one bear detached itself from the mass and began his walk. A large white bear striding over the ice towards us. Making his way across the distance. Growing as he neared, while behind him the great horde of bears moved further and further away. The large bear came closer, and as he approached, he opened his mouth wide, baring the sharp prongs of his teeth, and roared.

She doesn't love you. She doesn't love you.

Roaring louder still as he shrugged off his great white coat.

I saw him then, Jack, looming before me out on the ice where the coat had fallen. I turned quickly to where he had been standing on the rock beside me, but he was no longer there.

She doesn't love you.

Moving closer still.

I glided off the rock down onto the ice amongst the waves towards his shimmering figure.

She doesn't love you.

Menacingly near.

From out of the swirling sea of air, a fist formed, unbidden, from my open hand, and as he appeared to bear down on me, my arm rose and fell. Through the mist that enveloped my face, I saw him drop, rest easily on the hard cold ice. I heard the anguished wail the ice released. I stepped back just as the ice beneath him opened and took him in. As his body sank downwards, the ice above him closed over as though it had never opened, and further back, out on the horizon, all of the bears stepped, one by one, over the sharp edge of the frozen world.

CHAPTER 18

The days after Esther came back merged as one. The wind whipped the snow into outbursts of tenderness and anger. It sang at our doors and windows, it keened and it crooned. She loves you still, it chanted in my ear. She loved Jack, and she loves you still.

I held Esther near when she held me away. She took me in her arms, and I could hear the ice shear, scrape up against itself.

On one of those mornings, Esther roused me from my sleep. "Wade."

She was sitting up staring at me. She looked scared. "What is it?"

"Do you truly believe it was an accident?"

"I know it in my heart."

"Do you still love Tess?"

I sat up beside her, pulled the covers around us. "I love you."

"She was beautiful." She clung to the sheets. "Am I going to lose you?"

"Why would you ask such a thing? I could never leave you." I held her close while Esther shivered against me.

✦

The temperatures had a steady high of fifteen all week. I drove out to Cape Merry to see if the ice had broken on the river and the bay. Large pools of melt water spread across it like small lakes. Cracks, flaw leads, were evident on its surface. A creamy blue sky curved overhead while beneath the ice, radiation from the sun melted its underside. Two snow buntings flew from the rocks. Their white bodies disappeared into the background of snow.

Wade.

I turned to the sound of her voice. Tess's long dark hair. Her white tee shirt, her faded jeans. She stepped over the rocks. A gentle breeze rippled through her. Water dripped constantly off the chunky overlay of ice along the rocky shore. A shower sprayed down from a tall hanging ledge. The water caught in the sunlight releasing a splash of golden sparks.

"You came." I felt the warmth of the sun on my face. Underneath, the thaw began.

I cannot stay away. Ice broke free, shattered on the hard rocks. *I am waiting for the bay to break, the river to empty, Jack to be freed, sweep past. I will dive in and save him.*

"What about me, when will you rescue me?" The ice creaked loudly. Tess stood no more than two feet away. I could easily go to her, fall into her arms.

I rescued you already, but you slid yourself from my grasp.

"And if his body never surfaces?" The rocks glistened with the melt water, revitalized.

One way or another, I am going to Tadoule Lake and taking Jack with me.

"Is that what he'd want?"

Why don't you ask him?

She looked like she was going to leave. I didn't think I could allow her to. I would have to reach across and prevent her. But Tess didn't move. She stayed perched on the rock, surveyed the far reaches of the sky.

There has been no night since he left.

It was true. Daylight lasted for eighteen hours, and the night glowed with the promise of dawn.

"I take it as a hopeful sign."

All over, the snow had melted on the tundra. The semi-frozen ground gushed forth in reds and purples and yellows and oranges, blues and turquoises. I needed to tell her. Tess, I killed him. I did not seek her forgiveness but her blame, her unending blame.

"Tess."

Just at that moment, a thunderous explosion sounded. The ice heaved in front of us. An ear-splitting screech and the long deafening wail as the bay tore open, and Jack with all the strength he could muster pushed the broken sheet of ice above his head, upended its ten-foot thick layer before it wedged against the remaining ice and stuck tight. The low howl of his torment, and then the massive whoosh of air as Sandpipers, Godwits, Dowitchers, Terns, Loons, Bitterns, Eiders, Grosbeaks, Pintails, Mallards, Mergansers, Gulls, and Jaegers, rose from the rocks to cover the sky. And as the day went dark, the two snow buntings flew away in separate directions.

"I am at a loss." Esther sat at the kitchen table. All the papers she had gathered on Jack's disappearance, all her notes, were spread in front of her.

"Let it go," I advised her. "It all happened such a long time ago."

"It feels like it has yet to occur." She closed her eyes, sighed inwardly. "When did Tess leave?"

"Did she not tell you?"

Esther opened her eyes, looked at the world anew. "She started to, but then her story seemed to run out. I think I had exhausted her."

Tess left after break-up. After the ice tore itself apart and melted. After Jack's body failed to show up. The school year ended. Tess resigned her position, and she left. She did not say goodbye. Like Jack, she was here one moment and gone the next. I receded then into the small world she left behind. When Jack's body did not surface, I returned to work, but after my shift each day I went back home and remained there until the next. What I busied myself with before Esther came, I cannot remember. For a while, I busied myself with painful memories. My killing of Jack, my loss of Tess. Initially, I was overcome by those memories and my own existence seemed at risk. But that very act of being overcome, somehow, in time, led to the disappearance of those same memories. I learnt a new way of being in the world, a way that allowed me to glide across it surface while plunging to its depths. And thus I managed to carry on.

But now Esther has led me back to those memories, and where that will lead us I cannot tell. But I am very fearful, that much I know.

Tess and I searched for Jack together, and when we did not find him we parted. We did not speak or even see one another again. You would think, would you not, that Jack's disappearance might have brought us back together? But if anything, the opposite was true. We split further apart, and Jack was more present than he had ever been.

I assumed that when the ice melted his body would be found. I was prepared for my admission of guilt. But Jack refused to come back, and I remained at liberty if that term is in anyway applicable. In the beginning, when I met Esther, I thought that it was more than I deserved. My previous solitary life was to be my small and just sentence. But, perhaps, justice has been served after all. Perhaps, my meeting with Esther was exactly what I deserved.

✦

Esther never entirely returned from Thompson. Some part of her, some part I had never experienced, remained behind, may well have been taken back with Tess. And something of Tess had come home with her. It made its way through our house and took root. It followed us out to Bird Cove, drilled into the ice with the tip of the cutting tool. 43 cm, 27 cm. The ice was melting fast. It dripped from both our eyes.

The tundra burst into flower. It was the moment Marilyn had been waiting on, but, since returning from Thompson, Esther had little interest in plant life. Even before then, Marilyn could see it was waning. She had encouraged Esther in her search for Jack, but perhaps, she cautioned her shortly before she went to meet with Tess, she was taking it all a bit too far. Esther did not respond, but she was hurt by Marilyn's comment.

"She is just lonely," I reminded Esther. "She needs your company."

"Yes," Esther replied, "but does she give any thought to how lonely you must have been without the company of Jack? Those flowers will be back next year and the next. I am not going anywhere either."

As accidentally as they had met, they all but parted. Now, it was Jack, Tess, Esther and I. But for how long would that arrangement last?

Esther finished washing the dishes and dried her hands in her apron. She leaned against the sink. I sat at the kitchen table drinking tea.

"Could Terry Mitchell have been jealous of Jack because of Tess?"

"Tess?"

"She went with him to a community social once. Did you not know?"

There was so much about Tess I did not know. No, I did not know anything about other men she had known. She herself would never have told me about Jack's kiss. While Tess's past was clearly present, she rarely discussed it, nor I mine. The only glimpse I caught of it was during our visit to Tadoule Lake. Maybe my refusal to move there with her was a rejection of her past. Who is to know?

"No," I answered Esther, "I didn't know."

"If he was jealous of Jack being with his other girlfriend, maybe he was jealous of Tess too."

"It sounds like a long shot," I told her.

"It is what I am reduced to."

"What did Tess think had happened?"

"Tess believed she killed him, believed that by rejecting his love she had driven him to take his life."

I was horrified. Was it possible she had spoken to the same person at all?

"Tess did not reject his love."

"That is what she told me. She said she went to him for comfort only, to help her through your break-up. She knew he loved her, but she did not return this love. That day before he disappeared he had even said he would go and talk to you, that you were both being stubborn. For her sake, he wanted to bring you back together."

The shock of what she was saying struck me with a ferocity I could barely withstand.

"Tess was staying in his apartment," I insisted to Esther gripping the handle of my cup so tightly I thought it might break, but still I did not, could not, loosen my grip. "She had moved in with him."

Esther pressed against the edge of the sink with her hands as though holding down a truth that was rising to greet her. "She did not tell me that."

"Of course not," finally wrenching my fingers free and pushing the cup aside. My voice rising as I spoke. "You are living with me. How could she tell you that she rejected me, found solace in the arms of Jack?"

"Jack was going to bring you back together."

"Jack tore us apart."

"That very day he had determined to meet with you. If he had not died, he would have told you how she felt."

I jumped up suddenly, my chair screeched backwards on the wooden floor. My hands smacked on the tabletop. "He told me she did not want me back. That is what he came to say. Don't you see, Esther?" My fingers curled into calm fists. My voice quietened down. I owed Esther an apology. "I am sorry." I pulled my chair in and sat back down. "He didn't come to bring Tess and I back together. He came to tell me there was no way back."

"You didn't tell me he had come on that day." Her voice barely audible.

"I never told anyone." I tried to catch a glimpse of her across the room. I was putting a distance between us that could well be unnavigable, might never be traversed.

"Why not?"

"I couldn't. I was afraid of what people might think."

Esther leaned back as though to put even more distance between us. "But Tess, why did you not tell Tess that day she came to you to ask about him? Why not, Wade?"

"I didn't want her to know that I had spoken to Jack. I did not want to have to tell her what he had said. I hoped to learn for myself what she really felt. So, I told her I hadn't seen him, and then I could tell her nothing else."

"That day you saw him, did he give any indication of his plans? What did he tell you, Wade?" Esther, looked to me for help as if she had finally realized what I had been telling her all along, that the answers she was seeking lay with me alone. "Wade, I need to know everything that occurred."

If I could have led her away from this, I would have, but there was no turning back now. She was on the verge of discovery, that point at which something had to occur. We had to go forward now. Together. No matter how precarious our journey might be. Destined to catch up to one another or to leave one another far behind.

"Jack and I went for a walk."

"Bring me."

"It is long. The terrain is not easy in this weather."

"I want to go every step of the way."

Outside evening had already fallen. It was late.

"Tomorrow. We will leave in the afternoon. It was the same time of year. It was late June. Break-up was approaching."

That night I dreamt not about Jack as might be imagined but about Eb, Janice's husband. The husband, she confided to Esther, that she did not love. Eb who had crashed through the ice on his snowmobile believing her love was his. I saw Eb's arm reach from the hole. It was all I could see of him. I lay flat out to spread my weight and crawled slowly towards it then reached in to take hold of his hand. His flesh as cold as Tess's the first time we had met. He clasped my hand tightly, and I pulled. The freezing water shuddered as his body began to rise. I strained for every ounce of strength I possessed. The dark shadow of his head broke through the surface of the water. I pulled until his shoulders were free. Water soaked his hair, poured down his pallid face. He tried to say something but was too cold to speak.

"She never loved you," I told him.

His eyes stared. Drops of icy water gathered on his trembling chin. He let go my hand and sank back down into the water.

✦

The sun rose before five. Esther slept. I crept to the window. Outside the plants, the small trees, the shed, the discarded metal buckets, and wires were covered in frost. I dressed and went downstairs. I lit the stove to warm the chill of the night away. Our wood supply was almost exhausted. I made tea and drank it at the kitchen table.

Those days surrounding break-up I awaited my fate. I was resigned to the reappearance of Jack. In many ways, I would have been grateful for it. So many times I considered confessing. As self-serving as this may sound, I did not think Jack would want me to. Would not want my life to end as abruptly as his. Strong inescapable moments of panic, long hours of fleeting thoughts and swift sharp breathing. Then strangely the calm. If I struck Jack once, I struck him a thousand times. I felt the reverberation through my clenched fist, along my arm, into my nether recesses. I can feel it still. It is so incredible that at times I have to wonder if any of this really happened at all. Perhaps, I could ascend my stairs and enter my bedroom, find it empty. No trace of Esther as there is no trace of Tess.

One week the Churchill River was covered in ice, the next it was all water. I watched it daily. The snow pack melted. The ice cover began to thaw. With additional water, the levels rose, stream flows increased, and the ice thickness decreased. The forces exerted on the ice cover were almost unbearable. I shuddered beneath them. Large hinge cracks, parallel to the banks, developed reducing resistance further. I held my breath. The downstream forces continued to increase, and the ice cover began to move. The huge sheet of ice eventually fractured, broke into pieces, floated towards the bay, was swept away. The birds came in their millions. The river had swollen and flooded its banks. For weeks, great chunks of ice floated in the bay, tinged pink and blue with the setting and rising sun. Yellow and orange sheets suspended in disarray. Tess had gone and left us like this.

The house felt extraordinarily quiet. The crackling of the wood burning in the stove sounded like the melting of brittle frazil ice. Esther and I would set out late afternoon. The sun would reach its peak and begin its fall. Over the last few weeks, activity had continued at the range. Vehicles came and went. But it too was quiet now this early morning. The snow was slushy. I saw tracks towards my left. Fox. A trifling breeze ruffled my hair. I had talked so little since Jack's death. When Esther moved here first I found words difficult. They were caught inside of me like an ice jamb at the curve of a river. But in time they dislodged themselves, began to flow again. But who could I talk to now? If the fox had turned the corner of the shed and showed any interest, I would have done my best to begin discourse. I walked aimlessly in the snow. Small white flowers bloomed amongst the exposed willow shrub. The dead were coming back to life.

I returned to the house and waited on Esther to wake. She rose around seven thirty, and we had breakfast. The day progressed slowly. The sun dawdled in the sky as though it had nowhere to go. Esther and I passed our time in idle talk and small household chores. Tess was waking in Jack's arms. Her skin felt warm to his touch. The moist snow sparkled under the sun's glare. Esther ironed clothes. I swept the floors. Later Tess and Jack dressed, ate breakfast. A kiss passed between them. I watched Esther work. The look of concentration on her face. The strength in her arms.

"Why wait?" she finally asked. "Let us go now?"

But Jack had not come yet. He was still with Tess.

"We need to measure the ice first," I told her quietly.

She looked across at me, laid down her iron. "Of course we do." She went to the back hall and returned with our coats. We drove out to Bird Cove. It was here the last reported sighting of Jack had been made. Neither Esther nor I said anything about this, but I knew she watched out as though she might see him at any moment. I cautioned her about walking on the ice. Melt water gathered in pools across its surface, but Esther would not be deterred. We made our way out carefully. It felt as though this immense sheet of ice could float away at any moment and take us with it. Our breaths crowded in front of us. I stooped with the auger.

"Let me," Esther requested. It was the first time she had ever asked for it.

I showed her how to use it, the pressure to apply. She turned the handle, and the cutting tool began its journey downwards spewing out the particles of ice it cut away. I saw the sag of her upper body as the tool cut through. She withdrew the tool and flight, wiped them clean. I handed her the gauge, and she slipped it through. I held it for her while she measured.

"Thirteen centimetres," she said.

I nodded. We both knew that it was the final measurement we would take. Back in the truck, Esther filled out the form. I put the auger back in its case and stashed it under Esther's seat.

Jack would be smoking the last of his cigarettes. He would shortly step out to buy more. I turned on the engine and drove us home. Esther went in to make lunch while I brought in the last of the firewood and stacked it neatly by the stove. I stopped on one of my trips to the shed and listened. I could hear Jack in the distance. He was starting his journey towards us.

We ate lunch and went about our business. For the rest of the afternoon I listened to his footsteps as they came nearer. Finally, I heard him approach our home, and I went inside to Esther. "It is time to go."

Esther buttoned up her jacket and stepped out on the front porch a few moments later.

"This way," I said and led her out onto the tundra. Over the thick melting snow, the stretches of bright flowers that had recently emerged, the small plants flush with their crimson and burgundy leaves. We walked into a world part-quenched, part-aflame. Esther followed my path in silence. I walked back through each long day of every arduous year and did not stop until I had arrived at that place where I had met Jack before. When I had turned around and found him standing there before me.

"Why have we stopped?" she asked.

I looked around the empty tundra. "This is where I met him. I had been out walking by myself. I turned around, and there he was."

Hello Wade.

I turned with Esther to where he now stood. "Jack, you came."

I could not have stayed away. He smiled, ran his hand through his wavy hair. *Is this Esther?*

"It is."

You are a lucky man. He smiled again. *You'll have to watch her closely. A woman like that is hard to find.* He started walking back. *Come on,* he shouted over his shoulder.

"We can go now," I told Esther.

She nodded, and we set off after Jack. We caught up with him and walked alongside.

The years have been kind to you, he said.

Jack did not look a day older himself.

"What was he like when you met him that day?" Esther asked, linking her arm in mine.

"He seemed fine," I answered. "A little more serious than usual, but that was not to be unexpected. He told me he needed to talk. I asked him how he got here, and he told me he had walked. Strangely, he didn't seem tired at all. I remember being surprised by that."

"What did he speak about?" Esther walked jauntily along as though we were out on some pleasure excursion. Jack walked the other side of her and listened closely. For a while, I thought he might even link arms with her too.

"In the beginning we didn't say much. Jack smoked. I walked with him in silence. I don't think I knew what to say. I was angry with him, furious really, yet when I saw him my anger seemed to fall away."

Esther tugged at my arm in comprehension. The snow was heavy beneath us. I hoped she would be able for the long walk ahead. We neared the rocket launch. The gates were open. A few trucks were parked inside.

What's happening here? Jack asked.

"They're sending another rocket up."

Jack looked surprised. *I'd like to see it.*

"Perhaps you'll get the chance."

I lost a lot of chances. He spoke matter-of-factly.

"I am sorry."

Jack didn't respond. He seemed to quicken his pace. Esther and I did our best to keep up with him.

"We passed the rocket launch," I told her. "Jack mentioned something about the time we had climbed on the roof of my house to watch the rocket take off. He seemed intrigued by the notion of seeing the rocket go up into the air but not having seen it come back down, as though it were possible it was up there yet."

"Maybe it is."

Esther would like to believe in this as much as Jack. She had dreamed the same dream as him after all.

"No, it is not up there still. It fell unseen by us. It fell back to earth, exhausted." Jack slipped ahead of us again. "I asked him then why he had taken Tess away from me."

"You are certain he did that?"

Jack slowed down, his head half-turned, listening. Drops of melted snow dripped from the small branches of the willow. My feet sunk deep in the ridges of snow. It seemed to cling to me as though it was trying to hold me in one place.

"I lost her. When she left me in anger, there was an easy route back. She could have retraced her steps, or I could have followed after them."

Why didn't you? Jack shouted back. *That was what she wanted.*

"I didn't because I could no longer see them."

"What do you mean?" Esther asked.

"Jack filled them in. He blew snow across them until they vanished. Tess could not find her way back, and I could not find my way forward."

I could as easily, now, I thought, have been talking about Esther and I.

Jack stopped, turned around. *Don't listen to him, Esther.* Small wisps of cloud hung in the sky like shredded fragments.

"Is it possible that you blew the snow in there yourself?" Esther spoke gently. Jack smiled at her. He waited for us to catch up and walked alongside Esther again. The protruding rocks glistened with water.

"You loved her Jack," I told him. "That's the long and the short of it." A light breeze rose, offered some small but desirable resistance to our progress. "He loved her, Esther. There is no way around that."

Yes, Wade, I believe I did. Jack acquiesced. *But I would not intentionally have taken her from you.*

"I could not let you have her." The tiny stalks and leaves quivered. A sheltering cry as the snow geese blew across the sky.

She didn't love me, Wade. She loved you.

"No, Jack, she didn't love me. She could never say she did. She was leaving me. She was going to Tadoule Lake without me."

You wouldn't go with her.

"She wouldn't stay with me."

Esther looked to the geese, the expanse of their departure. "If the sun were hot enough, as it surely is, would the geese drop like a heavy fall of snow, melt before we could catch them?"

"No," I answered. "You are mistaking them with love."

We continued our arduous walk towards the bay. "Would you have gone with her, Jack?"

Jack pulled out a cigarette and lit it. *She didn't ask me to?*

"If she had, if you were in my place?"

Jack inhaled, blew the smoke upwards. *You know I walked out on Ang.*

"I heard."

My son.

"I know."

To this day, I cannot explain it adequately. He flicked ash into the snow. *That Christmas I went back I saw him. The man Ang was with was more a father to him than I. She had every right to be angry with me, but Ang was beyond anger by then. She was shocked when I turned up, but she didn't send me away. I offered to repay her for the support I ought to have been giving her in the past, but Ang refused. You have forfeited that now, she said. And I could see I had. Is it feasible for us to try again? I wondered. Ang shook her head. I asked her to consider it. Some day he may come to look for you, she said. It will be his choice then.* Jack's voice shook as he spoke. The cigarette trembled between his fingers. *Would I have gone with Tess? I will never know.*

And if his son ever did come to look for him, what would he now find? I had left that absence behind too.

I turned to Esther. "He came all this way to tell me she didn't love me. He said she wanted me back, but she did not need me. He told me not to return."

No, Esther, no. Jack sought to protest.

"It is true, Jack."

No, Wade. That did not occur.

Oh yes, Jack, it occurred. It occurred as surely as you are standing there. It occurred as surely as my arm rose into the air, as surely as you disappeared beneath the ice.

"Do you not remember?" I looked past Esther to where Jack strode by.

I remember everything, Wade.

"No, Jack, none of us remembers everything. Even I know that. I am loath to say it, but I think that death has interfered with your memory, or perhaps, Jack, it has heightened it too much."

"Why would he do that?" Esther looked at your back as you forged ahead of us.

"Because he loved her. He wanted Tess for himself. He had lost Ang. He was determined not to lose out in love again."

Esther slipped slid her hands into her pockets. The afternoon pressed ahead slowly. The land beneath us was harsh and unwelcoming. "Tess did not tell it that way," she said.

The breeze stiffened. The sun's rays seemed to cool. "Tess was not there."

We pushed through drifts of snow that had gathered like waves. The snow teetered at the tops of our boots. Jack was far ahead now. I feared we would lose him altogether.

"Recently, Wade, I think I have never been here, that you have been with Tess all along." She stepped on a submerged willow shrub and stumbled. I reached out and took her arm, helped her through.

"It is the other way around, Tess is the one who has never been here, that it is you I have been with all of the time?"

Esther regained her balance. We cleared the row of drifts. "No, Wade. That is not it at all." She shook snow from her boots. The ground ahead was deeply rutted. There was no path that I could see. The best we could do was follow in Jack's tracks, but they were scarcely visible as though he had blown snow into them after him. "You still love her."

"I still have love for her, but it is you Esther I am in love with."

What if I were to say I did not love you?

Did she really speak these words, or was it the rush of air across these tattered lands? Was it the wind through the limbs of the risen plants, the tongues of the rocks, the mouths of the opening waters?

I do not love you.

Jack himself was stopped in his tracks. I saw him up ahead. In a land devoid of echoes, the words bounced against him, reverberated in my ears. *I do not love you.*

Esther looked tired. She was slow in her stride. We still had a long way to go. The shore was not discernible. I wondered if we would ever make it.

I said it to Eloise eventually.

"What Jack?"

What I have been saying. I do not love you. I finally told her although she knew it all along. She had to hear it from me. He looked implanted on this land as though he had grown out of it. *Eloise did not love me either,* Jack went on. *She may well have thought she did, but she did not. Perhaps I should have told her that too.*

I owed it to him. Tess had told me that, and I had said it myself. Jack had to hear. Eloise had his baby. It was twenty-four years too late. Would I be with Tess still if I had followed through on my words? The sun slid lower in the sky. A shimmering of cloud formed on the horizon. The white snow lost some of its sparkle.

"Jack."

The snow was heavy going. It rose above our knees in parts. Something moved off to the side. I caught a glimpse of brown.

"A snowshoe hare," Esther said.

Its white winter coat was already changing colour. A transformation.

What, Wade?

Jack did not seem to notice the hare. His own pale skin looked greyer than usual as if he was transforming too.

"I don't know how to tell you."

After what you have done, Jack said, how is it possible that you cannot find a way to speak?

I watched the hare. Somehow, despite its browning fur, it managed to fade into the snow. It was gone.

"Eloise had a baby." The words fading from my mouth in a similar way.

Jack walked ahead, trudging through the snow, then stopped. He did not look at me but to the bay that was somewhere out there in front of us.

You are telling me this, he said. The breeze blew through his hair. The sun seemed to drop further still. *Why did she not tell me?*

"You said yourself you did not love her."

Did the ice rise to greet you Jack or did you sink within it? One moment you were there, and the next you were gone.

"Jack!" But there was no sign of you. "Jack!"

"What is it?" Esther asked. The snow above her knees, the breeze unsettling her strands of hair. "You called out Jack's name."

"He's gone."

Esther forced her way over to me. "This must be hard on you," she said. "Do you want to go back?"

"There is no way back," I answered her.

"There is always a way back."

But Esther, that is where you were wrong. You and I were going forward, and there was nothing now that could stop us.

"It will get dark. We must keep going if we are to reach our destination."

I started off again through the snow. Esther followed.

"He kept speaking of his love for her, and hers for him. He was unstoppable."

"Why would he do that?"

"It was all I could hear."

We cleared the drift. The snow was only ankle deep now. We proceeded onwards. Esther and I, minute specks of movement in this never-ending desert of ice. The struggle of the journey expended what little energy we had. We did not speak for some time. Esther wandered with difficulty through the rough terrain of memory. I searched for Jack in vain. Perhaps, I had been right all along. Perhaps, I should never have told him about Eloise's baby.

Esther paused to catch her breath. "Whoever we are," she said, "we are alone. It is just you and I." She looked around, back to where we had come from, forwards to where we were going. The snow had thinned to a bare covering of ice. Shiny pools of water spread like maps in front of us, reflected in the soft yellow of the sun. Chunks of rock tore from the earth, white, grey, black, brown, flesh. Strands of prickly sedge, clumps of tundra grass. "That day," she said, "it was just Jack and you." She looked for my response. I nodded. "It must have been late when you got back?"

"Yes, I remember it was." I felt the cold rise off the late afternoon ice. It enveloped my body.

"Jack?"

"Wait Esther," I advised. "I will take your arm and we will walk again. We will journey as Jack and I journeyed that day."

Esther held out the crook of her arm, and I took it in mine.

"I fell behind," I began again. "Jack seemed in a hurry. Eager to reach the frozen bay. I struggled to keep him within reach. Yet, somehow, whenever he spoke, his words reached my ears. They bombarded them, tormented me. He kept telling me how insignificant my love for Tess was in comparison to his. Repeatedly, he spoke of Tess's intense love for him." Ahead of us I could finally see the shore. Gordon Point. I showed it to Esther. "We are nearly there."

"Can this be true?" She brushed hair from her face.

True that we are nearly there, Esther? True, the depth of Tess and Jack's love? You have met Tess, have you not? You have seen her with your own eyes. And shortly, I sincerely hope, you will see Jack too. Although he is nowhere visible, I am confident he will reappear. If not, has not all of this been in vain?

Rejuvenated by our proximity to the bay, we picked up our pace, walked as swiftly as was possible. Twenty minutes more, and we were there. The point where land and water meet. It looked untouched from the day I was last here with Jack. The rocks, the frozen surface, the large pools of melt-water. I tried to find the exact rock we had stood upon. I walked the shore in search of it.

Wade.

Whose word, Esther's or Jack's?

Is it possible Tess kissed me?

The words rose from the ice like evaporating water. Something which had previously been there had altered beyond recognition, was no longer to be seen.

"I could not bring myself to tell you this before now," Esther said.

I saw it then. The rock. I was certain of it. I stepped up on it and helped Esther up alongside me.

"We were standing here," I said looking out to the very place I had looked out to with Jack.

"We were in the bar, dancing. It was as if someone leaned in, and I felt lips on mine."

"Jack told me to look. All across the bay, large swells of air rose, waves of mist, cresting, breaking."

"I longed to return it."

"As we watched, a group of bears emerged, stood up. Pale, wan creatures."

"It was as if something potent had been laid upon my lips. Something that would never wipe away."

"And then everywhere across the bay, more and more bears arose, appeared, until the ice was filled with them. Standing tall, moving in a slow dance."

She kissed me.

Standing there amongst the bears, there he was. Jack.

She kissed me.

"No, Jack," I called across to him. "You leaned in and kissed her. You told me so yourself."

She kissed me.

The bears moved in around him as though to protect him. The mist drifted all about. I could barely make him out. His face, his black hair floating behind the wavering air.

"It was down at the Churchill Bar. You had a beer or two too many. Someone had introduced you earlier in the night. You had talked a while then you went to play pool."

She kissed me.

"Later on you bumped into her again. You talked some more. You had no idea what you were saying, but Tess was laughing. She looked pretty. She stopped laughing and stood there looking at you, smiling. You leaned in and kissed her."

"Someone leaned in and kissed me."

I turned towards Esther. Like me, she stood astride this rock above the solid sea. Her mouth awash with words.

"What Esther?"

She pointed then. "I see him."

Esther!

"He is calling my name."

I turned to Jack. He was beckoning to her.

"No! No!"

"I hear him, Wade."

"Esther, no."

She moved as though she might step down to join him.

Esther. His voice as vaporous as the mist. His hand reaching towards her.

"NO!"

"I must."

"NO! NO!"

And still Jack beckoned. She would leave the rock, join him upon the ice. He would lean in, and they would kiss.

"NO! NO!" The anger surged within me. The white bears closed in around him as I climbed down from the rock, through the mist, over the heads of the swarming bears, into their midst where Jack sheltered, my hand clenched, my arm raised.

"NO!"

As I walked out on the ice, I saw that Jack was no longer there. The bears melted into the distance. I turned around to search for him, and, as I did, the ice suddenly fractured, opened under me, and as I slipped below through the freezing water, I saw him beneath me, welcoming me to him with open arms.

✦

I do not know how we made it home. When I awoke in my bed, I could not say for certain whether I was alive or dead. In many ways, I have felt like that for years. Esther, or someone resembling her, lay alongside me holding my hand. I tried to speak, but she shushed me. She placed her fingers on my lips. And then like everything else, she disappeared.

CHAPTER 19

A few weeks later, the ice was gone. The snow melted off the tundra completely. The ground ignited. A carpet of moss and vetch and sedge, every flower imaginable it seemed. The grey rocks rusted in lichen. The sand and gravel beaches gave way to soft petals of blue, white, indigo, violet. The marshes were moist and ripe with life. We awoke to merlins and northern hawks perched on the poles around our property. Families of Arctic fox wrestling and fighting. Millions of migratory birds descended. The train station was thronged with visitors from all over the world. This was normally one of Esther's most favourite times of the year. Marilyn tried to get her to accompany her out to see the wildflowers and birds, but each time Esther refused. Eventually, Marilyn gave up on her.

When the ice cracked, Esther told me it had awoken her.

"It was like my heart exploded."

"It is not possible that you heard it from here."

"Oh but I did," she insisted. "It woke me from my sleep. I heard it echo in the darkness.

For weeks afterwards, we drove out late at night to different parts of the bay. Bird Cove, Cape Merry, Sloop's Cove. We sat on the rocks in the light that ceased to fade. We watched the icebergs float on the bay, listened to the ice sheets grate against each other, the metallic clinking of fragments churning on the tides. We barely spoke any more. We had lost all appetite for words. Jack's name was never mentioned. On return from these late night excursions, we would retreat to our bed. Esther slept on one side turned away from me, and I slept on the other. The screeches, the cries, the wild calls of birds and animals outside. The endless day, the night that never came.

By mid-July, the waters were fully open, and the first ships came for their tonnage of Red Spring Wheat. I worked as much as I could, took whatever extra shifts were available. I drove out early in the morning, returned late in the evening.

Exactly what Esther had seen out at Gordon Point, I did not know, but I knew she had seen more than she wished to. I, for my part, had hoped I could somehow undo my actions of the past. But such a thing is not possible. Esther's paperwork had been put away, and had not reappeared.

In July, the temperatures reached their peak. We continued to endure the uncertainty of who we were. I arrived home one evening as a truck pulled away from our house. Esther stood at the door. A man waved as he drove past. I recognized his face but could not place it. I pulled in in front of our house.

"Who was that?" I asked Esther. The enormity of a person's existence seemed to bear down upon her.

She stepped off the porch onto the dusty ground. I closed the door of the pickup. It slammed as though making a comment of its own. Esther looked out at the vast field of tundra. The sun shone brightly, warmed the earth.

"He was from the range," she said.

I remembered him then. He was the man I had spoken to the time I had entered the range when the gates were left open.

"What was he doing here?"

Esther wore a short sleeved blouse. She rubbed at her lower left arm. Her freckles were evident. Like Arctic animals, they had darkened during the summer months.

"They will soon be ready to launch the rocket. He wanted to give us warning."

"When?"

"Two, maybe three weeks."

I walked over to Esther, put my arm on her shoulder. She did not respond. Since that evening at Gordon Point, neither of us had discussed what had occurred beyond the surface events. We were both afraid to. Afraid that our emotions would give way as easily as the ice had done. I rubbed her upper arm, felt goose bumps erupt upon it. Her near invisible hairs rose in protection. I took my arm away and walked inside. Esther stayed out for some time later. When she came in, I talked vaguely about my day at the terminal, the comings and goings at the port. How one of the belts had broken down, and how loading was delayed for over two hours. Esther may or may not have heard. She peeled potatoes for supper.

We eat silently, read in the living room afterwards. Later, I made tea. Then we retired for the night. We walked the stairs to our bedroom. Washed ourselves and brushed our teeth. Undressed for bed. We read a while, then Esther asked if I was ready to turn out the lamp light. She twisted the switch. The pale light of summer spread through the room. We lay quietly, listened to our breathing.

"Wade." Esther's quiet voice a short while later.

"Yes."

"I am pleased about the rocket. I am looking forward to it." The bed creaked as she turned towards me. "We will watch it, won't we?"

"Of course." I turned on my side. "Why would we not?"

"I don't know. I just thought ..." Her voice trailed off.

She was thinking of Jack and I up on the roof.

"We will watch it together."

Esther forced a smile. She reached out, brushed my hair from my forehead. "Good." She kissed my cheek lightly, turned away. When we fell asleep, I do not know.

The town was filled with talk of the launch. The terminal overflowed with it. The first in over twenty-five years. Many people here had never witnessed one. The rocket was sending instrumentation out to do some upper atmosphere research. Beyond that, little was known. I brought back whatever tidbits of information I could to Esther. She thrived on them. The man from the rocket range had told her little. It was a mere courtesy call, she said. She hadn't known what to ask him.

Esther herself never went to town now. Whatever provisions we needed, I bought on my way home from work. I believed she was afraid of running into Marilyn or Janice. What could she tell them if they asked how her investigation was going? But there was more to it than that. Esther was becoming as alone as they were, as alone as she once had been. It had been my greatest fear. The closer we came to Gordon Point, the more distance we had put between us.

The first of the white whales swam into the estuary. Soon the river and bay were filled with them. Thousands of whales diving and rising, singing beneath the water. I went out with Esther late one evening to watch them. We stood on the rocks at Cape Merry. The winds lashed upon the shore. We braced ourselves against them. Large waves crashed down on the rocks in front of us, broke on the backs of the whales. Their pale white creamy bulk sunk and rose up through the surface. We had to raise our voices to be heard above the gusting wind.

Are they the souls of the dead, Esther may have wondered, *sinking to the depths, rising in defiance? Are they there to give us hope or to pull us to the nadir of despair?*

She was searching for Jack, I am certain of it, while I sought out Tess's presence in the winds. The ragged outline of the moon was visible in the cloudy sky. I remembered the time Tess and I had climbed inside the skeleton of the whale. We sat crouched inside looking out at the world through the whale's jagged ribs. I do not think I ever really stepped out of the whale that night. I do not think that either of us ever did. It was too comforting a place. Even then, as I looked at the waters, at the pods of whales, at Esther, I saw it all through thick jagged rows of broken bone.

Esther's eyes were closed when I looked. Her face was held out in offering to the wind. But I did not close my own. I turned my gaze to the ashen misshapen moon as though Tess and I had found the whale's heart inside its skeletal frame that night and discovered it was not flesh but pallid bone and had cast it to the heavens to remind us and to watch over us forever.

✦

Driving home one evening, I met the man from the rocket range. The launch was only a few days away. Two pickups had passed me on the narrow road shortly before. The road was in very poor condition after the winter. My tires dug into the ruts, juddered free. His vehicle approached slowly. I pulled in on the side and lowered my window. He pulled up alongside and lowered his in turn. He nodded over, seemed to remember me. I asked him if the launch was going as planned.

"Depends on the weather," he replied. "If it's a clear evening we'll have lift-off."

"And after that, what then?"

He shrugged. "No one seems to know. This is more like a test run really to see if the range is still up to it. It might be the last rocket ever to fly from here. It might be the start of a whole new program."

"What about you, what do you do after the launch?"

"That depends how it goes. One way or another I'll be here a while analyzing the results. Then I guess it's back to Guelph." He scratched his nose, looked over towards my house. "And you, the rocket shoots high above where you live, and then what, life goes on?"

"That's about it." I ran my hands over the steering wheel. "They've been here before lighting up the sky. We've had armies, governments, settlers, traders, scientists, tourists, the likes of me, the people who were here in the first place, the plants and animals who were here before that, the land and sea itself."

There was Jack, I could have told him. He shot high above my head and life went on. There was Tess. Instead, I thanked him for calling over to tell us about the impending launch.

"No problem," he said. "I figured you'd already have heard about it in any case."

We didn't know what else to say to each other. That first evening we met, I recognized in him the same need to communicate that I had felt, but neither of us really knew how. We were like astronauts, I thought, meeting on a distant planet, with nothing in common other than our species, feeling obliged to commune.

"Take it easy," I said.

"You and all."

We pulled up our windows and drove on. He might return, and we would become friends. I might never see him again.

Esther had been tense for days. She had not been sleeping well. Many times, I awoke to find the bed empty. Sometimes, I found her by the window looking absently into the near dark and other times in the kitchen sitting at the table. The night before the launch, I could not find her at all. Eventually, I decided to look outside and saw her standing next to the shed. She barely moved when I opened the door.

"Esther," I called lightly. "Are you alright?"

She turned. Her parka was pulled on over her nightdress, her boots over her bare feet and legs. "I'm fine," she said. "I just can't sleep, and when I do my dreams disturb me."

I went back for my coat, put it on over my pyjamas, and rejoined her. The moon hung high in the sky, shed its pale yellow light across Esther's face. She looked unwell.

"We should never have gone out there," I said. This was the first time either of us had mentioned that day.

Esther looked at me in confusion. She seemed about to say something then stopped herself. She rubbed her forehead, then stuffed her hands deep into her pockets. A coyote howled.

That was my heart, I heard her say, although Esther did not look as though she had spoken a word. She furrowed the brow she had rubbed. She moved from foot to foot as though the cold from the earth was penetrating her.

"I thought you were going to die," she said. "I thought I would never see you again."

"I'm sorry."

My apology seemed to irk her. "We should not be living here," she snapped. "Neither of us have the skills necessary to survive here."

"It may not be too late to leave if that is what you want."

"I don't know what I want. There was a time when people didn't have to think that way. They just survived. Your Tess could probably have told you all about it."

"Please, Esther." I did not want Tess here with us tonight. It was bad enough with Jack waiting to pounce.

"Her ancestors woke to the morning hungry, went into the day in search of food, found what they could, appeased their appetites as best they were able, replenished their energy through sleep and awoke to discover their hunger had returned. We want too much, Wade. But we do not know what it is we want, and so our wants can never be appeased."

Where I fell through the ice, it was shallow enough that Esther could clamber down and rescue me. With her assistance I got to my feet, scrambled back to shore. Esther took off my jacket, the clothing on my upper body and covered me in her parka. She wrung out the rest of my clothes and replaced them on me. Then she walked me back an impossible journey.

"What are we to do?"

Esther turned and walked towards the door. "Go back to bed, sleep if possible."

An owl hooted. As I turned to go back in, a light flickered through the darkness.

"Look." I pointed it out to her. "It's coming from the range. Someone is working late."

Esther paid no heed. "I am tired now." She opened the door and stepped inside.

I closed the door behind me. We ascended the stairs where slumber was a prospect.

Esther rose early the following morning. She took a hot bath. Steam drifted into our bedroom. I listened to the splash of water, and later the gurgling of the drain as the bath emptied. The cistern to the toilet flushed. The tap in the sink ran briefly. Esther came back in dressed in her dressing gown. She had washed her hair. It hung straight and wet. It never ceased to amaze me how different she looked when her hair was wet, almost unrecognizable, a different person entirely. She saw me watching her.

"You are awake. I'm sorry. I didn't mean to wake you."

"I was awake anyway," I said.

"I feel as nervous as though I was solely responsible for the launch myself."

"Perhaps it is to be expected."

Esther shook this idea away. "No it is not. My nerves are unreasonable." She took her dressing gown off and dressed. Her turquoise blouse and green woolen sweater. Her grey skirt.

I lay in bed after she had gone downstairs. I tried to see her emerging from the bathroom in her dressing gown, moving through the room, filling in space with her presence. I could hardly recall her. I had taken Jack's life in front of her, had I not? She had witnessed my raised arm, my clenched hand, my lunge towards him. There was no point asking her forgiveness for rightly she had nothing to forgive. And there was no point in saying I was sorry since no amount of remorse could reconcile the taking of Jack's life, the taking of our life together too. The ice had long since melted all around us, turned to water, seeped away.

From bed, I heard the truck start up. By the time I got to the window, Esther was gone. The exhaust fumes hung in the air, dark black clouds. I showered and dressed. There were so many uncertainties despite the constant fall of day into night. Fortunately, I did not have to go to work that day. Perhaps Esther had taken this into her deliberations, or perhaps she had not deliberated at all, had simply reacted to some internal stimulus. I walked out to where the truck had been parked and looked at the tire marks. I could smell the fumes still. There was a train leaving that morning. Esther could be planning to be on it. She had packed nothing, but

Esther would not wish to bring any part of her life here with her that she could leave behind.

The launch was to go ahead as planned. At seven forty-five that evening, countdown was to begin. The sky had been clear all week, the weather calm. Ships slipped into the port and slipped out again. Russian, Spanish, African, Middle Eastern. The world came to us and left us alone again. The train station was filled with people arriving and departing. American, Belgian, German, Indonesian. Coming or having come for the birds, the flowers, the whales. Some had even travelled here specifically for the launch itself. A pack of wolves had been wandering through the dump and town and had to be shot. For the first year in over twenty, the Ross's gulls failed to return.

I worked outside for the rest of the day, tidying, making small repairs trying to keep busy, to keep my mind occupied. They would be busy in the launch centre too, last minute details, checking, rechecking. The previous day, Esther and I had driven down the road towards the range. We parked a short distance away and watched through the open gate. A number of men were gathered around a crane. The rocket lay on a wooden palate on the ground. The rocket was lean and looked about fifteen to twenty feet long. Esther was surprised by its size. She had expected something larger. We watched them put straps around it at either end. The crane lowered a girder, and the straps were attached to it. As the men stepped back, the rocket began to ascend horizontally. It was jet black, its nosecone silver. "It's beautiful," Esther said. And it was, from its tailfins to the tip of the nose. The booster to launch the rocket was already in place on the launcher. We watched the slow process of lowering the rocket onto the launcher and positioning it in place. I told Esther what little I remembered about rockets. How the booster would burn briefly until it ran out of fuel a few miles up in the air, separate and fall back to earth. The rocket motor would next ignite before it separated too thirty miles high. After that the nosecone would be ejected and the remainder of the rocket holding whatever instrumentation was on board would continue upwards to conduct its experiment until it ran out of momentum and fell back down, a parachute opening to allow its safe return.

Right now, the few clouds in the sky seemed to rearrange, ready themselves for the evening lift-off. Like Esther walking from the bathroom into our bedroom, the rocket would move through the sky filling small portions with its mass and then it would be gone.

It was after five before I heard the truck return, heard the approach of my own relief. For now anyway, Esther was still here. She pulled into our driveway and parked. The launch was still two and a half hours away. We ate supper and waited. Esther told me she had gone to see Janice.

"I don't know why," she confided. "I couldn't get her out of my mind. A niggling feeling as though she were in trouble."

"And was she?" We were at the table, the dirty dishes remained in place.

"Are any of us any other way?" Esther looked resigned to this fact. "I went for a walk on the beach first since it was early. I saw two Arctic terns. One was perched on a rock, the other hovered beside it feeding it a small fish from its beak."

"These things still happen," I said.

"I read the signs warning of polar bears. It is a relief to know they have gone, have not yet arrived."

Esther was quiet a while. I waited then asked her again about Janice.

"She had just started work when I called in. She said she had been thinking about me. She thought she could get away

314

around eleven. I went to the library as usual, but I couldn't find anything to read, nothing that interested me. I whiled away my time looking through the shelves of books, skimming through magazines. I left at ten forty-five and waited for Janice by the large windows overlooking the bay. She got there about ten minutes after eleven. We walked down to the beach. I told her about the terns I had seen earlier. I probably shouldn't have. It made her think about Eb. She told me that the man who had asked her out before had called her again. She had said no, but she was thinking that if he called once more she might just say yes. I told her she should. She needed the company." Esther looked over. "I hope I did the right thing in saying that."

"Of course you did," I said.

Esther continued to look at me. "She told me something disturbing." Esther looked old. I really hadn't noticed it before. Her face was wrinkled, her hair turning grey.

"What is it?" I asked.

"Terry Mitchell. He *was* forced to resign. Someone died in custody when he was questioning him. She said she couldn't find out all the details. He was a petty criminal, a known drugs offender. He was reported to have fallen, may even have been under the influence of something, but there was some suspicion that Terry Mitchell may have used force. She said he was obliged to leave as a way of containing the damage. There were no charges laid against him."

"Maybe it was an accident," I said. I was trying to understand what impact this could have on Esther. "I think we should give him the benefit of the doubt."

"Doubt," Esther repeated. "That is the word." She stood up and started to clear away the dishes. "I decided to call in on Marilyn afterwards. I have treated her badly. I think she was annoyed with me in the beginning, but once we got talking her annoyance seemed to disappear." Esther put the dishes in the sink and turned on the tap. "She is going to leave."

"Marilyn?"

"She said she regretted not having left years ago when she was young. "Most of my life here," she said, "I thought I had made the right decision. It is only recently I realized it was a mistake." Esther turned off the tap, squeezed in some detergent and began to wash the dishes. "It was my doing," she said. "I caused her to see her mistake. Without me, she would have believed she had done the right thing." Esther began to cry. I went over to her and put my hand on her shoulder. She shrugged it away. "Please don't." I stood uselessly beside her. She leaned on the sink and wept.

At seven thirty, we climbed up on the roof. I held Esther's hand as she stepped off the ladder. The roof sloped gently next to the chimney, and we sat there with our backs against it. The sun would set soon. Already the light of evening was low. The launch rail pointed high into the sky. The black rocket looked majestic, dominated the vast wilderness as though it alone was the sole reason for the existence of the universe. A shiver ran through me. Esther couldn't take her eyes off the rocket.

"Do you remember the night we climbed up on these logs before the house was built?"

I remembered every moment of it. We had looked out at the distant lights of homes, the strange outline of the rocket range. "I was afraid the logs would be displaced, that they would come careening down burying both of us."

"Do you think they have?"

"We are surely testing their weight."

A truck drove in through the gates of the rocket range. Further in the distance, other vehicles pulled in on the road to watch. People would be gathered all around the town. Over by the Golf Balls, the Aurora Domes. It was starting to cool down. I had brought a blanket up with me and placed it around the two of us. Esther leaned in against me. Below us the blossoming tundra.

"Is there anything we cannot see?"

"You would hope it was so," I replied.

More vehicles gathered along the roadside. The large yellow sun sunk low in the sky. I felt the hard roof beneath me, the softness of Esther to my side. We sat together silently, the day coming to a close.

"That day out at Gordon Point, I saw him too." Esther eventually said breaking the prolonged silence.

"Yes. I know you did."

"I saw him fall through the ice." She looked at me sadly. The sun grew before our eyes, turned orange. The wiry sprigs of tundra grass caught aflame. The fire spread in all directions. The sun burned a deep red, soaked the sky. "You tried to save him, didn't you?" Esther needed to believe this. Nothing else could restart our lives. You clambered down off the rock and, reaching out your hand, you tried to save him."

If I was to wonder one thing only about that day, it would not be how I did what I did but what Jack thought as that terrible event befell him.

Esther had turned to look at me, was awaiting my response. Before my words could form a deafening roar filled the air. Esther quickly looked back to the rocket. Flames shot downward from the booster, curled outwards into plumes of smoke and fire as the rocket rose along the launcher and lifted into the sky. The house shook beneath us. Esther clung to me as though afraid the logs would finally give way and collapse from under us. The earth itself was shaking, venting some long pent up anger. The desperate roar grew louder, thundered all around. Dark smoke spread across the land. The scorching heat peeled at our skin. The rocket soared through the darkening sky burning a path through it.

"There *we* go," Esther whispered.

Shortly afterwards the rocket disappeared from sight. The plumes of smoke remained slowly dissipating.

"It looks like a path someone could walk on," I said indicating the trail of smoke.

Esther lightened her grip on me. The earth had steadied itself again. "They would set out upon it," she said, "but, bit by bit, it would disappear until they were left there stranded."

We sat on the roof watching the sky, clinging to one another. The rocket was nowhere to be seen. The sun had slipped over the edge of the world. And then we saw it, the parachute floating calmly downwards returning the remains of the rocket safely back to earth.

We went back indoors, and I lit the stove. The wood from my old home was almost gone completely. We sat in our chairs either side of it.

"Tell me what happened," Esther said. "Tell me what I saw."

I breathed deeply. A wave of heat from the stove hit the side of my face. It felt like some part of Jack's presence that had failed to turn to ash.

What response could I give? What could I tell you, Esther, that would reveal to you that which you most want to know? All along all I have asked of you was that in your search you would uncover the reasons for my actions. But Esther, my beloved, I have come to realize that there are no reasons, at least none we are capable of comprehending. What happened, I do not know. We could spend the rest of our lives investigating the circumstances, but in the end we would still be so far away from the truth that we may as well have never set forth.

"A respectful hunter makes offerings to the soul of the bear he has killed, and the bear seeks out such a hunter to be killed by in order to take those offerings with him into the hereafter."

"What are you saying, Wade?"

"I am telling you Esther, that I am the cause of his death, that I may even have killed him."

"You reached out to him."

"I raised my arm in anger. I clenched my hand into a fist. I believed that he had taken Tess from me, and it was more than I could endure. One moment, he was beside me on the rock and the next he was down on the ice in front of me. Turning on me. And as he approached, the anger surged within me. I climbed down to join him. *She doesn't love you*, were the only words I heard. Whether they were Jack's or my own, I couldn't tell. Hearing over and over again, *she doesn't love you*. I saw him come menacingly near. *She doesn't love you*. That was when I raised my arm towards him. And that was when he fell. The ice shattered beneath him, and he sank beneath it."

"He fell."

"I raised my arm and clenched hand towards him."

"Did you strike him, Wade?"

"Why would I do that if not to strike him?"

"To ward him off."

"Whatever happened, I caused his death."

"You didn't strike him."

"You don't know that, Esther. *I don't know that.*"

"Wade, he fell. The ice shattered beneath him. You did not intend for him to die."

"I don't know what I intended anymore. Everything was just happening before me. He was there on the rock beside me, and then he was there on the ice, and then I was on the ice beside him with my arm raised and my hand clenched into a fist. Oh, Esther, I have gone through this so many times in my mind. Over and over. Until I can be certain of nothing anymore except that he fell and the ice shattered and Jack disappeared beneath it. The ice closed over, and he was gone." I looked at Esther sitting across from me, attentively watching me. "For some length of time, I stood transfixed. Unable to move. And then I ran to where he had fallen through. I got down on the ice on my knees and pushed my hand through the broken ice into the freezing water extending my arm down as far as I could, but I couldn't feel him anywhere. I had to keep taking my arm out, alternating it with the other, as it was unbearably cold. But wherever he was, he was out of reach. I couldn't save him."

Esther rose and came to my side. "Oh, Wade." She rubbed the side of my cheek. Tears flowed from her eyes. "My love." She bent to kiss my lips. "You did what you could. You cannot fault yourself for that."

She wrapped her arms around me, and we stayed in that embrace, both of us weeping.

We walked back out to Gordon Point the following day. Back out to where Jack had fallen through the ice.

"He was my friend," I told Esther on the journey there. The sky was clear, and the sun shone brightly. The snow and ice had melted and the flowers were in bloom. The arduous journey of the previous time was now one of ease. "He was the only friend I had. I would never have wanted to harm him."

Esther's arm was linked through mine. She clasped me tightly. "I know that, Wade."

"I was afraid. Afraid that he had taken Tess from me and then, when he drowned, afraid that that I would be blamed.

And later, in my solitude, afraid of my own thoughts, of what I would find out about myself."

"It was an accident. You tried to save him. You saw how the ice was when you fell through. How easily it fractures. You Wade, you of all people, who have measured it for years. You know that."

"It is possible also, I was drowned in sorrow."

When we reached the place where Jack had drowned, I stood by the shore next to the rock we had been standing on, and took the gift that Tess had once given me from my jacket pocket. The white seal carved from the bone of the beached whale. I could see and hear her yet, "I have brought you a present." Then she shook the snow from her boots. It was evening, and I took her boots and her jacket and her gloves and placed them in front of the stove to warm and dry off. From that day forward, Tess and I were together constantly, until shortly before Jack's death when everything began to fall apart.

I held it in my palm and showed it to Esther.

"What is it?" she asked.

"It is a gift Tess gave me once. A seal made from whale bone. It is time to return it to where it came from."

I bent down to the water's edge with the seal cupped in my hand. "It is time to let them go," I said. "Tess and Jack."

Esther bent down beside me and reaching over, I took her hand in my free hand. "I loved Tess once," I told her. "But it is you I now love." ·

"I know that," Esther said squeezing my hand warmly.

And, as she did, I opened my other hand and the small white seal slipped from my palm, back into the water where it swam far beneath the surface until Esther and I could see it no longer.

Back at the house Esther threw the last of our wood on the fire. The last of my old home. We sat in our chairs either side of the stove and watched it burn.

"Esther, you are afraid of bears," I said, "and yet you came here to be with me."

"I was falling, Wade, and you saved me."

She smiled over at me from her chair. It was the first smile I had seen in weeks.

"Those bears have already drifted on the broken floes." I warned her. "They have been blown south by the winds into warmer seas. Their floes are melting now, and they are swimming to shore. Soon, they will begin their slow walk towards us."

Esther bent her legs up in the chair, wrapped her arms around them. "But for now we are safe, are we not?"

"What do we know, Esther? We step upon the ice and expect that it will withstand our weight."

"I am not too heavy for you, am I Wade?"

Oh Esther, my love, I was light for the want of you.

Esther stood, and I felt a chill run through my bones. The wood was all but burnt out. By morning it would be gone. She went upstairs and returned with her papers. She opened the door to the stove and thrust them in. We watched them catch alight. A burst of blue and yellow that lingered. For a brief moment in the flames, I thought I caught sight of him, his windswept hair, his beaming smile, the cigarette hanging from his youthful lips. Then Esther closed over the stove door, and he was gone.

ABOUT THE AUTHOR

Gerard Beirne holds dual citizenship of Canada and Ireland. He has published 7 books previously: three novels, three books of poetry, and a collection of short stories. He is a past winner of the the Hennessey New Irish Writer of the Year Award. His first novel *The Eskimo in the Net* (Marion Boyars Publishers) was shortlisted for The Kerry Group Irish Fiction Award, 2004, and was selected as Book of the Year by the Literary Editor of the Daily Express. His short story collection *In a Time of Drought and Hunger* (Oberon Press, Canada, 2015) was shortlisted for The Danuta Gleed Literary Award. A story from this collection was shortlisted for the Bord Gais Book Awards (Short Story of the Year) 2016. An earlier short story, "Sightings of Bono," was made into a short film (featuring Bono) by Parallel Productions, Dublin. Gerard lived in Canada for over 18 years and lectured at the UNB English Department. He now lectures at ATU Sligo, Ireland, (BA Writing and Literature Program).

NOTABLE TITLES FROM BARAKA BOOKS

FICTION

Blacklion
Luke Francis Beirne

Almost Visible
Michelle Sinclair

Shaf and the Remington
Rana Bose

NONFICTION

*The Calf with Two Heads,
Transatlantic Natural History in the Canadas*
Louisa Blair

The Great Absquatulator
Frank Mackey

Waswanipi
Jean-Yves Soucy

Printed by Imprimerie Gauvin
Gatineau, Québec